CHAPTER 1

S uzy sat back in her seat and tried her best to relax. Finally, after months of planning, they had done it. All the pain and torture, both physical and mental, were worth it. They had escaped.

She glanced at her daughter, Leanne, who was staring out of the bus window at the trees lining the road they were driving down. The child had a faint smile on her face. Perhaps, Suzy thought, Leanne was looking forward to her seventh birthday, even if it was a couple of months away. Or perhaps she was looking forward to seeing London for the first time. Suzy had bought nothing yet for her daughter's birthday for two reasons. The first was that Leanne changed her mind over what she wanted almost daily. The second, and main reason, was that if Suzy had bought something, she would have had to bring it with her. She needed to stay as mobile as she could.

With a smile that mirrored her daughter's, Suzy clasped the tote bag in her hands to her chest. This bag, along with a small suitcase in one of the baggage holds under the bus, was now all they had in the world. Everything else had been left behind. But, Suzy reflected as she looked again at her daughter, they had all they needed in those two bags. Along with each other.

Suzy closed her eyes and thought back over the day's events. The first was the phone call at almost seven in the evening. It had been her partner's phone. No one would call Suzy in the evening. No one called Suzy at any time of the day, not anymore. Not since Vince had slowly cut her off from her friends. He'd done it so gradually that by the time she had realized what he was doing, it was too late.

The phone call had roused Vince from his place on the sofa, as Suzy knew it would. When she asked him who it was, he had simply replied work, as he always did. Then he had left, not saying a word about where he was going or when he would be back.

She imagined him driving to his office, summoned along with his colleagues to deal with an anonymous tip off. But the tip off was only anonymous to Vince and his team, not to Suzy. She knew exactly who had made the call, and what he had said. She'd paid the man a fair amount of money to make it, and to ensure that he said exactly what she wanted him to say. The people Vince worked for didn't respond to any anonymous tip off, only those with certain words or combinations of phrases that would make them think it worthwhile to railroad the local police. It had taken Suzy months to put the phrases together, gathering snippets here and there, mostly when Vince was drunk and in a good mood, which was rare. But he had gradually revealed enough of them for Suzy to construct something meaningful to grab their attention.

The moment Vince's car had screeched around the corner at the end of their road, Suzy had leaped into action, getting Leanne ready for their big adventure. Then they had

THE HUNTER

THE PREACHER SERIES
BOOK 2

NATHAN BURROWS

First printing, 2023.

Nathan Burrows
Unit 130535
PO Box 6945
London W1A 6US

www.nathanburrows.com

hurried, moving like mice, down the alley by the side of their house. At the bottom of the alley was a taxi that Suzy had booked via one of the few remaining working pay phones in the area. The taxi took them to another taxi, booked from a different phone and under a different name. Then one final taxi to the bus station. They arrived for the evening bus to London with moments to spare. Just long enough to persuade a homeless man to buy her two tickets for cash so she and Leanne didn't have to enter the ticket office.

Suzy knew Vince could eventually trace their route, but by then, she and Leanne would have left London and be on the next stage of their complex journey. Speed was of the essence. At the thought of the journey ahead, Suzy allowed her smile to broaden. They had finally done it.

A few moments later, just as Suzy was drifting off to sleep, she heard the pneumatic hiss of the brakes of the bus. It juddered to a halt, and she looked out of the window to see only trees. This wasn't one of the regular stops, surely? She heard a commotion at the front of the bus and her heart sank. How had Vince traced them so quickly? It couldn't have been more than an hour since they had left Norwich. Suzy craned her neck and looked toward the front of the bus, hushing Leanne, who had just stirred from sleep.

It wasn't Vince at the front of the bus. It was a man wearing a balaclava. In one of his hands was a pillowcase. In the other was something that made several of the other passengers gasp with horror. A small, black pistol that he was waving around the interior of the bus.

"No one move," a man's voice said, the balaclava moving in time to the words. "Phones, wallets, purses. I want the lot."

CHAPTER 2

Caleb, who had closed his eyes the moment the bus had left Norwich, kept them closed as the bus ground to a halt with a hiss. He angled his head to one side as he heard the door slide open. A few seconds later, he felt the bus tilt to the left by less than a degree as someone—presumably the driver—got off. The next sound he heard, other than some muffled voices, was the distinctive noise of someone being struck with a fist, followed by the soft *crump* of a body falling to the ground. Then the bus shifted again as someone got back on. Someone who was smaller than the driver from the amount the bus dipped, assuming it was him who had got off. Then another tilt as another person climbed aboard before a collective gasp rolled through the interior of the bus.

"No one move! Phones, wallets, purses. I want the lot."

The voice was young, British, probably white. Caleb angled his head in the opposite direction, moving slowly and keeping his eyes closed. A collective gasp told Caleb several things. The first was that the young man was armed. The second was how the sound had come from all areas of the bus. It told him that the weapon was probably a gun. A knife wouldn't threaten the entire bus in the same way. Caleb's final assessment from the words that were spoken was that whoever it was who had spoken was serious. The timbre of the collective gasp only reinforced that assessment.

"In the bag! In the bag!" the man continued. Caleb imagined him carrying a gym bag or something similar down the bus, going from passenger to passenger until they had emptied their pockets. The voice continued its threats as it got louder, but Caleb was content to appear to be asleep. There was no need for him to open his eyes. Not yet.

Caleb was sitting five or six rows from the front of the bus, just behind a woman and her daughter. As he had got on board, the young girl had commented on the gray robe he wore, but the woman hadn't been keen on engaging.

"Why are you wearing a dress?" the child had asked in the innocent way that only children can.

"I'm a preacher," Caleb had replied, smiling.

When the child's mother had tried to hush her daughter, the woman had made no eye contact with Caleb. She was perhaps in her early thirties, wearing light-blue jeans, unbranded sneakers, and a shapeless burgundy sweatshirt over a slim frame. She had blonde hair tied up in an untidy ponytail, and her shampoo or body wash, perhaps both, contained lemon extract. Caleb also caught the faintest bruise on her left cheek, almost but not quite hidden under a layer of foundation.

The next voice that Caleb heard was the girl's. She didn't speak; she screamed. Caleb opened his eyes a few millimeters to assess the situation and saw the gunman standing just in front of the woman and the girl. He was pointing the gun directly at the woman.

Caleb pressed his lips together as he took in the situation through the faint slit in his eyelids. As he had thought, the gunman was young. He was wearing a balaclava, his eyes wide underneath the black fabric. Late teens, early twenties, perhaps? No more than that. Behind him, at the front of the bus, was another man wielding a gun. He looked much more assured than his younger colleague. The boss, for sure.

The guns the men were carrying were Glock 17 pistols. Simple, but effective, especially at short range. They were plastic and metal in construction, the slide and the firing mechanism made of metal and the grip with its magazine made of plastic. Caleb could see the bottom of a magazine in the grip, but there was no way for him to tell if the gun was actually loaded or had been made ready. The only way he could tell for sure was if the man holding it—or someone else—pulled the trigger.

"What's in the bag?" the young man shouted, pointing the gun at the bottom of the woman's seat. Caleb remembered she had been holding a cloth bag close to her chest when he had boarded the bus. She must have tried to hide it under the seat, perhaps not realizing that this would only draw attention to it. Caleb saw her shifting in her seat. "What's in the bag?" the man repeated, shifting the pistol in his hand so that it was pointing back at her. In his other hand was a pillowcase, an incongruous bright yellow color, weighed down with the possessions of the other travelers.

Caleb opened his eyes a fraction more to observe the way he was holding the pistol. The Glock 17 had no safety catch, but relied on a small lever on the trigger. The actual trigger couldn't be pulled unless the lever was depressed at the same time. Caleb could see that the pad of the man's index finger was pressing the lever in. A few pounds of pressure and the gun, if it was loaded, would fire. Caleb closed his eyes and offered a brief prayer for intervention, divine or otherwise.

Whether it was because of Caleb's prayer or not, to his relief, the woman leaned forward to get the bag. A second later, it was snatched from her grasp. The man diverted his attention from the pistol to look inside, giving Caleb the perfect opportunity to disarm him. Caleb usually took such opportunities as and when they were needed, but the risk to the other passengers was too great.

"Jackpot!" the man shouted to his companion at the front of the bus. Another opportunity that Caleb didn't take or need. He leaned forward slightly to see what was in the bag, trying to maintain the impression that he was asleep.

It was money. Lots of money.

CHAPTER 3

Less than fifteen miles away from the bus, Naomi Tipton was sitting in her small, bright red Mini. The car had been a graduation present to Naomi from her father, a reward for passing her law degree a few years previously. According to him, Naomi was the first in their family to go to a proper university, and she wished he'd been there the day she had finally passed the Professional Skills Course to make her a fully qualified criminal law solicitor. It had followed two hard years of on-the-job training, but the reward was more than worth the effort. With a lump in her throat, Naomi realized that the restaurant she was sitting outside was one of the last places she had been with her father before the cancer had taken him only a few months ago. If she'd realized earlier, she would have insisted her boyfriend meet her somewhere else. But if Naomi's plan went as she hoped it would, they wouldn't even get past the waiter showing them to their table and bringing them a carafe of water. Before the menus were even presented to the table, it was her intent to be back in the car a single woman.

With a heavy sigh, Naomi climbed out of the Mini and locked it. She wasn't looking forward to the next few minutes, but it had to be done. She'd arrived early, making sure the distinctive car was hidden from the view of the restaurant. A few moments after she had arrived, a sleek black BMW belonging to her soon to be ex-boyfriend, Mark, had slipped into the parking lot, much like he had slipped into her life. Naomi had known he wouldn't be late for their meeting. Mark was never late for anything. It was one way he showed he was in charge.

When they had started seeing each other, Naomi hadn't even realized she was in a relationship with him until it was too late. They'd been on a few dates, enjoyed each other's company. Mark worked in the city, not Norwich, but London. He did something with hedge funds. Naomi knew or cared little about what that involved. She'd not been looking for anything serious. Naomi was far from promiscuous, but the first time they had gone to bed together was more of a natural extension of a drunken evening between two single people than the start of a serious relationship. At least, that was how Naomi had seen it. But it wasn't how Mark had.

It had remained fun at the start. Their relationship, and Mark had made it clear by the third time they slept together that they were in one, had started like any other. But Naomi had never seen it as anything other than a temporary thing. Her plans were elsewhere, and Mark turning up at her apartment one evening with a bag claiming he'd had to move out of his own apartment hadn't helped.

She had been offered a job far away from Norwich, in Bristol, as a newly qualified criminal law solicitor. Naomi had every intention of taking the vacancy once she had finished working her notice period. When she had told

Mark of her plans, Naomi quickly realized two things—one of which she knew already, the other she suspected. The first was how quickly he could turn to anger. The second was that he didn't mind using his fists to express his anger. Even on her.

Naomi paused at the glass doors to the restaurant, steeling herself for what was to come. Through the plate glass, she could see Mark, wearing his trademark blue suit and brown shoes like most other traders in the city, flirting with a waitress. She remembered back to a meal in another restaurant. The waiter there, a good-looking young man who, according to his name badge, was also called Mark, had been very attentive to Naomi. She'd not thought he was flirting with her, but the other Mark had. He had dragged her to his car after the meal and almost thrown her into the passenger seat before simmering all the way back to his apartment. When they had gone to bed, the way Mark had been with her raised a red flag that she couldn't ignore. He had stopped when she had told him to, but Naomi wasn't convinced that would always be the case. The next morning, she had told him of her plans for Bristol. That's when he had hit her for the first, and in Naomi's mind, the last time.

She pushed against the door and made her way into the restaurant. When Mark saw her, a lazy grin spread across his face. He stopped talking to the waitress and gestured toward a table with an enormous bunch of flowers front and center. Naomi thought again of her father, a large man who had spent his life working on oil rigs and had a physique to match it. When she was a teenager and had started dating boys, he had offered her some sage advice, unwanted at the time.

Fists, then flowers. That's when you get out and you tell me. I'll sort it.

Except Naomi's father wasn't around to protect her anymore. She was on her own. Or at least, in a few moment's time, she would be.

CHAPTER 4

Leon blew air through his cheeks as he saw the money inside the bag. It was full of paper money, most of the notes rolled together and secured with elastic bands. When he saw the outer notes of the rolls were fifty-pound notes, he whistled. There had to be thousands of pounds in the bag. Most of the notes were purple twenty pound ones with a few light brown ten pound notes as well.

Leon glanced toward the other gunman at the front of the bus who he knew only as Syd. No one in their group knew whether Syd was his real name, and Leon had never asked the man. Syd was in charge, both of this job and also the group themselves. The other two members were spread out along the road, one a hundred yards toward the front of the bus and one the same distance toward the rear. There was little if any chance of anyone driving down the road, at least according to their reconnaissance, but Syd wasn't going to take the chance that their operation would be disturbed.

"If anyone turns up," he had said during their final planning meeting, "they're just people to be robbed."

Leon tried to grab the bag from the woman, but she was clinging on to the handle for dear life.

"Give me the fucking bag!" Leon said, forcing a snarl into his voice. Beside her, the woman's child started crying.

"Please, no," the woman said, imploring him with her eyes. "It's all we have."

"I said," Leon replied, tugging at the bag again, "give me the fucking bag."

The woman still wouldn't let go of the bag. Leon raised the Glock and pointed it at the child instead of the woman. That did the trick. As the child screamed, the woman let go of the bag and pulled the girl into her arms.

Leon took the bag and backed up the aisle to the front of the bus. When he reached Syd, he saw the older youth's eyebrows shoot up under his balaclava.

"What-cha got?" Syd asked, the question almost a single word.

"Look," Leon replied, glancing down at the bag. "Cash, and plenty of it."

"Sweet," Syd replied as he took the bag from Leon. Too late, Leon realized that he could have slipped a roll or two of the notes from the bag before he handed it over. "What you waiting for?" Syd said, nodding back down the bus. "Go on, get the rest."

Leon turned and made his way slowly back down the bus, trying to look menacing to hide his underlying fear. Several of the passengers glared at him as he did so, mostly the older ones. The younger passengers had the good sense not to look him in the eye. Leon started to feel good, powerful. Syd had been right. This was a buzz like no other. But the fear hadn't completely receded.

When Leon had heard he would need to prove himself

before he could even be considered for membership to the group, he'd been nervous. He'd heard various stories about the initiation rites of the local gangs. On his estate, there were two primary gangs, loosely allied with local rival football clubs.

Most of the time, the two gangs left each other alone. They co-existed on the subsidized housing estate in an uneasy truce, the residents who lived there were at risk because they were in the middle. Apart from the derby days when the two football teams faced each other on the pitch and the gangs faced each other in the streets, a grudging respect seemed to keep the peace. Leon wasn't interested in joining either gang. He was more interested in earning money than scrawling graffiti or fighting on recreation grounds. There was one option that was only whispered about. The man called Syd, who ran various business enterprises on the estate. He wasn't a hard man, but sat above the gangs and controlled the flow of drugs and stolen vehicles through the estate. Leon had heard Syd was putting together a new crew, and he had engineered a meeting with the man where, with his heart in his mouth, Leon had asked about joining.

Syd had been clear from the off—his group wasn't a gang. Gangs were for losers with no ambition. There were plenty of others who could spray their colored tags on walls and buildings in the estate they lived on, but that wasn't Syd's intention. He was a businessman and was more interested in hard cash than reputation. Which was why Leon was walking down a bus with a gun in his hand, threatening everyone on it.

Including, Leon reflected as he walked back to the seats where the woman without the bag was now crying, tears and snot streaming down her face, a man who appeared to be asleep in the seat behind her. The bus had all sorts of passengers, young and old.

But this passenger was the only one wearing a robe.

CHAPTER 5

Vince rolled his head from side to side, trying and failing to ease a crick in his neck that he'd had since the previous evening's session in the gym. He knew exactly what he'd done. It was the last dead-lift of his set and he'd been so desperate to complete it that he'd poked his head forward, which had resulted in instant pain and a dropped weight. Even an ice pack from the stupid cow in reception at the gym hadn't helped. Maybe when this job was over, he would go and see his chiropractor, even though he usually felt worse after visiting him.

"All teams. I have control of Yellow Burger," a male voice said in his earpiece. Vince tutted under his breath. He knew it was a computer that allocated their target's code names, but surely there was an over-ride button at Control to skip the stupid ones. "White baggy trousers, navy blue puffer jacket, black baseball cap pulled down low over his eyes."

Vince frowned. That didn't sound like Yellow Burger to him. The man who he and his team had been tracking for some months had only ever been seen wearing a thobe, a long garment worn by some Muslim men, and he usually wore a traditional kufi hat. Never a baseball cap. If Yellow Burger was on their radar as a terrorist, he could have ditched his usual clothes as part of a cleansing process prior to an attack of some sort. But that wasn't why Yellow Burger was on Vince's hit list. He wasn't a terrorist, but a high-level mercenary who was planning to attack the British cyber network with a program that would suck everything out of all the government agencies to be sold to the highest bidder. If the intelligence Vince's employers had was correct, and it usually was, there was a veritable queue of potential buyers.

"Confirm it's Yellow Burger, six four," Vince said into the small microphone sewn into his suit cuff. "Do you have a definite visual?" It could be just some random bloke leaving the flat, not their target.

"Wait, wait," the male voice belonging to a member of Vince's surveillance team replied. Vince did as he asked, knowing that six four would be adjusting his position to get a better look at their target. The problem with Yellow Burger was that he was surveillance aware and highly paranoid with it. They had only a few photographs of the man, which made tracking him difficult, if not impossible. That was why, when the call of a sighting had come in from one of their sources, Vince and his team had dropped everything to get to his location even though it had been several hours drive from their base in Thames House in London.

Vince stabbed his fingers at the screen of his phone and raised it to his ear.

"Hello, how may I help you?" the woman who answered asked. That was the standard greeting. It wasn't as if they could say *Secret Intelligence Service. How may I help you?*

"This is six six," Vince said, using his designated identifier. His department had six teams, all composed of six operatives, but only his team was authorized to take executive action. The other five found and followed people, but they didn't take them out. Only Vince's team did that, and it was something they did very well indeed. "How did we get notification?" There was a pause on the other end of the line while Control considered their response. Calls were always like this. Slow, formulated, and utterly meaningless to anyone who might be listening in.

"From a reliable source," she said a moment later. "They used an agreed identifier."

Vince thought for a moment. The agreed identifiers were used to ensure that any information received was genuine and from a known informer, of whom there were many. He couldn't ask for any more information on the phone, so he just disconnected the call and sat back in the passenger seat of the car to wait for six four. It took the other operative longer to respond than Vince wanted, but eventually, he did.

"Stand by, stand by. Target not confirmed as Yellow Burger. I say again, the target is not Yellow Burger. Sending visual now for ident."

Vince swore under his breath as he reached for his secure tablet. He swiped at the screen and brought up the photograph six four had just sent. It wasn't Yellow Burger, unless their target had lost around twenty kilos since he was last captured on film. At least the image six four had managed to get was a clear one, which would make Control's life easier.

"Six one and six two, stay on him in case he's connected to Yellow Burger," Vince said into his cuff microphone. A couple of clicks on the line told him they had received the message. "All other callsigns maintain control of the apartment. Yellow Burger could still be in there."

"No signs of life inside, six six," one operative said a few moments later. Then Control's voice came on over the radio.

"Earlier target not on any of our databases."

Vince swore again. The man's face would have been run through several facial recognition systems, a few of which would have the left-leaning public up in arms if they knew they existed. There was something off about this whole job. Vince could feel it. His earlier enthusiasm about a successful take down was evaporating.

"Six one, earlier target returning to the apartment," Vince's radio told him a few moments later. "Now carrying a carton of milk in his hand."

"For God's sake," Vince muttered, not caring if it was picked up on the microphone. They had just deployed a kill team to the back end of nowhere to watch a man get some milk.

CHAPTER 6

Caleb waited, listening as the thief walked down the length of the bus. He could hear the footsteps over the sound of the woman in the seat in front sobbing. The noise she was making was far from sadness at having lost some money. It was a sound Caleb had heard before. The sound a person makes when they have lost everything.

"You! Wake up!" Caleb felt a foot nudging his calf. The foot was tentative, with nowhere near as much authority as the voice. Caleb waited for a few seconds before opening his eyes. When he had opened them, he arched a single eyebrow in the youth's direction. "What have you got in there?"

The man with the gun was gesturing at the small cloth bag that Caleb had on his lap. Caleb looked at the gun, confirming his suspicion that it was a Glock 17, probably loaded, perhaps made ready. The youth was using it as a prop, not a threat. It would only take a split second for Caleb to put his hand over the youth's and disarm him with a vicious twist that would break either his finger or his wrist. Perhaps both. Then another split second to rack the slide back and put a round between the eyes of the man at the front of the bus. It would be an easy shot for Caleb. He'd shot people from much further away with similar weapons and not missed. Caleb rarely missed. Then the man who had just nudged him would be looking at the other end of the gun and the smoke trickling from the barrel before his compatriot's body had even hit the floor.

Caleb did none of these things. The bus was full of civilians. Children, women, and men who had no experience with guns. Perhaps one or two of them would have in the past, but Caleb had watched them all board and he was pretty sure they were all career civilians. If he started shooting, their reactions could be unpredictable and dangerous. That was one reason.

Another was that the young man who had just nudged his leg was not, in Caleb's opinion, particularly dangerous. He was trying very hard to project an aura of menace, but was falling well short. Caleb would be surprised if he had ever fired the weapon in his hand.

"I asked you a question, monk," the man with the gun said. Caleb said nothing, but just looked at him. "What's in the bag?"

Caleb, moving slowly, opened the top of the bag to allow the man to see inside it. There was nothing in there to interest a robber. Nothing of value to anyone other than Caleb. He knew the man would recognize some of the items in there. The cut-throat razor Caleb used to keep his head shaved, perhaps the whetstone that he used to keep the razor sharp. But there was no money, no wallet, not even a passport. Caleb did have one, just not in his bag. He kept it in an interior pocket of his robe, along with the little money he had, as he always did when he traveled on public transport.

"Where's all your stuff?" the young man said, raising the gun and pointing it at Caleb. His finger was outside the trigger guard, and Caleb knew he could snap it at the first phalangeal joint before it got anywhere near the trigger.

"This is all my stuff," Caleb said, keeping his voice low and, hopefully, non-threatening. "I travel light." If the young man recognized Caleb's Texan drawl, he didn't acknowledge it. They stared at each other for a few seconds, the young man's eyes flicking between Caleb's as if he was trying to work out what to say next. Then the other balaclava clad man at the front of bus shouted at his partner in crime.

"Yo, come on!" Caleb saw him whirling his index finger in the air, a universal military gesture that meant *Let's Go!* "Twenty seconds and we're out of here."

Caleb tucked away the gesture in his mind. It was an unusual one for a civilian to make. Perhaps he wasn't the only person on the bus who had served after all?

With a final look at Caleb, the young man with the gun moved on to the passengers in the seat behind him. Caleb closed his eyes as he heard the two elderly passengers struggle to put their valuables into the pillowcase. A few seconds later, he heard a young woman scream, but he kept his eyes closed. The scream was one of anger, mixed with fear, and he doubted she was in any danger. Caleb doubted any of the passengers were in any danger at all. When he had looked into the young man's eyes a few seconds previously, Caleb had realized one thing.

The gunman was just as scared as the passengers on the bus.

CHAPTER 7

Suzy took a deep sigh of relief when she realized that the two gunmen had got off the bus. She used the back of her hand to wipe her face before reaching into a pocket for a packet of tissues. When she handed one of the tissues to Leanne, the girl was just staring at the seat in front of them. No tears, no expression. Just a vacant look. Suzy didn't know if that was good or bad. Was it shock? Neither of them had ever seen a gun up close and personal before, and Suzy didn't know if Leanne had comprehended just how much danger they had been in.

That didn't matter anymore, though. The danger from the two men who had just robbed the bus had gone. They had left with a screech of tires and disappeared. The last thing she had seen of them was the brake lights of their vehicle flaring a few hundred yards up the road as they slowed for a bend. Then they were gone. But the real danger facing Suzy and Leanne hadn't gone. If anything, now that Suzy had lost the money she had been saving for so long, their position was even more precarious.

"Where's the driver?" a male voice from the front of the

bus shouted. A couple of the passengers got off and a few moments later, one of them got back on to address the rest of the passengers. "Is there anyone with first-aid training here?" It was the same man who had asked where the driver was. Suzy looked at him as Leanne stirred beside her. At least someone was taking charge of the situation. "And can anyone drive a bus?"

There was some movement behind her as another passenger got to his feet. Suzy turned to see an elderly gentleman with his hand raised in the air.

"I used to," he said with a nervous laugh. "A long time ago, but how hard can it be?" None of the other passengers reacted to him. The majority of them, like Leanne, appeared to still be in shock.

"I've called the police," another passenger shouted. "I've still got my phone. They're on their way."

"Leanne," Suzy said, shaking her daughter's shoulder. "Come on." When the bus had stopped, she'd not been able to get a signal on her cell phone, a burner bought for cash from the market, but it appeared somebody had managed to keep their phone from the robbers and get a signal.

"What is it?" Leanne replied, mumbling the words.

"We need to go, sweetheart," Suzy said.

Suzy got to her feet and tugged Leanne's arm. Around them, other passengers were milling about. Some of them laughed, nervous sounds that Suzy thought were intended to cover their shock. Just before she made her way to the front of the bus, Suzy turned around to look at the man who was sitting behind them. He just stared back at her with an impassive expression, his gray eyes giving nothing away.

She made her way past the other passengers, pulling Leanne behind her. Suzy knew they couldn't be here when the police arrived. That would be a disaster. Losing the bag with all the money was bad enough, but if the police knew who they were, that would be an end to everything before she and Leanne had even got to London.

With a few mumbled excuse me's, Suzy managed to get to the front of the bus. She made her way down the steps, hefting Leanne onto her hip as she did so. Her daughter had got so big, so quickly. It only seemed like a few weeks ago that she was a babe in arms. Now, Suzy could barely carry her down the steps to the ground where she put her down.

Suzy looked around, her head snapping from side to side. The bus had stopped in what looked like a country lane in the middle of nowhere. On either side of the road were thick tree trunks, their branches almost forming a tunnel over the roof of the bus. The robbers had chosen their spot well.

As Suzy looked toward the far end of the road, she thought she could see the flicker of blue lights approaching through the branches. They needed to go. But where? The only option was into the forest.

"This way, Leanne," Suzy said, pulling her daughter's arm. Their primary goal was to get away from the authorities, and slipping into the woods was the only option they had available. The rest, she would have to worry about later.

"But Mummy," Leanne said, resisting Suzy's arm. Suzy looked down at her daughter who was pointing at the bottom of the bus. "What about Boo Boo?"

Boo Boo, Leanne's favorite toy, had been stuffed into a bag as they had packed their things back at the house. Along with the rest of their clothes, the tattered pink elephant was in a suitcase that the driver had put into the baggage hold of the bus for them back at the station. Suzy looked back at the flickering blue lights, now much closer than before. They didn't have long.

"Boo Boo will be fine, Leanne," Suzy said with a lump in her throat. "He'll be absolutely fine. Now we need to hide, just like we practiced. Do you remember?"

With tears streaming down her face, Suzy pulled Leanne toward the trees. Her daughter resisted at first, but eventually acquiesced. As they approached the dark forest, Suzy saw Leanne looking back at the bus several times. She mouthed the name Boo Boo a couple of times, which broke Suzy's heart.

By the time they reached the tree line, they were both sobbing.

CHAPTER 8

The interior of the restaurant was cool and Naomi took another deep breath as she took in her surroundings. There was the faintest smell of food in the air that made her mouth water, but she had no intention of eating here. At the sound of the door opening, the waitress had glanced up and smiled at Naomi, as had Mark. But it was only the waitress's smile that was genuine. Naomi ignored Mark's gesture toward the table with the flowers and stayed where she was for a few seconds.

The restaurant had started life as a coaching pub at some point back in the mid sixteenth-century. It was located on the original main road that linked Norwich and London, built by the Romans not long after they invaded, to help the legions keep the troublesome locals north of the capital under control. Terrorized by highwaymen and all but impassable in winter, the route had not seen horse-drawn coaches for many years. But many of the hostelries, originally based every seven to ten miles along the route, had somehow endured.

Naomi neither knew nor cared for the restaurant's

history. Her attention was focused on Mark, who was staring at her as she stood just inside the door. She broke away from his gaze to look around the dining area. It wasn't busy, with only a single couple sitting in one corner sipping coffee. From recessed speakers in the ceiling, Sting was crooning about how much his poor heart was aching, and in the distance Naomi could hear the clatter of cutlery as the kitchen staff prepared for the evening diners.

"Naomi," Mark said as he approached her. She saw his eyes flicker from her head to her feet, and back again. She had deliberately worn a version of her work clothes, a smart business suit that was just slightly too informal for court, in an attempt to appear businesslike as opposed to alluring. But the effect appeared lost on Mark. "You look amazing." He leaned forward and she allowed him to kiss her on the cheek. As he did so, she caught the scent of his cologne in her nostrils. The familiar smell turned her stomach, but not in the way it once had.

Naomi allowed herself to be guided to the table, ignoring the flowers as she sat down. The waitress came across and fussed around them for a moment before placing menus in front of them and telling them she would be back in a moment to take their order. Naomi saw the faintest frown cross Mark's face when she declined a pre-dinner drink, but it was gone in an instant.

"You've had your hair done," Mark said, casting an appraising gaze over Naomi's new bob and smiling. She raised both hands to her ears and smoothed strands of dark hair behind them, an unconscious gesture her mentor had cautioned her against in the courtroom, unless she deliberately wanted her opposing counsel to know she was nervous. "It looks lovely." Mark's smile broadened. "Shows off your cheekbones very nicely."

"Thank you," Naomi replied automatically, her voice almost a whisper. Her mouth was dry and she wished she'd asked the waitress for a glass of water.

She took a deep breath. Prior to leaving her apartment, Naomi had stood in her bathroom rehearsing her words in the mirror, just as she did before every court case. But the words she had practiced earlier deserted her.

"Mark, listen," Naomi said, trying to put some authority into her voice.

"No, Naomi, let me go first," Mark replied, putting his hands palms out in a placatory gesture. "Please?" Naomi knew it would be no good to try to talk over him. Let him have his say. Then she could have hers. "The other morning, when we argued? That was stupid of me. It was the thought of you going to Bristol, me not being able to see you as often. That was all. It meant nothing." Naomi felt her eyebrows arching at his words. The sting of his palm across her cheek hadn't meant nothing to her. "It was a childish reaction and it will never, ever, happen again." Another thing her father had told her men like Mark said.

He was looking at her with an imploring expression, evidently waiting for, and fully expecting, complete forgiveness. If the situation hadn't been so serious, Naomi would have laughed in his face. She licked her lips, waiting to make sure he had finished. When she was sure he had, Naomi spoke.

"It's over, Mark." She paused as his expression froze. "We're done, you and I. Thanks for the flowers." She nodded at the bouquet on the table. "Maybe you could give them to your mum?"

As Naomi scraped the chair back and prepared to get to her feet, Mark's hands flashed down and grabbed both her wrists. She felt his fingers digging into the soft flesh of her forearms and gasped. The waitress, who had been approaching the table, paused before turning and walking away.

"What did you say, Naomi?" Mark hissed, trying to force a smile onto his face.

"I said, it's over, Mark," Naomi replied, trying to pull her forearms away. Knowing her next words were childish, she said them anyway. "What's the matter? Have you never been dumped before?"

Mark's grip tightened on her arms. "You don't get to say when it's over, Naomi," Mark said, his voice low. "That's not how it works at all. Now we're going to eat our dinner and then go back to our flat where you can apologize for what you just said." It wasn't their flat, it was Naomi's, and his claim to it wasn't lost on her.

"Is everything okay here?" a woman's voice said. Naomi looked up to see the female diner who had been sipping coffee with her companion standing a few feet from the table.

"Everything's fine," Mark replied on their behalf, not even looking at the woman.

"Are you sure?" she said.

Finally, Mark tore his gaze away from Naomi and looked at the customer. The woman was petite, almost tiny, and had an expression somewhere between bemusement and concern.

"Not being funny, pet,'" Mark said to the woman, "but this is nothing to do with you, so why don't you just fuck off." He turned his eyes back to Naomi and she could see the raw anger behind them. "This is personal."

CHAPTER 9

Caleb watched the woman and child from the seat in front of him as they stood in front of the trees. The child appeared to be upset about something. Not the fact they had just been robbed, but something more visceral than that. He was far from an expert on children, but it was the way she was crying almost inconsolably that piqued his interest. Perhaps the child needed the bathroom and that was why her mother was taking her toward the trees? Caleb looked over his shoulder at the tiny bathroom built into the bus. The green light above the folding door told him it was empty, so why weren't they using that?

He watched them for a few seconds, realizing that it wasn't a bathroom break. The woman was gazing at the trees, as if searching for a way through them. With a last backward glance that sealed Caleb's next actions, she stepped forward and into the tree line, pulling the girl behind her.

"Excuse me," Caleb said as he got to his feet. There was a passenger standing in the aisle, chatting with one of his fellow travelers. Whether it was Caleb's deep Texan accent, the fact he was wearing a gray robe, or that the passenger picked up on the intensity in his eyes, Caleb was unsure, but the elderly man took a step back with a look of surprise.

Caleb made his way down the bus, moving as quickly as he could without attracting too much attention to himself. He hurried down the steps at the front and into the open air. A few yards away, the driver was sitting on the grass verge being attended to by some of the other passengers. Caleb wouldn't have bothered. The man was conscious and appeared alert enough to be exchanging jokes with the passengers. Not only that but there were two police cars approaching rapidly. Caleb spoke to the driver briefly before he got what Caleb had asked for, a suitcase from one of the luggage compartments. Caleb then made his way to the spot where he had seen the woman and the child disappear into the woods.

He paused for a few seconds to look at the trees in front of him. The forest was predominantly composed of oak trees and while it had perhaps been managed at some point in its history, the random nature of the way the trees grew told Caleb it was now wild. Above his head, the rich canopies swirled in a soft breeze. Caleb would have preferred to pause for longer, close his eyes, and just appreciate the sound, but there was work to be done.

Caleb stepped through the gap in the trunks and took a few steps forward before stopping. He placed his hand on a gnarled trunk for a second or two, wondering what the tree may have seen in its history. Caleb had read about the British fascination with oak trees, some of which dated all the way back to when a Norman named William managed to replace his original nickname of William the Bastard with the more complimentary one of William the Conqueror. Oak trees had since hidden kings from rebels, been used to build famous warships such as Horatio Nelson's HMS Victory, and even provided the ink used to sign the Magna Carta.

"All from a single acorn," Caleb muttered under his breath as he took in his surroundings. Behind him, he could still hear the now muted voices of the passengers from the bus. He dropped to his haunches and studied the ground. The rain earlier had left the soil soft and pliable, and it only took Caleb a few seconds to find fresh footprints. Two sets, one large, one small. He pushed through the leafy ferns growing on the forest floor, his eyes alternating between the ground and the terrain in front of him.

The further into the forest he got, the more indistinct the footprints became as the amount of rain that had penetrated the canopy lessened. But Caleb didn't need footprints to follow people through a forest. There were plenty of other signs that told him which way the woman and the child had gone. Small, freshly broken twigs on the ground. Ferns with no raindrops on their leaves where they had been brushed away as someone had passed by. He hefted the small suitcase onto his shoulder before slowing his pace. It wasn't his intention to catch up with the woman and the child. Just to follow them. To make sure they were safe. If necessary, to watch over them.

He knew they were scared. Terrified.

But of what? Or of whom?

CHAPTER 10

Vince stared out of the window of their black SUV as the countryside flew by outside. They were on the A1, heading back to London along a road originally laid by the Roman Empire. The next set of invaders a thousand years later, the Normans, had probably used it as well to establish their dominance over the kingdom. But since then, England hadn't been invaded by anyone. The fact that this was in part because of people like Vince wasn't lost on him. As a member of MI5, his team was responsible for protecting the country against threats from internal agencies and individuals who might want to encourage foreign invaders. But Vince's team didn't just operate under the radar. There wasn't a radar that could even come close to detecting them, and as the sixth team, they were the very best of the very best. So how had they just been made idiots of?

They had stayed on mission for another few hours before finally deciding that the mission was a bust. Yellow Burger was nowhere to be seen. Vince doubted he'd ever heard of the small village they had spent the day in, much less actually been there. It wasn't the first time they'd been chasing a ghost. It was what they spent most of their time doing. But Vince's senses told him something was off about this.

Vince's tablet pinged with an incoming file. He swiped at the screen to open it and tapped on the play icon of the audio file. This was the call that had come into a GCHQ confidential hotline which had generated their team's deployment.

"Arif Hussain is staying at number fourteen, Glebe Close, in Spalding." It was a male voice, somewhat muffled. "This is Crouching Squirrel."

Vince almost laughed at the identifier. It was yet another stupid phrase spat out by a computer, but its purpose was to inform MI5 that this was a genuine confidential informant, not a random caller with delusions of grandeur. He frowned and replayed the voice file.

"What do you think, six?" the driver of the SUV asked. They didn't use their real first names when talking to each other, but Vince knew the driver's name was Stephen. He knew nothing else about the man. Any personal information was kept to themselves to avoid compromise. If the bad guys wanted to look for a man called Stephen in London, they could fill their boots.

"Where d'you think that accent's from?" Vince asked as he replayed the file.

"West country?"

"No, I think it's the other side. That sounds like a Norfolk accent to me."

"You should know," Stephen replied. "That's your neck of the woods, isn't it?" Stephen's question was, technically speaking, a breach of protocol, but Vince couldn't hide his accent any more than he could hide his face. He waited for the inevitable dig about inbreeding, webbed feet, or extra digits, but Stephen appeared to have more sense than that.

Vince sat back in his seat and stared out of the window. To his knowledge, there were very few confidential informants in the area he lived in. It was far from a hotbed of terrorism or fundamentalist ideologies. His sense of disquiet about the job was increasing the more he thought about it. Why would there be a call to GCHQ with a correct identifier from someone with an accent from where Vince lived?

Once they got back to Vauxhall Cross, the sprawling building on the banks of the Thames that housed the Secret Intelligence Service, Vince could instigate a proper review of the call and the mobile phone that made it. He would be able to identify where the call was made from down to within a couple of yards. He could cross reference calls to other numbers and read any text messages sent or received from it. The systems Vince had access to would even be able to suck out any photos taken by the device if it had a camera. There was nothing on the mobile phone that Vince wouldn't be able to see. He could have instigated the review through Control, but he didn't want to do that. If he did it himself, he could do it quietly without any traces being left on their systems.

Vince had always trusted his instincts, and they were telling him one thing about the supposed sighting of Yellow Burger.

Something wasn't right.

CHAPTER 11

Leon sat back in the passenger seat of the car, pulled the balaclava from his face, and grinned widely at Syd, who was behind the wheel.

"Awesome," Leon said, hitting the dash with the heel of his hand. "That was bloody awesome."

Syd grinned back at him, nodding his head.

"You did good, bro," Syd said, his accent marking him out as being from the East End of London. But Leon knew that while Syd might have been born within the sound of the Bow Bells, making him a genuine cockney, the accent was mostly affected. Once or twice, when Syd had let his guard down, Leon had heard it slip and a more cultured accent creep through that spoke of somewhere less deprived. "Getting that bag off that woman, that was mint, Leon," Syd said. "How much do you think is in there, Gary?"

Leon turned to the third member of their group, Gary, who was sitting in the rear of the car going through the pillowcase. At Syd's question, he glanced into the bag next to him. Leon could see rolls of notes piled on top of each other.

"I dunno, Syd," Gary replied, his accent definitely genuine. Gary was a couple of years older than Leon, wore the same dark clothing as the others, and usually acted as the muscle due to his bulk which was partially from working in the gym, partially from some additional steroids. "Got to be at least five grand, if not more. I'll sort out these phones and I'll count it up after."

"Sweet," Leon said with another slap of the dash. "Give me a handful. I'll help out."

Gary leaned forward and thrust five or six phones into Leon's outstretched hand. As Gary was doing in the back of the car, Leon first looked to see if any of them were unlocked. Any that were would be quickly checked for internet banking apps. People who failed to secure their phones often failed to secure their banking apps as well, and Syd had an anonymous cryptocurrency account that these unsuspecting people would deposit funds into on his behalf. By the time the phone owners and their banks discovered the theft, the cash would be long gone. But on this occasion, all the phones that Gary had handed to Leon were locked.

Leon thumbed at the screen of the first phone, an almost new and latest version of the iPhone, to be asked for a pass code. Putting his thumb over the camera to foil any security apps that might try to take his photo, he tried six zeroes, then the numbers one to six. When he got to the screen that told him the iPhone was disabled, and that he should try again in one minute, Leon flipped the protective case off the phone to remove the sim card. If he had been able to, he would have powered the phone down as well, but they wouldn't have the phones for very long anyway.

He went through the process for the other phones before turning round to Gary.

"Nothing on these, mate," Leon said. In reply, Gary held open a large pouch the size of a laptop for Leon to put them in. It was, according to the manufacturer's specifications, a complete Faraday cage that would block all signals both to and from the phones. The pouch would be dropped off later with one of Syd's friends who ran a phone stall in a local market. A few days after that, the street value of the handsets, minus Syd's friend's cut for cleaning them, would appear in one of Syd's business accounts. According to Syd, this would be a genuine transaction that he would even pay tax on. He had explained this to Leon one evening. Whether this was to show off his business acumen to Leon or because he wanted the younger man to know, wasn't clear but Leon had listened attentively.

In the back of the car, Gary had turned his attention to the wallets and purses. Leon watched him as, wearing purple vinyl gloves, he worked his way through them. Any cash went straight into another bag, and Leon saw him searching through them for anything else of value such as small bits of paper with four digits on them. There were several cash machines they knew of where money could be withdrawn out of the gaze of any cameras.

"Did I do okay, Syd?" Leon asked, turning to face their leader. "Are you happy with how it went?"

"Like clockwork, bro," Syd replied, an easy smile on his face. "You did good. Up for another in a few days?"

Leon smiled to himself before replying. To be invited onto the next job told him all he needed to know about his performance. If Syd wanted him along, it meant he was in.

"For sure, Syd," Leon said, looking out of the window as the forest started to give way to open countryside. In a few moments, they would be on a two lane highway that led all the way back to Norwich. "That'd be magic."

CHAPTER 12

Naomi felt the corners of her mouth start to twitch as, behind Mark's shoulder, she watched the female diner's companion getting to his feet. He was a large man, easily over six feet tall, and broad shouldered with it. Unseen by Mark, he made his way over to the table. When he placed his hand on the back of Mark's neck, it was large enough for her to see both his thumb and fingers on either side. In response to the movement, Mark jumped and tried to turn but the man's hand held him in place. With his other hand, the diner reached into his pocket and produced a small, black leather wallet which he flipped over. When the man placed the open wallet on the table, Naomi didn't need to look at it to see the silver crown of the police warrant badge.

"Did you just tell my Detective Sergeant to fuck off?" the police officer said. His voice suited his physique, a deep baritone that was filled with menace. "Only that's not very polite, is it now?"

"Let go of me," Mark replied through gritted teeth,

glancing at the badge. "I've got your number. I'll be reporting you for assault."

"Will you now?" The police officer smiled in Naomi's direction. "Let go of the young lady's arms and I'll think about it."

Mark turned his attention to Naomi, and the raw anger in his eyes only seemed to intensify.

"You bitch, you've set me up, haven't you?" he asked her. "You work with these muppets, I take it?" Naomi saw the policeman's knuckles whitening as he increased the pressure on Mark's neck. In response, Mark let go of her and Naomi had to resist the temptation to rub the small, painful indentations in her wrists his fingers had left.

"This can go one of a couple of ways, sunshine," the policeman said. He was a Detective Constable called Dave who according to his colleague, Sarah, was a sucker for a damsel in distress. "You can walk out of here like a good lad, get in that hairdresser's car of yours, and do one. Or I can arrest you for something and take you into custody. You'll probably resist arrest and I'll be forced to give you a good old-fashioned shoeing on the way to the nick." His grip on Mark's neck tightened further, and Naomi saw her hopefully now ex-boyfriend wince. "Which is it to be?"

"I'm going," Mark said, still shooting daggers at Naomi with his eyes. "But this isn't over, Naomi. It's far from over."

"Just take it like a man, mate," Dave said, still smiling at Naomi. "That's my advice."

"I don't need your advice," Mark replied, trying and failing for a steely voice as Dave let go of his neck. Naomi saw Dave turn his eyes to Mark, his smile hardening.

"I think you do," Dave said, his voice even lower. "If I hear you've been bothering young Naomi here in the slightest, then I'll pop round to see you for a chat. Are we clear?"

"Crystal," Mark replied as he used his hands to push his chair back. He stood and puffed himself up. Naomi knew he would be desperate to try to save face, but with Dave still towering almost a full head's height above him, it wouldn't be easy.

With the waitress hovering uncertainly near her till, Mark made his way out of the restaurant. A few seconds later, there was the roar of an engine which was followed by the screech of tires as he left the parking lot. Naomi blew her breath out of her cheeks and smiled at the two police officers.

"Dave, Sarah?" she said as she gestured to the chairs at the table. "Can I get you both a drink?"

"I think it's the least you can do, Naomi," Sarah said with a smile as she sat down. "A glass of Pinot Grigio for me, and just Pepsi for laughing boy here. He's driving." Dave just shrugged his shoulders, picked up his warrant badge from the table, and wandered off with his cell phone in his hand.

Naomi raised her hand to attract the waitress's attention. When the young girl approached, Naomi asked her to remove the flowers from the table and take them away before placing the drinks order. Sarah leaned forward and put her hand on Naomi's arm.

"You okay, babe?" Sarah asked. "You've got somewhere you can go for a few days, just in case?"

"I can go to my sister's place," Naomi replied. "Mark's never met her, so won't know where she lives."

"Any problems, you just shout." Sarah nodded at Dave who was still engrossed in his phone. "He'll be round like a shot, you know that. I think he quite enjoyed that."

Dave returned to the table with a wry smile on his face a few moments later just as the waitress arrived with the drinks.

"What have you done?" Sarah asked him, shifting her position to allow the girl to put the drinks down on the table.

"I just texted my mate in Traffic," Dave said, reaching for his Pepsi. "Your ex might be attracting their attention over the next few days. A gentle reminder that we're keeping an eye."

Sarah laughed as she picked up her own glass, clinking it off Naomi's. "Cheers, babe. Here's to being young, free, and single again."

Naomi smiled and she returned the gesture.

"Cheers to the pair of you," she said, her smile faltering as she remembered Mark's parting shot.

Naomi had a feeling she'd not seen the last of Mark just yet.

CHAPTER 13

Suzy clutched Leanne's hand firmly, as much for her own reassurance as the child's. They were following a rough path through the woods, perhaps made by animals looking for food. Every few steps there was a muffled sob from Leanne. Suzy knew they would have to stop soon. But they had no water, no food, no money. Perhaps she should have taken the time to get the suitcase with the rest of their belongings? In her desire to get as far away from the bus, and the authorities, as possible, all Suzy had managed to do was to get lost in a forest. She could see from the way the light was changing that it would be dark soon. As if reading her mind, Leanne finally spoke.

"Mummy?" she said, her voice plaintive. "I'm tired. Are we stopping soon?"

"Yes, Leanne," Suzy replied, almost on autopilot. "We'll stop soon."

As they walked, Suzy thought hard about their predicament. The most important thing was that they were safe, at least for the time being. Had they waited for the police to arrive, the moment her name had gone into any official database, Vince would know exactly where she and Leanne were. He could catch up with them at any point, that much she did know. Their faces would be recorded on a camera somewhere that would eventually ping up on a computer system. But she had been bargaining on being lost in the crowds of London before that happened. Although there were more CCTV cameras per head of population in England than anywhere else in the world, there were also plenty of places to hide from them.

Suzy's main concern was about the cameras owned by the authorities, as Vince's systems would be able to access them almost in real time. But she also knew that he would be able to trawl through privately owned ones, given time. He had once told her about a terrorism suspect who had been caught after the government's facial recognition software had picked him up on someone's video doorbell. But when questioned about how the footage had been accessed, Vince had gone quiet.

The path they were traveling down started to open out and become wider, confirming her thoughts about animals. A few hundred yards further along, it gave way to a small clearing with a ramshackle hut in the center. The hut was small, perhaps ten feet by six feet, and made of wood with a felt roof. But it was shelter of sorts.

Suzy approached the hut cautiously, Leanne shuffling along behind her. The walls were made of hewn logs, with wooden planks forming a door. There was no lock that Suzy could see, but she knocked softly on the door just in case it was occupied. When there was no reply, Suzy slowly inched the door open and peered inside.

"Mummy," Leanne said from her side. "I don't like it. It's scary."

"Shh, Leanne," Suzy replied as she waited for her eyes to

adjust to the gloomy interior. "There's nothing to be scared of."

Inside the hut was a variety of tools that Leanne didn't recognize. Some sort of hand axes, a scythe that looked as old as Suzy herself, but most importantly, there was also a wooden bed with a mattress and carefully folded bedding. Next to the bed was a table, and under the table were several large plastic bottles of water. Suzy sighed with relief at the sight. At least they could drink now.

"It's perfect," Suzy said to Leanne, forcing a smile onto her face. "We can stay here for the night. Look! There's a bed just big enough for you and me."

She waited as Leanne inched her way into the hut, her curiosity overcoming her fear.

"Does someone live here?" Leanne asked, her voice only just above a whisper.

"No," Suzy replied. "This is just somewhere for people to stay if they're working here." She nodded at the tools. "See? They use them to look after the trees." Next to the tools were bowls and several sets of cutlery, all covered in dust but otherwise clean.

"Where's the light switch?"

"I don't think there is one."

"But how will we see?"

"We won't need to see," Suzy said, making sure she kept smiling. "We'll be fast asleep. Do you want a drink of water?"

Leanne nodded her head and Suzy walked into the hut and picked up one of the bottles of water. The air smelled musty and thick, and she could see that no one had been in the hut for a while from the layer of dust that covered everything. The bottle of water was still sealed though, and Suzy drank from it gratefully once Leanne had her fill.

"I'm hungry, Mummy," Leanne said as Suzy patted the worn mattress on the bed.

"We'll have a massive breakfast in the morning," Suzy replied, although she had no idea where she was going to get it from. They might have bowls, but she had nothing to put in them.

"Promise?"

Suzy nodded her head.

"Sure, I promise. Now, come on." She patted the mattress again. "Snuggle in. Let's get a good night's sleep."

"Are there bears in these woods?"

"Nope, no bears anywhere."

"Monsters?"

"Monsters don't exist, Leanne."

"Are you sure?"

Suzy paused for a few seconds before replying. Monsters did exist, but not in the form that Leanne thought they did. One, in particular, who Suzy knew would be making every effort to locate them both.

"I promise you, Leanne, there are no monsters in these woods," Suzy replied. Vince would be miles away, so she wasn't lying. "Now close your eyes." She watched as Leanne did as she was told before tucking the bedding around her daughter. "Sweet dreams."

CHAPTER 14

Caleb squatted on his haunches and looked at the small hut in the clearing. It hadn't taken him long to catch up with the woman and her daughter, and he'd needed to slow his pace to remain unobserved. As he had followed them along the path, always remaining out of sight, Caleb had taken in the way the forest had changed as they had moved through it. The oak trees had become interspersed with beech and ash, and he had even seen some alder in the wetter areas. Caleb saw some large hazel stumps in the undergrowth between the mature trees, clear evidence of human activity. The stools had been coppiced, although not recently, for firewood or building material, and there were clear paths between them. Caleb had paused to examine the paths, tracing his fingers over the way the vegetation had been flattened.

In the clearing, the woman and the child had now ventured into the hut. It looked to Caleb to be a forester's hut, no doubt used by the same people who had coppiced the hazels, but from the look of the stumps, no one had done that for a while. He found a patch of ground with no stones and sat down, folding his legs underneath him before placing his small cloth bag down in front of him, and the suitcase from the bus behind him. Caleb stared at the hut, perhaps seventy five yards away, and thought again about the woman hiding inside with her daughter.

Around him, the forest gradually started to settle into the night. He could hear the almost silent whooshing of bat wings in the canopy above him as they darted around, searching for insects. A larger animal, most likely a deer or perhaps a badger, was making its way through the under-growth some distance behind him, but Caleb knew the animal would keep its distance. There was a faint breeze on his face which would carry his scent for hundreds of yards. Long enough to warn off any curious creatures. The light gradually faded, and before long his hearing and sense of smell were the only senses available to him.

Caleb settled in to wait. He had spent many hours in similar situations in his life. If anything, this was a very comfortable way to keep watch. He wasn't wearing a ghillie suit, hiding in a tree in a country where every other person in the vicinity would kill him on sight. He could get up and move around, relieve himself, or just sit and be.

As he sat, he contemplated his situation. This had not been how he had planned on spending the night. He should be in London, in a bed, preparing for the next stage of his journey to the west of the country. Caleb's ultimate destination was a town in Somerset called Glastonbury where he hoped to find something long since lost. But it seemed that quest would have to wait. Caleb lived his life in the moment, and that moment was now. He went where he was called, and he had been called here. Caleb didn't know why, not yet, but he knew he was in the right place.

Caleb slowed his breathing and closed his eyes, relying

on his hearing to alert him to anything untoward in the forest. He focused his mind, concentrating on inhaling and exhaling. As he did so, he murmured a version of a psalm under his breath.

"I will keep you safe from all hidden dangers." Caleb inhaled through his nose. "I will cover you with my wings and you will be safe in my care. My faithfulness will protect and defend you." His eyes flickered as he put all his focus into the words. "You need not fear any dangers at night or sudden attacks during the day."

When Caleb had finished reciting the amended psalm, he opened his eyes to see a large buck on the other side of the clearing upwind from him, close to the hut. Its enormous antlers were silhouetted in the half light, and beyond it, Caleb could see several does. The light wasn't enough for Caleb to see clearly, but the way the buck was holding its head told him that the animal was staring at him. Caleb nodded, half-expecting the buck to do the same, and the large animal melted away into the forest.

Caleb nodded his head again. He knew he was exactly where he was supposed to be.

CHAPTER 15

Vince's hand curled around the crystal whisky tumbler in his hand, and he whirled the amber liquid round and round. He watched his knuckles whiten and wondered idly how much pressure would be required to break the glass before lifting it to his lips and emptying the tumbler. Then he hurled the glass across the room. It smashed against the wall of his small London apartment, leaving a dripping brown stain on the wall.

"Bitch," Vince muttered, glancing down at the laptop on his knees. "Absolute bitch."

The screen of the laptop was showing him a view from his house in Norwich. He could see his lounge, devoid of life, before the view changed to the camera in his hallway. Also devoid of life. His house was empty, which meant only one thing. Suzy had disappeared and taken her daughter with her.

Outside his apartment, a one bedroom in Southwark that cost him more each month than the rent of his house in Norwich, the night had closed in like his mood. He'd spent a couple of hours after the mandatory team debrief looking on the various MI5 systems that he had unfettered access to. Not only did he have unrestricted access, but his privileges meant his actions left no trace.

Vince had been right about the caller who had reported Yellow Burger's location. According to his systems, the call had been made from Norwich city center, a couple of hours to the north of his current location. The phone the call had been made from was a burner, with no other calls recorded to or from the handset. No text messages, no photographs. Just a single call. Another system told him the phone had been bought from a market in Snetterton, a town around thirty minutes from Norwich. It had been bought for cash, from a stall with no CCTV, and no online accounting that Vince could find. In Snetterton market, cash was king. Almost certainly a pop-up stall that wouldn't be there if he visited the market although, ironically, he used similar shops himself all the time.

"Bitch, bitch, bitch," Vince muttered again. On the screen, the laptop continued to cycle through the hidden cameras he'd installed in the house he rented in Norwich. Every room was empty. The bedrooms, the kitchen, the lounge. Even the bathroom camera, where he'd enjoyed watching Leanne on more than one occasion, had recorded no activity since just after he'd left to chase the ghost that was Yellow Burger.

There were several things that Vince didn't understand. How had Suzy known the code word to authenticate the call? Whose was the male voice that had made it? And where, most importantly, was the bitch and Leanne? He couldn't give a shit what happened to Suzy, but Vince had plans for Leanne.

Vince got to his feet, stretching as he did so. He'd missed his usual gym session with everything that was going on, which irritated him no end as it put his carefully planned routine out of sync. Today should have been leg day, but that would have to be tomorrow now, and he would have to adjust the supplements that he took accordingly. One more thing for the bitch to regret when he caught up with her. And he would catch up with her.

Vince was a hunter. Not just that, but he was The Hunter, and if Suzy wanted to make herself the prey, so be it. All that would do is bring the inevitable forward. Vince's plans for Leanne were only weeks away. After she had served her purpose, what was left of her would be disposed of, but by then, she would be miles away and no concern of his. Vince would let the lease on the rented house in Norwich expire and disappear from the city forever, just like Suzy and Leanne were supposed to, before resurfacing somewhere new and starting over. Just as he had done so many times in the past. Although Vince was almost disappointed when things came to an end, it meant that a new beginning was just around the corner. And he enjoyed the build up just as much as the resolution.

He could just let them go. Suzy wouldn't have a pot to piss in, he'd seen to that. She would have to start over somewhere with nothing. Vince considered this for a while. That might be fun, he thought as he got to his feet to get the bottle of whisky, momentarily regretting smashing the glass. He raised the bottle to his lips and took a mouthful of the fiery liquid. Maybe tormenting Suzy for the rest of her life might be fun? Making her think she was safe, and then doing something subtle to let her know that she wasn't. That she would never be safe and would spend the rest of her life looking over her shoulder, wondering when he was coming for her and her daughter?

But if he let them go, he would have to accept the loss of

money and face from not delivering Leanne as promised. The people he worked with understood that these things happened. Vince wasn't bothered so much about the money, but he was very bothered about losing face, even if his had not been seen by his co-conspirators. But the concept was the same. He had a reputation to maintain.

"No," Vince muttered as he took another, smaller, sip. Fun as letting them run and try to hide might be, he needed Leanne and now had plenty in store for Suzy. She had made the decision to run and take her daughter with her.

For that she would pay.

CHAPTER 16

Naomi stretched and angled her head to get the shaft of sunlight streaming in through a gap in the curtains away from her eyes. She stretched, enjoying the feeling of release that the movement gave her, wiggling her toes underneath the thick duvet cover. For some reason, although she always slept better in her sister's spare room than in her own bed, Naomi still woke up early.

Throwing the covers from the bed, Naomi got to her feet and padded to the bathroom. A quick glance at her watch on the bedside table before she did so told her that it was just after six in the morning. Naomi's sister, a nurse working in the Norfolk and Norwich hospital, would be long gone. Naomi had offered to buy Jennifer a car on more than one occasion, but the offer had been declined every time.

"I like getting the bus," Jennifer had said the last time Naomi offered. "Besides, if I get a car then I've still got to put petrol in it, park it somewhere, and there's tax and insurance too. The bus is only a couple of quid a day."

Naomi washed her hands and made her way into the small lounge. Jennifer's flat was small but functional in a new build not far from the city center, and had a small balcony that overlooked the river running through the heart of the city. She smiled when she saw the empty pizza boxes and wine bottles on the floor. They had spent the previous evening catching up. As she gathered the trash together, Naomi recalled Jennifer's face when she had told her about what she had said to Mark, her smile broadening at the memory. Jennifer had told Naomi that she could stay for as long as she needed to, but Naomi hadn't yet decided what to do about her living arrangements. The flat she shared with Mark was rented in her name, and when he had moved in she had made it clear that it was a temporary arrangement. At least, she thought she had. But Mark seemed to only hear what he wanted to hear.

Once she had worked out which items went into which bins, Naomi spent a while tidying up the lounge before returning to the bedroom to get dressed. Jennifer's flat was only a twenty-minute walk from Naomi's office, and as long as she arrived there after the security guards started at seven, she would be safe. It wasn't their clients who required the law firm to have security. The ones that got off were happy, the ones who didn't tended to be incarcerated. But the families were a different matter. Regardless of the reason, having two large men controlling who could and who couldn't enter the building suited Naomi just fine.

A few moments later, as Naomi was sitting on the balcony with a coffee, her cell phone rang. She had been watching another early riser on a paddleboard making her way down the river and was just wondering if the woman on the board realized she was going with the tide when her cell sprang into life.

"Good morning, Naomi," a male voice said. It was Grant, their office manager, and Naomi's heart sank. She had been looking forward to getting to the office and catching up on some paperwork, but him calling at this hour meant there was some work to be done.

"It was a good morning, Grant," Naomi replied, making sure she kept a smile on her face as she said it, "until you called." She reached for her notebook and pen, knowing that the office would have to wait. On the river, the woman on the paddleboard was turning herself round. Even though she was some distance away, Naomi could tell from the look on her face that she'd not expected the tide to be quite so strong this far from the sea. "What have you got?"

"TWOC and Class B possession," Grant replied. Naomi scribbled on the pad. TWOC was taking without consent, probably a car, and Class B drugs included some amphetamines, cannabis, and the increasingly popular ketamine.

"Bit early, isn't it?" Naomi said, glancing again at her watch.

"He got nabbed in the small hours." She heard him sigh down the line. "Fifteen year old lad, so they had to wait for a responsible adult."

"Which nick?"

"Wymondham," Grant replied, pronouncing the town's name *windum*. Not for the first time, Naomi wondered why so many towns in Norfolk sounded so different to their spelling.

"Okay," Naomi said. At least they had decent coffee at Wymondham nick, probably because there were so many senior officers based there. "I'll head down there now. Can you let them know I'm on my way? And what's the lad's name?"

"Yeah, I'll let them know. The boy's name is Leon. Leon Brockwell."

CHAPTER 17

Leon sat on the hard bench that he'd been perched on for the last three hours. His mother was outside, smoking, her only contribution when she had arrived a slap on the head for Leon and a mouthful of abuse for the custody sergeant. At least the abuse had included a request for a duty solicitor. He looked up as the hatch in the cell opened.

"You alright in there, son?" the custody sergeant asked through the small rectangle. "Anything you need? Breakfast maybe? A full English might be a stretch, but I can probably rustle you up some cereal?"

"Nah, I'm good," Leon replied. The police officer at the door was perhaps in his fifties, with a kind face that looked tired at the same time. "Unless you just fancy letting me go, like?"

"Sorry, son," the sergeant replied. "There is the small matter of you nicking a car."

"I told you last night," Leon said with a sigh. "I didn't nick it. I borrowed it."

"And the weed in the glove box?"

"Not mine."

Leon saw the police officer look to one side and, from the way the man's face fell, he thought his mother was returning. The hatch was half closed, but through it Leon could hear his mother's nasal voice complaining about something. Leon sat back on the bench and pulled his hood over his head. At least they had let him keep his own clothes, minus his belt and shoelaces.

He'd been so close to being home the previous evening, he couldn't believe it. The car belonged to an old boy who lived just off the estate Leon lived in, and he'd borrowed it before when he'd run out of weed. Borrowed in the loosest sense, that was, but he had needed to get to the other side of the city to score. The car, a shitty old Nissan Micra the color of cow shit, was old enough to be started with nothing more than a screwdriver under the steering column to reveal the ancient wiring. But perhaps if he'd not run a red light in the full view of a marked police car, he wouldn't be here.

Leon's mother stomped into the cell, bringing her usual sense of tension with her. For someone so thin, bordering on painfully so in Leon's opinion, she carried a huge amount of energy, mostly negative. She was wearing a deep purple velour tracksuit that had been in fashion at some point in the eighties, and her thin peroxide hair was scraped back in a savage bun. He groaned under his breath as she paced in the small room.

"What are you moaning at?" she barked. He closed his eyes and ignored her, knowing she would carry on regardless of what he said or did. Sure enough, she launched into her usual narrative about what a waster he was, how much of a loser his father had been, and how the apple didn't fall far from the tree. It was her favorite phrase that he heard several times a day. Socks not in the laundry basket? Plates on his bedroom floor? Getting arrested in the middle of the night? It was all about the apple according to her.

Leon's father was, depending on how much booze his mother had consumed, a man called either Harry or Henry. She had no idea what his last name was, only that like all men she knew, he'd taken what he'd wanted and done one. Leon had long suspected that the act of union that had resulted in his existence had a financial element to it, but that was a suspicion he kept to himself.

His main concern was not about what his mother said but what Syd was going to say when he found out he'd been nicked. Leon had never been arrested before, although he'd been cautioned a couple of times for stupid stuff like every other kid on the estate. That was one of the things Syd said he liked about Leon. He was clean, and therefore less likely to attract the attention of the authorities. Which, given the line of work Leon wanted to get into, could only be a good thing. The more the police knew about you, according to Syd, the more interested they became.

Leon jumped at the sound of banging. He opened his eyes to see his mother standing by the metal door of the cell. A few moments later, the hatch opened.

"What now?" the custody sergeant said, his tone bored.

"Let me out," Leon's mother said. "I need another smoke."

With what Leon thought was a sympathetic glance at him, the custody sergeant sighed and opened the door.

CHAPTER 18

"Mummy?" Suzy stirred at the sound of her daughter's voice. What Leanne said next caused her to open her eyes and sit bolt upright, instantly alert. "There's someone here."

"Where?" Suzy said, her voice low and urgent. She flashed her eyes around the small hut which was barely lit from the sun coming through a couple of gaps in the door. "Where?" she said again, this time in a whisper. Leanne pointed her finger to the door.

"Out there," Leanne said. "I needed the toilet and had to go behind a tree." Her head went down and she looked at her lap. "I didn't want to wake you up. You looked so peaceful."

Suzy fought the urge to hug her daughter. She would, later, once she knew they were safe. She got to her feet, surprised at how rested she felt. When she reached the door, Suzy inched it open just enough to see through and into the forest beyond. It took her a couple of seconds, but she saw the outline of someone sitting down, facing away from the hut, perhaps seventy-five yards away.

Suzy puffed air out through her cheeks. It wasn't Vince, and it wasn't one of his goons. They didn't wear robes.

"It's the man from the bus," Leanne whispered, her eyes wide. She had crept up to Suzy's side without her noticing. "The preacher man."

As if he had heard them talking, the man slowly got to his feet. He turned to face the hut. Then he leaned down and picked up a bag before walking toward the ramshackle structure. As he approached them, Suzy saw he was carrying their suitcase. He stopped around ten yards away from the hut and placed it on the ground before taking a few steps back.

"You forgot something," he said, putting a hand out palm up in the direction of the suitcase. Suzy looked at him, not having taken too much notice of him on the bus. There had been other things on her mind at the time, both before and after the robbery. He was smiling at them, but at the same time, he wasn't. His grey eyes never left hers for an instant.

"Mummy?" Leanne said, her voice urgent. "Mum?"

"What?" Suzy replied, not taking her eyes off the man in the robe.

"Boo Boo's in that bag."

"I know."

Suzy thought for a few seconds. There was nothing about this man that was threatening to them. Somehow, he had followed them to this hut to return their bag and he'd been a victim of the robbery as well. Her decision made, she told Leanne to stay inside the hut before opening the door and stepping outside. Without saying anything, she took a few steps across the clearing, feeling the man's eyes on her all the way, before grabbing the bag and retreating back to the hut. Leanne's shriek of delight when she opened the bag and pulled out the tattered pink elephant was reward enough for the risk she'd just taken.

When Suzy turned her attention back to the man in the robe, he'd not moved an inch. She looked at him, trying to do it discreetly and without him noticing. Other than the brief conversation Leanne had with him on the bus, Suzy hadn't paid him much attention at all. Now he was close to her, she could see he was somewhere in his thirties, wiry without being bulky, and had a head that was shaved so closely she couldn't make out a hairline at all. Other than the robe, the most noticeable thing about him was his grey eyes which bored into her with an intensity she could almost feel. It wasn't uncomfortable, it was just strange.

"Thank you," she said. The man in the robe just smiled. "Um, why are you here?"

"I have to be somewhere."

"Did you follow us?"

"Yes."

"Why?"

"I was curious."

"About what?"

Suzy folded her arms across her chest, suddenly feeling vulnerable. The man's eyes continued to bore into hers and while the sensation it caused intensified.

"Would you and your daughter like some breakfast?" the man in the robe replied. "I've taken the liberty of gathering some things just in case."

Thirty minutes later, Suzy was holding a bowl in her hands, enjoying the warmth from the food in it. Next to her, Leanne was doing the same thing but staring suspiciously at the pale, stew-like food inside it. Between them and the man in the robe was a small fire that he had made and warmed the food on. Suzy and Leanne had watched as he had used a razor to whittle some kindling before holding a pot over the flames.

"What is it?" Leanne asked him, her eyes flicking between the bowl and Suzy's face. Whatever was in the bowls smelled delicious, and Suzy's stomach rumbled.

"It's a special recipe," the man in the robe replied. "It's made from fruits of the forest and, I promise you, you will love it. Try some." As she watched, he took a spoonful of the food and let out an exaggerated sigh of contentment. "Oh, my Lord. It's like manna from Heaven." Suzy saw Leanne take a tentative spoonful before smiling. Then her daughter started eating in earnest.

"Thank you," Suzy said as she lifted her own spoon to her mouth. The food smelled of mushrooms and perhaps nuts. She looked at him as his eyes hardened almost imperceptibly.

"So, Suzy," the man in the robe said, arching his eyebrows. The way he elongated the word *so* accentuated his southern accent. Suzy frowned, not remembering introducing herself to him properly. She had been too fixated on what he was doing to think about formalities like introductions. The vulnerability she had felt earlier returned. "Are you going to tell me who you're running from?"

CHAPTER 19

Caleb kept his face passive as he saw Suzy's face fall at his question. She glanced over her shoulder to where her daughter was whispering to her cuddly toy inside the hut before Suzy looked back at him. When she did, her face was resolute.

"Who are you?" she asked him.

"My name is Caleb," he replied, gesturing to his clothing. "As I said to your daughter on the bus, I'm a preacher. Hence the robe."

"Why do you think we're running from someone?" she asked him. Caleb let the ghost of a smile play across his face as he looked around the inside of the hut.

"Why are you here?" he said.

"We have to be somewhere," Suzy replied. Caleb's smile turned into a laugh at the sound of his words being repeated back to him.

"When we were on the bus," he said, letting his laugh and smile fade away, "you had a bag full of money that they stole. And the moment the police were on their way, you took your daughter into the forest, not even stopping to get your bag." He looked at her, seeing the frown on her face. "Do you read scripture, Suzy?"

"No," she replied, her frown deepening. "No, I don't."

"Flee for your lives. Don't look back, and don't stop anywhere in the plain. Flee to the mountains or you will be swept away," Caleb said, half closing his eyes as he recited the verse. Then he opened them fully. "It's from Genesis and pretty much describes what you're doing. Someone is trying to sweep you away. My question is who? Perhaps I can help you?"

Caleb saw a look of resignation cross Suzy's face, but she still didn't answer his question. He sat in silence, giving her time. She would tell him when she was ready.

"I can't tell you," she said in a whisper a moment later. Caleb nodded. He placed his bowl on the ground and reached out both his hands toward her. She looked at him uncertainly for a few seconds before placing her own bowl down. Then, after pausing for a few seconds, she took his hands. Caleb closed his eyes at her touch. Her skin was light and smooth, and he held her hands lightly for a moment.

When he reopened his eyes, he regarded Suzy in a new light. He had sensed a darkness surrounding her that was bleaker than he thought he'd ever experienced. She was in danger, as was her daughter, but he didn't think she knew quite how much.

"Who are you?" Suzy asked him a moment later. "Who are you really?"

"I am Caleb," he replied.

"And you're a preacher?"

"Of sorts, yes."

"But why are you here? Not here as in here in this forest, but why are you here in England?"

"I'm looking for something, but sometimes He sends me in a different direction."

"He?" Suzy asked with a frown. "Who's He?" Caleb just pointed his index finger at the sky and smiled.

"Him," he replied.

"God?"

"Some call Him that, yes. But He has many names."

Suzy's frown melted away as Leanne called out to her from inside the hut.

"I'll be over in a moment, sweetheart." She looked at Caleb and he could almost hear her thinking. He waited as she examined her nails, pulling at a loose piece of skin on one of her fingers. A moment later, her eyes met his. "You really think you can help us?"

"I know I can, Suzy. That's why I'm here. In this forest, not in England. But here."

"I don't remember telling you my name."

Caleb didn't reply, but just held her gaze. "Who is he, this man you're running from?" A silence developed between them. Caleb knew this was a pivotal moment. Either she told him and they took action, or she didn't and he would walk away. Just as the silence was becoming uncomfortable, she spoke.

"My partner." Suzy went back to worrying at her nails. Leanne called out again and, as if she was grateful for the distraction, Suzy got to her feet.

Caleb watched for a moment as Suzy spoke to her daughter just inside the door of the hut. He tuned out their words as they weren't for him to hear and just watched the way they interacted. Leanne held up her elephant to Suzy's ear and a moment later, there was a mock look of surprise on Suzy's face. Then she laughed and returned to sit next to Caleb.

"Boo Boo wants to meet you," she said when she had settled on the ground.

"And I want to meet Boo Boo," Caleb replied, turning to look at the door to the hut where Leanne was waiting. Suzy raised a hand and waved to her, and Leanne bounded over to join them.

A moment later, introductions properly made, Caleb turned to Suzy.

"So," he said in a low voice. "Shall we make some plans?" Suzy nodded, but her face was full of doubt. Caleb's eyes flicked between her and Leanne a couple of times. "You have a good heart, Suzy."

"How do you know?"

"A heart is not judged by how much you love, but by how much you are loved by others," Caleb replied with a glance at Leanne.

"Is that from your scripture?" Suzy asked him with a wan smile.

"No," Caleb replied. "It's a line from *The Wizard of Oz*. What we need is a yellow brick road."

CHAPTER 20

When Suzy had given Caleb her hands, she had almost jumped at the sensation that had swept through her. It was like a wave of relief, as if he was absorbing all her worries and fears. But when he let go of her, they all came crashing back with a vengeance.

"Tell me about him," she heard him say in a low voice. Leanne was sitting in the hut, drawing with some pens and paper Suzy had shoved in the bag at the last minute before they'd fled Vince's house. As if there was any doubt about whom he meant, Caleb continued. "Your partner." Suzy shot a look at the hut to make sure Leanne was still there before replying.

"He's a monster," she said in a whisper.

"In what way?"

"In every way." Suzy paused for a moment. "In every way possible." She paused again, unsure how to continue.

"What does he do?" Caleb asked, his voice matching hers in volume. "For a living, I mean?"

"That's part of the problem," Suzy replied. She looked up at Caleb. He was just looking at her, the expression in his gray eyes neutral. "He works for the security services. MI5. He'll be looking for me and Leanne with every tool at his disposal, which is pretty much all of them."

"Hence, running from the police into the forest," Caleb said. "No cameras. No way to track you both." Suzy nodded in reply.

"But he'll find us eventually," she said. "I just need to get us both out of the country before he does." Suzy took a deep breath and out of the corner of her eye, she saw Caleb glance at Leanne. "For her sake more than for mine."

"He's her father?" Caleb asked.

"No," Suzy replied. "He's not. Her father is, was, just a brief thing. I was very young. But yes, he uses her to keep me in line. It's like being in a prison, but one with no bars." When Suzy looked at him, she could see he understood her sentiment. "But I had to get away, before..." Her voice tailed away and she took another deep breath. "I can't let anything happen to Leanne."

"Has he been violent toward her?"

"No, not violent. It's worse than that."

A few seconds later, Caleb asked her another question. His eyes were no longer impassive but full of concern.

"Suzy, can you explain?" he said. She took a deep breath. Where on earth was she going to start, Suzy wondered. "Just start at the beginning," Caleb continued. She looked up at him, alarmed for a few seconds. Had she said that out loud, or could he read her mind? He had an amiable smile on his face, and she relaxed.

"He controls everything," Suzy said, her voice quiet. "Absolutely everything about my life."

Suzy spent the next few moments telling Caleb about how Vince had isolated both her and Leanne from everyone they knew. About how he controlled her money, her schedule, even when she ate. When she slept. Where she went. He said nothing, nodding occasionally to encourage her.

"My parents have both passed," she said with a sigh. "I don't have any siblings. And now? I don't even have any friends."

"Does he beat you?" Caleb asked. Suzy paused before replying.

"Yes, on occasion. But only when I deserve it."

Caleb opened his mouth as if to say something, but he closed it again. Suzy went on to tell him about how she had been planning their escape for months and months. Putting money away by telling him the shopping had cost five or ten pounds more than it actually had and pocketing the difference. When she had realized he never checked the receipts, that was when her planning started in earnest. Her only sanctuary was the garden shed which Vince never went into. Caleb smiled as she told him how she'd taken up gardening soon after their relationship began. If anything, Vince had encouraged this.

"It'll do you good to get some fresh air," she told Caleb he had said at the time. Then her voice tailed away, and she stared at her fingernails, reluctant to continue.

"You said something might happen to Leanne?" Caleb prompted after a moment had passed. Suzy sighed again.

"Vince was away at work when the post came," she said. "Last week, it was. I'd been thinking something was going on for a while. He'd not been that interested in Leanne, but then one day he started taking photos of her on his phone." She glanced up at Caleb, whose face had darkened. "I don't mean of her, well, you know. In that way. They were just normal photos. Anyway, one of the things in the post had to be signed for." Suzy paused again.

"Go on," Caleb said. "You can trust me, Suzy."

"I know," Suzy said. "But I opened it." She laughed, but there was no humor in the sound. "I knew he would kill me if he found out, but I couldn't help it."

"What was it?"

"It was a passport. For Leanne. But wasn't a British passport. It looked similar, but it was an Estonian one." Suzy saw Caleb frown. "It had her photograph in it, but a different name and an address I didn't recognize."

"I don't understand," Caleb said. "Why would Vince get her a foreign passport?"

"There's only one explanation that I can think of," Suzy replied, her voice breaking. "He was planning on trafficking her. That's why I had to get away. Before he gave her to a pedophile gang or something like that. The moment I saw the passport, I knew we had to get away as soon as we could." When Caleb looked at her, there was a darkness in his eyes that was almost palpable. He said something, but Suzy didn't catch what he said. "I'm sorry?"

"I said, they truly walk amongst us." Caleb cast his eyes down to the ground and closed them, seeming to be deep in thought. Or perhaps it was prayer, Suzy wasn't sure. When he looked at her again, the darkness in his eyes was even darker. "Are you a believer, Suzy?"

"In God?"

"In a God, yes," Caleb replied. She paused before answering his question.

"No," she said a few seconds later. "A God wouldn't let people like Vince do what he does." As she watched, she saw Caleb's face changing. The dark expression slowly gave way to another one. It took Suzy a moment to realize what it was. It wasn't anger. It was resolve.

"Perhaps he doesn't, Suzy," Caleb replied as he got to his feet. "Perhaps he doesn't."

CHAPTER 21

Leon slouched back in his chair and blew his breath through his cheeks. At least the interview room was marginally more comfortable than the cell. Next to him, in an identical plastic chair, his mother was rubbing her hands together, no doubt wondering when she could next have another cigarette. Leon looked up as the door opened and a woman was shown in by the custody sergeant.

"Leon, Miss Brockwell? This is Naomi Tipton, the duty solicitor," the police officer said.

"It's *Ms.* Brockwell," Leon's mother barked as the sergeant retreated, closing the door behind him. Ignoring her, Leon turned his attention to the new arrival.

She was much younger than he'd been expecting, mid-twenties at most. And she was more female than he'd been expecting as well. When he heard the word solicitor, Leon automatically thought of a middle-aged man, probably with a posh accent. When the solicitor opened her mouth to speak, her accent was neutral and her voice reassuring. Not what he'd been expecting at all.

"Leon," she said, smiling as she shook his hand. "I'm Naomi." He opened his mouth to reply, but wasn't sure what to say, so he closed it again. She turned her attention to his mother. "Ms. Brockwell, I'm pleased to meet you."

As Leon's mother shook Naomi's hand, he took a few seconds to examine her. She was perhaps the same height as he was, around five feet five or six. A shiny dark green business suit covered a slim frame, and her oval face was framed by a dark bob. Leon hadn't been expecting this at all. Not only was his solicitor a woman, but she was a very fit one as well. He felt a slow smile spreading across his face as he thought about how he would describe her to Syd and the others when he got out of here. But what she said next wiped the smile off his face in an instant.

"So, Leon," Naomi said as she sat down and looked at him across the table, arranging a pad and pen as she did so. "Have you been to a Young Offender Institute before?"

"What?" Leon said with a gasp. He looked at his mother, who was staring, open-mouthed, at the solicitor.

"You're looking at a two year sentence in one, possibly more," Naomi continued.

"You're joking?" The response to this from Naomi was an arched, perfectly plucked eyebrow and the response from his mother a clip round the ear. "Sorry," Leon said with a mumble, looking down in his lap.

"No, Leon," Naomi said, "I'm not joking. These are serious offenses." Her eyebrow returned to its starting position and her face softened. "But that's why I'm here. To make sure that doesn't happen." She leaned forward to study her notepad and Leon caught the faintest odor of perfume as she moved. "So, I've looked through the custody logs and it looks like they've taken good care of you. Is that correct?"

"I s'pose so," Leon replied.

"And you have a responsible adult here," Naomi continued, with a brief smile at his mother. Leon bit back a smirk at the thought of his mother being described as responsible. "So how about you talk me through what happened?"

For the next few moments, Leon did just that. He ignored the gasps from his mother when he related how he'd started the car and omitted to mention the drugs the police had found in the vehicle.

"I just wanted to get out and about for a bit," he said, not really caring whether or not the solicitor believed him. From the look on her face, she didn't. "I was going to take it back and leave it where I found it. But the Old Bill nicked me before I could do that."

"Right," Naomi said as she made a note on the pad. "So you had no intention of permanently depriving the owner of the vehicle? Let me give you a hint. The correct answer to that question is no."

"Um, no."

"Leon, repeat after me. I had no intention to permanently deprive the owner of the vehicle."

"I had no intention of permanently depriving the owner of the vehicle."

"That's close enough," Naomi replied. "Remember that phrase."

Leon sat back in his chair and tried to relax. Perhaps things would not be as bad as he'd thought. He regarded Naomi with a confidence that was growing with every second. Not only was his solicitor fit, but she seemed to know what she was talking about. But he groaned at her next question.

"Tell me about the drugs the police found in your possession?"

CHAPTER 22

Vince's fingers moved across the keyboard so quickly they were almost a blur. He was sitting at his desk in Thames House, inside the horribly imperial Neoclassic building that housed the Secret Intelligence Service. Its location, and the nature of the people who worked within it, had to be the worst kept secret in the world. It had always been an ugly building, and when MI5 had moved in during the mid-nineties, the security upgrades had made it even uglier.

Behind the dual high-resolution screens on Vince's desk was a large window subdivided into smaller windows by grilles that let around fifty percent of the available light outside into his office. It was triple glazed for security purposes which was, as a rocket attack by Irish dissidents on the MI6 building over the river in Vauxhall some years previously had shown, effective. Beyond the window, Vince could see the steel and granite arches of Lambeth Bridge with its distinctive pineapple-shaped obelisks on either end. The bridge was carrying traffic across the muddy brown waters of the River Thames, but he paid the steady stream of distinctive red London buses and black cabs no mind. He was looking for someone who almost certainly wasn't in London.

On the screens in front of him were various feeds from CCTV cameras, not dissimilar to the ones he'd been looking at the previous evening. But these feeds weren't of the interior of his house. They were all external feeds. A quarter of one screen showed the approach to Norwich Station. Another quarter housed an external view of the city's bus station. The other two quarters showed views from inside trains and buses respectively. Vince wasn't watching the feeds though. The computer was doing that for him which, seeing as the feeds were playing at quadruple time, was just as well.

When he had sat down first thing that morning, he had uploaded a clear photograph of Suzy, followed by one of Leanne to one of the systems he had access to. He'd taken them both a few months previously, using the pretense that they both needed new passports as Suzy had managed to lose their existing ones. But she'd not lost them. They were in a drawer in Vince's apartment in Southwark. Once uploaded, the software measured a number of features on both their faces. The distance between Suzy's eyes. The depth of her eye sockets. The contours of Leanne's lips, ears, and chin. Then it converted these measurements into a unique mathematical formula that was as distinctive as a fingerprint, or more so if you believed the techies. The software, originally written by a Chinese tech firm, had been borrowed from them a year or so ago before being dramatically improved by the egg heads employed by the intelligence services.

Vince glanced at one of the quarters and watched as the feed paused for a split second and the software drew a green box around the head of a passing commuter. Then it drew some more lines inside the box before flashing them once in a bright red color. It then drew another box around someone else, and the process continued. He had instructed the software to search only for Suzy or Leanne, not to identify everyone it saw as it generally did. That search was much easier to delete afterward, using the administrator privileges he had negotiated with a senior member of the cyber team who had a penchant for young prostitutes. The younger the better. The cyber team member was quite keen for neither his wife nor his employer to know where and on whom he spent his disposable income and had been only too happy to help Vince. The fact Vince had only found out when he'd hacked the agency's databases to remove any trace of his own activities was ironic, and served to reinforce the man's own stupidity for not doing it himself.

With the software scanning hundreds of people every moment, Vince continued to type. He was entering text into another piece of software, this one focused on voices. The standard of voice identification wasn't as good as it was for faces, but that wasn't what Vince was entering. He was putting in words and phrases that either Suzy or Leanne might say, so names of friends, locations, toys. After each word or phrase, he hit the *Enter* key, building up a bank of phrases that could then be compared against pretty much every single phone call that happened in England. If a number of them occurred in the same call, it would generate a hit. The more that were used in a single call, the higher priority it would be allocated. He stopped typing and set the search parameters for the last three days, and then instructed it to keep a watching brief before clicking a button to send the data package down to the Government Communication Headquarters, another horrible government building full of people like him.

Well, Vince thought as he interlocked his fingers to stretch them, not quite like him.

CHAPTER 23

"You see, Leanne," Caleb said as the child walked next to him, careful not to get her feet wet in the small stream they were walking along side, "the thing about streams is that they always lead somewhere."

"Like the yellow brick road?" Leanne asked him.

"Just like the yellow brick road," he replied. It had taken a while, but he and Suzy had managed to explain some of the plot of the film to her. Caleb glanced down at the child who was clutching Boo Boo to her chest while behind them, Suzy followed with her suitcase slung over her shoulder. Caleb had offered to take it, but Suzy had declined.

"So where does this stream go, then?" Leanne asked.

"We'll see," Caleb replied, "but it has to go somewhere."

They walked on in silence for a while, Caleb enjoying the sights, sounds, and smells of the surrounding forest. At one point, he paused and dropped to his haunches.

"Look, Leanne, can you see that?" he said, pointing at some small indentations in the soft earth.

"What is it?" the girl asked, her curiosity getting the better of her.

"Rabbit footprints. You can see where he or she has hopped through the forest. Perhaps they live round here somewhere?" Caleb saw Suzy smiling as Leanne's head flashed from side to side for the next few moments, no doubt hoping to glimpse a rabbit.

It was perhaps twenty minutes before they reached a junction where the stream fed into a larger one. It wasn't big enough to be called a river, but Caleb knew there was a village further along the banks. As the sun had risen earlier that morning, he had heard the faint sounds of habitation through the clear forest air. A dog barking, car doors slamming. The hiss of brakes from a lorry or perhaps a bus. People had lived next to water for millennia, and Caleb was sure it was no different in England. They followed the languid water as it flowed at the same pace they walked. A moment later, as they rounded a bend in the waterway, Caleb saw the first buildings. They were residential, large houses mostly build of red brick with formal gardens.

There was one type of building he was looking for as the ground beneath their feet gave way to an asphalt path and a few hundred yards later, a sidewalk of sorts. It wasn't long before he saw a large rectangular tower appear above the roofs of the houses. Caleb could see that it was slightly tiered, with each level being narrower than the one below, and an arched window with louvers on it was set into the wall closest to them. Apart from the crenellated parapet at the very top, the walls were covered with flint stone, as were so many church towers in the area. He could imagine the bells in the tower ringing out across the countryside, calling worshippers to prayer. As they approached, the rest of the church came into view. It was much larger than he had thought it would be, given the apparent size of the village it served. Caleb stopped for a moment to stare at the ornate building. Its bells were silent and the only thing Caleb could hear was birdsong.

"We're going to a church?" Suzy asked as he took in the scene.

"Not to the church, no," Caleb replied. "But I'm looking for the man who works there." Caleb caught himself, having forgotten for a moment that things had changed over the years, even here in this small corner of England. "Or woman, of course."

They walked around the exterior of the church in silence, even Leanne seeming awed by the building. As they walked, they saw no one. Caleb knew it was about seven in the morning, and was surprised not to see so much as a dog walker.

"It's quiet, isn't it?" Suzy asked Caleb. He was about to reply when there was the sound of a car door closing from nearby. Caleb turned to see a middle-aged man with a shock of white hair making his way up a path leading from the parking lot to the main church entrance. What made the man distinctive was not his hair, but the long black flowing robe he wore and the white rectangle of an ecclesiastical dog collar around his neck.

"Excuse me, Father?" Caleb called out, taking a few steps toward him. The vicar stopped and stared at Caleb, his eyes moving up and down Caleb's own robe. "Do you have a moment?"

"Are you here for matins?" the vicar asked with a quick look at his watch. "Only I'm running a bit late."

"No, we were hoping to speak to you about something," Caleb replied. He noted the fleeting look of disappointment cross the vicar's face and wondered how large his congregation was. From the deserted nature of the village, Caleb didn't think any of them attended the early services.

"Of course. Can you give me a few moments?" The vicar glanced at his watch again. "I just need to bash out a swift psalm ninety-five to keep Him happy upstairs."

"Venite, exult emus Domino," Caleb replied, causing the vicar's face to break into a broad smile. Ignoring the vicar for a second, Caleb turned to Suzy. "It's the first verse of the psalm. 'Oh come, let us sing unto the Lord.'"

"Oh, superb," the vicar said, still smiling as he took in Caleb's robe again. "I wasn't sure if you were, er, one of ours. Would you like to join me?"

"No, thank you." Caleb shook his head in response before nodding at the church. "I'd be as welcome as a wet shoe inside one of them."

CHAPTER 24

Naomi watched the purple tracksuit Leon's mother was wearing shake as the woman extracted a cigarette from the packet. Almost as an afterthought, she held the pack out in Naomi's direction.

"No, thanks," Naomi said, shaking her head. "I don't smoke."

"Nah," the woman replied, squeezing one eye closed as she lit the cigarette with a small disposable lighter. "Didn't think you would, but I guess we owe you." Naomi laughed to herself. She'd never been offered payment for her professional services before in cigarettes.

"Where's home?" Naomi asked her. The reply was accompanied by a cloud of smoke.

"Lark's Cross," she said. Naomi hid a grimace. Lark's Cross was about the most deprived area of the entire city, guarded by two high-rise tenement blocks at the center. Leon wasn't the first client of Naomi's from the estate, nor would he be the last. "It's a shit hole, but it's our shit hole."

"How are you and Leon getting home?"

As Naomi said this, the door to the police station

opened, and Leon emerged, blinking into the watery sunlight.

"Bus, I s'pose." Leon's mother extracted a phone out of her pocket to check the time. To Naomi's surprise, it was one of the latest iPhones. "Leon? You got some cash?" Leon patted his pockets theatrically.

"I've lost my wallet, Mum," he replied. "I think it's round at Syd's place."

"I'll give you a lift," Naomi replied, almost without thinking. When she saw the look of surprise on the woman's face, she added, "I'm going that way, anyway."

"Cheers, Judge Judy," Leon said with a broad smile, making Naomi laugh out loud. "That'd be magic."

The three of them made their way to the parking lot next to the police station. Naomi was keen to give Leon's mother enough time to finish her cigarette. When she turned to look at Leon, he still had a wide smile plastered on his face.

"I'm not sure what the grin's for, Leon," Naomi said. "You've still got a caution. It's not like you've got off scot-free."

"Yeah, but you got me off of the drugs stuff."

"I didn't get you off anything," she replied, struggling to keep the corners of her mouth from twitching. Leon had suggested to the dour-faced traffic officer that the bag of marijuana belonged to the elderly gentleman who owned the car. When the police officer had said that, given the gentleman in question was a retired teacher in his seventies, it was unlikely, Leon had replied it could be medicinal. The innocent look on his face had caused Naomi to suddenly become very interested in her notes so the traffic officer didn't see her laughing. "You know a caution is a serious matter, don't you?"

"Doesn't it get sealed when I'm eighteen, though?" Leon asked, his smile slipping slightly.

"It does, but your name's now in the system. There're loads of jobs that, if you go for them, you'll have to declare the caution and what it was for."

"What jobs?" Leon asked, his tone scornful. Naomi paused before replying. The chances of Leon joining the military or the police were slim to none.

"I'm just saying, that's all, Leon," Naomi said as she blipped the locks to her car. When he realized the bright red Mini was hers, his grin reappeared.

"Sweet car," he said. "Like shit off a shovel, these are. I, er, I borrowed one once."

"You won't be able to smoke in the car, Ms. Brockwell," Naomi said to Leon's mother, who was about to light yet another cigarette.

Just under thirty minutes later, with Leon's mother's knee bounding up and down in the passenger seat, Naomi pulled off the A11 and aimed the Mini at the two large tower blocks that marked the center of the Lark's Cross estate. As she drove into the estate proper, Naomi glanced in her rear-view mirror to see Leon slouching down in the seat. By the side of the road, two youngsters in hoodies stood astride bikes that were far too small for them, eyeballing the car as it drove past. They looked to be a couple of years younger than Leon, and even though their faces were half-hidden by the hoods of their clothing, Naomi could feel the animosity in their eyes.

"They're the Bricknell brothers," Leon said. Naomi looked at him again in the mirror to see he was doing his best to hide his own face. "Right couple of twats, they are."

"Mind your language," Leon's mother spat over her shoulder. Naomi was just about to say something about the fact the two boys on the bikes should be in school when she thought better of it. "Left at the bottom of this road."

Naomi drove on, slowing to allow the car to ride over the potholes in the road rather than breaking an axle on them. The street was lined with cars on both sides, minimizing the amount of room Naomi had to navigate the craters, and she could see the squat terraced houses on either side. In the space of a few hundred yards, she had counted three sofas, two washing machines, and even a shopping cart full of car tires in front gardens. At some point, possibly for around six months after it had been built in the nineteen fifties, the estate had probably been quite smart. But those days were long gone.

She turned left at the bottom of the road, as instructed, and then pulled in a moment later, as instructed by Leon's mother.

"We're just here," she said, pointing at a house that was almost indistinguishable from its neighbors apart from the garden. To Naomi's surprise, it appeared well tended, with a small lawn and a few flowers bravely attempting to bring some color to an otherwise monochrome landscape.

"Thanks, Judge Judy," Leon said as he got out of the car, bouncing as he did so.

"Yeah, thanks for the lift," Leon's mother added as she got out, her cigarette packet in her hand. "See ya."

Naomi sat in the car as the pair made their way down the short path leading to the front door. She saw Leon pause for a second before bending over and pulling something from what passed as a flower bed. When he raised his other hand to wave at Naomi, she saw the remnants of a weed in his hand. She waved back, grateful they'd not invited her into the pokey little house for a cup of tea. The chances were, in Naomi's opinion, that her car wouldn't still be there when she came out.

She drove off slowly, glancing from left to right at the houses as she did so. They glared back at her, almost sullen in the sunlight. Naomi liked Leon, despite his crimes, and seeing where he lived, she had sympathy for the lad. Growing up in a place like this couldn't be easy, and it was a long way from her own middle-class upbringing, where the most outrageous offense was a resident taking too much off a hedge between neighboring houses.

Leon's mother had hit the nail on the head, Naomi thought as she approached the road leading out of the estate with some relief.

The place was a shit hole.

CHAPTER 25

Suzy sat down in a tired armchair in the vicar's lounge, suddenly feeling exhausted although she'd slept for hours the previous night. She could see Caleb and the vicar, Father Martin, talking in hushed tones in the tiny kitchen that was next to the lounge. Leanne was busy drawing on a piece of paper with some crayons that Father Martin had rustled up from somewhere. Suzy watched her for a moment, considering how resilient her daughter was, before taking in the rest of the room. The house they were in, the vicarage, was a new building, but Father Martin had somehow made the lounge look like it belonged decades earlier. The walls were festooned with pictures, mostly depicting religious scenes, and in one corner there was a horrific statue of a woman with her arms outstretched and a dagger thrust into her chest. Suzy was still watching Leanne, hoping she wouldn't notice the statue, when the two men walked into the room and sat down.

"So, Caleb's appraised me of your, er, your situation,"

Father Martin said, looking at Suzy with a compassionate expression. "But you're safe now, Suzanne."

"Suzy," she replied with a wince. The only person who called her Suzanne was Vince, and it was usually a precursor to something else. A slap, or perhaps a fist.

"I'm sorry, Suzy," Father Martin said. "But there is a shelter near the city that has space for you and young Leanne. I've spoken to Joan, the woman who runs it, and we can take you there this evening."

"Thank you," Suzy said, her voice almost a whisper. She looked at Caleb, who was sitting, motionless, in an armchair as tired as her own. His eyes were closed, and she could see his lips moving almost imperceptibly. Was he praying? "But I have no money to pay for anything."

"You don't need to pay for anything," Caleb said. When she looked at him, his eyes were still closed. As if he felt her gaze on him, he opened them and blinked a couple of times. "It's all taken care of by the charity that owns the shelter. Father Martin?"

The vicar looked at Caleb at the sound of his name and Suzy sensed, rather than saw, a look of deep understanding between the two men. A wave of reassurance swept over her. Finally, she felt safe.

"I was wondering if I might borrow some clothes," Caleb asked the vicar. "Some old ones, perhaps? I have some business to attend to in Norwich." He pronounced the name of the city in two distinct syllables, the second rhyming with witch.

"It's called Norwich," Father Martin replied with a slight smile. "Rhymes with porridge."

"Norwich," Caleb said slowly, prompting a laugh from the vicar.

"That's it. You almost sound like a local." It was Caleb's turn to laugh.

"I doubt I'll ever sound local," he said, "but I would like to fit in a bit more before I open my mouth."

"Of course, Caleb," Father Martin replied. "We're around the same size. I'm sure I can find you something less conspicuous than a robe." Another meaningful look passed between them before the vicar looked at his watch. "I've got the morning Eucharist shortly," he said as he got to his feet. "But after that, we'll have lunch. There's a chicken in the fridge, and I'm sure I've got enough potatoes for roasties all round. How does that sound?"

"That sounds amazing, Father Martin," Caleb replied with a smile in Leanne's direction. "Why don't you point me in the right direction and I'll do the prep."

A few moments later, Suzy and Caleb were sitting in the kitchen, which, like the lounge, appeared to belong to a much older house. Suzy watched as Caleb used a small stone he'd produced from his cloth bag to sharpen a paring knife. When he started peeling the potatoes, his hands moved so quickly they were blurred.

"Wow," Suzy said in admiration. "Where d'you learn to do that?"

"I've always been good with a knife," Caleb replied with a wry smile as the peelings dropped to the scarred kitchen table.

Suzy paused for a moment, wondering how best to say what she wanted to. "Caleb?" He looked up, pausing with a potato in his hand while his eyebrows rose. "I just wanted to say thank you. For what you're doing for me and Leanne?"

"It's nothing," Caleb replied, returning his attention to the task at hand. Peelings rained down on the surface, and within seconds, another potato was laid bare.

"I thought you were heading for London," Suzy said a moment later.

"I am, at some point."

"But you said you had some business to attend to in Norwich?"

Caleb looked at her, and Suzy felt the temperature in the room drop by a degree or two. As if he sensed this, Caleb smiled at her.

"I do," he said, fixing her with his gray eyes. "I'm going to visit a friend."

CHAPTER 26

"I'm just heading out for the evening, Mum," Leon called over his shoulder. As usual, his mother didn't even acknowledge the statement. Long ago, they had agreed that she wouldn't get on his back about being out every evening in return for him continuing to bring money in. Nor did she ask him where it was coming from.

As he made his way down the street his house sat on, past all the other almost identical terraced houses, Leon still had a spring in his step after what had happened at the police station. He was itching to tell Syd and the rest of the crew, but he knew he couldn't. Not without giving away the fact he'd been nicked for something so stupid. In some circles, having a record was worn as a badge of honor, but not in the circle Syd ran. He wanted the attention of the authorities on him and his crew to be at an absolute minimum, a fact Leon understood well.

He cinched his hood further over his face as the looming tower that Syd ran his operation from came into view. Syd had appropriated one of the four apartments on the top floor by persuading the previous resident that an exchange of council flats would be in everyone's best interests. Leon made his way into the building after punching a four digit PIN into a panel next to the door to gain access and waited for the lift to grind its way down from the top. Unlike the lifts in the other tower, this one wouldn't stink of piss when it arrived. Syd wouldn't stand for that. Leon slid his hood down and stared at the camera in the elevator car's corner. It was the only working CCTV camera on the estate. Despite the council's best efforts, any that were installed seemed to break as soon as the installation crews had left the estate. Within a few seconds, once his identity had been confirmed by whoever was manning the CCTV screen in Syd's apartment, the doors closed and the lift started its struggle back up to the top of the block.

"Leon, my man," Syd's voice boomed as Leon entered the hallway of his apartment. The air was thick with the fug of cannabis and sweat, even though most of the windows on one wall were open. "I want to chat with you. What's happening?"

"Not a lot," Leon said, walking into the lounge where the oxygen was even scarcer. He waited for Syd to point at a chair before sitting down. "Same old, same old. You know?" Leon settled into the chair, separated from Syd by a low coffee table that was scattered with empty beer cans and an overflowing ashtray.

Syd nodded sagely, as if he knew exactly what Leon was talking about. He shuffled forward in his chair and threw a packet of rolling papers onto the table, fixing Leon with an easy smile as he did so.

"You going to put one together?" Syd said, sitting back in the chair. Leon smiled as he pulled three papers from the packet. He licked one of them, fixing it to another and placing the third across the middle. Syd had never asked him to skin up a joint before, and from the red haze in the whites of the man's eyes, it wasn't his first of the evening.

Leon pulled a cigarette out of a packet he kept just for this purpose, licked the seam, and peeled the paper apart before emptying the tobacco into the papers on the table. Then he pulled out a small Ziplock bag with a brown lump of cannabis resin. It was all he had after the police had confiscated his stash of the good stuff in the car.

"What on earth is that?" Syd said as Leon held a lighter to the lump to soften the resin.

"It's all I've got, Syd," Leon replied, preparing to crumble some of the sugary-like substance onto the tobacco. "It's my emergency stash. I've run dry."

"No, wait," Syd said, laughing. "I can smell the diesel off that from here." He tossed a similar bag onto the coffee table, but this one had shredded green material in it. "This stuff is way better than that crap. I got a full ounce of that from my boy in Ipshit," Syd said, using the colloquial name for Ipswich, the town that had hosted Norwich's football rivals for over a century. "My regular shipment is due in tomorrow, and it's not been smuggled over the channel in a tank of diesel like your gear was."

A few moments later, Leon handed Syd a large joint. Although he'd been nervous about putting it together under the scrutiny of Syd, he was pleased with it. It was firm from the rolled tip to the cardboard roach in the base, but not so firm that air couldn't be drawn through it. Leon watched as Syd lit the end, taking a couple of puffs on it before inhaling deeply.

"Not bad, my man," Syd said a few seconds later after exhaling a cloud of smoke toward the ceiling where it rolled around in the still air. He handed Leon the joint. "So, I've got a proposition for you. Something longer term than rolling buses."

Leon took a couple of small hits on the joint before handing it back to Syd, who had picked up a guitar and was finger-picking the opening to a song Leon didn't recognize.

"Sure," he said, trying to keep his voice as nonchalant as possible.

"You were good on that bus, Leon," Syd said, his face half hidden by the smoke. "So I figured you deserve a promotion." Leon kept his face impassive at the news. "Unless you want to keep dick or collect plates for the rest of your life?" Keeping dick, or acting as a lookout for Syd's drug dealers, was how Leon had been earning most of his money for almost two years. Syd also ran a chop shop on the estate, and he regularly needed license plates from legitimate cars to cover the stolen ones.

"You want me to run a trap house?" Leon said. Syd had four areas, or trap houses, where drugs were sold across the estate.

"You got it, Leon," Syd said. Leon let a smile spread across his face at the news. He didn't want to seem too keen, but keen enough. The risk of trapping was getting caught, which meant the money was much better, but Syd hadn't lost a dealer to the Old Bill yet. The estate belonged to Syd, not the police. "You think you're ready?" Syd handed the remnants of the joint back to Leon.

"You know I'm good for it, Syd," Leon said, taking a puff on the joint that burned his lips. He stubbed it out in the ashtray, the last puff always the privilege of the maker. "I won't let you down."

CHAPTER 27

Caleb's stomach grumbled as he took a deep breath in through his nose. The smell of the roast dinner that Father Martin was putting the finishing touches to in his small kitchen reminded Caleb how long it had been since breakfast. He had made sure that Suzy and Leanne had their full share of the stew he had prepared for them earlier that morning, and by the time they had eaten their fill, there was little left. He didn't mind being hungry. The pangs in his stomach were offset by the knowledge that both Suzy and Leanne had nothing. Caleb had been far hungrier in his life than he was then, but at the same time, he was looking forward to eating.

"Is there anything I can help with?" he asked Father Martin, who was just measuring some gravy granules into a jug.

"No, I'm fine, thank you," the vicar replied. "Not much to do now. I'd say we'll be eating in about thirty minutes." Caleb nodded in response.

The two men stayed in an almost companionable silence for a few minutes. Both Suzy and Leanne were upstairs in the vicarage's spare bedroom having a pre-lunch nap, and Caleb knew that the excitement of the last couple of days had finally caught up with them. He watched as Father Martin stirred the gravy before covering the glass jug with tin foil and placing it in the oven. The aroma of cooking chicken and roast potatoes when he opened the door intensified, and Caleb's mouth started watering. Father Martin closed the oven door and sat opposite Caleb at the kitchen table.

"Caleb, may I ask you something?" he said. Caleb nodded in reply. He'd been expecting some questions about his background at some point, and now was as good a time as any. "Do you believe her?"

"Who, Suzy?" Caleb asked, realizing as he asked that there could be no one else the vicar was referring to.

"Yes."

"I think so, yes," Caleb replied. He didn't think so. He knew the moment he had touched her for the first time that there was danger surrounding her, but Caleb didn't think the vicar would understand this. "Why do you ask?"

"It's just, well, I don't know," Father Martin replied with a sigh. "It all seems rather, er, fanciful. A mysterious secret service man called Vince floating about somewhere in the shadows who's after her and Leanne. I take it you've not actually met this man?"

"No," Caleb replied, hiding a flash of irritation by closing his eyes. He didn't understand why, as a man of the cloth, Father Martin wouldn't take Suzy's story at face value. "I have no doubt she's telling the truth." This, at least, appeared to placate the vicar somewhat. "Tell me about this shelter?"

"It's on the outskirts of Norwich," Father Martin said. If he'd noticed Caleb changing the subject, he didn't show it.

"It's run by the diocese but all done discretely. For obvious reasons."

"Do you know Norwich well?" Caleb asked, taking care to pronounce the city name correctly.

"My previous parish was there," the vicar replied. "It's known as A Fine City. Nice enough place. They used to have a pub for every day of the year and a church for every Sunday." Father Martin laughed. "I guess they had their priorities right back in medieval times."

"Do you know a road called Lancaster Way?"

"No, I don't think so," Father Martin said, getting to his feet. "Wait there a sec, I've got an A to Z somewhere." Caleb waited as the vicar rummaged in a drawer, pulling out a dog-eared book. Father Martin flicked through it, turning first to the index in the back and then to the relevant page. He handed the book to Caleb and pointed at a road on the page. "That's it just there. Not the nicest part of Norwich, though. Why do you ask?"

"I have a friend who lives there."

"Really?" Father Martin looked down at the map in Caleb's hand. "Are you sure you have the right road? Only that's the Lark's Cross estate."

"Yes, that's where my friend lives. I take it there's only one Lancaster Road in Norwich?"

"Unless they've built another one since that book was published, yes. Although looking at the A to Z, it's probably quite out of date. I'll check on the internet for you after lunch."

"Thank you, Father," Caleb said, turning the book over in his hand. "I don't suppose I could hang on to this for a while, could I?"

"Of course," Father Martin replied with a short laugh.

"It's been in that drawer for years. We do have sat navs here, even in this part of the country."

The two men looked up in unison at the sound of someone walking into the kitchen. It was Leanne, her soft elephant clutched under her arm. She looked sleepy and had a crease on her cheek from a sheet.

"Hey, Leanne," Caleb said, a broad smile appearing on his face. "How are you doin'?"

"I'm hungry," Leanne replied, yawning as she spoke. "When's lunch?"

"As soon as your mother gets here," Father Martin replied. Leanne's eyes widened, and she looked a lot less sleepy in an instant. Then she turned and ran out of the room. A few seconds later, Caleb could hear her thumping up the stairs of the small house. "I have to say, Caleb," he said, turning to face him. "If your friend lives on the Lark's Cross estate, well..." His voice tailed away.

"Well?" Caleb said a few seconds later, keeping his voice light.

"Well," Father Martin replied with a curious expression on his face. "Let's just say you must have some interesting friends."

CHAPTER 28

Vince stifled a yawn as, on the projector screen in the stuffy conference room, yet another target's face appeared.

"This is Orange Snowball," Vince's boss said from his position of power next to the projector. There were a few muffled groans at the name from some of the other agents in the room. "He's a known member of National Action and we've got some intelligence that links him to both The Base over the pond and also the Loyalist Volunteer Force in the Republic of Ireland. Looks like he's trying to make some new friends overseas." Vince raised his hand and waited for his boss to acknowledge him.

"Shouldn't Six be looking at him?" Vince asked, referring to MI6, who were in charge of international threats.

"They are, Vince," his boss replied. "This one will be a joint operation with them." This time, the groans weren't muffled. None of the men and women in the room particularly enjoyed working with their counterparts from Vauxhall. "We think that Orange Snowball is meeting with a known player from the Republic this weekend, so we're going to pick him up on Saturday morning. They're attending a football match, so it will be challenging. Six has the visitor. We have this one."

On the screen, a young man glared out at the room. Mid-twenties, white with a shaved head. He was staring at the camera with an insolent expression, obviously trying and failing to intimidate whoever was taking his picture. It wasn't a covert photograph, but a police one that revealed the tattoos sneaking up onto his neck from his collar. Vince sighed. He hated scrotes like this one. Scum of the Earth, the lot of them. Vince's key problem with them was that they were usually too stupid to get even close to the threshold for his squad to do what it did best. Make them disappear.

"Who's playing?" another agent asked.

"Liverpool versus Chelsea," Vince's boss replied. "You'll be in the Liverpool end." There was another collective groan around the room, with someone muttering about how much they hated Liverpool. Vince couldn't have cared less about football, but trying to follow a target at such a crowded event was a challenge he was looking forward to. He started planning it in his head as his boss moved onto the next piece of shit they had an interest in.

Twenty minutes later, the briefing finished and Vince made his way from the conference room with the rest of his team. They had another planning meeting later in the day, but that was a couple of hours away, and he was hungry. One of his team suggested lunch in The Marquis of Granby, a dingy pub close to Thames House, but Vince wasn't in the mood. There was someone he wanted to check in on.

"Can I help you?" the blonde waitress said as Vince approached the counter. He had left Thames House twenty minutes ago and made his way to the Pret A Manger he was now standing in. He had taken a shortcut across St John's Gardens, a small park near the building where probably every other person in the park had a very high security clearance.

"Can I get this toasted, please?" Vince replied, handing the woman a cheese and ham sandwich in a paper bag. This was Samantha, who knew nothing about Vince at all. By contrast, he knew almost everything about her.

"Sure," the waitress said as she took the sandwich from him. Vince took a step back and watched as she handed the sandwich to a colleague. Samantha was twenty-four and lived in a tiny rental apartment in Neasden in the north of London. She was petite, standing only five feet three, and had a tattoo on her left leg that she'd not told her parents about. While she served another customer, Vince pulled his phone from his pocket to check Samantha's text messages. Then he looked at her e-mails, checked her Facebook instant messages. There was nothing really of interest, other than a reminder from her mother that it was Samantha's sister's wedding anniversary coming up, and some flowers would be nice.

Vince was just looking at the latest photograph Samantha had sent to her would-be boyfriend, a lad called Alex who worked behind the bar in a pub just down the road, when she delivered his sandwich. He swiped the photograph away and looked up at her. Vince much preferred the version of Samantha he had just been looking at to the clothed version now looking at him.

"Here you are, sir," Samantha said, her eyes betraying her lack of interest. That was fine by Vince. She would be very interested in him later.

He took the sandwich to a table and sat with his back to the wall, watching Samantha out of the corner of his eye.

She and Alex hadn't slept together yet, not helped by the fact he lived with his parents and she had a flatmate. But the flatmate was going away for a couple of days, and tomorrow night was going to be the night. Samantha was going to give Alex her spare key to her apartment, but she couldn't find it.

Samantha finished serving another customer before disappearing into the kitchen area of the restaurant. Vince pulled his phone from his pocket. She would be standing outside the rear fire door, smoking a Marlboro Light, something else she'd hidden from her parents. Vince's phone pinged. It was a message from Samantha to Alex.

We still on for tomorrow night?

It only took Alex a moment to respond, and Vince imagined the man lingering by his phone like a puppy waiting for a treat.

I can't wait. Could do tonight if you want?

Vince imagined Samantha puffing on her cigarette, wondering what she was thinking. He was tempted to answer on her behalf, letting Alex know she couldn't wait to be his dirty little fuck toy, but that would spoil the surprise.

Not tonight. Having a quiet night in. I can't wait either. Make sure you bring something to wear.

"Filthy little slut," Vince mumbled as he finished his sandwich.

He got to his feet, balling the paper bag up and tossing it in the bin on his way out of the restaurant. As he did so, he reached into his pocket and ran his fingertips over the key inside.

"Sorry, Alex," he said to himself, "but I'm going to be spoiling your fun a little."

CHAPTER 29

Suzy looked out of the window of Father Martin's car at the trees rushing past them. Beside her, in the rear seat of the car, Leanne was whispering something in Boo Boo's ear while Caleb and Father Martin were having a hushed conversation about something in the front seats. She tuned them out, grateful to have some time to think.

The first problem of their safety appeared to be taken care of. Although she barely knew Caleb, he had an air of confidence about him that was infectious. It was as if, as long as he was about, nothing could happen to them. But Suzy also knew that if Vince caught up with them, there would be nothing Caleb could do. She thought about her so-called partner for a moment, wondering how far he had got in terms of tracking her and Leanne. Her original plan had been for them to be in London by the time he'd discovered they'd gone. Then it was to be another bus to Dover and across the channel to France, somehow. Suzy hadn't been able to plan that part of their escape, other than hoping the immigration authorities were more concerned about people traveling illegally to England, not in the other direction.

But now she was in a car, heading to Norwich and a place she didn't know. All she could do was to put her faith in Caleb and Father Martin. Women's shelters, Suzy knew, were discreet by design and they were well used to hiding women like her. But could they hide her from Vince with all the resources he had at his disposal? All it would take would be a single slip up, and he would be there with his colleagues. And if Vince caught up with them, Suzy knew her fate would be sealed. He would never let her go again, and she would never see Leanne again.

"Mummy, are we nearly there?" Leanne said, looking up at her with tired eyes. Caleb turned and looked over his shoulder at the sound of her voice.

"It's about half an hour," he said, smiling at Leanne, "so not too much further."

"What will you do, Caleb?" Suzy asked him. "When we get to Norwich, I mean?" He was wearing jeans and a hoodie, both borrowed from Father Martin, and the difference from the robe was remarkable. With his shaved head, he could have passed for a football hooligan.

"I'm going to drop in on a friend," Caleb replied, earning a sideways glance from Father Martin. "But first, I'll make sure that you're both safe and sound."

"Will we see you again?" Leanne said.

"Of course you will."

"Promise?"

Suzy smiled as Caleb reached his hand back with his little finger extended.

"Pinky promise," he said. Suzy's smile broadened as she watched Leanne hook her finger with his. They shook, solemnly, and Leanne returned to whispering to Boo Boo

"Are you okay?" Caleb asked Suzy, his eyes meeting hers.

"I'm nervous, Caleb," Suzy replied. But she was far more than just nervous and, from the look on his face, he realized that.

"You'll be okay," Father Martin said. "This place we're going is very secure. They've never had any problems with ex-partners or husbands."

Suzy thought for a moment. She was pretty sure they'd never had any ex-partners or husbands like Vince, but he would have to find them first. She knew that the first places he would check would be the rail and the bus station. Suzy had no real friends to speak of, not anymore. Vince had seen to that. He'd been subtle about it, and by the time Suzy realized what he was doing, it was too late.

He wouldn't let her use any form of social media. Too dangerous, he had said, given my job. He had blocked all her friends on her phone, so any texts or calls to her never got through and then changed their contact numbers without Suzy realizing. So when she needed someone to turn to, someone to ask for help, there was no one. She couldn't communicate with anyone.

Could Vince have tracked her to the bus station? She'd bought the tickets using cash, paying a homeless man to get them for her so that she could avoid the CCTV cameras in the ticket office. It had been, she reflected as the trees continued to rush by outside the window, ten pounds well spent. The guy who'd bought the tickets hadn't asked her why she wanted him to buy them for her. He'd been far more interested in the tenner he'd just earned.

Suzy reached out and put her arm around Leanne, who snuggled into her, clutching Boo Boo to her chest. When

Suzy looked down a moment later, her daughter was fast asleep without a care in the world.

"I should be so lucky," Suzy muttered under her breath. She knew Vince was out there, searching for her with almost unlimited resources at his disposal.

CHAPTER 30

Naomi's fingers were trembling as she stabbed at the screen of her phone. The doorbell to her flat rang again, and a few seconds after that, there was a hammering at the door. Then the letterbox was pushed open from the outside. It made Naomi jump, and she knocked a mug from the sideboard. It fell into the sink, the handle breaking.

"Naomi," Mark's voice came through the small aperture in the door. "For God's sake, let me in. I just want to talk."

"Come on, come on," Naomi muttered. Finally, her finger hit the right button.

She glanced around the hallway where bundles of trash bags full of Mark's clothes were piled up. There was also a large cardboard box with the rest of his personal possessions, including his treasured collection of commemorative glasses from the local beer festivals he'd never taken her to. Naomi had spent the last couple of hours packing up all his stuff. Her plan had been to put the bags and the box in the garden, and then text Mark to let him know he could collect them when he wanted. At least she'd had the front door locks changed before coming back to the flat that morning, but her sister had been right. She should have brought someone with her.

Finally, after what seemed like minutes but could have only been a few seconds, a familiar baritone voice answered the phone.

"Detective Constable—"

"Dave, it's Naomi." She cut him off before he could continue. "It's Mark. He's here." There were another furious couple of thumps on the door as Mark shouted her name again.

"Where are you?"

"At my flat."

"I'm on my way. Five minutes, tops. Just stay put."

Her hands were still shaking as she disconnected the call. She leaned back against the wall of the hallway and took a deep breath. Mark was leaning on the doorbell, but Naomi did her best to ignore the noise. She walked back into the kitchen and checked that the back door leading to her postage-stamp sized garden was locked. When would Mark get the message that she wasn't going to speak to him?

The morning after the incident in the restaurant, Naomi had started getting calls from unknown numbers on her mobile. Knowing it would be Mark, Naomi had ignored them. Then she had seen glimpses of his black BMW, always in the periphery somewhere. But she knew it was him. Then, when she had returned to her flat that morning, there had been an enormous bunch of flowers on the doorstep. Mark would have seen them in the bin when he walked to her front door.

"Naomi, please," Mark said through the letterbox. His voice was more measured, almost but not quite plaintive. "You're overreacting. Come on, let's just chat about this."

Naomi opened her mouth to reply before remembering the advice she had dished out to many clients since becoming a lawyer.

"No comment," she whispered under her breath.

"Please, Naomi?" Mark said as if he had heard her. She walked into the lounge, needing to sit down. The adrenaline coursing through her was making her feel faint. As she sat in the armchair, she saw a shadow flitting across the window. It was Mark. He had his hands on the glass, either side of his face, trying to see inside. "Naomi? I know you're in there." His voice was more muffled now, but it was still audible.

She fiddled with her phone, turning it over and over in her hands. This was ridiculous. The first thing she was going to when she got back to the office was file for a restraining order against the man. He had no right to threaten her like this, not in her own home.

A moment later, there was a screech of brakes outside her flat. Naomi heard a car door being flung open, followed by the sound of an argument. She held her head in her hands as she listened, pressing her phone against her forehead. The argument didn't last long, and it was followed by a more gentle knock at the door.

"Naomi?" It was Dave. "Your ex is sitting in his car like a good boy. Can you let me in?"

Naomi leaped to her feet and ran to the door. She opened it to allow the police officer in, closing it as soon as he had crossed the threshold. Then she flung her arms around his broad shoulders, trying not to cry with relief.

"And then a hero comes along," she heard Dave singing in an awful impression of Mariah Carey. She relaxed her arms and looked at him.

"I wish I didn't need a hero," Naomi said. She saw Dave looking at the bags in the hallway.

"That his stuff?"

"Yes," Naomi replied. "I was going to put it in the garden for him to collect when he just turned up."

"Why don't you put the kettle on?" Dave said with a wry smile. "I'll help him load the car."

Naomi walked into the kitchen, retrieved the broken mug from the sink, and put the kettle on. While she waited for it to boil, she rummaged around in a drawer before emerging with a sample tube of Superglue which she placed next to the mug to fix later. When Naomi returned to the hallway, Dave was standing in the doorway, flinging the bin bags full of clothes into the front garden. Beyond the garden, Naomi could see Mark sitting at the wheel of his BMW, his face like thunder.

"What's in the box?" Dave said as he threw the last bag of clothes into the garden.

"Bits and pieces. His beer glass collection, other stuff like that."

Dave picked up the box and took a few steps onto the path. Then he hefted the box, ensuring it landed on the concrete path. Naomi heard glass smashing. When she looked at Dave, he was grinning.

"Whoops," he said, his grin broadening.

CHAPTER 31

Caleb looked through the windshield at the house that Father Martin had just pulled into. It was in a village called Thorpe on the outskirts of Norwich. Caleb knew nothing about house prices in England, but he could tell from the size of the ones they'd driven past that it wasn't a cheap area. Far from it.

When they had arrived at the large gates of the house, a small camera with a blinking red light stared at them for a moment before they slowly swung open. Caleb nodded in appreciation at the ten foot high walls surrounding the property, topped with shards of broken glass. Not very friendly, but given the purpose of the house, a good idea.

"You'll need to wait in the car, Caleb," Father Martin said as the tires of his car crushed the gravel in the driveway. "You won't be able to come in. Even I'm not allowed in the actual house, and I've known Joan for twenty years."

He nodded in response as Father Martin parked the car. There was enough space in the drive for perhaps four or five cars. Dominating the gravel space and ornate gardens was a two story house made of red brick with imposing gables on either side of a central section punctuated by small windows. A security light had burst into life as they had entered the driveway, even though it was still daylight and Caleb could see the curtains moving at one of the large ground floor windows.

"I'll see you soon, Suzy. Maybe a day, maybe a couple," Caleb said before turning to Leanne. "You too."

"You'd better," Leanne replied with a smile. Her face was full of innocent enthusiasm. "You promised, and it was a pinky promise."

"I've never broken a pinky promise in my life," he said, returning her smile.

Caleb watched as Suzy and Leanne got out of the car. Leanne was staring up at the house while Father Martin retrieved their bag from the trunk, and she slipped her hand into Suzy's as they made their way to the door. As they approached, it opened to let them in and Caleb caught a brief glimpse of a gray-haired woman in a floral dress before the door closed.

As he waited, Caleb examined his surroundings, working his way from the car outward in five-yard rings. It was an old habit, drilled into him many years ago, but a useful one to understand a new location properly. It wasn't until he got to the third ring that he noticed something. There was an oak tree near the wall that almost overhung the wall. But Caleb noticed any branches near the wall itself had been lopped off, and there was a small passive infra-red sensor attached to the trunk, facing the wall. Caleb was too far away to see any wiring, but he knew it would be linked to a camera somewhere. He nodded in appreciation. Whoever handled security knew what they were doing.

Caleb waited, closing his eyes for a few moments and thinking about his next steps to help Suzy and Leanne out of their predicament. He had three courses of action, as far as he could see. The first, as always, was to do nothing. That wasn't an option. In terms of a second and third course of action, he had little in the way of plans other than be nice or don't be nice. When he got to where he needed to go, he would put some meat on the bones of the latter two. He needed to do some reconnaissance, which was never time wasted.

A few moments later, Caleb heard the crunch of footsteps on the gravel, and he opened his eyes to see Father Martin walking back toward the car.

"They're all sorted," he said as he climbed into the driver's seat. "Joan and the girl who works with her will look after them."

"Do they have physical security?" Caleb asked a moment later, staring at the house. He could see CCTV cameras under the eaves of each gable and wondered whether they were linked to the motion sensor he'd noticed a moment ago.

"Not as in an actual person," Father Martin replied as they waited for the gates to re-open. "But the place is like a bloody fortress, and Joan's got panic buttons installed that link straight to the police." He started laughing. "She's allowed to test them once every three months, but she bakes for England before she does. Pretty much every police officer in Norwich responds, desperate to get their hands on her cake."

"Do the police know it's a shelter?"

"I'm not sure." Father Martin frowned. The gates started to swing open. "I guess they must. You're thinking about this Vince chap?"

"Yes. If he's as resourceful as Suzy says, he might be able to track her that way."

"Suzy and Leanne will be moved on in a few days," Father Martin replied a moment later as he eased the car back onto the road. The light was beginning to fade, and a pink hue was coloring the sky in the distance. "Joan and the other shelters never leave the women in the first one they get to as it's usually the closest to the men they're trying to get away from. So you'd better make sure you get back to see her and Leanne before then."

"I will," Caleb said.

The two men drove in silence for a while as the large houses outside gave way to open countryside. They entered the outskirts of Norwich a while later, the houses here very different. They were much smaller for a start. Father Martin pulled over in a small street and stopped the car. He turned to Caleb.

"This is the edge of the Lark's Cross," he said with a solemn expression. "I would drive you into the estate, but I like my car the way it is."

"I understand," Caleb replied. "Thank you, Father, for all your help." They shook hands and Caleb had picked up his cloth bag, making to exit the car, when he felt the vicar's hand on his shoulder.

"This friend of yours, Caleb," Father Martin asked. "Who is he exactly?"

Before he replied, Caleb reached into his pocket and pulled out a battered black leather wallet. He opened it and examined a student ID card through a scratched plastic window.

"His name's Leon Brockman," Caleb said. "He's lost his wallet. I'm just going to return it to him."

"Well, aren't you the Good Samaritan?" Father Martin said with a smile.

It faded as Caleb felt his face harden. "Not really."

CHAPTER 32

Leon adjusted the bag on his shoulder and slouched against a low wall belonging to a house that had more kitchen appliances in its garden than most houses had in their kitchen. At the end of the street, he could see two of the youngers, junior members of Syd's organization, slowly circling the deserted street on bicycles. They were lookouts, both for customers and the Old Bill.

In Leon's pocket was a burner phone and the two boys on the bikes had its number on speed dial. The second it rang, Leon was to run. He had several routes available through the alleys between the tightly packed houses on the estate. Any drugs left in his bag were to be ditched, but any money kept. You couldn't be nicked for having money.

Night had almost fallen, and the streets of the estate were bathed in a weak orange glow from the street lamps. Perhaps every other one was lit. Syd didn't want the areas he operated in being too well lit, and the council weren't about to venture onto the estate to fix the ones shot out with air rifles. Leon was nervous. More jittery than he had been on the bus, even. He was now running a trap house, and he wasn't even sixteen. All the others running trap houses were in their twenties. Syd must really believe in him, which meant he absolutely couldn't mess this up.

In his pocket, his phone vibrated with an incoming text message. He fished it out and looked at the screen.

Cus.

A customer. The youngers had stopped a car driving down the street and verified that the driver was kosher. If it was someone they didn't recognize, they wouldn't have sent the message. No verification, no deal. That was how Syd operated. He wasn't running a supermarket.

Leon waited as a car rolled down the street. As it approached, he stepped forward so the driver could see him. The car stopped and the driver's window went down. Leon didn't even look at the guy behind the wheel. As long as he had cash, Leon couldn't care less who he was. One thing he did know was that his car, a battered Ford Fiesta, was a wreck with almost as much rust as bodywork. When Leon was old enough to drive, there was no way he would be seen in something like the car in front of him.

"Alright?" Leon said, finally glancing at the man in the car. He was white, early-twenties, and his entire outfit looked to be from Primark. "How much you after?"

"I've got twenty quid," the driver replied, licking his lips. "What can I get for that?"

Leon sighed. Syd's product wasn't sold by price. It was sold by weight.

"Brown or green?" Leon asked. Cannabis resin or marijuana leaf. He knew before the driver replied he would go for brown. It was cheaper, less potent, and would last longer. Leon reckoned the customer was a student from the University of East Anglia on the other side of the city.

"Brown," the man in the car said.

"I can do you an eighth for twenty."

"Really? That's expensive."

"You think?" Leon replied with a sneer. He started to move away from the car. The man in the car could bugger off as far as he was concerned. Leon wasn't about to start haggling with Syd's product.

"Alright, alright," the driver said when Leon was a couple of feet away from the Fiesta.

A moment later, the car was moving down the street with a cough of black exhaust smoke. Leon watched as the driver performed an erratic three-point turn, obviously not wanting to go any further into the estate than he had to. Leon didn't blame him, although he couldn't see anyone wanting to car-jack such a shitty vehicle.

He glanced up at the top of the tower block to Syd's apartment. Had Syd seen Leon complete his first sale as the boss of a trap house? He hoped so, and had to resist the temptation to raise his hand and wave at the window, just in case Syd was watching.

In his pocket, Leon's phone buzzed again. He pulled it out, expecting to see a notification of another customer. They would come thick and fast now that night had fallen. But it wasn't a notification of a customer.

Stranger Danger, the message read. Leon's eyebrows went up. Few people visited the Lark's Cross estate, but there was at least one visitor on the way. The youngers had a sense of the Old Bill that was almost supernatural, but Leon moved down the street anyway. He stopped by an alleyway that led between two of the terraced houses. If he had to, he could run down the alley and lose the visitor in seconds. When he reached the alleyway, he stepped back off the road and into the darkness.

A few moments later, the visitor appeared in the gloomy streetlights. He was wearing jeans and a hoodie, but Leon couldn't see his face in the poor light. But the youngers would have got a good look at him. Leon made a mental note to speak to them at some point to see what they thought.

The man walked down the street, both hands deep in the pockets of his hoodie. If he knew about Leon hiding in the shadows, he made no obvious sign. He passed within about twenty feet of the alley Leon was hiding in, but didn't so much as glance in his direction. The man didn't seem in the slightest bit concerned about his surroundings, which was unusual on the Lark's Cross estate.

Leon watched, wondering if the man realized how much danger he was in, as a shiver ran down his spine. It was as if someone had just walked over his grave. He laughed the sensation away as the phone buzzed again in his pocket.

Cus.

It was time to get back to work.

CHAPTER 33

Vince sat in his car with his laptop perched on his knee, the screen resting on the steering wheel. On the passenger seat, his phone sat on top of a takeout menu. The screen was showing a feed from a camera he'd installed a couple of days previously. He glanced at the screen a couple of times, seeing that Samantha's bathroom door was still closed. Vince closed his eyes, imagining her in the bath, soaking in the bath bombs she'd ordered online the day before.

He breathed in through his nose, trying to conjure up what the website said were cool citrus and comforting florals. She'd taken a large glass of wine into the bathroom with her, and he could see her sipping from it in his mind's eye. Vince would have put a camera in the bathroom when he'd visited Samantha's apartment, but he'd not found anywhere to hide it properly. So his imagination would have to do for this part of the evening's entertainment.

Vince was parked in a large parking lot in Brent Park, in a shopping complex that included a huge Tesco supermarket next to a large Ikea store. Behind the Ikea store,

Vince could just see the top of Wembley Stadium's iconic arch, lit up in the night sky. The supermarket was busy, a constant stream of cars and customers, and no one took a blind bit of notice of him. He was only a few minutes' walk from Kingfisher Way, the residential street where Samantha was currently soaking herself in citrus and florals.

His laptop pinged with an incoming warning, as did his phone. Vince reluctantly opened his eyes and gazed down at the laptop screen, knowing it was the same message on both devices.

"Bingo," he said when he saw the message on it. The burner phone that had been used to make the hoax call, which Vince was now sure Suzy had engineered, had just been activated. On the screen was a map of the United Kingdom with a small red pin in the east of the country. Before he zoomed in on the pin, Vince knew its location. He also knew he'd been right. The call had been made from Norwich. He zoomed in as far as he could to see the pin hovering over a square in the center of the city known as Hay Hill. He knew the area well. It was close to the large modern library and near to the marketplace where, according to the tourist guides, cheap trash had been sold since the eleventh century. As he watched, the pin disappeared. He switched windows to check another piece of software to see if any calls or text messages had been sent and received by the handset, but there was no activity at all. It had just been turned on, and then off. Perhaps to check for messages? It didn't matter. He had its location and was a lot closer now than he had been a few moments ago.

Vince was distracted by movement on his phone screen. He closed his laptop down and put it on the passenger seat, picking up his phone as he did so. Samantha, her wine glass now empty, was making her way into the kitchen of her apartment. Her face was flushed, and she was wearing a pink, fluffy dressing gown that looked several sizes too big. On her feet was a pair of matching slippers, just as pink, just as fluffy.

"Very cozy," he muttered as he watched her refill her glass. Samantha took a large swig before topping it back up again. Vince felt his heart speeding up as she walked over to the telephone on the kitchen wall. He saw her picking up the handset and peering at a piece of paper tacked to the wall next to the phone. Samantha stabbed at the digits on the telephone and, a few seconds later, Vince's mobile rang.

"Hello, China Garden?" Vince said as he answered the phone and flicked it to speaker so he could still see the screen. There was no point trying to disguise his voice. This call wasn't one that would be recorded anywhere.

"Yeah, hi," Samantha replied, her voice slurring slightly. "Can I order some food for delivery, please?"

"Of course," Vince replied with a smile. "What would you like?"

"Um, can I have a Kung Pao chicken, plain boiled rice, and some prawn crackers please?"

Vince paused before replying as if he was writing the order down. As he did so, he looked at his own copy of the menu.

"So, that's a number forty-five, a number sixteen, and a number one hundred and twelve?" He heard Samantha giggling, and he saw her on the screen, peering at her own menu.

"Yep, that's right. And don't forget the fortune cookie."

"That comes to fifteen pounds and ninety pence," Vince said. "Cash on delivery?"

"Sure. It's number twelve, Peregrine Close. Just off King-fisher Way."

"It'll be around twenty minutes."

Vince disconnected the phone, grinning to himself as he did so. On the screen, he watched Samantha get a plate from her kitchen cupboard, placing it on the table. Then she crossed to her handbag and extracted a twenty-pound note from her purse, placing it on top of the plate. Then he got out of the car and walked around to the trunk.

A few moments later, carrying an empty insulated food box in one hand and a motorcycle helmet in the other, Vince was making his way down Peregrine Close. Samantha's apartment was at the end of a small block of apartments on the bottom floor. Her front door was hidden in darkness because, earlier that day, someone had vandalized the meager street lighting on the small road. Vince slipped the motorcycle helmet over his head as he approached the front door, the gloom also hiding the vinyl gloves on his hands.

He hefted the food box into the air, partially covering Samantha's view. Vince reached out and pressed the doorbell, listening as muffled chimes rang out from inside the apartment.

"Hang on," he heard Samantha call out. "I'm just coming."

The door opened, and she looked out, her eyes lighting up when she saw the box in Vince's hand. She was still wearing the pink dressing gown and had tightened it around her stomach before answering the door. In one hand was the twenty-pound note.

Vince dropped the box, kicking it inside the apartment as one hand shot out to cover Samantha's mouth. He used his other hand around her neck to push her back inside, closing the door behind him with his foot.

Samantha's quiet night in was about to get a lot noisier.

CHAPTER 34

Suzy looked through the window of her bedroom on the upper story of the house. Beyond the branches of the large trees that were moving slowly in the wind, she could see some of the other houses in the village. Like the one she was in, they each stood on their own ground. Most of them were surrounded by walls, but not as high or as treacherous as the ones surrounding this house. Many had gleaming cars outside, and most had at least one lit window, if not more. Suzy imagined the people inside the houses, living their lives peacefully, without fearing for them like she was. Parents would be putting their children to bed, reading them stories and tucking them in. Much like she had done earlier with Leanne, except the other children would be in their own beds, surrounded by their own toys.

Suzy looked at the adjoining door that led to the bedroom Leanne was sleeping in. The door was slightly ajar, just in case Leanne woke up, scared or needing anything. In her own bedroom was a large double bed, covered by a throw that looked as if it had been crocheted by an army of women. But Suzy couldn't even think about going to sleep.

A soft knock at the door made her jump.

"Hello?" Suzy called out. The door opened and Joan's head appeared. She was smiling warmly.

"Everything okay?" Joan said. Her voice was soft and reassuring. "I heard you moving about. I hope you don't mind me popping up?"

"Not at all," Suzy replied. "I mean, it's your house. I was just, er, just thinking about everything." Joan stepped into the room, closing the door softly behind her.

"As I said before," Joan said, "I'm always here to talk, if you want to. But I'm always here even if you don't want to."

Suzy looked at the woman, examining her as she did so. When Joan had ushered Suzy and Leanne into the house, she had introduced them to a young woman a few years younger than Suzy called Agnesa. Agnesa, according to Joan, helped run the house when they had guests like Suzy and Leanne. It had been Agnesa who had shown Suzy and Leanne around the house, with Joan only putting in a brief appearance as they ate that evening. Agnesa spoke little, and when she did, had a clipped eastern-European accent. The only information Suzy had been able to get from her was that she was originally from Albania, but this wasn't the sort of house where personal questions were welcomed.

Joan was, in Suzy's estimation, in her late sixties or early seventies. She was wearing a simple dress, which she could have made herself, with a knitted cardigan over her shoulders. Joan had a kind face, but underneath it was a hard resolve. In some ways, she reminded Suzy of Caleb. The gold cross that hung on a simple chain around her neck reinforced that, although Caleb wore no jewelry that Suzy had seen.

"Why do you do this, Joan?" Suzy asked, sitting on the

edge of the bed. Joan sat next to her, close enough to be comforting, but not so close that Suzy was uncomfortable.

"I have my reasons," Joan said, before tightening her lips. "But we need to talk about you. Father Martin's given me some details about your situation, but it would be helpful to know a little more about your plans."

"I was on a bus," Suzy said. Joan frowned, but her eyes remained kind. "It got robbed, and I lost all my money. So, my plans are shot to bits."

"Ah, I see." Joan appeared unmoved at the news. "Nothing we can't work around, I'm sure." Her frown faded, and a smile returned to her face. "What were your plans? Before you were robbed?"

"I was going to head to Dover and get across the channel somehow," Suzy said with a sigh. "I'd not really worked out how, but I'm sure there's a way. Everyone's looking for people coming in, aren't they? Not leaving." She swallowed hard, her mouth suddenly dry. "He's got no authority outside the United Kingdom."

"Your partner?"

"Yes." Suzy swallowed again. "Vince. He works for the government."

"Father Martin mentioned that, yes."

"He's got access to pretty much everything. National security and all that."

"I imagine he has," Joan said, again unperturbed. Suzy imagined the woman had heard it all before, anyway. "Well, you'll be stopping with us for a couple of days. But you can rest assured that this Vince won't be able to find you here. We're very much under the radar."

"Okay," Suzy replied, willing what Joan had just said to be true for both her and Leanne's sake.

"I have a friend who runs a similar place down in

Margate," Joan said, getting to her feet and smoothing a non-existent crease from the front of her dress. "I'll speak to her tomorrow. Why don't we see if we can get you and your daughter down there? I don't think she'll be able to help you get across the channel." To Suzy's surprise, Joan winked at her. "But you never know."

CHAPTER 35

Caleb sensed them before he saw them. A car had driven past him a few moments earlier, slowing down so its occupants could look at him before the vehicle turned into a side street. But Caleb hadn't looked at them. He didn't need to. When he got to the end of the road, he saw that the car had pulled over and the two men who had been in it were standing next to it. There would be a third man behind him, but Caleb didn't look to confirm it. He was either there or he wasn't. If he was, Caleb would deal with him. If he wasn't, he wouldn't need to.

"Alright, mate?" the larger of the two men said as Caleb approached. He was perhaps in his mid-twenties, white, and had acne scarring on his face. Both he and his colleague, who were leaning against their car, were wearing clothing similar to Caleb's, but much newer. Neither had the hoods of their hoodies up. Both men had white sneakers on, which Caleb thought was a mistake. It was hard to get blood out of white sneakers. "Where are you off to?"

Caleb stopped, slipping his hands out of his pockets so the men could see he was unarmed. Then he slipped his own hood down and nodded at the towers a few hundred yards away. He said nothing.

"Where you from, buddy?" the man leaning against the car said. He spoke with what to Caleb was an unusual accent, but Caleb knew the moment he opened his mouth, the feeling would be mutual.

"Texas, originally," Caleb said after a few seconds. The younger man glanced at his companion before laughing.

"Man, you are a long way from home," he said, his laugh fading. "We stopped because you didn't look local. Turns out we were right."

"You know this is a toll road, right?" the second man said. He'd not moved yet, but as Caleb watched, his hand slipped into the pocket of his jeans. "Which means there's a toll to be paid. You have them in Texas, right?"

"Sure do," Caleb replied. He could hear soft footsteps behind him, but they were far enough away to not be a concern. "I will always pay toll to those to whom toll is due. But not you two clowns."

There was a metallic click from the second man's hand, and a glint of light caught Caleb's eye. But he didn't need light to recognize the switchblade in his hand.

"Bollocks to this," the man said, pushing himself away from the car and stepping past his colleague. He was perhaps two feet in front of Caleb as he lifted the knife. "What-cha got?"

"Excuse me?" Caleb asked, looking the man in the eye as he adjusted the weight distribution in his legs. "What did you say?"

"Come on, let's see your wallet."

"I don't have one."

The man jiggled the knife, as if to draw Caleb's attention toward it. This also meant that his own attention was on the knife, not on Caleb. When he jabbed the knife toward him, Caleb pivoted into his assailant, turning his body so that his shoulder hit his chest at the same time as Caleb's right arm shot up and grabbed his wrist. The other man had only managed to take a half step forward when Caleb thrust his hips to the side and into his attacker's groin.

As the man bent in the middle, Caleb angled his wrist inward until the knife clattered to the ground and, using his other hand, pushed the man's head down to meet his knee, which was traveling upward, fast. The sound when face met knee was, in Caleb's opinion, most satisfying. The knife was spiraling away on the ground, courtesy of a kick from Caleb, by the time the second mugger had finished his step. As fights went, it was one of Caleb's shortest. But in his experience, the best ones always were.

Caleb leaped back, putting some space between him and the falling attacker. He put his weight on his back leg, turned to the other man, and held his hands up in a classic fighting stance. But it was only for show.

"You sure you want to play this game?" Caleb asked him. Over his shoulder, Caleb could see the third man who turned out not to be a man, but a boy. At first glance, Caleb thought it might be the man he'd come here to see, but it wasn't. The youngest of the three was staring at Caleb, open mouthed. He wasn't much in the way of reinforcements. "How about you just go home for a nice cup of tea?"

The first man who had spoken, whose sole contribution to the fight was taking a step forward by which time it was done, said nothing. He glanced at the man on the ground who had managed to get his hands up to his face, and then back at Caleb.

"Respect to those to whom respect is due, honor to those to whom honor is due," Caleb said, watching as a frown appeared on the man's face. "It's from Romans." The frown deepened. "In the Bible?" Caleb stepped over the prone man, who still had his hands clasped to his face, a thin rivulet of blood flowing from between his fingers. "Never mind," Caleb said as he continued toward his destination.

CHAPTER 36

Naomi watched as her sister, Jennifer, poured them both another glass of wine. The look on her face was one of intense concentration which made Naomi smile but, even though her hand wobbled, Jennifer was able to top up both glasses without spilling any. She placed the now empty bottle next to another one on the lounge carpet. The women were in Jennifer's apartment, Naomi having decided that she would stay for another couple of days before returning home.

"Chin chin," Jennifer said as she picked up a glass and handed it to Naomi.

"Cheers, sis," Naomi said, taking a sip. She grimaced. It was worse than the first bottle. "My God, that's rancid."

"Shut up and get it down you." Jennifer grinned at Naomi, who took another sip from the glass. "So, what's the plan with matey boy?"

"Mark?"

"Who else?" Jennifer sipped at her own glass and made a face, confirming Naomi's opinion of the wine. "Are you going to take out one of those restraining order things?"

"It's called a non-molestation order," Naomi replied, "but yes, I am. As soon as it's in place, I'll be out of your hair."

"You stay as long as you want, Naomi. It's kind of nice having you around." The two women sat in silence for a moment. In the background, a late-night music channel was playing on the radio. "At least I know you're not singing 'All By Myself' into an empty wine bottle." Jennifer giggled and reached out to rub Naomi's pajamas with her fingers. "But you have got the pajamas on already."

"That's the pot calling the kettle black," Naomi said, punching her sister playfully on the arm. "So have you, and you're just as single as I am."

"Yeah, thanks for reminding me." Jennifer sipped her wine. "Hey, I know what we should do?"

"Oh, great. Tell me, big sister, what should we do?"

"Less of the big, thank you very much. We should have a weekend away somewhere. Cambridge, maybe?" Another sip. "Somewhere we're not going to run into any arsehole ex-boyfriends."

"And do what?" Naomi relaxed back in her chair with a wry smile on her face. She thought she knew what was coming.

"We should book into a cheap hotel, or an Air BnB or something." Jennifer's smile now matched Naomi's. "Put our glad rags on and go out with one intention."

"What might that be, Jen?" Naomi said with a groan. She'd been right. Every time one of them broke up with a partner, which in Jennifer's case was far more often than Naomi's, Jennifer's suggestion was always the same.

"We should go out with the sole intention of getting well and truly laid." Jennifer started giggling. "Especially you."

"Why especially me?"

"What you need, Naomi, is a night of abandoned debauchery with a young stud muffin who you'll never see again in your life." Naomi's sister's giggles turned into a cackle. "We probably wouldn't even need to leave the hotel lobby. They're normally full of businessmen away from home."

"Nice idea," Naomi said, as she always did when Jennifer suggested this, "but it's not really my style."

"You've had one night stands before, though?" Naomi paused before saying anything. There wasn't much her sister didn't know about her. "There was that bloke, Tim, wasn't it? When you were at law school?"

"Two second Tiny Tim, you mean?" Naomi replied as she lifted her little finger up and wiggled it. Jennifer's cackle got worse, and she made a weird noise with her nose. "Did you actually just snort?" Naomi asked with a laugh.

"Stop, stop it," Jennifer said, using the back of her hand to wipe her cheeks. "You're making me cry."

Naomi folded her legs under her and regarded her sister. Although there were only a couple of years between them, Jennifer was definitely the big sister. Naomi had turned to her over the years for pretty much every crisis that had befallen her, whether real or imaginary. Even their mother had commented on it on more than one occasion, commenting that Jennifer was more maternal than she was. One thing the sisters did have in common at that moment in time was their terrible taste in men.

"Why are men such arseholes?" Jennifer said eventually.

"I'm sure they're not all arseholes," Naomi replied, more in hope than belief. "Maybe it's just the ones we meet who are? Aren't we supposed to all have a soul mate somewhere on the planet?"

"Mine had better turn up pretty soon." Her sister started

giggling again. "The rate I'm going, I'll be a virgin again before long." Then Jennifer started cackling. "It might be too soon, but have you put new batteries in your—"

There was a melodic sound as Jennifer's doorbell sounded. Naomi unfolded her legs and leaped to her feet.

"Food's here," she said. As she passed by her sister, Naomi ruffled Jennifer's hair. "Saved by the bell," she continued, laughing as she did so.

CHAPTER 37

Leon stuffed the two twenty-pound notes that his last customer of the evening had given him into his pocket and turned his back on the man. The customer, a middle-aged man who was doing a pretty good impression of a man just walking his dog, lived on the other side of the estate. Leon knew him by sight, and also knew that if the local rumors were to be believed, the man wasn't allowed within five hundred yards of a school or municipal playground. Not that Leon cared for rumors about things like that. The only thing he cared about was getting his bag full of money back to Syd's apartment. It would be a brave mugger who took Syd's cash, but there was also a rumor floating around the estate about some Albanians who were eyeing up Syd's area. Leon had no intention of becoming the first victim of a turf war.

After making sure the bag was secured, Leon made his way down the thin alley between the two houses that he'd hidden in earlier. The alley wasn't much more than a yard wide, and it was covered in weeds and rubbish. He was careful where he stepped. Although the alley was too skinny to be a regular part of any dog walker's route, he didn't want to step in anything. More likely would be stepping on a used needle left there by the skanks who couldn't wait to get back to their doss houses before shooting up.

Leon hefted the bag onto his shoulder. Although it was full of paper money, it felt as if it was weighing him down like it was coins. He had started the evening with fifty small bags of cannabis, all priced at twenty pounds a bag. Unless Leon had miscounted, there would be a grand in the bag, two hundred quid of which was his. If he did the same numbers for a week, that was over a grand in his own pocket —every week. Leon smiled at the thought of the money.

As he walked down the alley and turned into an even narrower passage that led between the gardens of the houses, he started doing some math in his head. Syd had at least two trap houses like the one he had run that evening. That was almost ten thousand pounds a week he was getting. Leon had no idea what Syd's costs were, but that was some serious coin right there, and it was before any supplemental income like buses. He knew the trap houses weren't run continually, which he assumed was a supply issue. If Leon could come up with a way of maintaining that supply, he could present it to Syd as a business proposition.

Maybe he could ask Syd about his supply line? Leon might be able to come up with a way of helping him maintain it so that he could run his houses all the time instead of only when he had product to sell. It was a long shot, he knew. Leon wasn't even sixteen, and he knew little about the business side of things. But he was more than happy to learn everything he could about it. It would be a better education than he would get at the crappy comprehensive school he attended on occasion. He was just mulling this over in his head when he walked out of the alley and onto the main road, almost colliding with someone as he did so. Instinctively, Leon grabbed the bag and held it to his chest.

"Jesus, bro'," the man he had almost walked into said. "You made me jump." Leon looked at him and the two others he was with, and relaxed. The older of the two men were brothers who he recognized, although he couldn't remember their names. But they were local, so would know who he was and who he worked for. Leon's grip on the bag loosened as he examined them. The oldest brother had blood smeared under both his nostrils and down the front of his hoodie.

"Man," Leon said. "What happened to you? You get jumped?"

"Yeah," the man replied, touching his nose gingerly. "There were four of the bastards from the other side of the city. Came over here on the nick. Isn't that right, Aaron?" The other brother nodded his head but didn't look convinced.

"Yeah, that's what happened," he said eventually. "Big bastards as well."

Leon looked at the pair of them, not believing a word of it. But it wasn't his business, so he just shrugged his shoulders and carried on walking. He kept his eyes and ears open as he approached the tower blocks in the estate's center. It wasn't until he was in the foyer of Syd's block, staring at the CCTV camera and waiting for the lift to be activated, that he was able to relax.

As the lift made its way slowly to Syd's floor, Leon smiled at himself in the mirror on the wall. It had been a successful night's work. He'd sold all his product, not been nicked or mugged, and was sure that Syd would gift him a bag so he didn't have to keep smoking his emergency stash.

One thing Leon did know for sure was that he was on the way up.

CHAPTER 38

Caleb looked up at the two monstrosities in front of him. They dwarfed the small houses on the estate proper, even though they were only twelve stories high. There were shops in Houston with more floors than these buildings. The walls were covered with some sort of cladding, no doubt designed to tidy them up, but they still looked gray and dank. He remembered a fire in London a few years previously where many people had died when the cladding had caused the building to incinerate itself, and he offered up a silent prayer for the individuals involved.

He wasn't sure which tower to look at. In terms of what he wanted to be able to see, either would suffice for his needs as they both overlooked the right part of the housing project, which was one of the roads he had just walked down. As he had passed the house in question, he had looked sideways at it to fix it in his head. In the end, he'd needed to use the house next door as his reference point, as the one he was interested in as his primary target was pretty unremarkable.

Caleb walked up to the door of the tower closest to him.

As he approached, the light worsened as the hulking building blocked out what little moonlight there was in the sky. The only light left was from the orange street lamps, and only around half of them seemed to be working. He could feel that he was being watched from somewhere, but that didn't matter to Caleb. You couldn't hurt a man just by looking at him.

The door to the apartment building was a heavy metal affair, dented in places but otherwise intact. There was a graffiti tag of some sort which covered half the door and the adjoining concrete wall. Scratched into the metal surface was a note regarding the ability of a presumably local resident called Jayne to perform oral sex. Caleb wondered if she lived in the building and had to look at those words every time she came home. He shook his head and pushed against the door, but it was locked.

Next to the door were two thin panels, one with a number keypad and one with a series of doorbell buttons. Only a few of the buttons had legible labels next to them, but Caleb worked his way down the line, pressing each button for a few seconds in turn. There were a series of voices through the thin metal grill covering the speaker, some telling him to go forth and multiply, others asking him what he wanted.

"Food delivery," Caleb called into the speaker, trying his best to sound English and not American. A few seconds later, there was a buzzing noise, and he pushed the door open. Whether it was someone just pressing the button or whether it was someone waiting for some pizza was unclear and irrelevant to him.

Caleb wrinkled his face as he entered the lobby of the apartment building. The air was sour and rancid, smelling of some sort of human waste. The linoleum floor was heavily stained and the way the fluorescent light reflected off a few of the stains told him at least some of them were fresh. Flyers for takeout restaurants littered the floor along with damp newspapers.

On the other side of the lobby were two elevators next to a door. Taking care to avoid the puddles of liquid on the floor, Caleb crossed to the elevators and pressed the Up button between them. Somewhere above his head, heavy machinery clunked into life, but he couldn't hear the elevator descending. But even if it was working, there was no way he was going to use an elevator in this place. As the machinery above his head fell silent, Caleb pushed against the door. He ignored a further note about Jayne's sexual prowess and stepped inside. As he had thought, it led to a stairwell.

The air inside was marginally cleaner than the lobby, as was the floor. Caleb doubted that many people used the stairs when the elevator was working. He started climbing the stairs, stepping over some used needles and syringes as he did so. The higher he climbed, the cleaner the air became. It was as if the rancid atmosphere gathered at the bottom of the apartment block. By the time he reached the top of the stairwell, Caleb was breathing hard, but he had got to the top of the building encountering no one.

At the very top of the stairwell was an access door to the roof space. It was secured with a rusted padlock that didn't look as if it had been opened in years. Caleb reached into his bag for a set of picks and kneeled next to the lock. Once he had selected the correct size one, he used a small tin of beeswax to lubricate the pick before inserting into the lock and sliding a tension wrench alongside it. He closed his eyes to concentrate so he could feel the pick sliding over the pins and a moment later, the lock sprung open. When he pulled the door open, a rush of fresh air swept into the stairwell as the hinges screamed in complaint. Caleb inhaled the breeze gratefully.

He stepped through the door and into the pale moonlight. The roof was cluttered with large ducting and other apparatus that served the building. Caleb turned to look at the door that he had closed behind him. Did he need to secure it? He thought not. If anyone opened it, he would know from the noise of the hinges.

Caleb stepped across the roof, clambering over some of the machinery until he reached the side of the apartment block he wanted. Surrounding the roof was a low balustrade which he kneeled behind before leaning his elbows on the lip.

Below him was the entire Lark's Cross estate, laid out like a model village.

"Time spent on reconnaissance," Caleb muttered to himself, "is seldom wasted."

CHAPTER 39

Suzy's eyes snapped open in the darkness. She blinked twice in quick succession, holding her breath as she did so. There was someone else in the bedroom. She could hear them breathing but couldn't see a thing because of the blackout curtains.

"Mummy?" Suzy breathed a sigh of relief at the sound of Leanne's voice. "I had a bad dream."

Suzy reached out and fumbled for the switch to the light on the bedside table. When it clicked on, she saw Leanne standing a few feet away from the bed. She was holding Boo Boo loosely at her side, and her face was creased from her pillow.

"Hey, baby," Suzy said, throwing the covers back and patting the sheet. "Snuggle in here. I thought we left a light on when you went to bed?"

"The shadows were scary," Leanne replied as she made her way toward the bed. "I turned it off."

A moment later, when Leanne was tucked up alongside her, Suzy asked her daughter about the dream.

"There was a bad man," Leanne whispered. "He was

chasing after us." Suzy stiffened in the bed. She had been so careful not to tell Leanne the true reason for their trip, describing it instead as a big adventure. At some point, they would have to have a discussion about why Vince hadn't come with them and why Leanne would never see Vince again, but Suzy wanted to be safe before they had that chat.

They had been watching television in Joan's lounge earlier that evening. Suzy had left Leanne for a few moments to make her a cup of hot chocolate before bed. When she returned, to her horror, Leanne was watching a news report about a horrific attack on a woman in North London. Suzy had turned the television off as quickly as she could, but she knew from the expression on Leanne's face that it was too late.

"Could you see who the bad man was?" Suzy asked her daughter, hoping it was the news report that had triggered Leanne's nightmare and not the fact that she had realized they were on the run from Vince. "Could you see his face?" If she replied 'It was Vince', her heart was going to break.

"No," Leanne replied. "He was kind of in the dark."

"You know it was only a dream, right?" Suzy said, stroking Leanne's hair. "That the bad man doesn't really exist?" She hoped Leanne wouldn't hear the lie in her voice.

"But I saw him."

"Where were you when he was chasing you?"

"In a wood."

"The one we were in last night?"

"No," Leanne replied. "Not that one. That was a safe wood. The one in my dream wasn't." Suzy continued to stroke Leanne's hair. It was possible that her daughter had picked up on what was going on, but Suzy didn't think she had. She hoped she hadn't. "Will you tell me a story? A fairy tale?"

"Sure. Which one?"

"The girl in the red hood."

Suzy sighed. She didn't really want to tell Leanne that story. Not when it was about a small girl being chased by a predator, even if the ending worked out in the girl's favor. She racked her brains for a fairy tale that didn't involve peril of some sort for a child, but was struggling to think of one.

"How about the princess and the pea? We've not done that one for ages." Leanne nodded in agreement, much to Suzy's relief. "Once upon a time, there was a prince. He was very lonely and traveled around the world to find someone like himself. A proper princess to share his life."

"What was the princess's name?" Leanne asked. Suzy could hear how tired she was from the way she spoke.

"I think her name might have been Leanne," Suzy replied with a smile. Every fairy tale they told had a Leanne in it.

She continued the story, her voice getting more sonorous as she did so. By the time she got to the part where the princess woke up, bruised and aching from the pea, Leanne was sound asleep. But Suzy continued the story, anyway.

"The prince and the princess got married and lived in an enormous castle," Suzy whispered as she turned off the light. She closed her eyes and put her hand gently on Leanne's head. "And they all lived happily ever after."

CHAPTER 40

Leon walked into Syd's lounge and placed the bag on the coffee table, which was strewn with beer cans and an overflowing ashtray. As was usual in Syd's apartment, a fog of cannabis smoke lingered in the air, but when Leon looked at Syd, he didn't look stoned. If anything, he looked energized.

"Leon, my man," Syd said with a broad grin. "How was it?"

"All gone, Syd," Leon replied, pointing at the bag. "Nothing in there now but cold, hard cash."

"Excellent. You've shifted that lot pretty quick." Syd's grin broadened. He reached for the bag and pulled out a handful of notes. Leon waited as he counted out ten of them. "Here you go. Two hundred, as promised."

"Sweet," Leon said. "Er, I was wondering if I could buy an eighth for myself?" He put the money into his back pocket, but kept one note out for Syd.

"Sure. You could have just sold one of those to yourself, though." Syd nodded at the bag.

"But I didn't have any cash until you paid me."

"Ah, got it." Syd was looking at Leon with a peculiar expression. "I'll just give you a sample to tide you over. Call it a tip for shifting that lot so quickly."

Leon waited while Syd crossed the room and opened a cool box in the corner. As he pulled out a small bag of weed, Leon could see that the cool box was full to the brim. Syd's supply run had obviously been a successful one.

"Thanks, Syd," Leon said, catching the bag as it was tossed in his direction. "Nice one." He waited for a moment, unsure what to do. Should he offer to put a joint together for him and Syd to share, or should he wait to be invited? In the end, Syd answered the question for him. "You in a hurry, bro?"

"Nah, not really," Leon replied. "You want me to put one together?"

"I'm not fussed myself. Fill your boots if you want to, though." Syd shrugged his shoulders as if he was indifferent, but Leon got the impression he really wasn't bothered. "I was going to run something past you."

"Sure."

Syd turned and walked to the other side of the lounge, where there was a door with a combination lock. Leon had seen the door before but figured it was where Syd kept the majority of his stash and his money. Leon followed, waiting as Syd entered the combination into the lock and opened the door.

"Come on in, Leon," Syd said as he walked into the room.

Leon followed the man into what would have originally been one of the bedrooms in the apartment. His eyebrows went up when he saw what looked like some sort of control center. Enormous twin monitors sat on a large desk with a powerful tower computer whirring away underneath it, and a reclinable chair completed the setup. The air inside the room was fresh and smoke free, and the surface of the desk was a marked contrast to the coffee table in the lounge. There was nothing on it apart from a keyboard and wireless mouse.

"Nice gaming rig, Syd," Leon said, whistling through his teeth in admiration. He had no idea how much the equipment would have cost, but it certainly wasn't cheap.

"It's not a gaming rig," Syd said as he leaned forward to wiggle the mouse. "Although I guess it could be."

The screens burst into life, filling the room with a warm glow. The left-hand screen had some sort of dashboard, with a complicated-looking series of graphs. Leon saw Syd run his eyes over the screen and he saw a couple of captions before Syd minimized the window to reveal a star-scape wallpaper. There was one for temperature, one for humidity, but the window was gone before Leon could see any more. On the other screen was a map.

"What do you think?" Syd said, pointing at an area on the map.

Leon leaned forward to look at the map more closely. It took him a moment to orientate where the map view was located, but he soon realized it was the main road between Norwich and Ipswich.

"You thinking about a bus job?" Leon asked. Syd nodded in reply.

"There's a rest area just here," he said, pointing his finger closer to the screen. "The bus from Norwich to Ipswich often pulls in there. It's got no toilet on it, so they stop for the customers to get out."

"Is it busy?"

"No, I don't think so. I was going to do a recce tomorrow if you're up for it? I've got some plates that need running

from the airport, but I can send one of the youngers."
Running plates was easy money. Syd would give Leon a list
of car makes, models, and colors, all stolen and hidden
away. Then it was just a case of wandering around the long-
term parking lot at the airport for cars that matched the
stolen ones, take a photo of the license plate, and send it to
Syd's chop shop. Bolt, the man who ran the garage, although
it didn't actually fix cars, would then make up plates for the
stolen cars. With a legitimate plate, the cars were invisible to
the police so they could be moved around the country at
will. At twenty quid a plate, it was easy money.

"Sure," Leon replied. He didn't have anything planned
other than staying in bed for as long as he could. After that,
he was free all day. "Why not?"

CHAPTER 41

Caleb reached into his cloth bag and withdrew two items that he had bought at a gas station just outside the Lark's Cross estate. Neither of the items were particularly high quality, but they would have to do. The first was a small pen flashlight which, when Caleb pressed the switch, cast more of a faint glow than a beam of light. The second was a pair of binoculars with a ten times magnification and twenty-five millimeter lenses. As with the flashlight, they were functional, but only just. But Caleb didn't mind. They would do the job he wanted them to do.

He laid Father Martin's street map on the lip of the balustrade, looking between the page he had earmarked and the roads below. Caleb rotated the map a couple of times until it was facing the same direction as the streets below. His eyes flicked between the map and roads. When he had located the street that his target lived on, he raised the binoculars to his eyes. Starting at the bottom of the street, Caleb worked his way along it until he saw the house next door to his target's. It was easy enough to locate due to the abandoned car in the front yard, covered with a light blue tarpaulin. When he had walked past the location earlier, the tarpaulin looked to be as old as the car underneath it which was sitting on tires long since deflated.

The house he was interested in was a mid-terrace. It had two windows, one on either side of the front door, and two upstairs windows he could see. There was a light on in one of the downstairs windows. From his vantage point, Caleb could see into the back-yard. Unlike the vast majority of the houses on the estate, his target's house and yard were in reasonable condition. It backed onto a small alleyway which was linked to other, even smaller passageways between the houses.

Caleb took the binoculars away from his eyes and looked at the general area of the house. If he had a platoon to assault with, he knew where he would deploy them. One squad with two fire teams to the front, and the same to the rear. They could approach via the houses on either side, and keep out of any lines of sight from the house until the last few seconds, by which time they would be knocking on the doors. Another fire team either end of the small road, with another mobile squad a few streets away for any mop up or crowd control operations needed. His command post would be up here where he could coordinate the action with an almost perfect oversight.

He took a few moments to consider other courses of action. He could put men on the roof of the terrace, moving along the tiled ridge and then fast roping in through the windows following flash-bang grenades. Caleb allowed himself a smile at the plan. It was a bit over the top for an assault on a small house. Then, just for fun, he considered how he would walk an artillery barrage in as his third course of action.

Caleb took a few moments to scan the estate below him, using his eyes initially to locate any movement. Once located, he raised the binoculars to his eyes to zone in. All he wanted to do was get an idea of the normal signs of life in the area. He saw an elderly woman walking a dog who didn't seem to want to be walked. There was a couple having sex in the alleyway behind a small group of houses. Was that Jayne, perhaps? Caleb smiled as he considered this, thinking back to the graffiti downstairs. Then he saw a couple of young men on bicycles, similar to the two he had seen earlier. They were different men, but acting in the same way, slowly peddling their bicycles around in lazy circles.

A car approached them, and they circled that too. It looked as if words were exchanged between the men and the driver. Then the car continued creeping down the road and Caleb saw one of the young men sitting stationary on his bicycle, using a phone. The car drove perhaps another hundred yards before stopping. Caleb saw another man emerge from one of the alleyways, a bag across his chest. He approached the driver's window and Caleb saw something being exchanged. The binoculars were not powerful enough to see what, but that didn't matter.

Caleb nodded in appreciation as the man with the bag faded back into the alleyway. The two men on the bicycles were the lookouts who were confirming the customer was genuine, meaning the dealer himself could remain out of sight. The alleyways would give him a myriad of routes to escape through should he need to.

"Very good," Caleb murmured to himself.

He returned his attention to his target's house and reconsidered his courses of action. Caleb had no section, no squads with fire teams. He certainly didn't have an artillery barrage, or a helicopter for a rapid extraction from the rooftop. All he had was himself and his wits.

But that was all he had needed for years.

CHAPTER 42

Vince drummed his fingers on the steering wheel of his Land Rover Discovery and stared at the long trail of red brake lights in front of him. They were complemented by a bright orange sky with wispy contrails from airplanes intersecting each other. It wasn't even six in the morning, and already the roads around London were jammed to capacity. He couldn't imagine doing this every day, as the vast majority of people in the queues probably did. They were like lemmings, all sitting in their cars listening to impossibly jovial idiots on the radio, just so they could get to their pointless jobs. Then, at the end of the day, they would do it all over again in the opposite direction. One day closer to death.

He cast his mind back to the previous evening, raising his hand to a deep scratch on the side of his neck. Samantha hadn't initially been as keen to play along with him as he'd hoped and had put up a spirited, if futile, attempt at fending him off. Vince wasn't concerned about leaving forensic traces like DNA behind, although he had scrubbed her nails with a brush and neat bleach, anyway. As she'd been unconscious, Samantha hadn't minded. Besides, there was no trace of Vince in any of the various systems the law enforcement officers used. No DNA, nor that of his family. No fingerprints. Nothing, not even a speck of him, existed anywhere. Vince had seen to that.

As he had left her apartment the previous evening, although it had been gone midnight before he was fully sated, Vince had texted the eager Alex from Samantha's phone.

I'm lonely. Come round now. Key's under the doormat.

It had only taken the young man a moment to reply to let Samantha know he was on his way, complete with something to wear. Vince had been tempted to hang about, just to see the look on his face when he saw the state of his ruined girlfriend-to-be, but that was taking things too far. Instead, he had just retrieved his camera, put the key under the mat, and waved goodbye to the woman from Pret A Manger.

Vince could have killed her. In fact, he almost had several times, but he'd stopped himself each time. Where was the fun in that? A few brief moments of suffering versus an entire lifetime of it? He drummed his fingers on the wheel again, wondering what the future held for young Alex and Samantha. Vince doubted very much indeed that it would be a shared future. As he waited for the traffic to inch forward, he considered what he might have been able to do to spice things up a bit. He could have left some of Alex's DNA dotted around some strategic location. Men of Alex's age were leaving deposits of it everywhere, so getting hold of some wouldn't be difficult. That way, when the police found it, which they would, Alex would be the prime suspect even though he'd never touched the woman. At least not in the way he'd wanted to. Maybe next time something like that would be amusing?

Knowing that he had a few days before the job in London with the shaven-headed idiot and his Irish counterpart, Vince had e-mailed his boss that morning to ask for a couple of days emergency leave claiming he was stressed and needed some downtime. Although he'd not heard from the man yet, he knew it wouldn't be an issue. MI5's human resources department was very receptive to such requests. It wasn't because they cared. It was because the department had been sued by both agents, moles, and everyone in between. The fact that was more of a factor wasn't lost on anyone, least of all Vince.

According to his laptop, the burner phone he was chasing had been activated at least twice since its original pin had appeared. Once again in Haymarket, and another time in Chapelfield Gardens, a park next to one of Norwich's two shopping malls. Both locations were favorite haunts for people on the fringes of the city's society and Vince was forming a picture in his mind of the type of person he was hunting. It was definitely a man. He'd run the voice recording of the original call through some more software, and there was no evidence it had been changed or moderated. When the pin had activated in Haymarket the previous evening, there had been a soup kitchen there where liberals and lefties tried to make themselves feel better by helping those less fortunate than themselves. They probably didn't realize that they were themselves only a couple of paychecks away from the same situation.

The sun was just beginning to appear above the horizon as the traffic started to clear and Vince could finally put his foot down and make better progress. He glanced at his watch. Norwich was a couple of hours' drive away, as long as he didn't get stuck behind a tractor when he got closer to the city. His first port of call was going to be the rented house he had shared with Suzy and Leanne. In the trunk of his car was an array of cleaning materials. Vince needed to clear the house as much as possible, including the network of cameras, before moving onto the primary reason for his visit.

Vince knew he had plenty of time to kill before he could start his search in earnest for the mysterious caller.

After all, animals only came out at night.

CHAPTER 43

Naomi squinted at the screen of her laptop. It was almost seven in the morning, and Jennifer was still sound asleep. But Naomi had woken early, needing the bathroom, and known there was no point going back to bed. Sunlight was streaming in through the kitchen window and glinting off the three empty wine bottles next to the sink.

The website Naomi was looking at was a familiar one. She had visited it several times in the past, but not as a proper user. It was called CourtNav, and was an online system for applying for a non-molestation order. Everything was online these days. Car tax. Banking. Household bills. Even domestic violence. She sighed as she looked at the screen, inviting her to set up an account. It felt very different to showing someone else how to complete the fields.

Naomi scraped the kitchen chair back and got to her feet to make some coffee. Did she really need to do this? In the cold light of day, it seemed extreme. After all, Mark had only hit her once. And it was a slap, not a punch. She waited for the water to boil and got two cups from the cupboard, putting a spoonful of instant coffee granules in each one, which was all Jennifer had.

"What if it was Jennifer?" Naomi said to herself. "What if it was the other way round?" She sighed again, knowing what the answer to her question was without even thinking about it. Her advice would be to fill out the form.

Naomi filled one cup with boiling water, leaving the other one ready for Jennifer, and returned to her place at the kitchen table. She stared at the screen, wondering what would have happened in the restaurant if Dave and Sarah hadn't been there. Or the previous day, when she'd had to call for help. Would Mark have broken into her apartment? Was he that violent? Naomi was quick to advise any of her clients in a similar situation that the potential for escalation was always there. She drummed her fingers on the table. What was so difficult about taking her own advice?

She pressed her lips together and started filling out the form on the website. Naomi knew hers wouldn't be an urgent case, so it would take a few days for Mark to be served the paperwork. She could call in a favor at the court and get them to deliver the forms to Mark. It would have to be done at his work, as she wasn't sure where he was living. That wouldn't go down well at all. Not with his bosses or his colleagues, most of whom were male. But that wasn't Naomi's problem. It was Mark's.

Naomi took a few moments to complete the witness statement, trying to keep it factual and unemotional. She'd been to enough hearings over the years to know that the judges preferred more formal writing, which many women, and indeed some men, found uncomfortable to write. When she had completed the form, Naomi clicked the *Save As Draft* button on the website and was in the process of closing the computer down when Jennifer appeared in the doorway.

"Oh, sorry, did I wake you up?" Naomi said, looking at her sister. She looked exhausted, as if she'd barely slept at all.

"No, you didn't," Jennifer replied with a yawn. "I think it was the smell of the coffee that did."

"Kettle's just boiled."

"Cheers." Jennifer walked across the kitchen, nodding at Naomi's laptop. "You're not working already, are you?"

"No, I was filling out the form for the non-mol."

"The what?"

"Non molestation order," Naomi said with a brief sigh. "But it seems a bit extreme when I think about it."

"Naomi," Jennifer replied. "You had a handprint on your face for days after he slapped you."

"But it was only a slap."

"Stop." Jennifer was staring at Naomi, her face hard and unyielding. "Would you listen to yourself? It always starts with only a slap. Do you know how many women come through my emergency room after an incident that started with only a slap?" Naomi looked at Jennifer and could feel a lump forming in her throat. She swallowed it back, determined not to cry.

"I know. I've already had that conversation." When Naomi saw Jennifer frowning, she continued. "With myself."

"So have you filled it out then? The form thing?"

"Yes."

"And you've submitted it?" Jennifer was crossing her arms and Naomi knew it was futile to lie. Her sister would see straight through it.

"I saved it as a draft. I'll do it later."

In response, Jennifer took a few steps toward the table, opened the laptop screen, and stabbed at the power button.

"You'll do it now," she said, putting both hands on Naomi's shoulders. As the computer started whirring back into life, Jennifer kneaded Naomi's neck.

"You're so bossy." Naomi leaned back into Jennifer's hands, enjoying the impromptu massage.

"That's what big sisters are for, isn't it? Now I'm not leaving here until you've submitted that form." Jennifer squeezed Naomi's trapezius muscles, making her groan. "Okay?"

"Okay," Naomi said. "Anything for a quiet life."

CHAPTER 44

Leon made his way through the school grounds, taking a shortcut to the location where he'd agreed to meet Syd. It was strange, being in the school grounds on a Saturday morning when there weren't hundreds of kids running around. He thought back to his first day here, when his mother had dressed him in a secondhand uniform she'd picked up at the thrift shop. Even now, years later, she was still skint. His mother didn't have any money that wasn't given to her by either the benefits system or Leon himself.

He glanced up at the shabby buildings that surrounded the playground. Leon had hated pretty much every minute he'd ever spent in them. The day before he turned sixteen would be the last day that he set foot in this place, anyway. He knew that. His teachers knew that. They were all just marking time until that day came.

Leon slipped through the gap in the fence, which was repaired almost weekly by the school's ground staff. He walked along a narrow path through the small woods at the back of the school, stepping over what looked like hundreds of cigarette and joint ends. Leon had many happy memories of these woods. It was here that he'd had his first sexual experience. Not actual sex, but close to it. It had been with a girl called Sandy, long since an ex-student of the school, and Leon grinned as he remembered it. It was, he reflected as he made his way toward the road where Syd would be waiting, the best thirty quid he'd ever spent, and he didn't care if half the boys in his year thought the same thing.

Syd was sitting in a car on the road, a small, dark blue Peugeot 307 that looked like an elderly lady's. Using cars like this one was part of Syd's strategy to stay under the radar. He could, he had explained to Leon one evening, drive a souped-up boy racer's car with an exhaust that rattled people's bones. But then every copper in Norwich would know who he was, and he didn't want that. Syd did have a modified Ford Focus, which was his pride and joy, but he rarely drove it. Leon couldn't see the point of having a car if you couldn't enjoy it, but he'd not mentioned that to Syd.

"Alright, Leon?" Syd said as Leon climbed into the passenger's seat. "You all set?"

"Yup," Leon replied. "Let's do it."

Syd put the car into gear and pulled away. A few moments later, Leon could smell the sewage treatment plant on the outskirts of Norwich as Syd pulled onto the outer ring road that encircled the city. The pungent aroma from the sewage pools made him reach for a packet of cigarettes.

"Bloody hell, that place stinks," Leon said, offering Syd a smoke from the packet.

"One way of making sure they don't build too many houses out this way, I s'pose," Syd replied as he took a cigarette from the packet. Leon leaned over and lit Syd's smoke before lighting up his own. The car was quickly filled with fine white smoke, but Leon was reluctant to crack open the window in case it let any of the horrible odor into the car. When they were a few miles past the treatment plant, Syd opened his own window to flick some ash out, so Leon did the same thing.

"You okay to work tonight, Leon?" Syd asked. "Had a good night last night, didn't you?"

"Sure." Leon shrugged, trying to hide his delight at being asked to run the trap house again. "Can I ask you something, Syd?" he said a moment later.

"Course, bro, you ask away."

"I'm not sure about this location."

"That's a question?" Syd said, giving Leon a sharp look.

"Kind of." Leon thought for a few seconds. "Okay, it's not really. More of an observation."

"Well, observe away, grasshopper."

Leon looked over at Syd, trying to gauge whether he was being sarcastic. When he saw a smile playing across the other man's lips, he continued.

"So, there're two things. The first is that we need to make sure the bus stops there. The only way to do that is to put someone on it, which increases the risk." Leon flicked his cigarette out of the window, watching the flurry of sparks in the wing mirror.

"I think it stops more often than not," Syd replied. "Loads of old people get on it from what I saw at the bus station. I told you that already."

Leon nodded in agreement. "So, it's what, fifty-fifty? Sixty-forty? In favor of it stopping?" Syd just shrugged his shoulders. "Which kind of brings me on to the second point. The bus is full of old people."

"Get to the point, Leon," Syd said. "I'm getting bored now."

"They're the wrong type of customer. We need people

who are going on holiday. Who've got stacks of cash. Passports. Credit cards. Decent phones." Leon punctuated each statement by tapping his hand on the dashboard. He'd thought long and hard about it the previous evening. "Not a bunch of old farts going to Ipswich to spend their pensions at the Bingo." His last statement made Syd laugh out loud.

"So, oh wise one, what would you suggest?" Syd said, still laughing. Leon got his phone out and opened his mapping app. He swiped to the pin he'd saved the previous evening and showed it to Syd.

"Where is that?" Syd said as the car veered onto the rumble strips at the side of the road. He corrected, swearing under his breath.

"It's a couple of miles to the west of your place."

"And what's so special about it?"

"Well, it's the route of the National Express coach from Lincoln to Stansted Airport," Leon replied, looking at the screen. "So the bus will be full of people loaded up for their holidays."

"Okay, I'm listening. But how do we stop the bus?" Syd glanced over at Leon briefly. "You thought that through, Leon?"

Leon let a smile play on his face.

"We'll need to get some empty suitcases for the takings," he said. "But then we can just wait by the side of the road."

"Oh, what, and the bus will just pull over?"

"Yeah," Leon said, beaming. "I'll show you when we stop, but there's a bus stop at the arse end of nowhere. It's a few hundred yards down from a lay-by on the other side of the road."

"Okay, grasshopper," Syd replied, flicking his eyes in Leon's direction. "Let's take a look. See if you're as smart as you think you are."

CHAPTER 45

Suzy stared out of the kitchen window, watching Leanne as she played a game on her own in the garden. Her daughter wasn't technically on her own, as she had Boo Boo with her, and from the way she was talking to the elephant, he was as engaged in the game as she was. Suzy had no idea what the game was about, other than it seemed to involve collecting acorns that had fallen from the large oak tree in the center of the garden.

"Is everything okay, Suzy?" a female voice said behind her. Suzy turned to see Agnesa, the young woman who helped Joan out, standing by the door jamb. She was wearing a pink tracksuit and had her jet-black hair tied up in a fierce ponytail that seemed to stretch her forehead. If Suzy tried the same style, she would have a headache in minutes.

"Yes, we're all good," Suzy said, smiling at Agnesa. In contrast to earlier conversations, all of which had been short to the point of being brusque, Agnesa made no motion to leave the room. "I've not really had the chance to thank you for your help."

"It's no problem," Agnesa replied, her clipped accent more pronounced than usual. "Would you like a cup of tea?" Suzy hesitated, not wanting Agnesa to be waiting on her, but then the young woman continued. "I'm having one."

"Yes, thank you." Suzy returned her attention to Leanne, who was now skipping around the base of the oak tree.

A few moments later, to Suzy's surprise, both women were sitting at the kitchen table. She had positioned herself so that she could still see Leanne playing outside over Agnesa's shoulder. Suzy wrapped her hands around her mug of tea, sensing that Agnesa wanted to talk about something. It took the young woman a few moments and when she spoke, her voice was clipped.

"I spoke with Joan," Agnesa said, looking at Suzy with a blank expression. "About your plans?"

"Ah, okay," Suzy replied. "She said we would go to another shelter. Further south?"

"Yes, I think so. But she told me your, er, what is the word?" Agnesa paused, frowning. "Future plans?"

"Yes," Suzy said, nodding her head and waiting for Agnesa to continue.

"My brother works for Balkan Trans. He drives lorries." Agnesa paused. "I speak to him. Spoke to him. He tells me that the lorry is never checked going across the channel. Back into Europe." She paused again. "The other way? Dogs. X-ray machines. Everything. But leaving England? Nothing."

"Right," Suzy replied, not sure where Agnesa was going with the conversation.

"He is driving to Poland later this week. He says he will take you and your daughter in his cab."

"Across the channel?" Suzy asked, barely able to believe what she was hearing.

"Yes. To France. Or Germany. Or Poland. No passport checks. He can take you where you want to go."

Suzy paused for a moment, letting the offer sink in. Agnesa was staring at her cup of tea, her expression neutral. Eventually, she looked up and met Suzy's eyes.

"That's really kind of him to offer," Suzy said, "but I have no money to pay him for the journey."

"He doesn't want money," Agnesa replied, shaking her head. "He makes the journey, anyway. You'll be safe with him. He's a big man. A good man. He'll look after you and Leanne."

At the mention of her daughter's name, Suzy glanced out of the window to make sure Leanne was still playing in the garden. When she saw Leanne and Boo Boo sitting up against the oak tree, a brief smile came to her face.

"That's incredibly generous, Agnesa," Suzy said. "Please thank him for us." She saw Agnesa frown.

"I don't understand."

"That's very kind." Agnesa nodded in understanding. Suzy paused for a moment before continuing. "What's your story, Agnesa?" She saw the other woman frown. "I'm not being nosy. I'm just curious."

Suzy thought she might have to explain the words nosy or curious when Agnesa spoke.

"I came to England on a small boat." Suzy saw a smile flash on her face, but it was brief. "To work in a hotel. But it was a lie." Suzy waited while Agnesa took a sip of her tea. "They wanted me to work as a laivre." She spat the unfamiliar word out. "A whore. So, I ran away." Agnesa's face hardened. "I am not a laivre."

Suzy had to resist the temptation to reach out and take her hand. "What a horrible story," she said. "I can't imagine how awful that must have been."

"It was no worse than your situation," Agnesa replied. "But not all men are bad. There are men like Father Martin and the vicar who brought me here." Suzy nodded in agreement as Agnesa looked out of the window.

"Do you have children?" Suzy asked. At the question, she saw a look of agony flicker across Agnesa's face.

"No," she said, her voice sharp and clipped. "I wanted to. But I can't. Not now." Agnesa got to her feet. The conversation was over. "My brother is leaving Folkestone in three days. The other shelter will take you to meet him at a motorway service station."

"Agnesa?" Suzy said as she also stood up. The young woman stopped and turned to face Suzy, her eyebrows raised as she was defying her to ask her another question. "I just wanted to say thank you. For everything you've done for me and Leanne. For everything you're doing."

There was the briefest flicker of a smile on Agnesa's face.

"It's no problem," she said. "We will keep you safe. I promise."

CHAPTER 46

Caleb walked out of the Lark's Cross estate, unmolested by young men on bicycles, as around him the residents got on with their days. Trash cans were being put out. Dogs were being walked. It all looked almost normal to him, apart from the fatalistic expressions on the faces of the locals. It was as if they had already given up on life and were just marking time until death which, Caleb guessed, many of them were.

It hadn't been the most comfortable night on top of the apartment block, but it was warm enough and hadn't rained, which made it immeasurably more comfortable than many of the reconnaissance missions he'd completed in the past. He thought he had what he needed for the evening ahead, which wasn't much.

From his vantage point on top of the block, he had seen his target get back to his house at around eleven the previous night, before resurfacing almost eight hours later. To his surprise, his target was much younger than he'd thought. Not that this changed Caleb's preferred course of action. It might change the outcome, though. Not Caleb's objective, but the outcome for his target.

According to Father Martin's map, Caleb was about two miles from the center of the city. With nothing else to do for the day, he decided to be a tourist. Using the tall spire of the cathedral as a marker, he walked slowly, taking in the environment as he did so. It changed within yards of the perimeter of the estate, as Caleb had seen all over the world. Poverty and riches could indeed live side by side, and often did. The shabby terraced houses gave way to much nicer houses. They were no larger than the ones on the estate, but they were cared for and had no kitchen appliances in the front gardens. Within a few blocks, the terraces gave way to semi-detached houses, which then gave way to much larger detached ones.

As he walked, Caleb thought about Suzy and Leanne. While he trusted Father Martin, this was based on the fact he was a man of the cloth. And Caleb knew only too well that not all men of the cloth were beyond reproach. Far from it. But in Father Martin's case, there was nothing that concerned Caleb other than the fact there was more to his and Joan's relationship than met the eye. Caleb had seen the way they interacted and their relationship was beyond platonic. Try as they might, they couldn't hide the intimacy he'd observed between them at Joan's house. It was ever so subtle, a glance here, a look there. But it was enough. That was none of Caleb's business. He was hardly a monk himself, and they would all be judged when the reckoning came.

What bothered Caleb was the fact he was some distance from Suzy and Leanne. There was a malevolence in their background, and Caleb could not sense its closeness. But it was there, there was no doubt of that. As he walked, Caleb went over the scant information that Suzy had provided about her partner. He was some sort of intelligence agent. Caleb had known several over the years. Some were so stupid it beggared belief. But some were so sharp you could cut yourself by looking at them. Caleb could only hope that Suzy's partner was the former, not the latter.

Caleb slowed his pace as he approached a series of flint covered walls. They had windowless archways and sat as a stark contrast to the modern building that surrounded them. He paused at an information board which was covered in graffiti, but Caleb could glean a few facts about them. Such as the fact they were built in the thirteenth century, almost three hundred years before Columbus had sailed the ocean blue. Caleb took a few steps forward, avoiding the litter and dog feces in the grass surrounding the structures, and pressed his hand on the closest wall, closing his eyes as he did so.

A few seconds later, Caleb pulled his hand back from the flint with a gasp. The images that had flashed across his closed eyes were many and stark. It was as if hundreds of years of memories had just fizzed in his head. Love. Laughter. Life. And despair. Poverty. Murder. He took a deep breath. This was nothing new. It was just the volume of the history that had surprised him. Caleb sighed again. Not every gift was welcome.

Closer to the center of the city was Caleb's ultimate destination. The cathedral. Every city, every town across the world, had a spiritual heart. In some, it was a simple building that represented spirituality rather than encompassing it. But this cathedral dominated the surroundings, its vast spire reaching a hundred yards into the blue sky. The closer he got to the building, the more imposing it became.

Caleb stood and looked at the cathedral, marveling at

both humankind's ability to build something so impressive in a time long before industrialization and at its need to raise a structure such as this. He turned his back on the building, a sudden wave of sadness sweeping over him.

Despite humankind's homage to its God, gestures such as grand churches ultimately made no difference. Evil still walked the earth, day after day, year after year, millennia after millennia.

And as long as evil still stalked humankind, it too would be stalked. Caleb walked away from the cathedral, deep in thought.

He had a job to do.

CHAPTER 47

Vince picked up his overpriced coffee from the barista, who had served it to him without so much as a single word, and made his way to the staircase in the corner of the coffee shop. He made his way up the stairs and chose an empty table next to the window. Under normal circumstances, he would have taken a table in the corner so that he could see the entire room and its occupants, but these weren't normal circumstances. Ignoring the uncomfortable feeling it gave him, Vince took a seat at a table next to the window.

He was in a coffeeshop on the corner of Haymarket, an area of Norwich that he guessed counted as a public space. From his vantage point, he could see the entire area which was surrounded by shops and restaurants, some modern, some not. There were a couple of market stalls dotted about as well. One had a red and white tarpaulin covering its occupants who were determined to spread the word of the Lord Jesus Christ, but few of Norwich's inhabitants seemed as enthusiastic. On the other side of the small square, overlooked by a statue of a contemplative looking man who was no doubt some sort of local dignitary, was another stall selling phone accessories. The statue's contemplation appeared to be unaffected by the traffic cone on his head and ribbons of bird feces covering his shoulders. But Vince was more interested in the group of men gathered around the statue's base than he was in the dignitary.

There were four of them. Vince estimated the youngest was in his twenties, and the oldest was perhaps in his sixties. What united them was their unkempt appearance and shared love of cheap but strong cider. Vince watched as one of them, wearing a long, heavily stained military jacket, raised a plastic bottle to his lips and drank from it. It wasn't even four in the afternoon, and they all looked two sheets to the wind already. He watched them, considering his next steps. In an ideal world, one of them would reach into his pocket, pull out a phone, and use it. Even just turning it on would be enough to trigger Vince's systems. But he knew this was far from an ideal world.

Instead, Vince tried to work out which of the four Suzy would be most likely to approach. He knew it was a stretch, assuming it was one of these men. There were more than four homeless people in Norwich. That much he had gathered from the many bundles of rags, flattened cardboard boxes, and other detritus that littered almost every empty shop doorway. Would she speak to the youngest of them on the basis that he appeared to be closest to her own age? Or would he speak to the oldest, hoping that he would take pity on her?

He sipped his coffee, which wasn't as nice as its price tag suggested it would be, and picked up his phone. Vince switched to the camera app and zoomed it as far as he could before he snapped photographs of the four men. He could put them through his software later, although he wasn't sure what use it would be to identify them. But old habits die hard.

At least the house he had been renting was now secure. Every possible trace of his, Suzy's, and Leanne's occupation had been removed. Their clothes were in garbage bags, sitting outside a variety of charity shops around the city. Suzy's and Leanne's belongings were also bagged and were now deep in the bowels of a recycling center a few miles away from the city. Vince had waited at the center to make sure those bags went into the crushing machine, as opposed to opened and scavenged from by the staff who worked there. Finally, he had scrubbed the house from top to bottom. It wasn't forensically clean, but it was clean enough. The lease had another couple of months left to run, but he could let it expire. When the realtors came round, they would find nothing but an empty house. Even if they tried to trace the original hirers, it would lead them to a shell company that had since been wound up. It was owned by another non-existent company based in Jersey, which in turn was owned by another shell corporation based in the Cayman Islands.

In the square below Vince, the four men drinking cheap cider had become five. The latest addition was a wild-haired man with a small dog. Was he the one with the phone? Vince watched, but all the new arrival did was sit down and produce a can of beer from one of his pockets. The dog, who looked every bit as bedraggled as his owner, just sat down on the steps the men were sprawled across. A small child, perhaps a year younger than Leanne, approached the dog, unnoticed by her mother. Vince saw the dog's tail thumping on the steps as the girl approached. Just as the child was about to pet the dog, her mother realized and dashed across, grabbing the child's wrist just before she could reach it. It was a tableaux Vince had seen before when Leanne had approached a dog on the beach one day.

Vince watched as the woman, her daughter now safely behind her mother's legs, spoke to the man with the dog. From this distance, they didn't look like angry words and as he watched, he saw the woman reach into her purse. She handed the man a note, gesturing to the dog as she did so. Vince didn't think for a moment that the man would actually spend the money on his dog.

But he had a very good idea which of the homeless people Suzy might have spoken to.

CHAPTER 48

Leon whistled to himself as the elevator approached, watching as the numbers counted down from the Syd's floor to the ground floor. On his shoulder was a full bag of product. Syd was trusting him with more than last time because he'd sold it so quickly. Even though Leon knew that was more luck than judgment, he was happy that Syd trusted him.

Their day out to surveil the potential sites of future bus robberies had gone well. Very well. To Leon's delight, although he hid it well, Syd's chosen location had turned out to be a bust. When they had arrived, the site had been full of lorries, so many that when the bus arrived, it could barely squeeze through them. Added to that were many families using the restrooms. Syd hadn't even waited for the bus passengers to start disembarking before leaving.

By contrast, Leon's alternate location was ideal. It was isolated, quite literally, a bus stop in the middle of nowhere. There was parking not far away on the other side of the road for a rapid extraction. And as it was a request stop, all they needed to do would be to hold a hand out to stop the bus.

They stayed there for almost fifteen minutes, during which time only a couple of cars passed by. By the time Syd dropped Leon back at his house a few hours later, they had everything planned except a date to enact the next robbery. It was a much more productive day than wandering round a parking lot looking for car license plates, even if he'd lost a bit of money to a youngster.

Leon continued whistling as the elevator descended, only stopping when he left the apartment block and walked onto the street. He glanced around him, more out of habit than anything else, but could sense nothing untoward. Picking up his step, Leon walked for a few moments until he reached his designated spot. It was a different spot from the previous evening, but right next to an alley between houses. Leon walked past the alley, glancing inside it briefly, and approached the two boys on bicycles at the end of the street.

"Alright?" he said when he reached them. They both replied in kind. Leon recognized both of the youths, but couldn't name them. He reached into his pocket and pulled out two burner phones that Syd had given him. As he handed them to the young men, he told them both that his number was the speed dial one. The younger of the two, who looked to be just into his teens but not by much, grinned as he pressed the button. A second later, Leon's own burner phone started buzzing in his pocket.

"Sweet," the young man said as he slid the phone into his pocket. "Let's rock and roll." He got onto his bike and wheeled away, followed by his colleague, who hadn't said a word. Not that Leon cared.

The first customer turned up less than ten minutes later. The way the system worked was that the lookouts would position themselves at the end of the street, next to a road that circled the entire estate. Any customers would drive,

bike, or even walk around the ring road until they encoun-
tered the lookouts who would, after vetting them, direct
them to the man with the bag. It meant they could vary their
routine every evening Syd's shop was open, which minimized the risk—according to Syd, anyway—but Leon knew
there were only so many roads leading into the estate. Leon's
first customer, a regular who he thought probably sold the
product on at a markup at the University of East Anglia,
took ten bags. Leon started whistling again, quietly, at the
excellent start of his evening.

Trade was steady, and Leon's bag was perhaps half
empty only an hour later, when things changed. The first
Leon knew about it was when a vehicle appeared at the end
of the road. It was boxy, an SUV of some sort, but it was too
far away for him to identify the make and model. He was
watching from the shadows as it pulled to a stop. That was
normal. Then both front doors opened and two men
stepped out. Leon instinctively took a few steps into the
alleyway, but he made sure he could still see the two men
from the car.

One of the bicycles moved around twenty feet away from
the car. Leon nodded in appreciation. He could see the lad
on the bike had his hand in his pocket, his finger no doubt
ready to speed dial his phone. The two men seemed to talk
to the other lookout. Then one of them lunged forward and
appeared to punch the boy on the bike. Both men then ran
to their car and, as the lookout who had been punched staggered back, his bicycle clattering to the pavement, put it into
reverse before it screeched back toward the ring road.

Leon stepped forward to get a better view of what was
going on. The boy who had been punched took a couple of
steps toward his colleague before slumping to the ground.

When the screaming started, Leon broke into a run.

CHAPTER 49

Naomi looked out of the window of her sister's flat at the setting sun beyond the river. The sky was just beginning to darken and a ray of light like a path was reflecting off the still surface of the water. She could see why Jennifer enjoyed living here so much. It was a serene view and wasn't one she would ever get bored with. Maybe Naomi should have a look for another flat somewhere similar? She thought about it for a few moments before deciding that if she moved, the thought that Mark had won would always bug her.

She'd received a text from a friend at the court earlier that day to let her know that the non-molestation paperwork had been delivered to him at his workplace. But there was no news on how it had gone down, just that it had been successfully delivered. Naomi reached for her phone. She should let Dave know about the non-mol. If Mark broke it, his would be the second phone number she called. The first would be 999.

"Hi, Naomi," Dave said a moment later. His voice

sounded strained, and there were other voices in the background. "You okay?"

"Yeah, I'm all good," Naomi replied. "Sorry, are you busy?"

"Kind of, but give me a few seconds." Suzy heard the voices fading into the background and, a few seconds later, the sound of Dave's footsteps became clearer. "How's things?"

"Like I said," Suzy replied. "All good. I was just phoning to let you know I took a non-molestation order out against Mark." She paused, but Dave said nothing. "It got served on him today."

"That's great news, Naomi," Dave said, and she could hear the smile in his voice. "Me and Sarah were talking about that earlier in the car on the way up here. We were convinced you would bottle it."

"I nearly did," Suzy replied, laughing. "Jennifer held me hostage until I submitted the form."

"Good lass. Are you still at her flat?"

"Yeah, just until the hearing." Mark would have two days from having the paperwork served on him until the court sat to decide the outcome.

"I've not seen your sister in months. She still in the Emergency Department?"

"She's still there," Naomi said. "You should pop in and see her next time you're at the hospital. She'd love to see you, I'm sure."

"You think?" There was the slightest hesitation in his voice as he replied. Naomi frowned. Had she missed something here? Dave wasn't the most subtle of men, and Naomi thought she detected something more than casual interest in his voice. She grinned to herself. Perhaps a spot of matchmaking was in order?

"I know she would. I told her about you coming to the rescue the other night like a proper hero. She was asking if it was the fit, ruggedly handsome detective out of Wymondham."

"Jennifer said that?"

"She did." Naomi could feel herself smiling. "I said, no, it wasn't that one. It was Dave."

"Very funny. Two seconds."

Naomi heard Dave's voice become muffled as he spoke to someone. It sounded like a female voice, so was probably Sarah, his partner. When his voice came back on the line, he sounded harried.

"Do you need to go?" Naomi asked him.

"No, I'm good. That was Sarah. She told me to wait here for forensics."

"You're at a scene?"

"Yeah," Dave replied, but offered no more information, and Naomi knew better than to ask any specifics. "What were we talking about again?"

Naomi smiled as she heard him trying to sound nonchalant. He might be a great copper, but he was a shit liar.

"We were talking about my sister."

"We were?"

"We were, Dave." She waited, but Dave didn't say anything for several seconds.

"Did you really tell Jennifer about the other night?"

"I said I did, yes."

"And what did she actually say?"

Naomi paused. Jennifer's response had been just what she had told Dave it was, but she had passed it off as a joke. Now Naomi wasn't sure, but she didn't want to make things awkward for either Dave or Jennifer if she was misreading things.

"I'm not sure," she replied, hoping that Dave wouldn't press her. "I can't really remember, to be honest." There was a pause on the other end of the line that was threatening to become uncomfortable. "Where's your scene, then?"

"City center," Dave replied, sounding relieved at the change in subject. "The underpass on Saint Stevens. It's a nasty one, though. A homeless guy."

"Any trade for me?" she asked. As in, had they caught anyone? In the background, Naomi heard a dog barking.

"No, we're a long way off that. Burglary gone wrong is what we're thinking." Naomi heard the sound of tires down the line. "I need to go, Naomi."

"Is that forensics turned up?"

"Um, no," Dave replied. "It's the Medical Examiner."

Naomi said goodbye to Dave and ended the call, staring at her cell phone. There was only one reason a Medical Examiner would attend the scene of a burglary and that was if it wasn't the scene of a burglary, but something else.

Like a homicide.

CHAPTER 50

After a few hours in the center of Norwich, Caleb had spent most of the afternoon back in his unofficial command post on top of the apartment building, watching his target's house through his binoculars. After he had left the city, he had stopped at a pub for some lunch near to the estate, asking the bartender for something traditionally British. The woman behind the bar had shrugged a heavy set of shoulders at him and just pointed at a section of the menu labeled Mains. Ten minutes after ordering, she had brought him a plate of sausages and mashed potatoes, complete with a jug of gravy so thick it could hold the spoon erect. It bore a passing resemblance to the food he had ordered, but to Caleb's surprise, it had tasted a lot better than it had looked.

On his way back to the Lark's Cross estate, he had stopped at a supermarket for some supplies, and even found some familiar items from home in the International section. Caleb had been prepared to stay at his perch all night if necessary, but just before four o'clock, his target had emerged from his house. Tracking him was easy enough at first, but as his target approached the neighboring apartment building, Caleb had struggled to keep him in sight as he disappeared through the main door.

For the next few moments, working methodically, Caleb had screened every window in the building, working from left to right and up and down, but there was no sign of him. He returned his attention to the front door and around twenty minutes later, just as Caleb was enjoying the last peanut butter cup in the packet, his target emerged, wearing a bag over his shoulder. Caleb tracked him as the young man walked through the estate before taking up position on a road. Caleb checked his map to ensure that he knew which road his target was on and made his way to the bottom floor of the apartment.

As he approached his target's location, Caleb stopped once or twice to recall the layout of the alleyways that bisected the houses. His intent was to approach his target through one of these alleys, pulling him back into it for privacy if necessary. Caleb made his way through the sprawling estate, using the alleys for cover, until he was within thirty feet of the young man. Caleb crouched down in the shadows and watched as several cars pulled up in quick succession. None of them stayed for long, just long enough to complete their transaction.

Caleb froze as his target took a few steps toward him in the alley. Certain that he couldn't be seen in the darkness, Caleb remained motionless, holding his breath. If his target came to him, so much the better.

Then there was a scream from further down the street. Caleb saw his target return to his original position and, a few seconds later, break into a run, heading toward the source of the noise. Caleb inched forward to the end of the alley, lifting his head to peer down the road. His target was running toward a figure on the ground. The scream intensified and became almost animalistic. Caleb had heard it before on more than one occasion. It was the sound of someone in trouble—a lot of trouble.

Breaking cover, Caleb started running down the road, following his target. As he approached the figure on the ground, Caleb saw a bicycle on its side, its wheel still spinning. A large black vehicle was at the end of the road, its tires screeching as it took the corner before disappearing from sight. The figure was clutching his lower thigh and even in the darkness, Caleb could see blood. He slowed his steps until he was standing next to his target.

"What happened?" Caleb asked. His target looked at him, fear etched on his face, but there was no recognition on it.

"He's been stabbed." The reply came from another young man, who was still astride his own bicycle. "They stabbed him in the leg."

Caleb crouched down next to the figure on the floor. When he looked at his face, Caleb realized that this wasn't a man. He wasn't even really a youth. At Caleb's arrival, his screams had faded away into sobs.

"Let me see," Caleb said, putting his hands over the young man's. "I can help." He gently removed his hands to be rewarded with a spray of blood that covered the front of his hoodie. Caleb didn't need to see the color of the blood. He knew it would be bright red. Arterial.

"Kneel next to me," Caleb barked at his target. "Make a fist and press here. Hard." He pointed at the injured youth's groin, but his target just stared at him with the same look of fear as before. "Leon!" Caleb barked. At the sound of his voice, Caleb saw Leon flash his eyes at him. "Come on, now!

He's bleeding out." Leon paused for a second, perhaps two, before springing into life and kneeling next to Caleb.

"How do you know my name?" Leon asked as he pressed his fist where Caleb had pointed.

"Later, but my name's Caleb, so now we're even," he replied. "Press harder."

The second youth dismounted his bicycle and kneeled next to Leon.

"What can I do?" he said, his voice high-pitched.

"Call 911," Caleb replied before checking himself. "Call for an ambulance. But give me your belt first."

"What?" the youngster asked, his eyebrows raised.

"Your belt. Give it to me." Caleb watched as he unthreaded his fabric belt uncertainly. He turned his attention to the injured youth on the ground. "You're going to be okay. You hear me?" The young man nodded, his face already ashen.

When Caleb had the belt, he wrapped it around the upper part of the young man's thigh. But he needed something to tighten it with. Caleb looked around, not seeing anything in the immediate vicinity. Then he noticed a small black pouch under the saddle of one of the bikes.

"What's in there?" Caleb asked. "Give it me. Quickly!" He watched as the young man whose belt he was holding ran to the bike, his phone pressed against his ear.

"Yes, the patient's breathing," Caleb heard him say. He undid the pouch and threw it to Caleb, who unzipped it with his spare hand and emptied the contents onto the ground. Several items fell out, including what Caleb had been hoping would be in there. Among the various rubber patches were three metal tire levers. He grabbed one, slid it into the belt, and started twisting.

"I'm sorry," Caleb said as the injured youth started screaming again. "This is going to hurt."

Caleb twisted the tire lever another full revolution and tucked it under the fabric of the belt. Then he put his hand on top of Leon's.

"Release the pressure, slowly." Leon did as instructed, and Caleb leaned forward to examine the wound. There was no arterial spray, which told him the makeshift tourniquet was doing its job. "I need your belt as well."

"Why?" Leon asked, but he was already undoing his belt.

"If the artery's completely transected, it could shrivel up and back into the body. If it gets past the tourniquet, the bleeding will start again."

By the time Caleb had placed the second tourniquet a few inches above the first, he could hear sirens in the distance. It could have been the sound reflecting off buildings, but he thought he could hear more than one.

"I need to go," Leon said, getting to his feet. Caleb's arm flashed out and grabbed his wrist.

"I'm coming with you," he said, making sure from his tone that Leon understood it wasn't a request.

"Who are you, man? And how do you know my name?" Leon asked. Caleb's grip tightened as he tried to free his wrist.

"I just saved your friend's life," Caleb said, fixing Leon with a stare. "I'm coming with you whether you want me to or not. Or we can both wait here for the police?" He leaned his head on one side and switched his stare to Leon's bag. "I'm guessing you don't want that."

It only took Leon a second to respond. He nodded his head at Caleb before replying.

"Let's go."

CHAPTER 51

Vince stared at his computer screen, flexing his right fist as he did so. The paper sutures on his forearm pulled, and he winced at the sensation. He should have killed the bloody dog, but he liked dogs—right until the moment they bit him. At some point, he would need to get the wound in his arm looked at properly, but he was quite satisfied with his running repairs.

On the laptop in front of him was the home screen of the Police National Database, a vast repository of information. It contained details of every crime, every criminal, and a lot of other information the public wasn't aware of was stored on it. Vince had read somewhere it had over two billion records, with an additional twenty thousand being added every month. But Vince was only interested in one record on the system.

The man with the dog had proven resistant to offering any information at all on Suzy and Leanne. Vince had followed him to an underpass that connected several busy streets in Norwich under a large rotary that the local council dug up and renovated every few years. It was a favorite haunt for drug dealers, alcoholics, and homeless people. Anyone using it after dark did so at their own risk.

The moment Vince had shown the man a picture of Suzy, he had seen the smallest flicker of recognition in his eyes. The gesture made all the man's subsequent denials useless. Vince tried money, then he tried alcohol. When the man with the dog had declined both opportunities, Vince tried violence. That worked, as it usually did, but it also provoked the mutt of a dog to attempt to protect his owner.

But none of that mattered to Vince now. He banished any thoughts of the man's broken body lying in the underpass with his stupid dog pawing at him and turned his attention to the screen. The homeless man had told Vince, eventually, that a woman who looked just like Suzy had given him money and a phone. She had asked him to do two things. The first was to buy two bus tickets, for cash, between Norwich and London. One adult, one child. The second was to make a call and read from a script. The time of the call had been important to her. It had to be first thing in the morning. No, the man told him, he didn't have a copy of the script. But the woman had been insistent that he read it verbatim.

"She had loads of money," the man had told him through broken teeth only moments before Vince snapped his neck like a twig. "I saw it in her bag."

Vince had started with the bus company's website to find out what time the bitch and her child had got to London. But there was an anomaly on the website, and it looked as if the bus hadn't completed the full journey. Then he checked the website for the Eastern Daily News to see what had happened to it. Perhaps it had crashed or broken down en route. A moment later, he was reading a report about an armed robbery. Vince had chuckled at the thought of Suzy sitting on the bus, thinking she was safe, only to be robbed at gunpoint and losing any money that she had squirreled away. The fact she'd managed to put some money aside irritated Vince. He'd thought he'd put a stop to all that sort of nonsense.

Looking at the screen in front of him, Vince navigated to the list of witnesses on the bus. Whoever had compiled it had helpfully put the witnesses ages in parentheses, but Vince couldn't see any passengers that even came close to Suzy and Leanne's ages. So had they actually been on that bus?

Vince switched systems and logged in to the bus company's back-end servers. It took him a few moments, but he found the digital archive of the CCTV cameras on the buses themselves. A few moments later, he was looking at the footage of the robbery. Vince nodded in appreciation at the way the two men subdued the passengers and methodically moved down the bus. About half-way down, he saw Suzy with Leanne sitting next to her. Although both of them were wearing hats, there was no need for him to run them through his facial recognition software. The man wielding the gun made his way down the bus collecting items from the passengers before he stopped at Suzy. Vince watched as they tussled over the bag she was holding before Suzy had to relinquish it. Just as the gunman said something to his colleague at the front of the bus, Vince saw the passenger behind Suzy shifting in his seat, even though he appeared to be asleep.

He rewound the footage on the screen and advanced it frame by frame. The other passenger, who was wearing a gray robe, appeared to brush against the gunman. Vince froze the screen and zoomed in on the passenger's hand.

"You sneaky bastard," Vince muttered as he saw the

object in the passenger's hand. Then he laughed at the thought of an armed robber having his wallet lifted by a man who'd not even appeared to open his eyes.

He shifted the camera to zoom in on the passenger's face.

"Who are you, my friend?" he said to himself

CHAPTER 52

Her stomach full, Suzy sat in the lounge of Joan's house, feeling more contented than she had been for months. Years, even. Outside in the garden, Suzy could hear Leanne's excited shouts as Agnesa walked around the garden with her. Dusk was falling, and Agnesa had asked Leanne while they were having dinner if she had ever seen a bat. All three women had smiled at Leanne's response. Apart from in a zoo which, according to Leanne, didn't count, no, she hadn't. Then Agnesa had offered to walk with her in the garden after dinner to show her where they flew around Joan's garden.

"She sounds happy," Joan said as she walked into the room. In her hands were two small glasses, both full of an amber liquid that looked almost like whiskey. She offered one of them to Suzy. "Sherry?"

Suzy took the glass, thanking Joan as she did so. Sherry wasn't something she'd ever tasted before, but, to her surprise, it was very sweet.

"It's been a while since I've heard her laughing like that,"

Suzy said, putting the sherry glass down on a small table next to her armchair.

"Does she know?" Joan asked, taking the armchair opposite. "About what's going on?"

"Not specifically, no," Suzy replied. "I've just told her it's a big adventure. But they pick up on things, don't they?"

"Don't they just," Joan said with a wry smile. Suzy thought about asking Joan if she had children, but when she remembered Agnesa's response to the same question, thought better of it. "How are you planning on telling her, if you don't mind me asking?"

Suzy sighed. She didn't mind, but at the same time, she wasn't sure what to say.

"I figured I'd get us both somewhere safe first," she said after a few moments. "Agnesa said her brother can help us get over the channel. Maybe once we're there and settled somewhere. That's when I'll tell her, but I don't think she'll be surprised." Suzy paused for a moment. "She'd been getting more and more uncomfortable around Vince over the last few months. Not wanting to be on her own with him, that sort of thing."

"I see," Joan replied, her face darkening. "Do you think he's ever, um…" Her voice tailed away.

"No, I don't think so. But it was only a matter of time."

"Where are you thinking of settling? You said France perhaps?"

"Yes, I think so."

"Do you speak French?"

"Well, I can ask where the post office is," Suzy replied, grateful for the change in subject. She could feel her first involuntary smile in a long time. "And if there's a cat on a wall, I can alert people to that fact."

"Très bien," Joan said, mirroring Suzy's smile. "Very good."

The two women sat in silence for a while, Joan fiddling with the gold crucifix that hung around her neck. A few moments later, Leanne burst into the room, followed by Agnesa, who was beaming.

"Mummy, Mummy," Leanne said, crawling onto Suzy's lap. "There were hundreds of them. One of them nearly flew into Agnesa's hair."

"Oh, no!" Suzy replied. "That wouldn't have been good. Whatever would you have done?"

"I would have helped set him free," Leanne whispered. "Very, very gently. Did you know bats' wings are like paper?"

"Well, I do now." Suzy ruffled Leanne's hair. "Right, munchkin. Time for bed."

Agnesa took a few steps forward as Leanne complained that she wasn't sleepy.

"How about I make you a cup of hot chocolate to take to your room?" she asked Leanne. "Then perhaps your mummy will read you a story when you've finished it and cleaned your teeth?" Agnesa glanced at Suzy, who nodded in agreement.

"Thank you, Agnesa," Suzy said. A moment later, it was just her and Joan in the lounge, and Suzy realized that the older woman wanted to talk more.

"Suzy, there's an organization we work with called Disciples de Jésus. We have a networking arrangement with them to place women like you." Joan leaned forward and pressed a piece of paper into her hand. Suzy glanced down at it to see an address written in spidery handwriting. "This is one of their properties in a town called Faulquemont, near the border with Switzerland. Agnesa's brother will drop you off close by, but he doesn't know the actual address. Nor should he."

Suzy could feel a lump forming in her throat as Joan continued.

"They will look after you while you get settled. But if you're willing to work with them, they can put you up for as long as you need to." Joan wrapped Suzy's hand around the piece of paper. "They're expecting you, but they know nothing about you. Not even your name."

Suzy attempted to say thank you, but all that came out was a sob. She let the tears stream down her face as she cried, all the tension of the last few days pouring out. Joan just sat in her armchair, saying nothing, but not letting go of Suzy's hand.

"How can I thank you, Joan?" Suzy said a moment later, using a tissue that Joan had conjured up from somewhere to dab her eyes.

"If you can help one other person, Suzy," Joan said, a kind smile on her face, "then that will be reward enough for me."

CHAPTER 53

With Caleb only a yard behind him, Leon made his way through the alleys between the houses, taking a circuitous route to the apartment block. Just before they had left the injured lad, his colleague had thrust an ancient cell phone into Leon's hand.

"They gave me this," he had said. "They said it's for the boss." As a set of blue flashing lights appeared at the end of the road, the young man started pedaling as fast as he could in the opposite direction. Leon had shoved the phone in his pocket and led Caleb into the alleyway, both men moving as quickly as they could.

Behind him, Leon heard several vehicles approaching and quickened his pace, as did his new companion.

"Need to move quickly," Leon gasped over his shoulder. "Get to safety." Caleb hadn't replied.

Five, perhaps six minutes later, both Leon and Caleb were at the door to the apartment block that Syd lived in. Leon punched in a code to release the door, and followed by Caleb, made his way to the elevator. When the door opened, he stepped into the lift and looked up at the camera in the corner. A few seconds after that, his burner phone started ringing.

"Who the hell is that with you?" Syd's voice barked down the line when he answered it. "And why are the bizzies crawling all over the estate?"

"One of the lookouts got plugged," Leon replied, looking at Caleb. "This guy saved his life. He's kosher, Syd. Let us up, would you?"

There was a pause before the elevator doors whined their way closed. Leon breathed a sigh of relief as the lift started ascending.

"You gonna tell me how you know my name, bro?" Leon said a moment later.

"Yes," Caleb replied. Leon looked at him, expecting him to say something else, but he didn't.

"Where d'you learn to do that shit back there?" Leon asked, trying a different tack. Caleb didn't reply, but just stared at Leon with cold eyes. Although he wasn't scared of the man, Leon was well aware that there was perhaps more to him than he'd first thought. "Where's that accent from? Are you American?" Again, there was no response.

The two men walked down the corridor from the elevator to Syd's flat. As they did so, Leon noticed Caleb touching the doors to the other apartments on the floor with the palm of his hand.

A few moments later, they were at Syd's door. Leon knocked, rapping on the door with his knuckles even though Syd would be expecting them. He saw the peep-hole darken as Syd looked through it, which drew a brief smile from Caleb that Leon didn't understand. Finally, the door opened, but Syd had left the security chain on it. He ignored Leon, directing his question straight at Caleb.

"Who the hell are you?" said.

"My name is Caleb. I need to speak with you."

"S'pose I don't want to talk to you?"

"That would be a poor choice." The tone of Caleb's voice chilled Leon.

"Syd, come on," Leon said. "This bro saved our boy's life."

"I only want to talk to you, Mr. Syd," Caleb said. "Just words, and they can't hurt a man, can they?" Leon waited as Syd considered Caleb's statement for a few seconds before closing the door. When it reopened, the chain was hanging loosely by the jamb.

"Never been called Mr. Syd before," Syd said as he stepped back to allow them both into the room.

Leon hung back as Caleb entered Syd's apartment. The American lingered, looking around him as if he were scanning the place, as Syd led them both into the lounge.

"Have a seat, bro," Syd said, pointing at the sofa. Leon sat down gratefully, the adrenaline from the previous moments dissipating as Caleb sat next to him. "So, speak." Syd was looking at Caleb expectantly.

"You have something that belongs to a friend of mine," Caleb replied. "I've come to get it back."

"And what might that be?" Syd replied. Leon could see him sneering, but at the same time, he could see the uncertainty in his eyes.

"A bag. From the bus." Leon saw Caleb lean back on the sofa, seemingly relaxing. "It had some money in it which she needs. So, I'd like it back. Please."

"What bus?" Syd asked. "I don't know what you're talking about, bro."

Caleb leaned forward and Leon noticed his eyes had darkened.

"I'm not your bro, Mr. Syd," he said. "Not now, not ever.

Now, quit the bullshit. I've asked nicely for the bag with the ten grand in it. And I'd like you to give it back."

"Weren't ten grand in there," Leon said with a laugh before realizing what he'd said. His eyes went to his feet, and he swore at himself under his breath.

"I rounded it up," Caleb replied. When Leon looked up, both Syd and Caleb were staring at him. "Shall we stop this dance?" Caleb asked, his eyebrows raising by a half an inch. "The bag?"

"Or what?" Syd shot back. "I don't give a monkey's what you done out there with my boy." He inclined his head toward the window before returning his attention to Caleb. "I don't owe you nothing."

"If anything is borrowed, it should be paid back. If what is borrowed is lost or injured, full restitution must be made," Caleb said. "It's from the Bible. Exodus, if you're interested. Your choice. Pay it back or suffer restitution."

Leon, who wasn't even sure what restitution was, remained silent, wondering how this would play out. He knew Syd didn't scare easily, but Leon's assessment of Caleb was that there was an inherent danger behind his cold eyes.

"Who are you, Mr. Caleb?" Syd said, leaning back in his own chair and regarding Caleb through half-closed eyes. Leon had seen him do this before and recognized the mannerism as a way of playing for time.

"I can be your best friend, Mr. Syd," Caleb replied. "Or I can be your worst nightmare. You strike me as a sensible man, so how about you decide which it's gonna be?"

CHAPTER 54

Caleb remained silent and watched as Syd leaned back again on his sofa and steepled his hands in front of him as if he was deep in thought. Caleb didn't care for the theatrics, but he was content to give this strange man time to consider his options. Although the last time he had seen him, Syd had been wearing a balaclava, Caleb thought he would come to the right decision. Eventually. And if he didn't? Well, Caleb had a plan for that as well.

"Or what, Caleb?" Syd said a moment later. Caleb, noting that he had dropped the Mr., mirrored Syd's theatrics with an exaggerated sigh.

"How about I put in an anonymous tip to the police?" Caleb said, watching Syd carefully. "To let them know about the cannabis farms at the top of a tower block in the Lark's Cross estate." Caleb had to force himself not to smile as he saw Syd's jaw tighten, almost imperceptibly. Leon, sitting to Syd's right, just looked confused. He obviously wasn't that far into Syd's inner circle. "I mean, it's a good setup," Caleb continued. "The other flats on this floor? No signs of life from the outside. No lights in the windows, no movement at all. I don't know how your social security system works, but I'm guessing you've acquired the flats somehow." A minor tic in one of Syd's eyes told Caleb he was on the right track. "But the doors are warm, so something's going on inside them. How am I doing so far?"

Syd didn't reply. He glanced across at Leon, who just continued to look nonplussed, before turning back to Caleb.

"Go on," Syd said after a few seconds. "I love a good story."

"With no residents in them, the power and water consumption probably looks normal to anyone watching. And it's not as anyone will look for a farm in an apartment block, is it? You're probably using the internal rooms for the main grow rooms, so there'll be no heat signature visible from the outside. No nosy neighbors walking by, wondering what's going on. Hydroponic system, I'm guessing. Automated mostly. How many apartments are you using?"

Caleb saw a slow grin spreading over Syd's face. "You know, that's not a bad idea. What do you think, Leon?" Syd looked at Leon, who just nodded in deference.

"Er, yeah," Leon replied. "Why not?"

Caleb put his hands on his knees and leaned forward. "Of course, if I'm wrong, then the police won't find anything. Will they?" He made to get to his feet. "So, no harm done. I'll leave you in peace while I make a quick call."

"Wait," Syd said, holding out a hand to Caleb. "Hold on a moment." He hissed something to Leon. Caleb didn't catch the words, but caught the intent. Not a word of this was to be repeated. "How do you know?"

It was Caleb's turn to smile.

"Terpenes," he said. "Unsaturated hydrocarbons produced predominantly by plants. The ones cannabis plants produce are particularly distinctive." Caleb sat back and steepled his own fingers. "I'm guessing you're using charcoal filters before venting the farms onto the roof of the apartment block. Right idea, as this high up, the smell will dissipate into the wind before anyone notices it. But I'm not just anyone."

"Seriously?" Leon said, shooting a look at Syd. "Is he right? You're growing your own product?"

"Shut up, Leon," Syd shot back, not taking his eyes off Caleb.

"My friend's bag?" Caleb asked. "If you would be so kind?"

"The bizzies won't give a damn, Mr. Caleb," Syd replied. "You call them all you want. I have contingency plans for them visiting. It would take them an hour to get inside the block if I shut it down. By the time they get this high up, there'll be nothing left for them to find."

"Bizzies?" Caleb asked.

"The plod. Old bill," replied. Caleb frowned in response. "The police, Mr. Caleb. What do you call them where you come from? Five-O?"

"Not since I was a boy," Caleb said with a smile. "We just call them the police. But I doubt they would find nothing, unless you have an industrial incinerator in one of the apartments?" He hardened his eyes and looked at Syd. "No, I didn't think you would have. If I was a, er, bizzie, I would just land a helicopter on the roof and send a tactical team down the fire escape. But I'm guessing you've thought of that eventuality, right?" The look on Syd's face said it all.

Caleb was just about to ask again for Suzy's bag, and the money it contained, plus what he considered a tip for the inconvenience, when a buzzing sound distracted him. He waited as Leon reached into a pocket and pulled out an ancient cell phone.

"It must be them," he said as he stared at the screen.

"Who?" Syd replied.

"The guys who sliced up the lookout. What do I do?"

"Give me that." Syd grabbed the phone off Leon and Caleb watched as he stabbed at a key on it. "What?" he said, pressing the phone to his ear.

Caleb waited, intrigued by the unexpected turn of events. While all he was here for was Suzy's money, this was a curious development.

"When?" Syd said a moment later. Then a few seconds after that. "Where?"

When Syd disconnected the call, Caleb could see the fear in his eyes, although he was trying hard to hide it.

"Who was that?" he asked Syd.

"They say they're an Albanian family interested in doing business with us," Syd replied, his voice shaking.

"What did they want?" Leon said, flashing his eyes between Syd and Caleb.

"They want to meet," Syd said, staring at the cell phone in his hand. "To discuss terms and conditions. Tomorrow night in the center of the estate."

"Sounds like you've got a whole bunch of problems, Mr. Syd," Caleb said as he stood up, brushing his hands down Father Martin's jeans. "Your empire could be about to come crashing down. No product, and no territory."

"Shit," Syd whispered. "What am I going to do?"

"You can start by giving me my friend's bag."

CHAPTER 55

The sun was just beginning to set as Vince drove past a weathered village sign welcoming him to Ranworth. It wasn't the most elaborate sign he'd seen and had only the village name and a simple silhouette of a boat and a church above it. Vince couldn't understand why people lived out in the sticks like this. He drove through the village, looking from side to side as he did so. There was a small shop complete with a post office, a pub overlooking a wharf that was full of hire boats, and as he came to the other end of the village, a church.

After he had reviewed the footage of the bus robbery, Vince had sat in silence in his car for some time, thinking. His concentration had been interrupted by a call to one of his burner phones from Hùng, a man who worked for Vince. Hùng wanted to know when Vince was dropping the girl off with him and his wife.

"There's a delay," Vince had replied, much to Hùng's irritation. But Vince couldn't care less if the man was irritated. He paid the man, and his wife, a lot of money for their services. They all knew it wasn't just the couple's services that were being bought, it was their utter discretion. Vince owned a caravan on the Norfolk coast, which was a perfect location to hide all sorts of things. Such as children waiting for someone to come and get them.

After reassuring Hùng that he would be paid in full and compensated for the delay, Vince hung up. His thoughts turned to Leanne, and the amount of money she had already cost him. It wasn't the cost of the property in Norwich, or his time, that concerned him. That was all part of the fun as far as Vince was concerned. But the tissue typing he'd had carried out on Leanne had cost a fortune. The first stage, the human leukocyte antigens testing, cost over a thousand pounds, but as with Hùng, there was a premium for discretion. But Vince wasn't going to go to all that time and effort with Suzy if her daughter didn't meet his needs. Fortunately for Vince, less so for Leanne, the girl had turned out to be a perfect match for a child in Russia of a similar age. A child with a congenital heart condition that wouldn't respond to surgery. A child with extremely rich parents.

Following the call, Vince had used Google Maps to find the closest civilization to the spot where the bus robbery had taken place. It would be the most logical place for her to go. He had studied the map for some moments to work out where she would head for. An internet search revealed that by the time she would have got there, the last bus through the village would have departed. So she would have spent the night in the village, surely? But where?

Vince turned the car around and headed back to the pub where he parked in the lot after checking for CCTV cameras. He glanced over at the boats, some of which were lit up as their inhabitants did whatever people on boats did in the evening. Perhaps, when the Russians had paid him, he could buy a boat? With the amount they were putting up for the delivery of Leanne, Vince could probably buy several. He made his way into the pub, pushing against the heavy door.

"What can I get you?" the bartender, a large woman in her fifties with far too much makeup on for Vince's liking, asked as he approached the bar. Vince looked around for cameras and saw a young family eating at one of the tables. The mother was particularly striking, in Vince's opinion at least.

"I'm looking for a friend of mine," Vince said, turning his attention to the bartender. "I think she stayed here on Thursday night with her daughter?"

"Not here, love," the woman replied. She glanced at the beer pumps in front of her before looking back at Vince.

"Are you sure?" Vince said. "They would have got here quite late? Had some issues with their transport."

"Nope." The bartender crossed her arms over her ample chest and looked down her nose at Vince. "Our accommodation's fully booked. Always is, this time of year. Middle of the boating season, see."

"Okay, thanks." Vince looked back at the family where the mother was trying to persuade her toddler to at least try a spoonful of food. "Could I get a pint of lager and a menu, please?"

The bartender unfolded her arms and grinned at Vince, revealing some seriously stained teeth.

"You grab a table, love, and I'll bring your drink over." She reached out and picked up a laminated menu, handing it to him with a theatrical wink. "The lamb's pretty good tonight."

A few moments later, sipping his lager, Vince watched the mother trying again to feed her child. Her husband was engrossed in his phone, much to her annoyance. She half rose to her feet to lean across the table, swiping at her husband's hand and giving Vince a perfect look at her backside.

"Dirty bitch," Vince muttered under his breath. "You dirty bitch."

"I'm sorry, what was that?" a female voice said. It was the bartender with a plate of food in her hand. Vince looked up at her, surprised both at the interruption and the speed of the food.

"Sorry, I was just thinking out loud," Vince replied. The woman put the plate down and gave him a strange look. She walked away without another word. Vince cursed himself under his breath. If she had heard what he'd just said, she would remember him, and he didn't want to be remembered.

Vince ate slowly, his gaze fixed on the mother as he did so. The bartender had been right about the lamb, but the mashed potato it came with wasn't anything memorable. He forced himself to concentrate, reluctantly taking his eyes off the mother. Where would Suzy and the man who got off after her go, assuming he was with her?

He finished his food and brought his phone out, swiping at the screen to bring up a screen grab of the man in the gray robe. He zoomed in on his face, trying to get a measure of the man. Across the pub, the young family was getting ready to leave. The mother looked to be angry with her husband, and Vince grinned as he imagined her being taught a lesson when the child was in bed. He knew how he would teach her a lesson, and it wouldn't be pretty.

The bartender returned to collect his plate, and Vince took the opportunity to ask her where else his friend and her daughter might have stayed.

"There's nowhere, really," the woman replied. "We're the only place that has rooms in the village. There's a shop and a pub, and bugger all else here." As she waddled away, Vince finished his pint and looked again at his phone. Where would a man of the cloth go to seek shelter? When it came, the answer was obvious.

"Oh forgive me, Father," Vince muttered as he got to his feet, "for I have sinned and it's been a long time since my last confession."

Vince was going to church.

CHAPTER 56

"You really going to help us out?" Leon said, glancing at Caleb as they rode the elevator down to the bottom of the apartment building. Slung across Caleb's chest was a cloth bag and in his hand was the bag full of money Leon had taken from the woman with the child during the bus robbery.

"Do you read the scriptures, Leon?" Caleb asked. He paused, but Leon wasn't sure what to say. "In the gospel of Luke there's a verse about negotiation. If your enemy is stronger than you, it suggests sending a delegation and asking for terms of peace. Chapter fourteen if you wanted to look it up?"

"What's the Bible got to do with it?" Leon replied.

"Everything, Leon" Caleb said. "I am quite experienced in negotiation. My terms of peace would be, I think, fairly attractive to whoever is looking to bring your friend Mr. Syd down."

"For a price," Leon muttered under his breath.

"Everything has a price, Leon. Especially freedom. But my fee will go some way toward securing my friends." Caleb patted the woman's bag and Leon eyed the cash inside it. "As will this."

Leon had listened, fascinated, as Syd and Caleb had agreed on their terms. Syd would return the money, along with a contribution for the inconvenience, in return for Caleb's help with the men who had stabbed the lookout. The two men continued in silence for a few moments. Then Caleb reached into his pocket and pulled something out. "I almost forgot, this is yours."

Leon looked down to see a battered brown wallet in Caleb's hand. His wallet.

"How d'you get that?" he asked, grabbing it from the man.

"You dropped it." Leon saw a half smile on Caleb's face. "On the bus."

"You stole it from me?" He saw Caleb look down at the cloth bag.

"There's a bit in the Bible about stealing as well, Leon," Caleb said. "It's somewhat frowned on. Worth a read at some point. Do you have a car?"

"Nah," Leon replied with a laugh. "Not one of my own. Why? You need one?"

"Yes."

"I can help you get one."

"What did I just say about stealing?" Leon saw he still had a half smile on his face.

"Does it say anything in your Bible about borrowing?"

"Probably."

"I've got a mate who's got a car. He lives just near me. I'm sure he'll lend it to you." Leon glanced at the bag across Caleb's chest. "For a price."

When the two men left the apartment building, Leon led Caleb back through a different set of alleyways, explaining that there might still be police hanging about following the stabbing earlier. It was pitch black, and they made slow progress through the alleys but eventually reached Leon's street.

"Wait here," Leon said to Caleb as they reached a lamp post near his house. He watched as Caleb slowly turned round in a circle, examining his surroundings. Then he nodded once. Leon shook his head as he made his way to his front door. When he reached it, he continued walking to a house a couple of doors down and knocked on it. While he waited for his friend to answer, Leon looked at Caleb. The man was still standing under the lamp post and was staring at Leon through the gloom.

"Leon, my man," a voice said as the door opened.

"Alright, Matty," Leon said, looking at his friend. From the way he was swaying slightly, it looked as if Matty had started the party early. The two of them had gone to school together, back when Leon used to attend regularly, but Matty was a couple of years ahead of Leon. "What's up?"

"All cool, bro," Matty replied. "You coming in? I got some wicked buds."

"I'm good, Matty. Hey, listen, I've got a mate who needs to borrow your car." Leon nodded in Caleb's direction and Matty leaned forward to look down the street.

"The fuck is he?" Matty asked.

"He's a mate of mine. Can he borrow it? He'll pay."

"What if he nicks it?"

"He'd be doing you a favor. He just needs to run to Thorpe and back, so it won't even move the needle. An hour, tops."

"How much?"

"Twenty," Leon replied. The price he and Caleb had agreed on was fifty, so Leon had some wriggle room to still come out on top. He watched as Matty considered the deal, but it didn't take him long. A few moments later, Leon was walking back to Caleb with the keys to Matty's crappy little Fiesta in his hand and an extra thirty quid in his pocket. He handed Caleb the keys and watched as he blipped the button. On the other side of the road, Matty's car lit up with two of the four indicators flashing.

"You'll bring it back, yeah?" Leon said as they made their way toward the car. He saw Caleb regarding the small vehicle with a mixture of curiosity and trepidation before leaning down and looking through the driver's window.

"Ah," Caleb said with a sigh. He turned to look at Leon. "Can you drive?"

"Not legally, but yeah," Leon replied. "Why? Can't you?"

"Not with a stick, no. You fancy driving me?"

Leon grinned before replying.

"Sure," he said, nodding his head. "For a price."

CHAPTER 57

"Busy shift, Jennifer?" Naomi asked her sister as she walked into the lounge, easing her shoes off her feet as she did so.

"Bloody nightmare," Jennifer replied. She sat down heavily in one of the armchairs before taking a deep breath through her nose. "Wow, something smells good."

"Yeah, I just threw something together for us." Naomi tried her best to look nonchalant. She wasn't known for her culinary abilities. "Just need to throw some pasta in a pot. You want me to plate up when it's ready?"

"Give us a minute. Glass of wine first, I think."

"Coming up."

Naomi got to her feet and padded into the kitchen, where a large iron dish full of beef bolognese in a ragu sauce was simmering on the stove. She walked past the stove, opened the fridge, and pulled out half a bottle of white wine, which she decanted into two glasses. Then she crossed to the recycling bin after rinsing the bottle and put the bottle into it, using it to bury the bag that the Deliveroo driver had brought the bolognese in. The aluminum tray that the actual food was in was already buried in Jennifer's wheelie bin in front of the apartment.

"Here you go, mate," Naomi said as she walked back into the lounge and handed Jennifer her glass. She sat down and folded her legs under her, waiting as Jennifer fiddled with the remote control to turn the television on.

"Mmm, cheers," Jennifer murmured, sipping her drink.

"So, why was it a nightmare at work?"

"Just really busy."

"Anything interesting?"

"Usual stuff. A selection of Norfolk's finest parading through the door. There was a smash on the A47 but nothing serious, and a bloke found wandering around the countryside with a stab wound."

"Really?" Naomi said, leaning forward. Although Norfolk wasn't the sleepy backwater some people thought it was, things like that were rare. "What happened to him?"

"No idea," Jennifer replied, navigating to the news channel. "Doesn't speak a word of English. I did meet that copper friend of yours, though. Derek, is it?"

Naomi glanced at Jennifer over the top of her glass.

"You mean Dave? Big guy?"

"Yeah, that's the one. He was trying to find an interpreter for the bloke, but he couldn't even work out what language the man was speaking. Dopey git."

"He's not dopey," Naomi said with a smile. "Did you talk to him?"

"Not really," Jennifer replied. "I was getting an old boy ready for theater. He had a foreign object stuck."

"Stuck where?"

"You don't want to know." Naomi could see the corners of Jennifer's mouth twitching.

"What sort of foreign object?"

"Potato."

"Stuck?"

"Very." Jennifer started laughing. "Apparently, he was walking round the kitchen naked and slipped over. The Maris Piper was on the floor, and well, just went pop right in there."

Naomi, who was about to take a sip of wine, burst out laughing and spilled some on her hand.

"Jennifer, that's awful," she said as she licked her fingers. "That so did not happen."

"That so did happen," Jennifer replied with a grin. "Okay, it wasn't today, but that sort of thing happens more often than you think."

Naomi, still laughing, put her wineglass down and got to her feet. "I'm going to put the pasta on."

"Did you know, Naomi, that some men use kitchen utensils to try to tickle their—" Naomi clamped her hands over her ears, giggling.

"La! La! La!" she said. "Not listening!"

Thirty minutes later, both women were lying back in their armchairs with empty plates balanced on the arms. Another half empty bottle of wine was on the floor between them. Naomi stayed where she was as Jennifer huffed before getting to her feet to clear the plates. When she came back into the kitchen a moment later, she was grinning at Naomi.

"Lying cow," Jennifer said as she sat back down.

"What do you mean?" Naomi asked, pressing her lips together so she didn't laugh.

"You seriously expect me to believe that you cooked that meal and tidied up after yourself? The last time you cooked, I was finding bits of dried out vegetables for weeks and the kitchen looked like a crime scene."

"I did cook it," Naomi replied, trying to look hurt. She had cooked the pasta, at least.

"Sure you did," Jennifer said with a smug smile in Naomi's direction. "But thanks for the supper, it was lovely. Just what I needed. Wherever you ordered it from."

In reply, Naomi picked up a cushion and lobbed it at Jennifer, careful not to send her wine glass flying. On the television screen in front of them, a somber-looking woman was talking into the camera. Behind her was a large house with a single police officer standing guard at the front door while white-suited technicians walked inside the building carrying boxes of equipment. Then the shot changed to another person.

"Hey, that's him," Jennifer said, reaching for the remote. "Derek."

"Dave," Naomi said as Jennifer turned up the volume. "He's called Dave."

"Hush you. I want to hear what he's saying."

Naomi leaned forward and watched as Dave, visibly nervous, read from a piece of paper in front of him. Behind him was a brand-new police station recently opened on the outskirts of Norwich.

"Police are urgently seeking witnesses who were in the vicinity of Ranworth Rectory between midday and approximately half-past one this afternoon. Anyone who was in the area at that time is asked to come forward directly to us to Crimestoppers, an independent charity who will treat your information with the strictest of confidence."

"What's happened?" Naomi asked Jennifer, who was tapping on her phone as the screen changed to a preview of the local football team's next match.

"Just looking it up now. Bloody internet's rubbish,"

Jennifer replied. "Hey, this Dave fella. Is he, er, well, a good friend of yours?"

"Why are you asking, Jennifer?" Naomi asked, looking at her sister, who was smiling into her phone.

"Just curious, that's all. He is quite easy on the eye."

Naomi grinned and opened her mouth to reply, but as she did so, she saw Jennifer's smile drop away in an instant.

"Oh my, that's awful," her sister said, frowning and scrolling the screen with her finger.

"What happened?" Naomi asked, all thoughts of Dave forgotten.

"That thing in Ranworth, they're saying it was a robbery that escalated into murder." When Jennifer looked at Naomi, her eyes were wide. "Someone murdered the local vicar."

CHAPTER 58

To Caleb's surprise, Leon was in fact a very good driver, considering he was too young to have had any formal training. But perhaps, Caleb thought as the young man navigated his way through the streets of the Lark's Cross estate and out into the city proper, it was more about avoiding the attention of the authorities. He had taken a circuitous route to leave the estate on the basis that there could still be cops floating about, but once they were on the main roads, Leon's confidence appeared to grow.

"So how come you never learned to drive properly, then?" Leon asked as he maneuvered the car over a complicated roundabout that made Caleb grateful he wasn't driving after all.

"I can drive properly," Caleb replied, "just not with a stick shift. Just never learned is all."

"Where're you from?"

"Texas, originally."

"Why d'you come over here? Texas is like miles away."

"It's a long story, Leon," Caleb replied as he watched the houses flashing past. The difference between the ones they were now driving past and the ones on the estate was stark. "But I have to be somewhere." They drove on, and the houses gave way to a parade of businesses, all closed apart from one small convenience store sandwiched between a charity shop and a bookmaker. "You ever been to the States?"

"Hell no," Leon said with a laugh. "I went to France once, on a school trip. But it was shit."

"Yeah." Caleb smiled, thinking back to his own adventures at school. "School trips can be like that."

"Not the trip," Leon replied. "The whole country. It stunk of piss."

Caleb's smile broadened at Leon's analysis of his country's closest neighbor, but the young man offered nothing further on the issue.

Outside the car, the houses and occasional shops gave way to open countryside, but from the number of open lots they passed in the darkness, Norwich's green belt was shrinking rapidly. It only took them twenty minutes, if that, but they soon arrived in the village where Suzy and Leanne were staying. Caleb recognized the village sign, important enough to have its own spotlight, which featured a man and a woman who appeared to be gardening. Leon slowed the car down to a crawl.

"Where am I going?" he asked, leaning forward to look through the windshield. Caleb didn't reply at first, not wanting to give the shelter's location away. It was further down the road, perhaps a few hundred meters away. Beyond it was a gas station, its lights still on.

"Pull into the gas station," Caleb said. Leon would have to drive past the shelter, giving Caleb the opportunity to look at it, and he could walk back from the garage without the young man seeing the exact location of his destination.

Leon did as instructed and, as they passed the shelter, Caleb kept his head pointing forward while he looked at the gate out of the corner of his eye. Something was wrong, and he felt himself stiffen before forcing himself to relax. The gate was open, only by a few inches, but it wasn't secured. Leon hadn't even stopped the car in the gas station parking lot before Caleb had opened the door.

"Hey, Caleb?" Leon called after him. Caleb, already a few steps away from the vehicle, turned. "You forgot your friend's bag."

"I'll be back for it. Wait here."

Without waiting for a reply, Caleb broke into a jog as he reached the main road. He covered the ground to the shelter in less than a minute and, when he arrived at the gate, he saw he was right. The gate was open. Caleb glanced round to make sure he was alone before pushing the gate and slipping through. Moving slowly to avoid making too much noise on the gravel, he stepped to the lawn and broke into a run. It wasn't just the gate that was open. It was the front door as well. Light was spilling out onto the drive.

Caleb stepped into the house and paused, closing his eyes for a few seconds. He got no sense that there was anyone inside but proceeded as if there was, just in case. Almost every light was on inside, and he made his way down a hall with oil paintings on either side, his footsteps muffled by the thick carpet. He passed a lounge, a study, and a kitchen. The doors to each were open, the lights in the rooms were on, and they were empty. Caleb noticed a large stain on the study's dark carpet, but he didn't linger. He was looking for Suzy, not critiquing the housekeeping.

At the end of the hall was a staircase with ornate wooden bannisters. Caleb made his way up the stairs, confident the lower floor was empty, and found himself in a similar corridor to the hallway downstairs. But the doors to the rooms were all closed, with the exception of one. He made his way toward the door, pausing just outside it. Like the other rooms downstairs, the lights inside were on. He heard the faint noise of tires on gravel coming from outside the house.

Caleb pushed at the door which opened without a sound. His chest tightened as he saw a figure lying on a bed. It was Suzy.

She had her hands clasped on her chest as if she was in prayer. But Caleb knew from the metallic smell in the air that she wasn't praying. He took a few steps forward, the world seeming to close in around him. All he could hear was his own blood rushing in his ears.

As he approached the bed, Caleb could see a dark halo on the bedding around Suzy's blonde hair. It was blood. Lots of blood. The deep, gaping wound in her neck was like a cruel smile. The world closed in further as Caleb sank to his knees. He reached out and took Suzy's hand. It was still warm. If he had got here earlier, he could have protected her. Caleb closed his eyes and wrapped his fingers around Suzy's. Through the rushing blood in his ears, Caleb could hear footsteps. He chose to ignore them. It could be a complete medevac team approaching, but there would be nothing they could do.

"Through this holy anointing may the Lord in his love and mercy help you with the grace of the Holy Spirit. May the Lord who frees you from sin save you and raise you up," he whispered under his breath.

Caleb took a breath, preparing to say the Lord's Prayer, when he was hit in the back by what felt like a sledgehammer. A shooting, excruciating pain shook his brain like it was a peanut in a jar, and he sensed a swarm of bees crawling under his skin. Unable to hold Suzy's hand anymore, Caleb felt his world starting to slide to one side. Then he realized it wasn't his world that was sliding. It was him. Just before he lost consciousness, Caleb heard a deep male voice shouting.

"Taser! Taser! Taser!"

CHAPTER 59

Vince pulled his hood up and hunched down as yet another police vehicle sped along a few streets away, its blue lights illuminating the houses it roared past. He was begrudgingly impressed by the speed of the response. There must have been some sort of automatic call placed when he had disrupted the power supply to the house that he'd not expected. But it didn't matter. By the time the first response vehicle had arrived, he had completed what he'd gone there to do and was making his way through the side streets. He'd secreted his car in the parking lot of a closed community store, a run-down building with no signs of cameras that was only a few minutes' walk away.

"Vince," Leanne said with a cry. "You're hurting my hand." He looked down at the child, who fortunately had slept through everything. Vince knew she would be a lot harder to control if she'd seen what he'd done back in the house. "Where are we going? I want my mummy."

"I told you, we're going on a brief vacation," Vince

replied, trying to keep his voice under control. "Your mother will join us soon."

"But I forgot Boo Boo," Leanne said with a cry. "He's still in the house."

"She'll bring Boo Boo, don't worry," Vince replied through gritted teeth.

Gaining access to the property had been much easier than he'd initially thought. Accessing the house's router had been child's play, and once he had access to it, he had access to the entire security network. Crouching down out of sight by the wall, Vince had taken a few moments to plan his assault. There didn't appear to be any back-up generator, so cutting the power would wipe out the cameras. The security system had a *Fire Alarm Response* mode which, when activated, would unlock the doors and windows to allow the inhabitants to escape. Once he was sure the mode didn't also sound an alarm, he activated it, opened the main gate to the property, and cut the power.

He'd not had anywhere near as much time as he had wanted to scope the property he'd just left properly. Under normal circumstances, he would have had an entire team surrounding the house for a few days. Observing the normal patterns of life. Who lived there? Who visited, and when? How long they stayed for? But when he'd arrived at the house and seen the enhanced security, he'd known instinctively that this was where Suzy was hiding with Leanne. What Vince didn't know was how long she would be remaining there for and, as a surveillance team wasn't an option, decisive action was required. Vince hadn't been expecting the old woman, but she hadn't been expecting a knife across her throat.

It wouldn't take the police long to link his activities at the vicarage of St. Helen's Church and the house he had just left. Although the vicar had proven much more resolute than the homeless man, the history that the dashboard camera in his car quietly collected had shown Vince exactly where the man had been. Vince had replayed the vicar's final trip turn by turn, tracing the journey with a map on his lap. It had showed the vicar's last destination and, although he had denied it before he died, the odds were that it was also Suzy's and Leanne's destination.

Vince was disappointed that his time with Suzy had come to an end earlier than he'd originally planned. Her ultimate demise, while satisfying, wasn't anywhere near as exciting as it could have been, but time had been of the essence.

As he approached the parking lot, Vince slowed his pace to do a quick survey of the area. It was a force of habit, nothing more, but he could see nothing unusual. He walked to his car, opening it the old-fashioned way with the key to avoid the blinkers and the headlamps coming on. He had planned out a route that would take him to the caravan where Hùng and his wife would be waiting to receive Leanne. The route which had no ANPR cameras or any other CCTV systems he could see. It would take perhaps thirty minutes, less if the roads were clear.

He buckled Leanne into the rear seat, ignoring her complaints. With any luck, she would be asleep within moments. He needed to change his clothes and shower away the blood from the elderly woman. He tutted under his breath. Arteries could be so messy.

Vince spent a moment in reflection before starting the engine. Once Leanne was safely in the hands of Hùng, Vince's work was complete. There were others who would take over from there. Leanne would be taken over to mainland Europe and from there to Estonia. Vince didn't care about that part of the journey, or where Leanne was taken from Estonia. As long as Leanne was collected from Hùng, Vince would be paid handsomely.

Vince knew his time in Norfolk was done, and he had no intention of returning. It was time to set up somewhere new. Time to find someone new. Someone fragile, a single mother with a child who could both be molded into what he wanted them to be. As long as the child's DNA matched someone else's, he could start again.

Vince started the car with a smile. He was looking forward to starting a new hunt.

CHAPTER 60

"I'm not shitting you, bro," Leon said to Syd. "That's exactly how it went down." Syd's face had finally gone from disbelief to shock. Leon sat back in Syd's armchair and blew his breath out of his cheeks. "What the hell do we do now?"

Leon had spent the previous ten minutes telling Syd what had happened earlier on. How he and Caleb had gone to Thorpe and parked in a gas station. How Caleb had left the car, leaving his belongings behind. And how a few minutes after that, every police officer in Norfolk, or so it seemed, had arrived.

"You're sure they nicked him?" Syd said, reaching for his rolling papers.

"Sure as I can be," Leon replied. "They drove right past me. He was in the back of a panda car, looked like he was cuffed to me."

"But what for?"

"No idea, but from the number of bizzies that turned up, it was something big."

Leon nodded at the two bags between them. One was

the woman's, still with the cash in it. The other was a cloth bag belonging to Caleb. Syd flicked the cigarette papers and a bag of weed across the table in Leon's direction.

"Put one together, bro," Syd said, reaching for Caleb's bag. "I want to know what's in here."

Leon picked up the papers and started constructing a joint as Syd upended Caleb's bag onto the floor. There wasn't much inside it. A gray garment of some sort, a small Bible, and a cut-throat razor tumbled onto the stained carpet, followed by a pair of tatty leather sandals. Then Syd reached into the bag and pulled out a battered navy-blue passport. On the front was a complex crest with the words United States of America on the front. Tucked inside the passport were a couple of crisp hundred-dollar bills that fluttered to the carpet. The last items shaken from the bag were a rectangular stone, maybe two inches in size, and a what looked to Leon like a leather belt.

"Man, he travels light," Syd said as he flicked through the passport. "Been about a bit as well. More stamps in this than my old man's stamp album." Leon watched as Syd replaced the bills inside the passport before prodding at the gray garment.

"That's the robe he was wearing on the bus," Leon said as he ran his fingers over the joint to check it was firm enough. "He was all dressed up like a monk or something."

"You're shitting me?" Syd said, his eyes crinkling. "He was dressed as a monk?"

"Yeah, like that Dally Lammy bloke."

"You mean the Dalai Lama," Syd replied as he took the joint from Leon. "He wears orange ones, though. Not mucky gray ones."

Leon just shrugged his shoulders in response. He watched as Syd lit the joint, puffed a couple of times, and took a deep draw on it. Tiny embers fell from the end and onto Syd's shirt before he brushed them away.

"What are we going to do?" Leon asked after Syd passed him the joint.

"We don't have to do anything," Syd replied. "We've got our money back and he's out of the picture."

"Yeah, but he was going to help us."

"He was going to work for us, remember?" Syd shot back, "as long as we paid him." Leon held his breath for a few seconds and exhaled, sending a plume of pale smoke toward the ceiling. "When did you and him become best mates, anyway?"

"He's a pretty resourceful bloke," Leon said, taking another toke on the joint. "I mean, he saved our boy out there. He rumbled your cannabis farms pretty quickly." He laughed, the laugh turning into a cough. "And he found us, didn't he?"

"No, Leon," Syd replied, leaning forward and holding his hand out. "He found you, and you led him to me. There's a difference, my friend."

Leon relinquished the joint and sat back, the first buzz of the powerful weed starting to tingle in his brain's periphery. Syd had a point. Caleb had lifted his wallet without him noticing. If it weren't for that, there would have been no way for Caleb to find him.

"I say we do nothing," Syd said with a note of finality. "If he comes back for the money in the bag, fine, he can have it. We'll keep it and the crap in his own bag for the time being and see what happens. Right?"

Leon knew there was no point discussing the issue anymore. He could tell from the expression on Syd's face that his mind was made up.

"What about that meeting tomorrow night?" Leon asked him. "What are we going to do about that?"

"I'll think of something," Syd replied. His eyes were closed, and he was resting his head back on the sofa. Leon picked up the remnants of the joint which was smoldering in the ashtray and, after puffing it back to life, took a couple of quick hits before stubbing it out.

Leon said goodbye to Syd and got to his feet. Syd didn't reply, and Leon wondered if he was asleep or just stoned. Closing the apartment door behind him, Leon made his way toward the elevator, glancing at the doors to the other apartments as he passed them. At some point, he really wanted to see the farms that Caleb had described.

He'd not said anything to Syd for fear of the older man taking the piss out of him, but Leon liked Caleb. There was something about the man that was difficult to pin down, something that made Leon want to try to at least help him somehow. Caleb had, after all, saved a young lad's life earlier.

Leon pressed the button to call the elevator and sighed. There must be something he could do?

CHAPTER 61

Naomi blipped the locks of her red Mini and walked toward the main door of the building outside of where she had parked. If her car wasn't safe in the visitors' parking lot of a police station, then it wasn't safe anywhere. She pushed the heavy doors open, grateful for the heat inside the foyer. Since the sun had set a couple of hours previously, there was a definite chill in the air.

The police officer behind the desk, who Naomi didn't recognize, made a show of not taking any notice of her until she had been standing at the desk for almost thirty seconds. It was a petty game some officers played to reinforce to their visitors who was in charge and it was, in Naomi's opinion, pretty pointless. The man behind the desk was perhaps in his late fifties, had sergeant's chevrons on his shoulder, and didn't look as if he would pass a fitness test any time soon.

"Can I speak to Detective Constable Hetherington, please?" she asked the desk sergeant.

"Not sure if he's in at the moment," the police officer replied.

"Well, his car's in the parking lot, so I think he probably is." Naomi's reply caused the sergeant to raise an eyebrow.

"And you are?" he asked, his eyebrow remaining in the up position.

"Naomi Tipton," Naomi replied. "Solicitor. Here about the case in Thorpe?"

"The double murder?" the sergeant said. Naomi blinked to hide her surprise. Leon hadn't mentioned that when he'd called her, desperate for her to help a friend of his. "That was quick. The suspect's still being processed."

"Hey Naomi," a familiar deep voice said from the other side of the desk. Dave's face appeared through a side door. "I thought I heard your voice. Can you let her through, Sarge?"

With a tutting noise, the desk sergeant pressed a button under his desk and the security gate separating the foyer from the rest of the police station clicked. Naomi walked through to join Dave, pausing by the x-ray machine in case the sergeant wanted to put her bag through it. But when she looked at him, he was engrossed in his paperwork, which she realized as she looked at it was a Sudoku puzzle.

"I didn't realize you were the Duty Solicitor tonight," Dave said, leading her through into the bowels of the police station. For a modern building, once visitors passed the security gate, it was surprisingly dingy. "Who called you?"

"I'm not the duty solicitor tonight, Dave," Naomi replied as they passed a noticeboard full of flyers for mandatory training, urgent notices, and several advertisements for the Police Federation. "I had a phone call."

Dave pulled up and turned to face Naomi.

"Who called you?" he said. She looked at him and noticed the fresh bags under his eyes. He looked more tired than she'd ever seen him before.

"A friend of the defendant who wishes to remain anonymous," Naomi said, noticing her voice had slipped into solicitor mode despite the fact she was talking to a friend.

"Did your friend happen to mention the suspect's name at all?" Dave asked, the ghost of a smile appearing on his face. "Only he's not said a word since he was arrested." He took a step toward Naomi and she caught the faintest odor of sweat coming from him. "Not even, I want a lawyer." They stood looking at each other for a few seconds. "This is bad, Naomi. Are you sure you want a part of it?"

"What's happened?" Naomi asked. "The desk sergeant said it was a double homicide."

"Yup, two women in a big house up in Thorpe," Dave said, continuing down the corridor. Naomi had to hurry to keep up with him. "Both had their throats cut. One in a bedroom, and we found another stuffed in a cupboard. The house had a panic alarm linked to us, which someone had set off. It could have been three women, though. There was another one who lived there, but she'd gone out for the evening. Lucky woman."

"Bloody hell," Naomi said, swallowing the lump that had appeared in her throat. She'd never dealt with a homicide before. The closest she'd come was a case a year or so back involving a bar fight that had seen a man killed with a single, unfortunate punch.

"When the response units got there, your man was there, praying over one of the bodies." Dave pushed open the door at the end of the corridor and led Naomi into the crew room. "Not had a murder in Norfolk in months, then we get four in the space of a few days. Like bloody London buses. Never one for ages, then two turn up at the same time."

"Are they connected?" Naomi asked. "The cases?"

"We're not sure," Dave replied, flicking the kettle on.

"Different MO. The priest was tortured before he was killed. I mean properly tortured. Never seen anything like it." Naomi fought the urge to give Dave a hug. She'd never seen the expression on his face before. It wasn't just exhaustion. It was horror. "The two women were killed with a knife, whereas the priest was battered to death like the homeless guy in Norwich. There's no obvious connection, but it's early days in the investigation. It's not helped by your mute friend." He put his hands on the small of his back and stretched. "You wait here. I'll see if they've finished processing him."

"You want a brew?" Naomi asked. Dave smiled, but it only made him look more tired.

"Thought you'd never ask, Naomi," he replied.

CHAPTER 62

Caleb folded his legs under him and sat on the thin, rubber covered mattress that lined his bunk. The only other piece of furniture in the cell was a stainless-steel toilet with a small washbasin. At least he had his own cell, which was in contrast to the holding cells used in his home country. The walls were painted lime green and were devoid of graffiti, while the only source of light was a small bulb enclosed in a metal cage on the ceiling. Even if it had been light outside, there was no window to let any natural light in.

He closed his eyes and thought back over the previous few hours. Since being tasered at the shelter, Caleb had been stripped, searched, poked, prodded, swabbed, and fingerprinted. His clothes had been replaced with a disposable white over suit that itched his skin and matching socks. He had complied with every request the police had made, apart from saying anything in reply to their many questions. He'd not even told them his name, knowing that the moment he opened his mouth, they would know he wasn't British. Caleb had nothing on him that could identify him.

He wasn't sure how the legal system worked in this country, but back in the United States there was an entire amendment devoted to the right to remain silent, and he didn't think it would be too different here.

Caleb wasn't prone to thinking in terms of what ifs, but under the circumstances, he couldn't help himself. When he'd got to Suzy's side, her hand was still warm. Her assailant must have been there only moments before he had arrived. After being cuffed and placed in the back of a marked police car, Caleb had watched as the police officers had searched the house, lights in the rooms turning on one by one as they went from room to room. He'd been hoping to see Leanne being shepherded to the ambulance that had arrived not long after the police, perhaps wrapped in a blanket and with Boo Boo tucked under one arm, but at the same time he knew it was a forlorn hope. What if he'd got there ten minutes earlier? It wouldn't have been Suzy's body lying on the bed, of that Caleb was sure. It would be whoever had killed her lying there instead.

Staying silent was, in Caleb's mind, the best course of action to take. It might delay his release if he said nothing, but he knew at some point he would be released. There was nothing to tie him to Suzy's murder from a forensic perspective. No murder weapon with his prints on it, no blood-soaked clothing. All he had done was discover the body and, while that wasn't a crime, it was going to be difficult to explain when he started talking. But Caleb knew that remaining silent as the various forensic tests were undertaken would—hopefully—eliminate him from the investigation and was the best course of action. The only problem with that was that every moment he was locked in a cell, Leanne could be being taken further and further away.

Caleb closed his eyes again and went over in his mind

everything that Suzy had said to him about her partner, Vince. He knew he worked for the security services. He knew the man was a monster. But beyond that, Caleb realized as he replayed the conversation in the forest they'd had, Suzy had told him little about this Vince. Caleb didn't even know his last name. He didn't even know Suzy's last name. Which was going to make tracking Vince, and by extension Leanne, very difficult indeed. But Caleb had undertaken more difficult missions than this one and succeeded. But there would be a way. There had to be a way. He had made Leanne a promise, and Caleb had never broken a promise, pinky or otherwise.

There was a metallic clunk from the cell door, and Caleb opened his eyes to see the inspection hatch had been thrown open. A pair of dark eyes were staring at him through the letterbox shaped opening.

"You need anything?" a male voice asked. "Food? Water?" Caleb just shook his head in response. The eyes stared at him for a few seconds. "Get to your feet. You've got a visitor."

Caleb unfolded his legs and stood, his fists held out in front of him with his wrists together, ready to be cuffed. The police officer who opened the door glanced at them.

"I'm taking you to a side room," the police officer said. "You won't be cuffed." He leaned forward and grabbed Caleb's arm just above the elbow, the firmness of his grip no doubt designed to reinforce who was in charge. Caleb didn't care, but just allowed himself to be guided from the cell.

The police officer took Caleb down the corridor of the holding cells and opened a door. Then he placed a hand on the small of Caleb's back and pushed him into the room. It was larger than his cell, although it was painted the same horrible green color. Inside the room was a chair in the corner, and a table with another chair in front of it. The only other thing that Caleb could see was a black rubber strip running around the wall of the room at waist height.

"Sit in the corner and don't move," the police officer said. He pointed at the rubber strip. "I'll be right outside and if that alarm goes off, I'll be straight in to beat the living shit out of you before the other coppers in the building all come and do the same thing. Understand?"

Caleb sat in the chair and slipped his hands under his legs, nodding at the police officer as he did so. He was a bully, nothing more, and Caleb hated bullies, but the odds weren't exactly in his favor at that moment. He watched as the police officer looked down the corridor and then took a step away from the door to be replaced by Caleb's visitor.

"Hello," the woman said with a bright smile. She stepped into the room as the police officer closed the door behind her. Her hand was extended toward him. "I'm Naomi Tipton." Caleb regarded her hand with curiosity, wondering if shaking it would attract a response from the monkey outside. He arched his eyebrows at the woman. "I'm your solicitor," she said, still smiling at him.

CHAPTER 63

Naomi kept what must have looked like a rictus grin on her face as the man in the side room regarded her. After what seemed like a full minute, but was in reality much less, he half stood and shook her hand. She looked directly into his eyes as he did so, wondering if she was looking into the eyes of a man who had killed two women in cold blood, perhaps others too. They were gray. Expressionless. But at the same time, infinitely deep.

"Please, make yourself comfortable," she said, gesturing at the chair. Then she sat down on the other side of the table and pulled her notebook from her bag, followed by a pen. She knew her fingers were shaking. It wasn't from fear. Naomi knew that the second she touched the alarm strip, the door would fly open, but she was still alone in a room with a man who had been arrested for murder. It was nerves at the thought of the situation she was in. How high the stakes were. "Do you need anything? Something to eat or drink?"

The man in the corner shook his head in response.

Naomi took a moment to look at him. His eyes were his most distinctive feature, with his shaved head a close second. He wasn't overly muscular, but she could tell from the thin paper suit he was wearing that he was in good shape. His handshake had been firm and confident, which she always appreciated. She thought he was older than her, but only by a few years, which would put him in his mid-thirties.

"So," Naomi said, trying to keep her voice professional and not squeaky. "You have me at a disadvantage." The man's eyebrows went up. "Well," she continued, "you know my name, but I don't know yours." Naomi watched as the man's eyes roved the room, going from one corner to the other in turn. Finally, his gaze rested on the door before returning to her. "We can't be overheard, if that's what you're concerned about. This is a room for interviews between solicitors and their clients, so no recording devices are allowed." Naomi tried another smile, but it felt false, so she let it slip away. "What should I call you?"

"My name is Caleb," the man said. It was Naomi's turn to raise her eyebrows. She'd not been expecting to hear an American accent.

"You don't sound local," Naomi said, scrawling the name down in her notebook. "Do you have a last name?"

"Just Caleb and no, I'm not local."

"Have you been arrested before?"

"Not in this country, no. You have disclosure here, right?"

Naomi paused with her pen over her notepad. His question had surprised her.

"We do, yes," she replied.

"So, the police will have told you they don't have anything on me?"

She said nothing for a moment. When she had talked to Dave in the crew room, he'd told her about the circumstances in which this man had been found and the custody sergeant had given her a copy of Caleb's custody record, but that wasn't formal disclosure.

"There are a lot of forensic tests that will need to be done," she said eventually, playing for time.

"They won't find anything," Caleb replied, his voice confident. "I was there, obviously, but I didn't kill her. The forensics will show that. Were the responding officers wearing body cameras?"

"They would have been, yes."

"Might be worth checking the footage. I'm pretty sure that the police are supposed to issue a warning before tasering someone, not after."

"They tasered you?" Naomi replied, her voice much higher than she'd expected. Dave hadn't mentioned that bit.

"Yes," Caleb replied. "In the back, as I was kneeling next to my friend, praying for her soul."

Naomi scribbled furiously in her notebook. If what Caleb had just told her was the truth, that was a whole new can of worms.

"Do you need medical attention?" Naomi asked.

"No," Caleb replied. "I'm good, thank you."

Naomi spent the next few moments trying to find out some more about Caleb. He answered some of her questions, but not all. He told her he was from Texas, but not why he was in England. All he would say on that front was that he had to be somewhere. He told her he was a preacher but wouldn't be drawn on his denomination. He was equally reticent about his relationship with the woman whose body he'd been found next to, saying only that she was someone he had met on a bus. The conversation was intensely frustrating, but at the same time, this strange man was growing on her.

A few moments later, just as Naomi was struggling to find questions Caleb would actually answer, he threw her by asking one of his own.

"Aren't you going to ask me who killed Suzy?" he said, gazing at her with his gray eyes.

"You know who did it?"

"Yes."

"Probably telling me would be a good idea then, yes. That's the sort of thing the police would probably quite like to know."

"His name's Vince. He sounds like he's an abuser at best and psychotic at worst. He works for the British secret service. The house she was in is a women's shelter, but he must have tracked her there and killed her before kidnapping her daughter."

Naomi stifled a groan at his words. Although the interview hadn't been going exactly as she had initially hoped, she'd not thought Caleb was living in a fantasy world. There'd been no mention of a child up to that point, let alone one which had been kidnapped. She turned the page in her notebook to start a fresh one.

"Okay, Caleb," Naomi said, injecting a note of professionalism into her voice. "Why don't you start at the beginning?"

"That's easy," Caleb replied, a slow smile appearing on his face. "In the beginning, God created the heavens and the earth."

She looked at him, shaking her head almost imperceptibly from side to side. The man was a complete nutcase.

CHAPTER 64

Caleb looked at Naomi carefully as she wiggled the pen between her fingers. When she did look up at him briefly, she had a look of confusion on her face as if she wasn't sure whether to believe him or not.

"Okay, let's go back to the bus. That was the first time you met Suzy, is that correct?" she asked him, making a note on her pad.

"Yes, that's correct. There was an armed robbery on the bus."

He watched as she laughed and put the pad on the table. She raised her hands to her face and rubbed her eyes. Naomi mumbled something under her breath, which Caleb thought was *I don't need this shit*, but he wasn't a hundred percent sure.

"Right," Naomi said, folding her arms over her chest, and smirking. "So, we've got an armed robbery, a mad secret service agent, two murders, and a kidnapping. Is that correct?"

Caleb didn't reply. No one had mentioned two murders in the house. He'd not seen the older woman who had answered the door when they had dropped Suzy and Leanne off and had hoped that she'd not been in the house when Vince had been there. Then he remembered the stain on the study floor. He closed his eyes and offered up a brief prayer for the repose of her soul, hoping that she had found peace along with Suzy. When he reopened them, he stared at Naomi until her smirk disappeared.

"Everything I'm telling you is correct," Caleb said, his voice determined. "You can check with your police colleagues about the robbery. Suzy and Leanne got off the bus before they arrived. I followed them into the woods."

"Why?"

"I was concerned for their safety."

"Very noble of you," Naomi replied, raising her eyebrows.

"When I spoke with Suzy, she told me about her partner Vince. How he abused her. Beat her." He saw Naomi flinch as he said this. It was brief, but noticeable. "She claimed that he was able to access computer systems and databases at will. The only way she could get away was to try to do it off-grid, which is why she left the bus before the police arrived." Caleb paused, wondering whether to tell the solicitor about the money that Leon had stolen, but he decided against that for the moment. "We went to a village and sought help. The person we spoke to took us both to the house in Thorpe, which is a women's shelter. I left Suzy and her daughter there, thinking they would be safe. How wrong was I on that front?"

"Tell me about the daughter," Naomi said, picking up her pen and making some more notes. At least now Caleb had her attention.

"Her name's Leanne, and she's seven or eight. Suzy was concerned that her partner was going to abuse her."

"He sounds like a nasty piece of work, this Vince. Do you know his last name?"

"No," Caleb replied.

"So, you went back to the house to find Suzy murdered?"

"Yes. The only thing I touched was her hand. That's why there'll be no forensics to suggest I killed her. The gate to the house was open, the front door was open. All I did was walk in and find Suzy." Caleb fought the urge to take Naomi's hand. He wanted to get a sense of how seriously she was taking him. "How long can the police keep me here?"

"Usually twenty-four hours before charging you, but that can be extended up to as much as ninety-six for a serious crime."

"Like murder?"

"Like murder."

Caleb sighed. That was four full days, by which time Leanne and Vince could be anywhere in the United Kingdom. They could be abroad. Caleb felt his heart hardening at the thought of why Vince had taken Leanne. It was unthinkable. He had to find her.

"Let's rewind back to after Suzy and her daughter left the bus. You went to a village?"

"Yes. To find help."

"And who was it who helped you?"

"The local vicar," Caleb replied. He saw Naomi frown as she scribbled in her notebook.

"What was the name of the village?"

"Ranworth, I think," Caleb replied, casting his mind back to the sign outside the church. "St Helen's was the name of the church. The vicar's name is Father Martin. He'll be able to back me up."

Caleb looked at Naomi, who had stopped writing. Her

hand was paused over her notepad and Caleb could see the nib of the pen trembling.

"Are you okay, Naomi?" Caleb said, leaning forward. The color had drained from her face and she looked as if she was about to pass out. When she looked at him a few seconds later, her eyes were wide.

"I just need to speak to someone," she said, getting to her feet. Caleb watched, concerned, as she bolted from the room.

Caleb sat back in his chair and blew air through his cheeks. What on earth was going on?

CHAPTER 65

Naomi was nervous, far more so than she usually was when she was sitting in on a police interview. She was sitting next to Caleb in one of the formal interview rooms. In the corner of the room, a small camera flashed a tiny red light every few seconds. If Caleb shared her nerves, he didn't show it. If anything, the man looked relaxed. Far more relaxed than he should be given that he was suspected of three murders.

Following his revelation that he had been in Ranworth and knew the murdered vicar, Naomi had run to the ladies restroom, thinking she was going to vomit. Had she just been sitting in a room with a multiple murderer?

"This interview is being recorded, both audio and visually," Dave's monotone voice said. She tuned him out as he went through the interview process, looking at Caleb as he answered most of Dave's initial questions. When she had returned to the side room Caleb was being kept in, after speaking with Dave for some time, Naomi had gone through everything with Caleb in minute detail. Her only advice to him had been to tell the truth. The more she spoke to him, the more she became convinced that he had just been in the wrong places at the wrong times. And if he was telling the truth, then time was of the essence. "Naomi?" she heard Dave say.

"I'm sorry?" she replied. Dave looked at her with a frown.

"I said, also present are."

"Oh, sorry. Naomi Tipton, solicitor." She forced herself to pay attention as Dave went through the preliminaries. No, Caleb had taken no drugs or alcohol recently. No, Caleb was not taking any prescribed medication. No, there was no reason why he could not be interviewed now.

"You have the right to free and independent legal advice and you are represented by Miss Tipton," Dave said, reading the script from his notepad. "Have you had enough time to consult with your solicitor before we start the interview?"

"Yes," Caleb replied. He turned to Naomi, and to her surprise, smiled at her. "She's very good." To her dismay, she felt her cheeks coloring.

A few moments later, Dave started the interview proper.

"The reason for the interview is that you've been arrested on suspicion of murder," Dave said. "Usually, at this point, I'd ask you what is called the responsibility question. I'd ask you, are you guilty of the offense?" He took a deep breath before continuing, and Naomi realized she was holding her own breath. "Are you guilty of the offense of murder?"

The red light in the corner of the room blinked at least three times before Caleb replied.

"No," he said, his voice firm and resolute. "No, I am not."

"Okay, Caleb," Dave said, his tone becoming more conversational as the meat of the interview began. "Let's start with the bus, shall we?"

Naomi listened as the two men talked. She occasionally made a note on her pad, but there was not a great deal to write down. Dave let Caleb do most of the talking, only asking occasional questions for clarity. Her client described taking Suzy and her daughter to the vicarage in Ranworth, and how the vicar there had arranged the place at the shelter in Thorpe.

"He drove us there," Caleb said, his eyes glancing between Naomi and Dave, "but I waited in the car. I didn't enter the house."

"What happened after that?" Dave asked.

"Father Martin gave me a lift to the outskirts of Norwich. He dropped me off to visit a friend."

"Who is this friend?"

"An acquaintance. I forget his name."

"Have you been to Norwich before?"

"No."

"So how do you know this friend?" Dave intoned the last word of his question with a sarcastic inflection

Naomi saw Caleb turn his eyes in her direction and raise his eyebrows. When they had spoken prior to the interview, he had promised that he would not lie to Dave about anything. But, Caleb had made sure to point out, there would be things that he wouldn't tell him.

"I'm not sure how Caleb's friend features in this investigation, DC Hetherington?" Naomi said, ignoring the dark look that crossed Dave's face at her words. "My client is keen to keep this interview about him and his actions, not his friend's."

"Where were you yesterday, Caleb?" Dave asked, flicking his notes to find an earlier page. "Between approximately twelve midday and half-past one?" Naomi saw Caleb frown, but it only lasted for a few seconds.

"I went into Norwich in the morning. But I stopped at a pub for some food on the way back to my friend's place. That would have been at about one o'clock."

"Which pub?"

"I'm not sure of the name, but the sign had a flower on it."

"The Heartsease?" Naomi said. "On Plumstead Road?" Caleb just shrugged his shoulders.

"Could be," Caleb replied. "It's next to a large supermarket."

"That would be the Heartsease," Dave said. "You're a braver man than I am, eating in there."

"I can't say I recommend the sausages and potato." There was a brief smile on Caleb's face as he said this, which served to lighten the mood. But it didn't last long. "What happened between twelve and one-thirty?"

Naomi and Dave had discussed telling Caleb in advance what had happened in Ranworth Vicarage, but Dave had been adamant that she should say nothing before the interview. If Caleb was involved somehow, and given that he was wearing clothes belonging to the vicar when he was arrested, he certainly was, then his reaction could be important.

"The body of a man we now know to be Father Martin was discovered at St. Helen's vicarage in Ranworth yesterday," Dave said, his eyes not leaving Caleb's. "He was murdered and the time of death is estimated at between twelve and one-thirty."

Naomi watched as Caleb closed his eyes. His lips moved silently, and she saw the knuckles of both his hands whiten. When he reopened his eyes a few seconds later to look at her, she felt the hairs on the back of her neck going up. It was as if the temperature in the room had just dropped by several degrees.

"I'd like to speak to my solicitor," Caleb said as the hairs on Naomi's arms also started rising.

"Interview terminated at," Dave glanced at his watch, "twelve oh three." He got to his feet and glanced at Naomi, his eyebrows raised. She nodded in response to let him know she was happy to speak to Caleb alone. Dave left, and both Naomi and Caleb stared at the red blinking light in the corner until it went out.

Naomi looked at Caleb, whose eyes were still piercing hers. She felt almost naked under his gaze. He put both his hands on the table, palms uppermost, before he spoke.

"Naomi," Caleb said, his voice so soft it was almost a whisper. "Would you pray with me?"

CHAPTER 66

Vince performed the usual security sweeps as he entered his apartment, even though he knew it was overkill. There were enough security systems to ensure that not even a mouse could wander round unnoticed, and unlike the systems in the house in Norfolk, his couldn't be disabled as easily. When he was sure everything was as it should be, he crossed to his kitchen and pulled a bottle of wine from his fridge. A moment later, he was booting up his laptop as he sipped from a glass.

The journey back to London from Norfolk after he had dropped Leanne off with Hùng and his wife had been uneventful. As he drove, he went over the previous few days' events in his mind. Vince was satisfied with his performance. He'd located his target, neutralized it, and swept away any accessory links on the way. It still wasn't perfect, the result, but it was satisfactory. The quiet resignation that Suzy had shown as he had drawn the knife across her throat had been a highlight. That resignation was his success. And he had kept his word. It had been Suzy's life or Leanne's, and Leanne was still alive. Vince was nothing if not a man of his word.

He booted up his laptop and perched it on his knee. Vince then opened a browser window before navigating to a single parent dating website he monitored. For a commercial operation, their security was pitiful, and he thought that he would have been able to access their backend databases without any of the toys that MI5 made available. But for the moment, he didn't need to be in their databases, so he logged into his fake account and started browsing.

He had decided that the location for his next hunt would be on the south coast of England. Apart from a few holidays, it wasn't an area he knew well, but it was well within two hours from London by car. He would have preferred the north-east of England as it had the highest single parent rate in the country, but it was just too far. But along the south coast, Brighton, Hastings, even Eastbourne were well within reach. Of the towns, Brighton was possibly the best location. It was a large town with plenty of anonymity. And looking at his browser, plenty of lonely women.

Vince narrowed down the search parameters for his browsing sessions to only include those profiles of women under the age of thirty-two. Then he further narrowed it down to include the words single parent within the profile. There were three hundred thousand people living in Brighton. Of those people, over thirty of them were under thirty-two and mentioned that they were single parents in their profiles. Vince scanned through them, filtering out those who weren't blonde, those whose declared dress size didn't meet his expectations and, finally, those he just didn't like the look of.

That process left him with three options.

"Eeny, meeny, miny, moe," Vince muttered as he flipped through the profile. "Catch a woman by the toe. If she hollers, let her go. Eeny, meeny, miny, moe."

Vince stared at the profile photograph in front of him that had appeared as he had spoken the last word, moe. The woman who was staring back at him was looking at the camera over a cocktail, a half-smile on her face. She was wearing a low-cut dress that he disapproved of and was standing in a bar or a nightclub. In the background, he could see the blurred figures of people dancing.

"Well, hello Rachel," Vince said as he read the profile. He was looking for any mention of the age of her child. A couple of lines down the profile, he found it. Rachel had a daughter who was twelve, going on thirty. Perfect. He went on to read what Rachel Parmenter, aged twenty-nine and living in Portslade, was looking for in her ideal man. Vince laughed as he read her wish list. If men like that actually existed, then Rachel wouldn't be such a lonely slapper, would she? He swapped to a new browser window, wondering how many times a day Rachel wished she'd kept her legs together when she was a teenager.

Rachel's Facebook profile was a carefully constructed lie showing a confident, happy young woman. Every photograph showed her enjoying herself. Sitting on the beach with a stupid grin and an enormous ice-cream. Laughing at a wedding reception, no doubt wishing it was hers. Holding her shoulder-length blonde hair in place as someone, probably her daughter from the angle of the photograph, took her picture on top of the sheer cliffs of Beachy Head near Eastbourne. The irony of that location being one of the most popular suicide spots in the country wasn't lost on him. But, despite the smiles, Vince could see the sadness in her eyes sitting behind them. She was perfect.

He opened up a new document and started making a profile. Within a few moments, he was building up a profile of Rachel Parmenter. Vince switched windows as he worked, sucking as much information about the woman as he could into the document. Some of the detail he needed, such as her phone records and her financial history, would need to be collated from the computers at Thames House, but there was plenty to be going on with in the public domain.

Vince whistled as he worked. He enjoyed this part of his hunts almost as much as the end of them.

CHAPTER 67

Leon wasn't just nervous. He wasn't even scared. The truth was, he was shitting himself.

It was almost nine in the evening, and he was sitting on a small bench near a small play area in the center of the Lark's Cross estate. There was a set of swings, a slide, a climbing frame, and a collection of empty beer cans left there by the teenagers who used it more than the smaller children on the estate did. In the small of Leon's back, the hard metal of his Glock 17 was pressing into his skin. Syd had told him it was important to bring the gun to this meeting, not to actually use but in case it was needed as a show of force. He glanced at the time on his phone. Would the Albanians be on time?

Leon cast his mind back to the conversation he'd had with Caleb where the older man had spoken about negotiation. He couldn't remember the exact words Caleb had used, but it was something about terms of peace. Except the gun sticking into his back wasn't very peaceful. On another bench, close to Leon's, Syd was sitting. He was also looking at his phone, and Leon wondered if he was as terrified as he was.

They had talked about getting some of the other lads on the estate involved, but Syd hadn't wanted to do that.

"This is a business meeting, Leon," Syd had said when they'd discussed it earlier. "We can't turn up mob-handed, can we?" Leon had disagreed, making the case that the Albanians had not only turned up mob-handed, but knifed one of their lookouts. That was hardly the prelude to a business meeting. "We'll just meet them and see what they have to say." When Syd had said that, Leon had seriously considered just saying no, but he knew what the result of that would be. Instant dismissal, and all his hard work to date would have been for nothing.

Leon looked up as a set of headlamps approached from one of the roads leading to the center of the estate. It was the same SUV that he'd seen just before Syd's lookout had been injured, Leon was pretty sure. It pulled to a halt and stayed where it was for a few seconds, its engine ticking over. Then the front doors opened and two men stepped out, followed by another two men from the rear doors.

"Bollocks," Leon muttered. There were four people in the car, which meant he and Syd were outnumbered by two to one. He watched as Syd got to his feet, put his hands out, palms up, and walked toward the men. As his boss approached, Leon saw one man from the car take a step forward, the other three fanning out behind him. A moment later, Syd and the front man were deep in conversation. Leon could tell from the way Syd was shaking his head from side to side that the conversation wasn't going Syd's way. He could hear raised voices, but he couldn't make out what they were saying.

As Leon watched, one of the three men standing behind

their boss reached into his jacket. When he pulled his hand out, Leon saw the silhouette of a handgun in his hand. It didn't look like the one he was carrying. The barrel looked longer, and he realized it had a silencer attached to the end. The man who had produced the gun handed it to the one who had been talking to Syd.

"What the hell?" Leon said. What was he supposed to do? If one of them had a gun, then they could all be carrying. He saw Syd throw a desperate glance in his direction. Leon's mouth had dried out in an instant and he could feel the adrenaline coursing through him. A classic fight-or-flight reflex. Leon's problem, which was effectively Syd's problem, was that he was thinking more about the flight element than the fight element. He was fifteen and carrying a gun he'd never actually fired. How could he go up against four grown men? Four men who were almost certainly armed?

Syd threw Leon another, even more desperate, glance as the men from the car shuffled their position, hiding the man with the silenced gun from Leon's view. If the men from the car knew Leon was there, they were ignoring him. Maybe he could use the element of surprise? Leon knew this was his make or break moment. He swallowed, his mouth like sandpaper, and reached behind his back for his own Glock. When he tugged it, the barrel caught in his waistband. He'd shoved it too far down the back of his pants.

Leon swore, looking down at his waistband and taking his eye off the horrible tableaux in front of him for a split second. Then he heard a loud coughing noise, followed by the sound of a body crumpling to the floor.

He looked up but all he could see were three of the men from the car.

Leon couldn't see Syd anywhere.

CHAPTER 68

Caleb watched as the gun dropped to the ground and disappeared under the car. It was followed a split-second later by the length of wood he'd thrown at the man holding it. When he'd thrown the wood, a piece of two by four he'd grabbed in the alleyway, at first he didn't think he'd thrown it hard enough, but when it hit the gunman on the side of the head, he had dropped like a stone.

As he slumped to the ground, letting out a noise that was something between a groan and a cough, the other three men with him reacted. Caleb stepped forward, lunging toward the man closest to him. As he did so, Caleb raised his left leg into a low sidekick, driving the point of his big toe into the back of his opponent's knee. As the man dropped, all power to his leg gone in less than a second, Caleb used his forward momentum to drive his right knee into the bridge of the man's nose, where it connected with a satisfying crack.

The next thing Caleb sensed was a blinding flash of white light behind his eyes and a searing pain in the side of his head. One of the other men had moved far quicker than he'd expected and punched him. Hard. Caleb instinctively pulled his forearms up to his face before feeling a bone-jarring impact on his forearm as the follow up blow was deflected. He lashed his foot out, aiming a slant thrust kick at his assailant's stationary foot, but the man danced away from it. Caleb wasn't bothered that his blow hadn't landed. He'd created some space between them.

Caleb took a few steps back before crouching down. He could feel a warm trickle running down the side of his head just above his ear. The man who had punched him must have been wearing rings or using brass knuckles. He regarded his two remaining opponents, focusing on the one who had landed the blow. He was next. Caleb's foot brushed against the piece of wood he'd used to drop the gunman. Without taking his eyes off the two men, Caleb reached down and grabbed it. As he did so, the man who was yet to be involved reached into his jacket pocket. Caleb tensed, half expecting a gun, but when his hand re-emerged, he saw a brief glimmer of light from a blade. That was good. It would mean he would be focused on the weapon, not on Caleb.

The man advanced, holding the knife out in front of him. He took a couple of steps to the side, angling his body to around forty-five degrees. He was holding the hand without the weapon vertically. Caleb hefted the wood in his hand, trying to keep both men in view at the same time. If they had any sense, they would move even further apart than they were. In his peripheral vision, Caleb could see Leon hopping from foot to foot, unsure what to do. Caleb hoped he would stay where he was. He didn't want the boy getting in the way or trying to get involved.

The man with the knife moved first. He lunged forward,

extending his off hand out toward Caleb's face. It was a classic prison-style attack. Caleb stepped in toward him, noticing a look of surprise on the man's face as he did so. He dropped the piece of wood, hooking out one hand to grab the man's upper arm and wrapping his other hand around his wrist to control the knife. Then Caleb stepped to the side to move into a two on one position where he had complete control of the man's arm.

He pivoted to put the man with the knife between him and the other assailant just as the other man moved in with a wild punch that glanced off the side of Caleb's head before landing on the other man's neck. By the time it had bounced off Caleb's head, it had lost much of its momentum, but it still provoked a cry from the man Caleb was holding.

Caleb swept his leg round, hooking it behind the knife man's ankles and sweeping them from under him. As Caleb pivoted round, he placed his hand on the back of the man's head before rolling him off his hip and into the air. Then he shoved down as hard as he could on his head to make sure that it was the man's face that hit the ground first. Caleb scampered to the side to retrieve the piece of wood before leaping to his feet and swinging it in a move that Nolan Ryan would have been proud of.

The wood passed in front of the one remaining attacker, missing his face by inches. He arched his back to move his head away from the wood, which was exactly what Caleb wanted him to do. If the wood had actually connected with the man's head, it probably would have killed him, and no one was going to die today. Caleb used the momentum of the swing to bring the wood back round before driving it forward like a sword into the man's solar plexus.

The look on the man's face was one Caleb had seen many times before. Complete shock. The blow to his diaphragm would have caused it to go into immediate spasm, rendering him temporarily unable to breathe. He took a couple of steps backward before sitting down on the ground. Caleb could have moved in with a kick to the head to take him out of the equation completely, but he could see from the look on his face that the fight was over.

CHAPTER 69

Naomi watched through the window of the microwave as the cheese melted on top of the emergency macaroni dish she'd picked up on the way back to her sister's flat. A bottle of white wine was chilling in the fridge and she was tempted to open it. It had been a long day, but the risk was that if she did, it would be empty by the time Jennifer got back from work.

"Sod it," she muttered under her breath. She could message Jennifer to tell her to get another bottle. Just as Naomi was reaching into the cupboard for a glass, her phone began vibrating on the kitchen worktop.

"Hey, Jennifer," Naomi said as she answered the call. "I was about to message you."

"Let me guess," her sister replied. "You were going to tell me you're going to crack open the vino, so if I want some, pick some up on the way home?"

"Am I that predictable?" Naomi replied with a laugh.

"Yep, always. Can you do me a favor, though?"

"What's up?"

"Can you nip to the corner shop and grab me a bottle

and something to zap in the microwave? I'm going to be late leaving work and they'll be closed."

"Sure," Naomi said, glancing at the microwave. It wouldn't take two minutes to nip down the road. "What's going on?"

"There's some sort of major incident going on in Norwich. Four men got the crap beaten out of them on one of the estates. That, and the fact half the night shift hasn't turned up. But that's not why I'm going to be late. I'm going for a quick drink with someone after work."

"And who might that be?" Naomi asked, a slow smile spreading across her face.

"Never you mind, you nosey cow," Jennifer replied. "Listen, I need to go. It's really busy here."

"Okay, no worries," Naomi replied. She didn't know how her sister managed to cope with the pressure of working in such a busy emergency department. At least when Naomi was having a bad day, it didn't really mean much. In Jennifer's case, a bad day meant people died. "Of course. Are you okay?"

"I'm fine," Jennifer said, but Naomi could sense the stress in her voice. "Two secs."

Naomi heard a male voice in the background asking Jennifer something. From the other side of the kitchen, there was a loud ping as the microwave announced her dinner. Her stomach grumbled in response.

"Sorry," Jennifer said when she came back on the line. "That was your mate, Derek."

"Dave?"

"Derek, Dave, whatever," Jennifer replied, and Naomi was grateful to hear her sounding less stressed than a few seconds previously. "He's making me a brew, bless him."

Naomi groaned. Dave had many strengths, but making tea wasn't one of them.

"Just be nice and pretend it's lovely," she said, prompting a laugh from her sister.

"Don't worry, the minute his back's turned, it'll be straight down the sink," Jennifer replied.

"Is that who you're going for a drink with?" Naomi asked. "Would it be Dave, by any chance?"

"You have a good day?" Jennifer replied, and Naomi could tell from her voice she was smiling. The next time she spoke to her properly, she could get all the details then, so Naomi said nothing about the change in subject.

"Not too bad," Naomi said. "Busy, you know how it is." She thought back over the day, remembering the look of relief on Caleb's face as Dave had told him he was free to go. The CCTV footage from the supermarket had confirmed Caleb's movements and the fact he was nowhere near the vicarage at the time the vicar was murdered. That and a still from a passing dashboard camera showing a man who clearly wasn't Caleb entering the house where the women had been killed had done the deal. In the absence of any meaningful forensic evidence, Dave had told her, they had nothing to keep Caleb in custody for.

"Sure," Jennifer said. Naomi could hear the sharp, insistent ringing of a landline in the background. "Hey, listen. I need to go. The phone from ambulance control's going off. You'll grab me something from the corner shop, right?"

"Of course," Naomi replied. She was about to end the call when she thought of something else. "Jennifer? Those four men? Where were they hurt?"

"Um, Lark's Cross. The ambulance had to wait for a police escort to go in and get them."

Naomi ended the call, deep in thought. When he'd been

released from police custody, Naomi had offered to give Caleb a lift to wherever he needed to get to. She recalled his face hardening as he had replied.

"Could you drop me off near the Lark's Cross estate?" Caleb had said, a stony expression on his face. "I've got some business I need to attend to."

All thoughts of her supper forgotten, Naomi made her way to the door of Jennifer's flat, grabbing her car keys as she did so.

CHAPTER 70

"Caleb," Leon whispered. "Come on, man. We need to get out of here." In the distance, he could hear approaching sirens. Leon didn't know what type of emergency vehicles they would be, but even if they were ambulances, they wouldn't come onto the estate without the police.

He hooked his arm around Caleb's and pulled him toward the alleyway between two houses. Caleb looked at him with what was almost a blank expression. It didn't look as if he recognized Leon and a thin stream of blood was slowly making its way down the side of his head. Was he concussed?

"That shit was unreal," Leon said as they stumbled into the entrance of the alley. "Where d'you learn to do that?" Caleb didn't reply. He slipped and almost fell, causing Leon to tighten his grip on his arm.

Leon wasn't sure what to do. His priority was to get away from the incoming emergency vehicles. There was no way he was going to be caught with a gun that was still stuck in the seat of his pants. He'd not been able to free it at all, but hadn't needed to once Caleb had weighed in. But equally, Leon had not tried to assist Caleb in the fight even without the gun, and for that, he felt bad. Not that the man had needed any help. A split second after the fight had started, Syd had turned tail and fled, much to Leon's surprise.

"This way, mate," Leon said, pulling Caleb deeper into the shadows. Where should he go? He pushed Caleb gently against a wall on one side of the alley and, once he was sure he wasn't going to topple over, pulled his phone from his pocket.

"What?" Syd said a few seconds later when he answered. It sounded to Leon as if the man was running, or at least walking fast. He was out of breath, almost panting.

"Where are you, man?" Leon said, keeping his voice low. The sirens were growing louder.

"I'm lying low for a while," Syd replied. "I'm going to a mate's house for a couple of days, just until things die down a bit."

"Seriously?" Leon replied, incredulous. Syd was running away?

"What's it to you, bro?" Syd shot back. "You got any sense, you'll get off the estate as well. The old bill will be looking for us both."

"What about Caleb?"

"What about him?"

"He's hurt," Leon said, glancing at Caleb, who was still in the same position he'd left him against the wall. "He's got, like, a head injury." There was a silence on the end of the line and Leon glanced at the screen to see if Syd had discon-nected the call.

"Take him to the hospital, then," Leon heard Syd say

before an electronic click told him that he had now ended the call.

"For God's sake," Leon muttered. He reached out and grabbed Caleb's arm again. "Come on, man. Let's get going." He was going to have to take him to his own house and get him cleaned up. But his mother was going to do her nut. She would want to know why Caleb couldn't get medical help, and the number of blue lights that were beginning to flash amongst the tightly constructed houses of the estate would be a dead giveaway.

Leon led Caleb through the alleyways that intersected the houses, taking a roundabout route to his street. Caleb followed him wordlessly, but as long as he was still moving, Leon wasn't overly concerned. If he collapsed or anything like that, he would have to leave him where he was but could at least call in Caleb's location. Leon owed him that much, as did Syd, but his mentor had shown a different side to his personality. One which Leon didn't really care for. When the chips were down, that was when decent men stepped forward, not turned and ran.

A few moments later, Leon led Caleb to the entrance of the alleyway directly opposite his house. He could see from the lights in the windows that his mother was home. Leon would have some explaining to do, but he couldn't leave Caleb. He'd still not said a word, and that wound on the side of his head looked nasty in the poor light of the street lamps.

Leon glanced up and down the street. At the very end, a police car was slewed across the road, preventing access to the central part of the estate. But the coast was clear to his house. He took a couple of steps forward, pulling Caleb behind him, when he heard a car door opening.

"Leon?" a woman's voice said. "Leon Brockwell?"

Leon looked up to see the solicitor who'd bailed him out standing by a small red car. She had her hands folded over her chest and was looking at him with an expression that was somewhere between curiosity and anger. He saw her gaze flick to Caleb and then back at him.

"Do you want to tell me what the hell is going on?"

CHAPTER 71

Vince stared in horror at the screen in front of him. On it was a single image taken from the dashboard camera of an interfering member of the public. It was hazy and not the best quality, but it was him. Of that, there was no doubt. The screen showed him about to enter the gates of the house where Suzy and the old woman had been hiding.

He couldn't delete the image. Even the access rights he had to the Law Enforcement Data Service wouldn't allow him to do that. The only thing he could do was adjust the image subtly. The cursor dashed across the screen as he widened the distance between the eyes of the man on the screen by a fraction and pulled the chin down by a few centimeters. It was all he could do, and it should throw any facial recognition software off the scent, albeit briefly. He'd been so careful not to get caught by any of the many cameras between where he had parked the car and the house itself. It seemed every other house had CCTV cameras, complete with doorbells that recorded passersby. It wasn't as if he could walk down the street with a balaclava on.

Vince left the image and flipped to the crime report itself. The local police had found a man at the scene and arrested him on suspicion of murder. When he had first read this, Vince had smiled. He couldn't have arranged the misdirection better if he'd tried. Vince brought up the body camera of the arresting officer.

"Naughty, naughty," he said as he watched the police officer using his taser seconds before issuing a warning. Vince returned to the crime report to see the man they'd arrested was called Caleb, no surname given. He clicked on the small photograph of the suspect to enlarge it. As he had thought, it was the man from the bus, but at least now he had a name. "Hello, Caleb," Vince muttered. "So, who the hell are you?"

He switched back to the crime report and started reading the forensic summary. A broad smile spread across his face as he read through it. Damn, he was good. There was a forensic convention known as Locard's principle. Every contact leaves a trace. Unless you were Vince, that was. There was no significant forensic trace at all. They had a few fibers from some gloves that were now in a trash can in central London and a partial footprint from a pair of sneakers that were now in two different trash cans, again in London. The knife he had used was at the bottom of the Thames, where it would never be found. And even if the knife, the gloves, or the sneakers were recovered, there was no obvious link between them and the crime, let alone between them and him.

Vince brought up the recording of the interview with Caleb. He pressed play and, as he watched the gorilla who was doing the interview go through the motions, Vince turned his thoughts to Caleb. How much of a loose end was he? He knew Suzy from the bus, had left the bus with her, and taken her to a place of safety.

"No," Caleb said on the screen when the police officer asked him if he was guilty of murder. "No, I am not." Vince raised his eyebrows. He was American?

The police officer went on to talk about the murder at the vicarage. Vince frowned. He'd not been expecting them to make that link so soon. It didn't materially matter. He'd reviewed the LEDS entry for that investigation and that was cleaner than this one. But the common thread that linked them was this American on the screen. What had Suzy actually told him? Vince narrowed his eyes and stared at the man. He might have to go back to Norwich and tidy up this particular loose end. That would be a shame—he was very much looking forward to meeting young Rachel Parmenter and had already put several things in place to facilitate that —but Vince figured his trip to the south coast could wait. Rachel wasn't going anywhere in a hurry.

Vince changed screens again to review the arrest record of Caleb. To his annoyance, he saw the police had released him earlier that evening. He checked the notes of the investigating officer, along with the comments from the Crown Prosecution Service. Both agencies were pretty sure Caleb was involved to a greater extent than he was letting on, but they had no solid evidence to keep him, so had to cut him loose. Vince tutted, irritated by the rules being followed so rigidly.

He needed to find this Caleb. Hunt him down, find out what he knew. And, if necessary, which it almost certainly would be, neutralize him. Vince knew he had the tools at his disposal to find the man, even if he only had a first name. But that would take time, and Vince didn't have that luxury.

A shortcut was required, and Vince knew just the one he needed. He checked the interview record to make sure he had the right information. The mysterious Caleb might be in the wind, but his solicitor wouldn't be and she would know where he was.

Vince logged out of LEDS and opened up a fresh document. It was time to create a new profile. His fingers hovered over the keyboard before he began to type.

Naomi Tipton

CHAPTER 72

Naomi watched as Leon's mouth opened and closed like a goldfish. Next to him, Caleb was regarding her with a bemused expression. He was bleeding, a thin rivulet of blood on the side of his head.

"Well?" she said, taking a step toward Caleb. "What happened?" She reached her hand up to Caleb's face and tilted his head to one side so she could see his injury. There was a cut on his temple, not far from his eyebrow. It was perhaps an inch across, not particularly deep, and the blood was already beginning to dry.

"I fell over," Caleb said, looking at her with a faint smile. His voice was soft.

"Of course you did," Naomi replied with a frown, "and I'm going to be the next Queen of England." In the distance, Naomi could see a uniformed police officer standing by his car, its lights still flashing off the houses. He was looking in their direction. "What's going on over there?" she asked, looking at Leon as she did so.

"Er, there was a fight, I think," Leon replied. "I was going to take Caleb to my house, but my mum's going to go spare."

He was shuffling his feet and Naomi could feel the tension radiating from him. With a quick glance at the police officer, she made a decision.

"Right," Naomi said, turning her attention back to Caleb. Behind him, the police officer was walking down the road toward them. "Caleb, get in the car. And Leon? Go home." She nodded at the police officer. "Quick, before he gets here."

Naomi saw Leon's head jerk round and stare down the road. He mumbled something under his breath and, with a grateful nod in Naomi's direction, shot across the road. A few seconds later, his front door slammed behind him. She held Caleb's arm and guided him toward the passenger seat of her car, waiting until he was settled. The police officer was perhaps twenty yards away. Naomi didn't want him to get a close look at Caleb, so she walked toward the approaching man.

"Good evening, officer," Naomi said with a smile as she reached the police officer. He was an older man, perhaps in his late forties, and had the weathered face of a man who had seen everything. The equipment hanging from his utility belt didn't disguise his paunch and Naomi couldn't help but wonder when the last time he had been in a foot chase. Whenever it was, it wouldn't have lasted long. "What's going on over there?"

"Evening, ma'am," he replied. Naomi watched as he ran a practiced eye over her from top to toe before he looked at her car. She kept her eyes on him, not wanting to draw his attention to Caleb. "You look familiar. Do I know you?"

"Not professionally, no," Naomi said, forcing a light laugh out. "I'm Naomi Tipton, one of the duty solicitors. You might have seen me at the station."

The police officer's expression changed to one of recognition. He clicked his fingers together and grinned.

"That's it," he said. "I knew I'd seen your face before." Naomi couldn't say the same back to the man. She didn't recognize him at all. "You don't live round here, do you?"

"No," Naomi said. "I just had to pop some paperwork in for a client."

"Yeah, that makes sense," the police officer replied. "I bet you've got a fair few clients on this estate." They shared a conspiratorial smile, and he nodded at the car. "Makes sense to bring some protection. That your fella?"

"Um, yes," Naomi replied. She looked round to see Caleb with his head resting against the seatbelt. His eyes were closed, and he was hiding the trickle of blood behind the material of the belt. "He's had a couple of beers, though."

The police officer raised his hand to his earpiece and frowned. A few seconds later, she watched as he used the microphone pinned to the front of his vest to respond.

"I need to get going," he said. "Make sure you come and say hello the next time you're in the nick." The police officer nodded at Caleb. "You'd better get him home and into bed."

Naomi watched the police officer as he ambled back toward his marked car. Whatever the message had been on the radio couldn't have been urgent, or perhaps that was just the speed he normally used. She got into the car and sat behind the wheel, watching the officer for a moment before starting it.

"Thank you," Naomi heard Caleb say.

She glanced toward him, but he was still resting his head against the seatbelt, his eyes closed. He had obviously been involved in the fight, which meant that depending on what had actually happened, she was almost certainly breaking the law. Naomi mulled over the law in her mind. Assisting an offender depended on the offender having committed a relevant offense. She had been in court with more than one person facing those charges, and knew from bitter experience that when found guilty, the courts took a rather dim view of that type of behavior. Three years in prison was the starting point.

"What the hell am I doing?" Naomi muttered under her breath as she put the car into gear.

CHAPTER 73

As Naomi drove, Caleb replayed the fight with the four men back in the estate. He knew he'd made several mistakes, and the pain in his head was reminding him of one of them. Caleb hadn't been punched that hard in years and had forgotten how disorientating it was. He was aching in the left side of his chest as well, but didn't remember getting hit there. It must have been while he was still dazed from the blow to the side of his head. At least at that point in the brawl, no blades had been produced. If they had been, it could have been a different outcome. There were a lot of important things just under his ribs where the ache was, all of which would not react well to a knife.

Caleb mentally rewound the images in his head until the four men were standing in front of him. He adjusted his movement to account for the fact that at least one of the men—the one who had hit him—was a lot quicker than he looked. Caleb tried a couple of variants of his choreography until he found the one that would produce the ending he wanted. One without him ending up with a headache.

"How are you feeling?" Naomi asked from the driver's seat. Caleb turned to look at her, but she had her eyes fixed on the road ahead.

"Sore," he replied, "but I'll live."

"What happened?"

"There was an altercation."

"Obviously." Naomi glanced across at Caleb for a second or two before turning back to face the windshield. "Was Leon involved?"

Caleb thought back to the sight of Leon struggling, and failing, to pull the weapon from the back of his pants. There was a reason that was a poor place to store a pistol.

"He was there," Caleb said. "But he wasn't involved in the altercation."

"Who was the other guy?" Naomi asked. Caleb said nothing at first, figuring that Naomi would realize at some point there had been more than one of them.

"Just a would-be mugger. He was threatening one of Leon's friends, so I stepped in. But he was all hat and no cattle. Not much of an altercation, truth be told."

"Quite the good Samaritan, aren't you?" A barked laugh escaped Naomi's lips. "Is that what you do? Just wander the world saving people in distress like some of sort of Jack Reacher character?"

"Jack Reacher's way bigger than me," Caleb said, a slow smile on his face. "But he's just corn fed. I think I could take him down if it came to it."

"I doubt that very much," Naomi replied. "Unless he's the Tom Cruise version, not the other lad." When Caleb looked at her, she was smiling as well. She paused for a moment, her smile fading, before she asked him another question. "So, how do you know Leon?"

"I bumped into him a few days back," Caleb said, omitting any more information such as the circumstances. "You?"

"He's a client, obviously. But I can't tell you any more than that."

"Or you'd have to kill me?" Caleb's response caused another smile. That was two, in quick succession, both of which Caleb had enjoyed seeing. "Why did you do what you did back there? Send Leon into his house and lie to the policeman?"

"I didn't lie to the policeman," Naomi replied. "I was just economical with the truth."

"That's not an answer, Miss Tipton," Caleb said, extending her name into a pronounced Texan drawl. Three smiles.

"I don't know," Naomi said a moment later, slowing the car and putting on the turn signal. "Acting on instinct, I guess. My sister's always telling me I should do that more often. Be a bit more spontaneous."

"Do you think your instinct's right on that one?" Caleb asked her as she pulled the car in at the side of the road. She stopped the vehicle and took her hands from the wheel before turning to look at him. In contrast to the Lark's Cross estate, the road they were in was well lit and he could see a slight frown on her face.

"You're somehow mixed up in three murders, Caleb." He opened his mouth to protest, but she raised her hands palm out to silence him. "I know, I know, you're innocent of all of them. But you're involved somehow and then the next time I see you, you've been brawling in the street." She put her hands back in her lap and looked at him for several long seconds.

"I'm kinda hoping there's a but coming," he said. Four smiles.

"There is a but coming, yes," Naomi replied. "I'm just not sure what it is." She bit her bottom lip. "There's something about you that makes me want to, I don't know quite how to put it. Help you, maybe?"

"That wasn't what I was expecting you to say," Caleb said, raising his eyebrows. It had been years since anyone had said they'd wanted to help him, if at all. It was usually the other way round. "But I appreciate it." He nodded once and looked through the passenger window at the small apartment building Naomi had parked next to. "This your place?"

"Yep," Naomi replied as she opened the car door. "I was staying with my sister for a while, but I live here. I don't think my sister would appreciate me bringing a strange preacher man home. Besides, she's out on a date tonight, so it's probably better if I leave her to it. I'd better text her."

"Now I'm strange?" Caleb was aiming for a fifth smile, but all he got in return was a brief nod of Naomi's head. She was engrossed in her phone, and he liked the way the light from the screen lit up her face. "How come you were staying with your sister?"

Naomi's expression changed ever so slightly as she replied. Hardened almost imperceptibly. It was the briefest of looks, but Caleb caught it. He usually did.

"I had a rat problem," she replied, "but it's all sorted now." She didn't look at him as she spoke, but rummaged in her purse before pulling out a set of keys. "Come on up. Let's get you cleaned up."

CHAPTER 74

Leon lay back on his bed and stared at the soft green glow of his cell phone screen. He scrolled through the icons aimlessly, checking his WhatsApp messages as he did so. There was nothing from Syd. Leon had sent him several messages over the course of the evening, and they had been read from the two blue ticks, but no replies.

"For God's sake, man," Leon muttered under his breath. Why was Syd ghosting him? What had he done wrong?

As it had turned out, there was no reason Leon couldn't have brought Caleb back to the house. His mother was out, almost certainly in the pub, getting hammered. She would stumble in after chucking out time and haul herself into bed, or turn up in the morning looking shamefaced and hungover, claiming she'd slept on a friend's sofa and not really caring whether Leon believed her or not.

What was going to happen next, Leon wondered as he put his phone down. Syd would come back at some point, no doubt claiming victory. But what if the Albanians came back? More of them, and better prepared? Caleb might not be around next time, and even if he was, he was only one man. A smile spread across Leon's face as he remembered the way he had dispatched the four men who had clambered out of the car. Maybe he could teach Leon how to fight like that?

Leon picked up his phone again and opened up his browser, searching for martial arts gyms near him. He could join one, learn how to look after himself like Caleb could. Maybe beef himself up a bit at the same time. A few moments later, he had found a bloke called Ian who ran a gym round the back of one of the industrial estates on the edge of the city. Looking at Ian's photo on the website, he was a seriously hard-looking bloke and Leon was tempted with the offer of a free introductory session.

He put his phone down again and stared at the ceiling. In a few short months' time, he would finish school. Leon had no plans to stay on at college or get some crappy apprenticeship that paid next to nothing. His original plan had been to see if he could work for Syd full time, kind of as his chief of staff or second in command. That's the only reason he'd done the bus job. To prove to Syd that he was capable. Not just that, but he had some ideas about how to maximize their profit margin. And if Syd was growing his own product? Well, no reason why Leon couldn't teach himself about how to do that better as well.

Leon let his thoughts drift, knowing he was too wired after the excitement of the evening to sleep. He imagined a scenario in which he and Syd were equal partners. Where he wasn't working for Syd, but with him. They could gradually expand the farming side of the operation, take over more apartments in the complex. If what Caleb had said earlier was true, they could persuade more tenants to move out and take over two floors. Three, even. There were plenty more places in Norwich where they could sell weed, and London was only a couple of hours down the road. If they met any resistance, Leon could dispatch them with a few well-placed kicks or blows, just like Caleb.

But a few moments later, Leon's daydream evaporated. Who was he trying to kid? He was fifteen, barely old enough to shave. The chances of him becoming a drug lynch pin in Norwich or anywhere else were few and far between. He heard a man shouting outside. Not an unusual occurrence on the estate, especially when the pubs closed. There was a cackle of female laughter in response. Leon's heart sunk. His mother was back.

Leon lay still as he heard the front door opening before being closed quietly. That was a good sign. When his mother was properly drunk, it would be slammed shut. He heard her moving about downstairs, fetching herself a glass of water. Then the stairs creaked as she made her way up the stairs. He closed his eyes and turned over just in case she decided to check in on him, but she didn't. A moment later, he heard her bedroom door close.

He sighed, swearing under his breath as he did so. A few days ago, things seemed to be looking up. Now, in the space of a single evening, it had all gone to shit.

CHAPTER 75

Vince drummed his fingers on his desk in frustration. Naomi Tipton was proving a rather elusive woman, and he'd not been able to find out much about her beyond the basics. Nothing on LEDS, although given that she was a solicitor, that wasn't a surprise. He had her address from her driver's license, but as far as social media went, there was nothing. She didn't use any of the usual platforms, nor any of the more discrete ones. Not that Vince needed that level of detail. He just enjoyed digging into people's lives as they lived them on the internet so he could contrast their drab reality when he finally met them. Vince had what he needed already. He just needed a plan.

Closing the laptop, Vince got to his feet and poured himself a glass of vodka. According to the man who had given him the bottle, it was one of the finest vodkas ever to leave the original Stolichnaya distillery when it was based in the Moscow State Wine Warehouse. The man then started telling Vince a convoluted story about Putin coming to power, but Vince had closed him down. He had no interest in the man's story, nor really the vodka, but the man had just paid Vince an eye-watering amount of money for an off the books piece of executive action, so the least he could do was accept the gift.

The fundamental problem that Vince had was time. He couldn't take any more time off work, especially as other teams were closing in on a target they'd been tracking for months. When the target was confirmed, it would only be Vince's team who would be involved in the takedown and there might not be much notice. Returning to Norwich so soon would be a risk. But even riskier was what Vince didn't know. Which was how much Suzy had told this Caleb about him, and the only way he could discover that was to find Caleb.

Vince was still irritated with the speed that Caleb had been released, especially as he'd not provided the police with anything other than his first name. Vince sipped his vodka as he pondered how Naomi Tipton had pulled that off. He thought back to the body camera that showed Caleb's arrest. She must have negotiated with them, pointing out that shooting a man in the back with a Taser while he was praying was neither necessary nor proportionate. A quid pro quo of sorts.

Even if he went to Norwich and visited young Naomi, there was no guarantee that she would know where Caleb was. Vince wasn't bothered about her not telling him if she knew—he could be quite persuasive when he needed to be —but she might not actually know. Or he could just leave them alone. The worst case scenario was that Suzy had told Caleb about him, and he had told Naomi, who had told the police. But where would that leave the police? With an altogether fanciful sounding story about a man who lived in the shadows.

Vince refilled his glass and mulled things over for a while longer. When he'd applied to join the security services, part of the application process had been to complete a Belbin exercise to find out their team roles. While Vince had thought at the time it was a waste of time and money, he had to agree that his apparent role as a Completer Finisher wasn't that far off the mark. According to the report, he was the one who polished and scrutinized work for errors—striving for perfection in an imperfect world. And the thought that Suzy might have told someone about him was one of those imperfections. Caleb needed to be found and taken out of the equation, and the only way he could do that was through Naomi.

He tilted his head back and drained the glass in one motion, grimacing at the bitter taste. If this was what people in Russia drunk for enjoyment, they could keep it, Vince thought as he patted his pocket to check his car keys were there.

It was time to pay Miss Tipton a house call. Best case was that she would know Caleb's location and tell Vince where he was. Worst case was that she didn't know where he was, and Vince would be back at square one.

But either case meant he and Naomi could have some fun together. Vince wasn't going to kill her, though. That would just bring more unwanted attention, potentially his way. Besides, women were so much more satisfying when they were broken.

CHAPTER 76

Caleb angled his head to the side so he could see the wound in the small mirror he was holding. He balanced the mirror on Naomi's coffee table by leaning it up against a bottle of wine and used one hand to push the edges of the skin together. With the other hand, he squeezed the tube of Superglue gently so that a bead of the liquid glue appeared at the end of the nozzle. Then he touched the bead to the top of the wound and watched in the mirror as it rolled down the skin edges. Caleb repeated the motion for the bottom edge of the injury before holding the skin edges in place for twenty seconds or so. When he removed his fingers, the wound was almost invisible. He nodded at his reflection in satisfaction before replacing the lid on the nozzle, although he doubted Naomi would want to use it for anything else. The mug in the sink might have to stay busted.

He was sitting in the den of her small apartment, freshly showered and dressed in a pair of sweatpants and a t-shirt that Naomi had found for him. They were male garments, but she offered no explanation for whose they were, nor had he asked. Naomi was in the shower and he could hear the water through the thin walls.

Naomi's apartment was, by US standards, tiny. He had only seen the den he was currently in, the bathroom, and the kitchen where he had found the tube of glue. There were two other doors, so he assumed there were two bedrooms, but that was it. Caleb liked it, though. Naomi had obviously taken great care in choosing the decor, and it was decorated tastefully. Definitely a female apartment from the soft pastels on the walls. The den was only large enough for a single sofa, the coffee table, and a large flat screen television.

Caleb got to his feet and crossed to the mantelpiece to look at the photographs on display above the modern-looking gas fireplace. There weren't many. One of Naomi with a woman who he assumed was her sister, the nurse whom Naomi had earlier threatened to ask to call round after work to check on him. In the photograph, the two women were on a beach in front of deep blue skies and a verdant ocean. Almost certainly not a British beach. They were both smiling at the camera, complicated-looking drinks in their hands. There was another of just Naomi, wearing a mortar board and clutching a scroll of paper in her hands. She had an excited expression on her face, part laughter and part relief. The only other photos he could see were a small one of an older couple, and one of a black and tan Dachshund looking mournfully at the camera. Caleb tilted his head slightly to one side. From the look of the fine layer of dust on the mantelpiece, there had been a further photograph there until recently.

"They're my parents, and the dog was called Biscuit," Naomi's voice said from behind him. "In case you were wondering." Caleb turned to look at her. She was wearing a pair of sweatpants similar to his, but much better fitting, and a loose t-shirt. Her hair was damp from the shower and she had tied it up into a loose ponytail. Naomi nodded at the bottle of wine on the table, the small mirror still leaning against it. "I'm going to have a glass of wine. Do you want one?"

"Why not?" Caleb replied with a smile. He saw her face drop.

"Oh, I wasn't thinking. Maybe you shouldn't have one with a head injury?"

"I don't think a glass of wine will kill me, Naomi," Caleb said. "And if you're having one, it would be rude not to keep you company."

It took Naomi a few moments to notice Caleb's self-administered repairs. By then, they were sitting next to each other on the sofa. Her eyes widened and her eyebrows shot up.

"Oh, my God," she said. "What did you do?"

"I hope you don't mind, but I used the Superglue in the kitchen."

"You glued your head closed?" Naomi said with a laugh, her eyebrows raising even further. "Are you serious? Let me see."

Naomi unfolded her legs and kneeled on the sofa next to Caleb. He tilted his head slightly to allow her a better look. She shuffled forward and put her fingertips next to the wound on the side of his head. Caleb winced.

"Oh, sorry," Naomi whispered. "Is that sore?"

"No," Caleb replied. "Your fingertips are freezing."

"That'll be from the wineglass."

He hadn't just winced from her fingertips, though. As she had shuffled forward to kneel next to him, she had pressed one of her breasts against his upper arm. He could feel the firmness of it still through the thin material, but she made no effort to move away.

Caleb sat still as Naomi examined his head. Out of the corner of his eye, he could see a small vein pulsing in the side of her neck. He couldn't help but count her heart rate. It was over one hundred and twenty beats per minute. Much too fast to be normal.

A moment later, she shuffled again and turned to face him.

"Are you hurt anywhere else?" she asked, her eyes flicking between his. "You were holding your chest in the car."

"I think I took a whack to my ribs at some point."

Naomi's eyes flickered down to his t-shirt.

"Come on, take it off. Let me see."

"I'm fine."

"Don't argue. I'll need to be able to tell Jennifer I've looked you over properly."

Caleb paused for a moment before slowly easing the t-shirt over his head. He saw Naomi's eyes widen as she reached out to touch his right shoulder.

"Is that a bullet hole?" she asked him as her fingers stopped just short of his skin.

"Not anymore."

"Can I touch it?"

"Sure." Caleb jumped as her fingertips touched his skin, causing Naomi to do the same thing. He started laughing. "Sorry, I couldn't resist." The vein in her neck was still pulsing.

"And this one?" Naomi's fingers brushed against his abdomen where a thin line of scar tissue was lined with small, ugly puckered holes. "What happened here?"

"I cut myself shaving," Caleb replied with a wry grin. "I

thought you were interested in any fresh injuries, not my old ones."

"I am, sorry," Naomi replied, a faint flush appearing on her cheeks. "Where else are you hurt? Any aching anywhere?"

Caleb pressed his lips together to stop the smile he could feel building. If he answered that question honestly, he would probably get a slap to the face.

CHAPTER 77

Naomi helped Caleb ease his t-shirt back over his head before returning to her original position on the couch. She was itching to ask Caleb more about the various scars on his body, but sensed he didn't want to talk about them. The only fresh injury she had seen had been a slight reddening of his chest wall on Caleb's right hand side. Naomi had pushed and prodded, with no idea what she was looking for, but Caleb hadn't seemed to mind, so she was sure it wasn't serious.

"Do you want another glass of wine?" she asked him. He nodded in reply.

She got to her feet and walked into the kitchen, pausing to turn the thermostat on the wall down by a couple of degrees. When she returned with a fresh bottle of white wine from the fridge, Caleb was sitting with his eyes closed and his hands resting on his lap. She resumed her position at the other end of the sofa and took a moment to look at him. He looked very serene, almost peaceful. Then, as if he sensed her gaze on him, he opened his eyes and looked at her.

"Sorry," Naomi said. "You looked like you were praying, so I didn't want to interrupt."

"That's very thoughtful, Naomi, thank you."

"Were you? Praying, I mean?"

"Kind of. More reflecting than praying." Naomi leaned forward and topped up their wine glasses. "Do you ply all your clients with wine, Naomi?" he asked her.

"You're not a client anymore," Naomi replied with a laugh. "If you were, I would bill you for this conversation. And the wine." She sipped from her glass and looked at Caleb over the top of the rim. "Tell me a bit more about yourself."

"What would you like to know?" Caleb raised his own glass, but Naomi wasn't sure that he actually took a drink from it. She paused before replying. There was a lot she wanted to know, and there was a lot she would never have the nerve to ask.

"Where are you from?"

"Texas."

"Where in Texas?"

"A two horse town in the middle of nowhere that you'll never have heard of."

Naomi took another sip, wondering what to ask him next.

"Have you always been a preacher man?"

"Not always, no. I kind of fell into it."

"What did you do before?"

"Nothing important."

"Bloody hell, you're hard work, Caleb." Naomi started laughing. "You're not really the sharing type, I guess."

"No, it's not that," Caleb replied, finally reaching for his glass. "But all that's in the past. And the future's not happened yet, so all that's left is the now. Do you read scripture, Naomi?"

"Um, no. Not really." Naomi looked at Caleb, wondering where he was going with the conversation. He had an almost playful expression on his face.

"Luke, chapter nine, verse sixty two."

"Right," Naomi replied, a half smile on her own face. "You might have to help me out a little?"

"No one who puts a hand on the plow and looks back is fit for service in the kingdom of God."

"Okay," Naomi said. "That makes sense. Don't worry about the past."

"There's also Matthew, chapter six, verse thirty-four." Naomi raised her eyebrows at Caleb. "Therefore, do not worry about tomorrow, for tomorrow will worry about itself. Each day has enough trouble of its own."

"Have you memorized the entire bible?"

"Only the good bits," Caleb replied, his smile broadening, "and the bits that say what I want to say."

Naomi laughed at his response. "That's not a bad way to live, I guess."

"It works for me."

"So, carpe diem is how you live your life. Is that right?" Naomi asked. "No past, no future. Just now." She emptied her wineglass and placed it on the carpet next to the sofa, folding her legs under her as she did so.

"That's not quite what carpe diem means, Naomi," Caleb said. "May I take your hands?"

Naomi paused for a moment, looking at Caleb's hands which were extended toward her.

"Where are we going, Caleb?" she replied as she slipped her hands into his. His skin was warm. Comforting.

"While we speak, envious time has already fled. Seize

the moment, trust in the future as little as possible." Caleb's voice was soft, almost a whisper.

"Is that in the Bible?" Naomi replied, her voice also soft.

"No, it's from a Roman poet."

"Where are we going, Caleb?" Naomi asked again.

"Nowhere you don't want to go, Naomi. Just trust in yourself."

Caleb's eyes were closed. They sat in silence for a moment, Naomi trying to quell the thoughts that were rushing through her head. She could feel a warmth in her core that was growing by the second. Her heart was thumping hard in her chest. She wanted to kiss him. But she couldn't. Could she?

Then, the thoughts in her head dissipated, leaving nothing but an innate desire she didn't think she'd ever experienced before.

"Carpe diem it is, then," she whispered as she leaned forward.

CHAPTER 78

Leon swore under his breath at the insistent ringing from his bedside table. He opened his eyes, realizing it was still dark outside, and grabbed the phone. According to the screen, it was just before six in the morning and it was Syd who was trying to get hold of him.

"What is it, man? You know how early it is?" Leon said as he answered the call. It wasn't just the fact that it was early that was bothering him. It was the fact he'd barely slept a wink all night. Every time he closed his eyes, thoughts and images rushed into his head. Ones where the outcome of the previous evening were different. One in particular that kept haunting him saw Leon holding his Glock in front of him, smoke drifting from the barrel as an Albanian lay dead on the ground. The same Glock that was currently under his mattress.

"I need your help, bro," Syd said. His voice was fast and clipped, and Leon wondered what he had snorted. "I need you to go round to the flats and refill the water containers for the plants." So Caleb's suspicions had been true after all.

"I got stuff to do, Syd," Leon replied. A few days ago, he would have seen the request as a huge step up. A move closer to Syd's inner circle of trust. But now, Leon wasn't so sure.

"It won't take you long, mate," Syd said. "I'll see you right for your time."

"Why can't you do it?"

"I got business." The way Syd pronounced the word business was truncated, sounding like *bidness*.

"What business you got at this hour, Syd?" Leon asked. There was a silence on the other end of the line. Syd wasn't used to being questioned, especially by an underling, but Leon didn't care. He couldn't get the sight of Syd's face just before he left him and Caleb out of his mind's eye.

"My business, Leon, is my business. Not your business." There was an edge to Syd's voice that would have been a warning before, but Leon wasn't feeling it. "Can you help out or not? 'Cos there're plenty of others who will."

"Why d'you run, Syd?" Leon said, sitting on the edge of his bed and massaging his temples with his free hand. "We had a wounded man, and you just did one."

"I had to get off the estate, man," Syd shot back, the tension obvious in his voice. "The bizzies were all over the place. You know that. After the stabbing and what happened last night, it's not safe for me to be there at the moment."

"But it's safe for me, right?"

"You're just a kid, Leon," Syd said. "You're not even old enough to shave. They won't look twice at someone like you."

Leon paused before replying. The phrase *someone like you* had been delivered with what sounded like contempt.

But it wasn't Leon who had run away. He had stayed to help Caleb, get him to safety. If it had been Syd who was hurt, Leon would have helped him. But would Syd have helped him? Leon shook his head slowly, knowing the answer.

"I got stuff to do, Syd," Leon said. "You'll have to find someone else." His finger hovered over the screen, preparing to end the call.

"You're shitting me," Syd barked down the line. "After everything I've done for you? You ungrateful little bastard." His voice changed, became more conciliatory. "Come on, man, please? I'll make it worth your while."

"I told you, Syd, I've got stuff to do today," Leon replied. "Talk later, yeah?"

Leon ended the call before Syd could reply. He stared at his phone for a few seconds, wondering if he would phone back, even if it was just to abuse him. But the phone remained silent. He put the handset back on the bedside table and put his head in his hands. Had he just burned the bridges he'd spent months building?

Knowing there was no point trying to get back to sleep, Leon padded to the bathroom, careful to tip-toe past his mother's door. The last thing he needed was her banging around, somewhere between still drunk and hungover, at that time in the morning.

Twenty minutes later, Leon was sitting at the kitchen table, munching on some dry toast. He used his phone to scroll through his socials, but there was nothing interesting. He brought up the website for the local paper but, as usual, it was full of people whining about something or other. His attention was drawn briefly to an article about a new striker his local team was apparently interested in, but almost certainly wouldn't be able to afford.

Outside the kitchen window, the sun was just beginning to illuminate Lark's Cross. He crossed to the window to put his plate in the sink and looked out at the gray monotony of the buildings outside. Leon took a deep breath and nodded. He had just decided something.

Somehow, sometime, he was getting off the estate.

CHAPTER 79

Caleb lay back on the bed and laced his fingers behind his head. He was in Naomi's spare bedroom, which was barely large enough for the single bed he was lying in. Outside the window, he could hear birds singing as they welcomed the new day. By his reckoning, it was some time after six. Caleb stretched, enjoying the sensation of release the movement gave him.

His thoughts drifted back to the previous evening, and Caleb smiled. What had happened was not what he had expected at all. When Naomi had kissed him, at first she had been tentative. He hadn't exactly protested, but at the same time, he'd responded in the same way.

"Are you sure about this?" he had asked her more than once. She hadn't replied and within a few quick moments, it had been too late to ask her if she was sure. She obviously was. So sure that they'd not even moved from the sofa. Caleb had been as gentle as he could, knowing that she wanted more than just sex. Naomi had said or done nothing to that effect, but Caleb could sense it. He had slowly transferred their actions away from his pleasure and towards hers. If Naomi had noticed, she said nothing. She'd not said anything until some moments after they had finished. They were entangled on the sofa, her astride him and still breathing hard, when she had whispered in his ear.

"Let's go to bed."

Caleb had climbed out of her bed only a couple of hours ago, leaving Naomi sound asleep, a half-smile on her face. Their second time once they had moved to the bedroom had been much slower, but at the same time, more absolute, if that were possible. There hadn't been a third time. Not for Caleb, at least, but he hoped there had been for Naomi. He'd done his best on that front. His grin spread as he remembered the feel of Naomi's body and the way she tried so hard not to make any noise. In his opinion, it only made things more erotic when soft moans did escape. He had wanted to stay, but he knew she would be better off waking up alone.

Reluctantly, Caleb forced himself to concentrate on something else. It was a new day, and he had work to do. His primary objective was to locate Leanne and ensure her safety. His secondary was to locate Vince and deal with him appropriately. Ideally, both objectives would be achieved at the same time. But Leanne could be anywhere, and Caleb didn't know where to start.

He tried to think like Vince. If he was going to kidnap and hide a child, where would he put them? Thinking this way didn't come easily to Caleb, but he tried as hard as he could. The child was either with Vince, or he had an accomplice or accomplices who were hiding her for him. It was an unfortunate fact of life that there would be people who would do that. Caleb thought it would be reasonably close by, purely for logistical reasons. Vince had taken her from the house, presumably under duress, and the longer the transportation time, the higher the risk.

Caleb needed to find Vince, and quickly. But the difficulty there was that if the man was in fact a member of the security services, he would be hard to find. It wasn't as if Caleb could just go to wherever their headquarters was and just ask for him, was it? The chances were the man wasn't even called Vince. Caleb had no photographs of him for reference. He didn't even have a description of the man.

He sat up in bed, frustrated. Finding people was hard enough, but chasing a shadow was next to impossible.

Caleb heard the toilet flushing through the thin door of Naomi's guest bedroom and, a moment later, the sound of the shower starting up drowned out the birdsong outside. He closed his eyes, briefly entertaining the idea of seeing if Naomi would allow him to join her, before discounting it. His stomach grumbled, and he realized he'd not eaten since the previous afternoon. Rummaging through Naomi's kitchen for food, even if it was for a breakfast for both of them, seemed presumptuous.

He got to his feet and stretched again. Coffee would be good. Or would Naomi prefer tea, like so many Brits seemed to? The only problem with that was that he wouldn't know how to make it their way. He'd noticed a coffee percolator in Naomi's kitchen the previous evening, which he was much more familiar with.

Caleb made his way to the kitchen, pausing at the bathroom door for a few seconds and allowing his earlier fantasy to return, if only briefly. He found filter papers and cups in a cupboard, but it took him longer to locate the coffee grounds. A moment later, the percolator was gurgling.

He sat down at the kitchen table to wait for Naomi and his thoughts turned again to Vince. If he couldn't find him, and this was the most likely scenario, he was going to have to try a different tack.

Caleb was going to have to make Vince find him.

CHAPTER 80

Naomi gasped as she put her hand under the shower before reaching for the tap to increase the water temperature. She shivered a couple of times while she waited for the ancient boiler to burst into life. A moment later, steam clouded the shower cubicle as the pipes in her apartment rattled and she stepped inside gratefully.

When she had woken up, Naomi had initially thought she'd had some sort of lucid dream involving Caleb. As her head had cleared, she realized it hadn't been a dream at all. She'd not dreamed about them together. It had actually happened. On the pillow next to her, there was still an indentation where his head had been. Naomi had sat up, clutching the duvet to her chest, to see where Caleb was. Had he just crept away in the night? Naomi had heard of people doing that, but no one had ever done it to her. She'd not put herself in a situation where that was a possibility before. But she could see through her bedroom door that the door to the guest bedroom was closed. Naomi always left it open to let the air circulate, so she had known he must be in there.

Naomi had lain back in her bed for a moment, pulling the duvet over her head. What had she done? She barely knew the man, and she had welcomed him into her bed. Naomi grinned for a second, remembering what they had done on the sofa before they'd made it that far, before a fierce blush made her face burn. He was injured. Wounded. And she had all but molested him. Naomi had laughed briefly before putting her hands over her face, mortified.

As she let the hot water cascade over her, Naomi wondered what the etiquette was for the morning after you had slept with a virtual stranger. Should they both ignore what had happened? Make some small talk but not mention it? And then, when the small talk was exhausted, go their separate ways? Jennifer would know, but she was the last person Naomi was going to tell about what she and Caleb had done. Naomi could imagine the look of horror on her sister's face as her normally restrained sibling confessed to a one-night stand.

You did what? Jennifer would say before collapsing into laughter. *You little slut!* Then she would demand to know all the details. What they had done. How they had done it. And, inevitably, whether she had enjoyed it.

Naomi lathered her body, almost as if she was washing the previous evening away. But she wasn't. Naomi had enjoyed it very much indeed, not that anyone would ever know. Except perhaps Caleb, who had seemed to know exactly what she wanted.

A few moments later, her hair damp, Naomi wrapped herself in a dressing gown and stepped out of the bathroom. There was a glorious scent of fresh coffee in the air and she walked into the kitchen to see Caleb sitting at the table.

Naomi met his eyes before looking away, ashamed and embarrassed. When she looked back at him a few seconds later, he had a wry smile on his face.

"Mornin'," Caleb said, extending the word into a drawl.

"Good morning," Naomi replied, automatically, as if he was someone she had just met at a bus stop.

Caleb got to his feet and pulled out a chair. He gestured for her to sit down as he poured her a cup of coffee.

"Milk? Sugar?" he asked her. She nodded as she sat down, not able to meet his eyes.

"Yes, please," Naomi said. "Um, listen, Caleb. About last night?" Might as well get it out in the open. "I've, er, I've not done that before."

"Are you serious?" Caleb replied, and she could sense the smile in his voice. "Only for a virgin, you sure seemed to know what you were doing."

Despite the awkwardness she felt, Naomi laughed.

"No, I'm not a virgin. I mean, I wasn't. I have done, er, *that* before." She looked at him, shamefaced. "Just not with someone I barely know."

"So?" Caleb said, his eyebrows raised.

"How do you mean, so?"

"So what, I guess. Happens all the time, I reckon."

"Oh, God, this is difficult. What must you think of me?" Naomi could feel a lump forming in her throat but had no idea why. Caleb reached his hands across the table and took her hands in his. Naomi took a deep breath, remembering what the same gesture had led to the previous evening.

"What I think is this, Naomi." Caleb paused, and she looked up at him, this time holding his gaze. "I think that last night you saw an opportunity for some intimacy which you wanted. Perhaps even needed." His eyes bored into hers as they had done last night, and she felt incredibly vulnerable yet safe at the same time. "And you took that opportunity. Where's the harm in that?"

Her eyes glanced at the wound on the side of his head.

"But you're wounded. I feel as if I took advantage of you. I mean, it was kind of me who started it."

"I was hardly a reluctant participant, Naomi," Caleb said. The way he said her name sent a flutter through her chest.

"Can I ask you something?" she said.

"Ask away."

"Um, was it a one off, or do you think it'll happen again?"

"Can I finish my coffee first?" Caleb smiled, and Naomi started laughing. But her laughter was cut short by the chiming of a bell toward the front of the apartment.

"Oh, shit," Naomi said, staring open-mouthed at Caleb. "There's someone at the door."

CHAPTER 81

Vince adjusted his position in the rear of his car, trying to make sure that he couldn't be seen by the woman he was watching if she turned around. He was parked around a hundred yards away from the door he had been watching for the last hour or so and, apart from a couple of dog walkers who had been more interested in what their dogs had produced than anything else, the woman was the first person he had seen.

He raised his phone, using his fingers to zoom in on the screen, and tapped a couple of times to capture the woman at the door. Although the windows were heavily tinted, the phone's camera was powerful enough to retain enough detail through the dark glass. He knew who it was from her Facebook page. Naomi's sister, Jennifer, was much less concerned about her on-line presence than her sibling. Vince waited, still holding the phone aloft, for the door to be answered. When it did open, Vince captured several pictures of Naomi herself, wearing a dressing gown and a surprised expression on her face. Then the door closed behind Jennifer as she entered the apartment. According to the clock on his phone, it was just before seven in the morning. From the expression on Naomi's face, an early morning visit from her sister was unusual.

Vince clambered over the seat and back into the front of the car. He drummed his fingers on the steering wheel a couple of times before starting the engine. It wouldn't be long before the surrounding streets would be busy. If anything, he was surprised at the lack of people about already, but a change in location was required. His plan was to park his car in the parking lot of a restaurant the next street over, and double back to take up a position at a bus stop close to Naomi's apartment. Jennifer, and hopefully Naomi, would have no choice but to drive past him.

As he drove, Vince tapped at his phone screen until he found the number he was looking for. A few seconds later, a male voice came through the speakers in his car.

"Emergency Department?" the voice said.

"Hi," Vince replied, lowering his voice by an octave or two. "Is Jennifer there, please?"

"Hang on." The sound in the speakers became muffled, but he could hear the man who had answered the phone. "She's not in until eight. Can I take a message?"

"No, I'll try her cell," Vince replied before thanking the man and ending the call.

Vince found a parking space near to the bus stop, but when he looked at it, there were several seniors already waiting. He was reasonably inconspicuous in the car and had a good view of the road leading from Naomi's apartment, so he decided to stay put. With cars parked on both sides, the street wasn't wide enough for her sister to turn her car around, so this was the only way she could come.

While he waited, Vince brought up the browser on his phone and navigated to a realtor's website he'd found the previous evening. The page was a couple of years old, but it showed Naomi's apartment before she had bought it. As well as photographs of the interior, there was also a floor plan. Vince took a moment to review it, but there wasn't a great deal to review. Two bedrooms, a lounge, bathroom, and kitchen. One way in, one way out, unless she left through the garden which Vince doubted she would do. The smaller of the two bedrooms was neighbored by other rooms, so if he needed to be noisy, that would be his room of choice. Vince didn't want any nosy neighbors hearing him and Naomi enjoying themselves through the walls.

But, tempting as it was, Vince didn't think that getting to know each other that way was a sensible option. He'd had to re-evaluate his plans somewhat. Naomi was a solicitor, not some down-beat woman with no friends or people to look out for her. Any assault on her would be investigated with much more enthusiasm by the local law enforcement officers. And if he made the visit into a terminal event, the heat it would bring down would be intense. Vince didn't want or need that level of attention. He just needed some information from her, so he would have to be more subtle.

In the trunk of his car, Vince had a bag with all the equipment he would need. Among the kit were several listening devices, including his personal favorite, the Endura black box recorder. The recorder wasn't as good as the ones he used for work, but they were more than capable for his needs. Around the size of a packet of cigarettes, they could record for weeks with their built-in voice activated microphones.

He scrolled through the photographs of Naomi's apartment. One could go inside the housing of the stove. One could be placed in the bathtub's paneling. The lounge and bedrooms wouldn't be as straightforward, but who looked in the frame of their sofas or beds routinely? A couple of zip ties would do the job. The only downside was that he would need to retrieve them to gain access to the recordings as opposed to having the audio uploaded to a server some-where, but as they could be bought online, they were as good as untraceable. If he used any of his work kit for the same purpose, they wouldn't be.

Vince wasn't bothered about that element, though. He thought he would only need a day or two of surveillance to get the information he needed. The only problem would be if he didn't find out Caleb's location that way, he would need to think of another method. Perhaps going back to Plan A would be required after all? Vince smirked as he put his phone down on the passenger seat. He had plenty of zip ties in the trunk for that eventuality as well.

CHAPTER 82

"What is it exactly I'm looking for, Syd?" Leon pressed the cell phone against his ear and looked at the contraption in front of him. He was in Syd's kitchen, staring at the cupboard under his sink.

"You see the reverse osmosis unit?" Syd replied. Leon looked at the device under the sink. Several large, empty water barrels were standing next to it.

"I think so, yeah." Leon had decided that he would help Syd out just one last time, not feeling ready just yet to make the break completely. After all, he still needed money. But he was planning on speaking to his career advisor at school to ask if it was too late to apply to stay on at college. Once he had a proper plan, he would tell Syd to stick his business where the sun doesn't shine.

"There's a small tap on the pipe and a thin blue hose. Stick the hose in the barrel and turn the tap. That's it."

Leon did as instructed and, a few seconds later, was looking at a pathetic dribble coming from the hose.

"How long is it going to take to fill the barrel?" he asked. "There's not much flow."

"There won't be," Syd replied. "Probably an hour per barrel. Then it's just a case of swapping out the empty barrels in the flat with the full ones. Everything else is automatic."

Leon glanced at his watch. He could fill this barrel, then get the next one going while he nipped back home for breakfast. He would be back in plenty of time for the final one.

"You owe me for this, Syd," Leon said. He heard Syd laughing down the line.

"Yep, I do. You know me, Leon. I always pay my dues." Leon made sure Syd had disconnected the call before he replied.

"Yeah, sure you do."

Leon wandered around the apartment while he waited for the barrel to fill. It was the first time he'd been there without Syd or another of his cronies hanging around. Whether that was a sign of Syd's increased trust in him, or a sign that the man was desperate, Leon wasn't sure. He watched the television for a while but soon got bored.

He walked into the lounge and across to the key cabinet on the wall. Leon checked his phone for the combination that Syd had texted to him and opened the cabinet. He wanted to have a proper look at Syd's operation. Maybe he could come up with a few ways to optimize it? Syd was coming back that day and Leon was planning on talking to him properly—about his plans for college.

With the keys to the three other apartments on the floor in his hand, Leon left Syd's place and made his way to the first one. He remembered Caleb placing a hand against the door and Leon repeated the gesture. But he couldn't feel any difference in the temperature of the door like Caleb had been able to. Leon opened the apartment door and stepped inside.

The interior was almost a mirror image of Syd's place. Leon made his way to the master bedroom, which is where Syd had told him the plants were growing. He pushed against the door, which opened with a subtle hiss as if it was hermetically sealed.

"Bloody hell," Leon whispered as he took in the sight in front of him. There were perhaps twenty plants with thick, lush foliage. They were cylindrical, their flowers reaching up toward the LED lights hanging from the ceiling. The windowless room stunk, the air almost fetid with the unmistakable cloying smell of cannabis. In the room's corner, Leon saw the water barrel he would need to replace. There was a pipe leading to the large tray the plants were sitting in, and a cable leading from the barrel to a power extension cord which was full of timers.

Leon took a few moments to explore the small room, making sure the door was closed to keep the odor in the room. On the ceiling were large silver extraction ducts fed by a fan that looked just like the fan in Leon's bathroom, apart from the charcoal filter. On the floor, a series of desk fans were pushing the air around the room. The primary limitation that Leon could see was the fact all the devices in the room were being powered by a single socket.

Closing the door behind him, Leon looked around the rest of the apartment. The room that would have been a lounge was full of drying racks, currently empty, and a marine dehumidifier sat silently in the corner. The second bedroom just had a desk and boxes of small plastic bags that Leon recognized as the ones used to sell the product. On the desk was a set of digital scales. Both the kitchen and bathroom were unused and empty.

Leon made his way back to Syd's apartment, thinking hard. There was a lot of wasted real estate in the apartment. The second bedroom could, if the windows were properly sealed, be a second growing room. In the drying room, there was plenty of space for more racks, especially if they were vertical instead of the horizontal ones he'd just seen. The kitchen could be used for preparation if they installed some opaque film on the windows. If the other two apartments were mirror images of the one he had just seen, they might double the output. And why not put one of the osmosis machines in the kitchens to water the plants directly instead of lugging heavy barrels of water around?

By the time he got back to the apartment, Leon had got several ideas to run past Syd that evening. He made a few notes on an app on his phone while he waited for the water barrel to fill to the top before placing the hose in the next barrel.

Leon hadn't changed his mind about going to college. But maybe there was a middle ground? He smirked as he closed the front door to Syd's apartment before locking it.

Perhaps he could study horticulture?

CHAPTER 83

"Hey Jen," Naomi said as she saw her sister standing at the door. "Come on in."

She stepped back to let Jennifer walk inside, closing the door behind her.

"I just thought I'd pop in on my way to work, Naomi," Jennifer said as she breezed through into the kitchen. "Make sure everything's okay. My God, that coffee smells amazing."

"Do you want some?" Naomi asked, following Jennifer into the small room. To her dismay, she saw two mugs in the sink next to the broken one. When she had scampered around the flat after shepherding Caleb into the spare bedroom, she'd missed them. "I've, er, I've had two cups already." If her sister thought differently, she didn't show it.

"That would be magic," Jennifer replied, sitting down at the table where, a few moments earlier, Caleb had been sitting. "So, you're okay? You look tired. You've got enormous bags under your eyes."

"You look great too, Jennifer," Naomi said with a sigh. "I'm fine." She fetched a clean mug from the cupboard. "Why wouldn't I be?"

"I'm just checking. After your random text message last night."

"I just thought I'd stay out of your way, that was all." Naomi let a smile play across her face. "How did the date go?"

"It wasn't really a date. Just two friends meeting for a drink after work."

"Sure," Naomi replied. "Of course it was. Are you seeing him again?" It was Jennifer's turn to smile.

"I bloody well hope so," she said, grinning broadly. "We went to the Last Pub Standing on King Street. Had a few beers and then he walked me home like a proper gentleman."

"Dave's a good bloke, Jennifer," Naomi said as she placed Jennifer's mug in front of her. "You could do a lot worse."

"I just wish I'd seen your text saying you were staying here before I'd said goodbye to him." Jennifer started laughing before reaching across the table and putting her hand on Naomi's. "Are you sure you're okay, sis? Only you really do look shattered."

An image flashed across Naomi's mind's eye of the previous evening as she remembered being on the sofa when Caleb slid her t-shirt up before kissing her breasts. She shook her head to try to dissipate the memory of that moment, the following moments, and the following hours, but she could feel the color rising to her cheeks.

"I just didn't get much sleep, Jen, that's all." Naomi slid her hand out from under her sister's and got to her feet. She fussed with the coffee maker for a moment so she could keep her back to Jennifer. Naomi knew she had done nothing wrong, but she wasn't about to own up to Jennifer that she had slept with Caleb, a man she barely knew. Not when he was in the next room.

"As long as everything's okay, sis," Jennifer said. Naomi allowed herself a smile. Everything was more than okay just now.

Naomi and Jennifer chatted for a while, Naomi returning to the table when she thought her face had returned to normal. Finally, Jennifer finished her coffee and got to her feet. The two women hugged and Naomi saw her sister to the door, promising that they would catch up properly soon.

Once Naomi had closed the door behind Jennifer, she breathed a sigh of relief.

"Oh thank God," she whispered. Naomi closed her eyes briefly, imagining a scenario in which Jennifer and Caleb were talking over the kitchen table. How mortified would Naomi be if that had happened? "But it didn't," she told herself, remembering what Caleb had said about living in the moment the previous evening.

Naomi padded across to the spare bedroom door and cracked it open. Inside the small room, Caleb was sitting cross-legged on the bed, a wry smile on his face. He was wearing Naomi's spare dressing gown, which was too small for him. In the corner of the room, his clothes were neatly folded in a small pile.

"How did that go?" Caleb asked her, his smile broadening. "Did your sister suspect anything?"

"Nope," Naomi said, tightening the belt of her own dressing gown. "At least, if she did, she didn't say anything. Are you hungry?"

"Starvin'," Caleb replied, accentuating the drawl as he had done earlier.

"I was going to order a breakfast for delivery. Do you fancy a full English?"

"Sure, sounds good to me. What's in it?"

Naomi listed the ingredients, ticking them off on her fingers as she did so.

"Eggs, bacon, sausages, obviously. Beans and mushrooms. Toast and black pudding are optional."

"Black pudding?" Caleb asked.

"Um, it's a kind of cake made out of pigs' blood and some other stuff. Onions and herbs, mostly." She saw Caleb frowning as she spoke. "I'm guessing that's a no to the black pudding?"

"It doesn't sound like my cup of tea," Caleb replied, attempting an English accent. Naomi laughed.

"Come on, let's go back to the kitchen. You can work your magic with the coffee maker while I call for a delivery."

A few moments later, they were sitting back around the kitchen table in the same position they had been in when Jennifer had arrived.

"So," Naomi said. "Where were we?" She watched as Caleb thought for a moment.

"You were asking me if last night was a one off, or whether it would happen again."

Naomi felt her face flushing. Why on earth had she asked the man that?

"I was?" she asked. Caleb didn't reply. "Sorry, I'm not sure where that question came from."

"Nothing to apologize for, Naomi," he said with an amiable smile. "If it does, it does. If it doesn't, it doesn't. How about we just see what happens?"

Naomi stared at her coffee to hide her embarrassment. Living for the moment was all very well, but was it normally as awkward as this? She scraped her chair back and got to her feet.

"I should get dressed," she said, her voice almost a whisper. As she walked past Caleb, he reached out and took her hand. She looked down at him to see him smiling at her. "What are you grinning at?" she asked him as the corners of her own mouth started twitching.

"Did they say how long the breakfast would take?"

CHAPTER 84

Caleb interlaced his fingers and stretched them, taking care not to dislodge Naomi's laptop that was balanced precariously on his knee. He wasn't used to using a track pad, and his forearm was aching from just a few minutes of using the computer.

On the screen was a map of the village where Suzy and the woman who ran the shelter had been killed. Caleb studied it for some minutes before switching the view to a satellite one. He zoomed in, keeping the house in the center of the screen, and examined the surrounding area.

"What are you looking for?" Naomi said, looking over his shoulder. She was standing just behind him, and he could smell the shampoo in her hair.

"I'm trying to work out this Vince character's movements," Caleb replied. A few seconds later, he pointed at a patch of land on the screen. "He would have parked his car there."

"How do you know that just from looking?" Caleb glanced up at Naomi and she leaned forward, resting her chin lightly on his shoulder. He traced a route on the screen from the light brown patch of ground to the house, and back again.

"I reckon this is the route he would have taken. It doesn't look as if there's much in the way of street lighting, and the parking lot's not overlooked, so it would be easier to get Leanne into the car." Caleb didn't add it would be the route he would have taken. "Do you think the police will have searched it?"

"I doubt it," Naomi said. "They did have a suspect in custody, after all." He could tell from her voice that she was smiling. "Why? What are you thinking?"

"It's a long shot, but he would have been struggling with a child at the time. He could have dropped something."

"You want to go up there? Have a look around?"

"Probably not a good idea." Caleb zoomed the map out until almost the whole of East Anglia was visible. "I'm struggling, Naomi. Where would someone hide a child?" He wasn't expecting her to answer. Caleb's gut feeling was that Vince would try to avoid the usual routes out of England and into mainland Europe. He assumed that was Vince's planned destination for Leanne, but even that was a thin assumption and based solely on what Suzy had told him about the passport. That made a boat the most likely option, but from where? Caleb took a deep breath. He was starting to feel overwhelmed.

Caleb was about to ask Naomi where the largest ports in the area were when the doorbell rang.

"Breakfast's here," Naomi said, pecking him on the cheek. "Shut that down and grab some plates."

As Naomi went to the front door to collect the food, Caleb stared at the laptop for a few seconds before closing it. He forced himself to clear his mind, resolving to take a break and come back to the problem with a fresh set of eyes and a full stomach. He could hear Naomi talking to the delivery driver, and his thoughts drifted to what they had been doing earlier. There had been none of the urgency of the previous night. It had almost been like Sunday morning sex. Slow and languid. Caleb smiled, remembering the way Naomi had started giggling after they had finished.

"Sex is like comedy," she had said, her cheeks flushed with two dime-sized patches of redness.

"How so?" Caleb had asked her.

"It's all about the timing." She had closed her eyes and taken a deep breath. "And yours is very good indeed."

Caleb's daydream was interrupted by Naomi returning to the den.

"That's not getting the plates, is it?" she said with a laugh. "Come on, put that down and let's eat. I'm starving, and it's all your fault."

He forced a smile onto his face and put the laptop down on the sofa before getting to his feet. It was time for a new cultural experience, but when he looked at the food Naomi was laying out in the kitchen, he almost did a double take.

A full English breakfast looked less like sustenance and more like a heart attack on a plate.

CHAPTER 85

Vince made his way back to his car, thinking about what he had just seen. When a moped had arrived a few moments earlier with a distinctive large orange box on the back, the driver had been only too happy to accept a twenty-pound note to let Vince deliver the food to Naomi's apartment. It was almost an hour since her sister had left, alone, and there had been no signs of movement since.

"It's a surprise for my girlfriend," he had told the bemused looking youngster. But when Vince took the bag of food from him, he realized there was more than one serving in it. That meant there was someone else in the apartment with her, which meant he would have to change his plans. When he'd been doing his research on Naomi, he'd not been able to find anything about a partner.

Vince's original plan had been to greet her with a smile and insist on bringing the food into her apartment. He'd used the technique several times in the past, and it had worked more often than not. He knew his smile could be quite disarming, and most people were too polite to say anything. By the time they realized it was a horrendous mistake, it was too late. Vince was inside. The door to the outside world was closed behind him. But the fact there was someone else with Naomi negated that plan. Regardless of who it was.

When Naomi had answered the door, Vince had studied her carefully. She wasn't even dressed, which definitely meant that whoever was inside the apartment had spent the night.

"Breakfast for two?" Vince had asked her, noticing a slight flush appear on Naomi's face as she answered. She was much more attractive close-up than the few pictures he'd been able to find on-line, was not wearing a speck of make-up, and her hair was mussed up as if she had just got out of bed. Vince felt himself harden as he imagined her naked body under the dressing gown she was wearing.

"Um, yes," Naomi had replied, taking the food and starting to shut the door as if she sensed his thoughts. "Thank you." And with that, she closed the door in his face.

Vince muttered an obscenity under his breath. He paused next to her car before kneeling down as if tying his shoelace. Confident he couldn't be seen from the apartment, he slipped a magnetic tracker in the wheel well. It was something, at least.

When he slipped back behind the wheel of his car, Vince checked his phone to make sure the tracker was working properly. He stared out of the windshield for a while, wondering what to do next. He needed to get Naomi on her own. But who was she with?

Vince reached into the back of his car and grabbed his laptop. A few moments later, having logged into his work account, he brought up a browser window with a tool called AddSearch, a bespoke piece of software written by some eggheads down at GCHQ, the British government's communications headquarters in Cheltenham. He entered Naomi's address and sat back to wait as the software did its thing, looking in a wide variety of databases for activity connected to the address. Most of the databases allowed AddSearch access on the grounds of national security. Those that didn't just weren't made aware of the access the software had.

While he waited for the search to complete, Vince thought again about Naomi. He remembered the smell of the food he had delivered to her earlier, and his stomach grumbled. Now that he had the tracker on the car, he didn't have to maintain eyes on. That was the reason he had planted it. To give him some space for less overt surveillance. There was a greasy spoon cafe a couple of streets away. He could head there for a bite to eat in a few moments.

A few moments later, Vince had a complete list of individuals connected to the apartment's address. But since Naomi had purchased the apartment, nothing had been listed in another name. No mobile phone, no utility bills, no credit searches. Whoever was with her wasn't a long-term arrangement. Vince closed the laptop, tempted to punch the steering wheel in frustration. But the years he had spent working for the security services had taught him one thing.

Patience might not be a virtue, but it was certainly a necessity. Vince's problem wasn't really a matter of patience, though. It was a matter of time, and he knew he had little of it.

CHAPTER 86

Naomi smiled as she watched Caleb push the plate away from him, defeated by the enormous breakfast.

"Oh my word," he said, rubbing his stomach theatrically. "I thought the meals in Texas were big, but that was a monster."

"You enjoyed it?" she asked him. Her own plate was empty, but she'd given herself a much smaller helping. Depending on what Caleb's plans were, Naomi was planning on hitting the gym later in penance for both the wine the previous evening and the breakfast. Although, she thought as she reached forward for his plate, she had already worked off quite a few of the wine's calories.

"I can feel my arteries hardening as we speak," Caleb said as he sat back in his chair. Naomi got to her feet and loaded the dishwasher after scraping the plates clean. "Have you got plans for today?" he asked her.

"I was probably going to nip into the office for an hour or so," she replied. "Maybe go to the gym after. You're more than welcome to stay here, though." She looked at him, realizing that she had no idea where he was living. "The pub that my sister went to last night is only down the road. We could go there for a drink?"

"We could," Caleb replied, but Naomi didn't think he sounded that enthusiastic.

"It's called the Last Pub Standing," Naomi said, trying to sell the idea to him. "There used to be sixty-odd pubs on the road it's on. Back in the old days. Now it's the only one left. It's a two-minute walk."

"I was going to visit Leon and his, er, friend, Syd."

"On the Lark's Cross estate?"

"Yes. This Syd lives in one of those towers."

Naomi frowned at the thought of people living in those monstrosities. But she knew that most of the residents had little to no choice. Social housing was social housing, and those that required it had little say in its location.

"I'll give you a lift," she said. "It's on the way. Well, kind of." The Lark's Cross estate was in fact in the opposite direction, but Naomi didn't mind.

"Are you sure?" Caleb asked. "That would be most kind, thank you, ma'am." Naomi grinned at his choice of words.

"I think we're probably past the ma'am stage now, aren't we?" she asked him, earning a smile in response.

A few moments later, Naomi was sitting in her bedroom, applying some make-up. She was dressed in a pair of navy-blue jeans with cotton sneakers and a loose-fitting cream blouse. Casual but at the same time, smart. A pair of simple gold stud earrings completed the ensemble. Although she didn't think she would see anyone else in the office, if there was someone else there, she didn't want to be seen in gym gear. The firm she worked for was some years away from that. As she dusted her face with foundation, she could hear Caleb getting dressed in the spare room. From the little she knew about the man, she was under no illusion that they were at the start of a long relationship. He seemed to live a much too transient lifestyle for that, but she allowed herself to daydream for a moment, anyway.

Being a Sunday morning, the roads between Naomi's apartment and the Lark's Cross estate were almost empty, and they made the journey in no time at all. Even Naomi's sat nav overestimated how long it would take them by some moments. As they approached the area, it was as if the skies above them darkened.

"Take the next turning on the left," the sat nav intoned as they turned into the estate.

"What a depressing place," Naomi said as they made their way to Leon's road. She shivered involuntarily. "Can you imagine having to live here?"

"I've lived in worse places," Caleb replied. She turned to look at him, but he was staring out of the passenger window. As the sat nav announced they had arrived at their destination, Naomi pulled in to the curb outside Leon's house.

"I'll wait here," she said. "Make sure he's in before I abandon you at the gates of Hell." Caleb flashed her a quick smile as he exited the vehicle. A moment later, Naomi could see him talking to Leon's mother. In between puffs on her cigarette, Leon's mother pointed toward the towers that dominated the drab surroundings.

"He's at his friend's apartment," Caleb said when he returned to the car. "I can walk from here."

"Call me when you're done and I'll come and get you," Naomi replied as she kept a nervous eye on three young men in hoodies a hundred yards away who were pretending not to look at them. Caleb's quick smile came back as she handed him one of her business cards. "My cell's on the back. Are you sure you're okay walking from here?"

"Yes, I'm sure. Is it alright if I come back to your place tonight?" He looked at her and she felt a shiver of delight at the way his eyes met hers. "I owe you a takeout meal, after all." Trying for a nonchalant expression, she nodded in response. But the way his smile broadened told her that her attempt at nonchalance had failed.

She waited for a few moments until Caleb had walked past the three hoodies unmolested before executing a three-point turn, keen to get away from the estate. When she reached the road leading from the area, she breathed a sigh of relief and tuned her car radio to a local radio station. When she realized they were playing a song by the Black Eyed Peas about tonight being a good, good night, she turned the music up to sing along.

If Caleb liked Chinese food, she knew just the restaurant to order from. They could eat, relax, drink some wine. And then what?

Naomi raised her voice as she sang along, tapping the steering wheel in time to the music. Tonight was going to be a good, good night indeed.

CHAPTER 87

Leon was just relaxing in Syd's couch, smoking a joint and listening to something bizarre from his record collection, when Syd's bell rang. Groaning, he got to his feet and made his way to the small monitor that would show him who was in the lobby. When he saw it was Caleb staring up at the camera, he grinned.

"Caleb, my man," Leon said into the intercom. "Come on up." He leaned forward and pressed the button to allow Caleb to access the elevator. After unlocking the front door, Leon returned to his position on the couch and relit his joint.

A few moments later, the door to the apartment opened and Caleb walked in. The first thing he did was start waving his hand in front of his face.

"It stinks in here, Leon," Caleb said, wrinkling his nose. "Can't you at least open a window or something? You smell like you want to be left alone."

Leon inclined his head toward one of the windows in the wall.

"Over there," he said, closing his eyes and leaning back. "Fill your boots."

"Put that out, Leon," Leon heard Caleb say a few seconds later as a soft draught blew in through the now open window. "I need your help."

Leon crushed out the joint and sat up. Caleb needed his help?

"Sure," he said, shaking his head to clear his head. "You want a drink?" He paused, searching for the right word. "A soda, maybe?"

"Thank you."

Leon made his way into the small kitchen, almost tripping over the barrel of water that was now almost full. He swore as he realized he'd forgotten about it and then barked his shin as he kneeled down to turn the water supply off. The sharp pain in his leg worked wonders to clear his head, and by the time he returned to Caleb with a couple of cans of Coca Cola, he was feeling much less messed up.

"What do you need help with?" Leon asked him as he sat back down on the couch, trying his best to look alert.

"If you were going to smuggle someone out of the United Kingdom, somewhere locally, how would you do it?" Leon thought for a moment before replying.

"Smuggle them to where? I take it you mean with no one knowing?"

"Estonia, ultimately," Caleb replied. "So mainland Europe first. And yes, with no one knowing. That's kind of what smuggling means."

"Um, let me think for a moment." Leon wracked his brains, wanting to help Caleb but unsure whether he could or not. He sipped his can to buy some time. "It would have to be on a boat, I reckon." Caleb nodded and Leon continued, encouraged. "I mean, I don't think there are any ferries to mainland Europe from round here. I think you'd have to go to Harwich for that, and that's hardly local. Or subtle." He continued thinking for a moment, but couldn't come up with anything to add. "What the hell are you doing smuggling people to Estonia, anyway?" Leon started giggling. "What sort of crazy shit are you involved in?"

"Leon, listen to me," Caleb barked. The steel in his voice stopped Leon's laughter instantly. "I'm trying to stop a child from being taken against her will to another country. A child who might be being trafficked by a pedophile ring."

"Shit," Leon whispered. "You serious?"

"As serious as the business end of a .45," Caleb replied, his voice still hard.

"Okay, okay," Leon replied, licking his lips. "So, if I was going to do that, I'd get a charter out of somewhere. There's got to be loads of places in Europe where a boat could sneak in unnoticed."

"Where can I charter a boat from?"

"It would have to be a big one to get all that way, so most of the smaller places round here wouldn't work. Probably Great Yarmouth. Maybe Lowestoft?"

"Are they far?"

"About half an hour to Yarmouth," Leon said, taking a sip of his drink. Caleb hadn't even opened his. "Lowestoft's a bit further, but not much. We should ask Syd. He moves stuff to and from Europe occasionally."

"Is he here?"

"He will be, in a bit, yes." Leon had texted Syd not long before Caleb's arrival and he'd replied to say he would be there in an hour, maybe less.

"Okay," Caleb replied, nodding.

The two men sat in silence for a few moments. Leon

thought about rolling another joint, but dismissed the idea almost instantly. He didn't think Caleb would appreciate it.

"So, this Syd," Caleb said after a while. "He's your friend, right?"

"Yeah," Leon replied. "Friend and, er, business partner."

"Partner?" Caleb had a wry smile on his face. "You're what? Sixteen?"

"Fifteen," Leon mumbled.

"You want to run with the big dogs, right?" Leon watched as Caleb's smile faded away. "You want to know what I think?" From the expression on Caleb's face, it was clear he was going to tell Leon, anyway.

"Sure," Leon replied, his voice almost a whisper. Caleb spread his hands out to encompass the apartment.

"This is the bit where I'd normally ask you if you read scripture," he said. Caleb's smile almost returned, but his eyes were still ice cold. "But I'm guessing you probably don't." Leon nodded in agreement. "You're better than this, Leon. You're sitting in a low-life drug dealer's apartment, watering his plants. Robbing buses for him. Doing his dirty work. And for what? A bit of cash and the very realistic prospect of prison?"

"You don't know me, man," Leon said, trying to defend himself from the onslaught. Caleb's eyes continued to bore into him. "You don't know me one bit. I've got plans. Big plans."

"I'm a very good judge of character, Leon," Caleb replied. "It's a skill I have." He placed his hand on Leon's sternum and the younger man flinched at the contact. "You have a good heart in here." Leon could feel his chest start to heat up under Caleb's palm. Then he raised the same hand to tap the side of Leon's temple with his index finger and the heat transferred to his head. "And you have a fine brain in here. You need to use both to come up with some new plans."

Leon took a deep breath, considering what Caleb had just said. He was looking at him, but the ice cold of his eyes had warmed, almost softened. Leon felt strange, almost spaced out, and he wondered if the cannabis was coming back for a second rush. Or was it Caleb's words? Was it Caleb's touch?

"You trying to convert me, preacher man?" Leon said with a smile. He could still feel the heat from Caleb's hand on his chest and on the side of his head.

"Not my style, Leon," Caleb replied as Leon closed his eyes, relaxing into the unfamiliar sensation in his body. "You can find your own way."

CHAPTER 88

As she had done a hundred times before, Naomi reversed her car into the small space in the underground parking lot her law firm shared with the other occupants of the small office block. There were three companies in the block. Her own, a realtor on the second floor, and a marketing company on the top story. The average age at Naomi's firm, except for her, was far higher than the other two firms, but they all got on most of the time. The only conflict Naomi could remember was a brief argument over the parking spaces, but as it was a Sunday, there were only a couple of cars in the lot.

She blipped the locks to her car and made her way to the corner of the lot where her key card allowed her access to the elevator. Naomi was still humming the song she'd been listening to in the car and, when the elevator arrived, the moment the doors closed, she started singing again.

Laughing to herself, Naomi entered her office, which was thankfully empty. She didn't want to be making small talk with any of her colleagues when she was in such a good mood. They were a dour bunch at the best of times, and

Naomi had tried unsuccessfully on more than one occasion to persuade the partners to hire some interns just to bring the average age down and liven the place up a bit.

After logging onto her computer, she quickly scanned through her e-mails, flagging a couple to look at in more detail the next morning. Then she reviewed her diary. She would be in the office on Monday and Tuesday, then in court, probably for the rest of the week. One of her clients, a nasty individual who lived near the coast but traveled around the county to steal, was due in court for aggravated burglary. The burglary element was undeniable. He'd been caught red-handed inside an empty property, a second home on the North Norfolk coast, when the neighbors had seen a flashlight bobbing about. The police who had responded had found a knife near the property with his prints on it. Naomi's entire defense against the aggravated element was that he didn't have it on his person at the time of his arrest.

Naomi crossed to the filing cabinet to retrieve the man's file. She spent a few moments reviewing it, and her notes for the court case, but there wasn't much she could add. She just hoped her client brought a bag with him to court because the chances of him returning home were slim to none. Naomi had been surprised the man had made bail, but perhaps he would do them all a favor and just do a runner. She looked at his mugshot on the file. He had a thick neck covered in spidery tattoos and broad shoulders which, with his shaved head, made him look as guilty as sin.

She sighed, placing the file back in the cabinet. After making a mental note to speak with one of the senior partners before the trial to make sure she wasn't missing anything obvious, she let her thoughts drift to Caleb. She wanted to speak to him, but he had no cell phone. She could call Leon and ask to speak to him, but that would probably come across as needy. Naomi put her hand on her chest and tried to do an impression of her mother.

"Naomi Tipton," she said with a broad grin. "You've been a very, very naughty girl." Then she laughed to herself, knowing she had every intention of repeating her sins. "Carpe diem indeed," she whispered.

Once she had locked the office, Naomi made her way back down to the parking lot. She let herself daydream for a few moments before checking the time on her phone. She could nip into the city to buy some new lingerie? Something spicy to entertain Caleb, perhaps? Naomi hadn't treated herself to something like that for years. Mark hadn't seemed to notice things like that, she thought as she unlocked her car. He'd been much more of a wham, bam, thank you ma'am kind of man. But Caleb was different. Very different.

Naomi let a smile play over her face as she threw her phone onto the passenger seat before fishing in her purse for her key fob. Then she gasped as she felt a piece of hard, cold metal pressing against the back of her head.

"Hey, Naomi," a male voice said. "How was breakfast?"

CHAPTER 89

Caleb looked at Syd's monitor, which was currently showing pretty much the same map he'd been looking at on Naomi's laptop earlier.

"That's Great Yarmouth there," Syd said, wiggling the cursor over a town on the map. "It's where the River Yare empties into the sea. The mouth of the Yare. So Yarmouth. And it's wide, so it's great. Get it?"

"Yes," Caleb replied, unimpressed with the impromptu history lesson.

"The River Yare goes all the way back to Norwich, so in your hypothetical scenario, this person could hide anywhere along its length," Syd continued. Caleb sighed, knowing his task had just got more difficult with more options to consider. "But I would just hide them in Yarmouth and take them straight to the charter." From his position on the sofa, Leon could be seen nodding enthusiastically.

"Tell me about the charter firm you've used," Caleb said, glancing at Leon. "For your, er, operations." It was Syd's turn to glance at Leon, and Caleb could tell he wasn't impressed that Leon had told Caleb about that element. "They're discrete, I take it?"

"For a price, very," Syd replied. "There's a bloke in Caister, just north of Yarmouth, who operates a fishing boat that'll reach Holland. Proper shitty boat it is, but it gets the job done. He's been doing it for years, so is pretty much part of the furniture. Henry, his name is, and he's a proper nasty bastard. But he'll move anything for a price."

"Even people?"

"Like I said, he'll shift anything for a price."

"What's his background?" Caleb asked.

"Prison, mostly," Syd said with a laugh. "He did a ten stretch for armed robbery a few years ago, but has kept his nose clean since. The boat was his dad's, and the word is the family's been shunting drugs back and forth for generations."

"Can you introduce me to him?"

"You'll have to pay to play." Syd reached for his rolling papers and pulled three out of the slim cardboard box.

"Why doesn't that surprise me?" Caleb muttered, getting to his feet. "I'm going to get some fresh air if you're smoking that."

"I can call him, set something up," Syd said, licking one of the rolling papers. "How do we get in touch with you? Leon says you don't own a phone."

"I'm staying with Naomi Tipton for the time being," Caleb replied. "Leon's got her number." He saw Leon's eyebrows go up at the statement, but the young man had the sense not to say anything.

He made his way to Syd's front door, keen to not spend the rest of the day smelling like a marijuana factory, and up the fire escape to the roof. Caleb stepped out into the fresh air and inhaled deeply, realizing it might be too late to not stink of weed.

At least they had made some progress. He sat down on a heating duct close to the edge of the roof and stared at the estate that sprawled out below him. The chances of this Henry character also being Vince's point of contact were slim, but it was the closest he had to a lead. Caleb considered his courses of action.

The first, as always, was to do nothing. That would see Leanne being trafficked to Estonia and then disappearing. An easy option for him to discount.

Caleb's second and third options depended on Henry. If he was Vince's point of contact, the chances were he wouldn't tell Caleb, anyway. Why cut off an income stream? Caleb imagined the payoff for smuggling people as opposed to drugs was much larger. So he might need to approach it another way and develop courses of action for that eventuality. Or he might not be connected to Vince at all, which threw up a range of other possibilities, depending on who else he knew. Caleb couldn't imagine that Henry was the only person operating in that particular space, so he might need to follow that spider's web to see where it went.

He sat in silence for some moments, his eyes closed, and enjoyed the soft sunshine on his face. Caleb breathed deeply, relishing the fresh air. Then he got to his feet, figuring he'd been up here more than long enough for the two men in the apartment below to have smoked several joints. But by the time he got back downstairs, the air in Syd's lounge was still thick with aromatic smoke. Caleb didn't want to stay a moment longer than he had to.

"Leon, could you call Naomi for me?" Leon looked up at him from his position on the sofa. On the other side of the room, Syd was strumming on a guitar, humming under his breath. He watched as Leon raised his phone, stabbed at the screen, and held the phone to his ear. Twenty seconds or so later, he frowned.

"No reply," Leon said, holding the phone out toward Caleb as if to prove it.

"Can you try again, please?" Caleb replied. He watched as Leon did as he had asked. This time, there was no delay before his frown reappeared.

"It just went straight through to her voicemail."

CHAPTER 90

"Don't answer that," Vince barked as Naomi's phone trilled on the passenger seat. "Hands on the steering wheel where I can see them." He examined her in the rear-view mirror, pleased with the look of utter shock on her face. That was just where he wanted her to be. He waited until the phone stopped ringing before continuing.

"Take the battery out," he said, his voice low and full of menace. Naomi's hands were shaking as she picked up the phone, and it took her a couple of tries to disconnect the battery. "Now the SIM card." It took her even longer to get the tiny sliver of plastic out of the phone, but when she had managed it, she replaced her hands on the wheel without being prompted. That was good in Vince's eyes. She was compliant already. Although, to be fair to the woman, most people were when they had a gun to their heads.

"Who are you?" Naomi said, her voice stuttering.

"Shut the fuck up, Naomi," Vince replied, pressing the pistol harder into her scalp. "Just answer me this. Where is he?"

"Who?"

"You know who." He examined her in the mirror. Her face was drained of color, almost as white as a sheet. "Where is he?"

"Please, I don't know who you're talking about." She swallowed and blinked back tears.

"I'm looking for Caleb," Vince said with a snarl. "Where is he?" In the mirror, the expression in her eyes changed ever so subtly.

"You're Vince," she said. It wasn't a question.

Vince had to resist the urge to slam the pistol into the back of Naomi's head. What she had just said told him plenty. The bitch Suzy had talked. She had told Caleb about him. And he, in turn, had told Naomi, which had dramatically changed both their life expectancies. Not in a good way.

"Yes, Naomi," he replied after taking a few seconds to compose himself. "I'm Vince. Now tell me where Caleb is?" She didn't reply, but just shook her head in response. He slipped his free hand around the seat and encircled Naomi's neck, squeezing it gently. "Tell me."

"I don't know, I swear." Naomi's voice had gone up an octave, and a tear squeezed its way out of the corner of her eye.

"This can go one of two ways, Naomi," he said. "You can tell me where he is and I'll leave you in peace. I'll just walk away and you'll never see me again unless you talk to the police. Do that and you'll spend the rest of your pathetic life looking over your shoulder, wondering if today's the day I'm coming back for you." He increased the pressure on her neck slightly and saw her eyes widening in response. "Or you can carry on lying to me and I'll kill you. Not here, not now. No, after we've had some fun together." He saw her blinking rapidly in the mirror. "Only it won't be much fun for you, I can promise you that. Then you'll just disappear." He blew softly on her neck as he tightened his grip more. "Into the air," he said, dropping his voice to a whisper. "It'll be like you never existed. What's it to be?"

"I'll tell you," Naomi said, her voice almost inaudible. "Please, I'll tell you."

Vince relaxed his grip on her neck, making sure he left enough pressure on it to remind her his hand was still there. He felt her swallowing under his fingers.

"Where is he?"

"He's in London," Naomi said. "I dropped him at the station after he was released by the police. Now, please, let me go. I won't say a word to anyone, I promise."

"Where in London?" Vince asked her, more to gauge her reaction than anything else. He knew she was lying, but how far would she try to take it?

"I don't know," she replied. "Please, just let me go."

Vince smiled at her in the rear-view mirror. She'd made the right choice, not to elaborate on the lie. But she was still lying.

"Who was the second breakfast for, Naomi? Was it for Caleb?" Vince asked her. He saw her eyes widen again, almost imperceptibly. Bingo. It wasn't until she had lied about Caleb's location that the penny had dropped. Vince was disappointed in himself. He should have put that together much sooner.

"No, it was for my boyfriend," she replied. "Mark." Clever, Vince thought. Keep the lie as close to the truth as possible.

"Is that the same Mark you broke up with a few days ago? The one who texted his best mate complaining that you were a frigid bitch?" He saw Naomi close her eyes as if in resignation. "Crap in the sack, I think is what he said. Like a corpse in the bedroom. Is that what Caleb thinks as well?" He tightened his grip on her neck as Naomi tightened her grip on the steering wheel. "Does this Mark know you're sleeping with someone else already?" Her knuckles were as white as her face, and Vince knew it would only be a second or so before her hands flew to her throat to try to relieve the pressure. Sure enough, as his grip got tighter, Naomi's fight-or-flight instinct kicked in. Vince wasn't bothered about her scratching him. No one would ever find her body to get any DNA from her fingernails.

"Shh," Vince whispered in Naomi's ear as he continued to increase the pressure. He knew she would have a rapidly diminishing field of vision if she opened her eyes, a black circle closing in. He waited until her hands started flapping instead of scratching. Then, a few seconds after that, they fell into her lap.

Working quickly, Vince released Naomi, shoving her against the steering wheel. She gasped like a newborn baby, an instinctive reflex to get as much oxygen back into her body as she could. He produced a pair of zip-ties and fastened her wrists behind her back, making sure they were secure before he opened the car door. He stepped out and opened the driver's door.

Vince grabbed Naomi by the hair and pulled her from the car. He half-dragged her to the trunk, her legs scrabbling for purchase on the concrete floor of the parking lot. By the time he had opened the trunk, she was still gasping for air but was moaning as well. He bent her over, cramming her upper body into the trunk before sweeping her legs up and folding them into the space. She started wriggling, but had no space to move.

"You said you'd let me go," she said, just as he was about

to close the trunk. Her voice was rasping. "If I told you, you said you'd let me go."

Vince paused and looked down at Naomi.

"You weren't the only liar in that car, Naomi," he said, meeting her stare. "But I promised you something, didn't I? If you lied to me?" She just stared back at him, her expression a mixture of fear and hate, but more the latter than the former. Vince smiled. He loved a fighter. Just before he slammed the trunk shut, he leaned forward to whisper in her ear. "And I always keep my promises."

CHAPTER 91

Leon looked at Caleb. For the first time since he'd met the man, he looked concerned. Syd was still strumming away in the corner of the lounge, oblivious to everything. He'd smoked most of the joint that he'd put together, with Leon only having a couple of puffs.

"You okay, man?" Leon asked Caleb. He didn't respond at first, but paced up and down the lounge for a few seconds. "Caleb?"

"I'm not sure," Caleb replied. "Something's not right."

"Maybe Naomi's busy with something," Leon said. "She could be tied up at work or something?"

"On a Sunday? No, something's not right." He stopped pacing and looked at Leon, the concern on his face obvious. "I can feel it."

"What do you want to do?" Leon asked. He saw Caleb look over at Syd.

"Does he have a car?"

"Yeah," Leon replied. Syd had a rarely used Ford Focus RS, the staple of many a boy racer in the United Kingdom. The previous owner had modified it with various bits of metal and plastic to make it what Syd called original, but Leon couldn't see the point himself. It was only a car, but everyone on the estate knew it was Syd's, which meant it was left alone. "Yeah, he has."

"Is it an automatic?"

"No," Leon said, knowing what Caleb's next question would be. "But I could drive it if you want?" He nodded at Syd, who was still humming to himself. "If that's okay with Syd?"

Leon watched as Caleb walked across the lounge toward where Syd was sitting.

"Syd, I need your car keys," Caleb said, his hand out in front of him, palm up.

"What?" Syd looked up at Caleb through rheumy eyes. "What for?"

"I need to check on someone. Keys?"

To Leon's surprise, Syd put his guitar to one side and started rooting round in his pocket for his car key. He handed it over to Caleb without a further word and picked the guitar back up, positioning his fingers on the fret with exaggerated slowness. If it had been Leon who had asked, it would have been a two word reply.

"Let's go," Caleb said to Leon, walking past him to the front door of the apartment.

The two of them remained silent as they rode the elevator down to the first floor. Caleb seemed lost in thought, and Leon didn't feel able to ask him any of the questions that were rattling round his head. Where were they going? What were they looking for?

Leon blipped the locks for Syd's bright blue Focus and they got in. He remembered to turn the stereo off before starting the car and when he started the engine, the modified exhaust rattled like an angry swarm of bees in a tin can. Syd's car was hardly subtle.

"Where are we going?" he asked Caleb, who was looking at a crumpled piece of cardboard he had pulled from his pocket.

"Do you know where Palace Street is?" Caleb asked. Leon didn't, but he pulled his phone out and a few seconds later had brought it up on the map.

"It's near the cathedral," Leon replied as he put the vehicle into gear. "What do you think might have happened?"

"I don't know," Caleb said, his voice distracted, "but there's a darkness coming. I can feel it."

Leon looked through the windshield at the skies over their head. It was grey, but not particularly forbidding.

"It doesn't look that bad," he said. "Might get some rain later, I s'pose."

"It's not that kind of darkness, Leon," Caleb replied.

Confused by his response, Leon focused on the road in front of him. The traffic was light to start with, but the closer they got to the cathedral, the busier it got. When they arrived on Palace Street, a narrow road with a flint-lined wall on one side and black beamed medieval buildings on the other, Leon saw Caleb staring out of the passenger's window. Leon drove slowly down the road with the older buildings gradually giving way to more modern ones.

"There," Caleb said, pointing at the newest building on the entire street. "That's the one."

Leon pulled into the curb next to the red-brick building and put the hazard lights on. The car hadn't even come to a complete stop before Caleb was out of the vehicle and running across the road. Leon watched as he jabbed at one of the doorbells on a panel outside the building before jabbing at all of them. A moment later, he turned and shook his head at Leon before making his way down a ramp to the side of the building. Leon had seen the ramp as he had pulled up, but a low bar across his meant he couldn't take the car down it.

Caleb was out of Leon's sight for only a few moments, but when he returned, his entire demeanor had changed. The look of concern that Leon saw earlier had been replaced by an entirely different expression. Leon thought back to what Caleb had said about a darkness coming.

From the look on Caleb's face, it was already here.

CHAPTER 92

Naomi forced herself to take deep breaths in through her nose and out through her mouth, just like she had learned way back in school when she had suffered from panic attacks. She remembered the school nurse, a woman who seemed to the children to be as old as the hills but was probably only in her late fifties or early sixties, sitting her down on a chair with a brown paper bag.

Hold the bag like this, the nurse had said, showing Naomi how to hold the bag by the neck and breathe into it. *Nice and slow, in through your nose and out through your mouth.*

Fighting tears, Naomi tried to replicate the technique, but there was a massive difference between a panic attack brought on by a harsh word at school from a fellow pupil and one that comes on after being kidnapped by a man who she knew had killed at least three people.

As the car rumbled along, Naomi gradually managed to slow her breathing down. It was still rapid, and didn't seem to be affected by the way her heart was thumping against her ribs like a caged animal. In the movies, she would be able to trace where they were heading by the speed and motion of the car, but Naomi had no chance of that. It was all she could do to breathe.

She wriggled a couple of times to see just how much room she actually had, which was hardly any. The trunk of her Mini was not exactly spacious. That had been one of her father's concerns about buying the car in the first place. Naomi was on her side, her legs folded, and her hands were tied fast behind her back. There was some give in the ties that Vince had used, but not a massive amount, and the plastic was unforgiving.

Was there some sort of quick release mechanism inside the trunk, she wondered? Naomi didn't think there was, and she couldn't see one, anyway. Even if there was, how was she going to reach it?

She could feel the panic rising in her chest again as the car lurched to the right-hand side. Naomi screamed as she was pressed up against the carpet lining the trunk. When she realized that the scream helped to dissipate her panic, she screamed again. She had no idea where they were, but surely if a pedestrian heard a woman screaming from a passing car, they would call the police. Wouldn't they?

"Help me!" Naomi shouted as loudly as she could. She used the couple of inches of room she had to try to bang her feet against the car's side. "Someone help me!"

A few seconds later, just as Naomi was about to scream again, she saw an orange flashing light inside the trunk. It was followed by a continuous red one. The car started to slow, and she realized it was pulling over. Perhaps Vince would just abandon the car and run off? Maybe he was having second thoughts about what he was doing? Naomi knew from her work that sometimes criminals bottled their crimes at the last minute and cancelled them. But Naomi knew it was wishful thinking. He had already killed three people. She needed to come up with a plan for when he eventually untied her, and one she could implement before he did anything else.

The car came to an abrupt halt, and she heard the driver's door opening. There were a few footsteps and then the trunk was flung open. Before Naomi could react, Vince reached down and wound something around her head. She could feel the material being forced between her teeth and she struggled as much as she could, but Vince was too strong. Over his shoulder, she could just make out the branches of some trees. He must have pulled over somewhere remote to silence her.

"I would have thought you've had more sense than that, Naomi," Vince said, leaning forward to talk to her. Flecks of his spittle flew out of his mouth, landing on her cheek, but she couldn't even move enough to wipe them away. "Now shut up. We'll be there soon and I'll show you how much of a gentleman I can be." Even though his face was silhouetted against the bright sky, she could see the menace in his expression as well as hear it in the tone of his voice.

Then the trunk was slammed shut. More footsteps, and she heard the car door closing. Fighting against tears, Naomi tried her hardest to fight the tight band that was crushing her chest. She was going to die. He was going to kill her. And the thought of what he would do to her before that ramped up the pressure three-fold.

Probably for the first time in over twenty years, Naomi started to pray.

CHAPTER 93

Vince chuckled as he thought about the look of absolute terror in Naomi's eyes as he had slammed the trunk closed. He should have gagged her back in the parking lot, he realized, and his laughter faded away. Perhaps he was losing his touch? Most of the time, when he was transporting people in the trunk of a car, they were either dead or unconscious and soon to be dead. He shook his head.

"Schoolboy error," he muttered to himself. "Get a grip, Vince."

He was parked at the side of a road that lead through a large, wild park in the center of Norwich. The signs had told him it was called Mousehold Heath when he had entered it, and there were quite a few people taking advantage of the sunshine to walk their dogs or go running. But the park was extensive enough to find a deserted spot easily.

Vince leaned forward and jabbed at the screen of the in-car entertainment system in Naomi's car. It took him a moment, but he worked out how to bring up the sat nav. He selected the option for Recent Destinations and looked at the list. Although his tracker showed the same information, it wouldn't list any exact addresses, only locations. He studied the screen for a moment, trying to work out whether it listed all of Naomi's recent destinations or only those she had programmed the sat nav to take her to. Deciding it was the latter, he tapped on the most recent entry.

17 Falcon Road, Norwich

He brought up the maps app on his phone and entered the address before switching to street view.

"Jesus wept," Vince said under his breath. "What a shit hole." What on earth was Naomi doing visiting there? Vince couldn't see how Caleb had any connection with the council estate, either. He thought back to the transcript of the police interview. Caleb had definitely said he'd never been to Norwich before. But there was something pricking at Vince's memory. Was it something about a friend in Norwich? Vince would have to wait to get back to his laptop, which was in his own car, to check, but the more he thought about it, the more he thought he remembered Caleb saying that. The nasty little house on the screen must be where this friend lived. Either that or it belonged to a client of Naomi's.

Vince sat back in the seat and thought for a moment. Naomi had left her apartment, visited this address, and then went to the office. His tracking app confirmed that. So if she was lying about Caleb's location, which Vince was one hundred percent sure she was, that meant Caleb was in one of two places. Either still at her apartment, or at the address on the screen. He drummed the steering wheel for a moment. Both locations were on opposite sides of the city.

Which should he go to first? Or should he secure Naomi? He still had access to the house in Norwich he had shared with Suzy and Leanne. Although he didn't have the keys with him, he was confident he could get inside and, technically, he still rented the property. Although he would need to sanitize it again once Naomi's stay there had come to an end, that wasn't a drama.

An additional consideration was the fact that the longer he drove around with her in the trunk of her car, the more risk he was taking. She could dislodge the necktie he'd used to silence her and start screaming again. The trunk lid could fly open, although he doubted it would. But the risk was there. The time it would take to secure her properly at the house would be minimal, and he could even give her a taste of what was to come when they had some quality time together.

On the other hand, the longer he left it before he confronted and neutralized Caleb, the greater the likelihood that he would have moved on. But unless he left Caleb in place once he had dealt with him, which he was loath to do, he would need some room in the trunk for disposal.

Three options. His old house, Naomi's apartment, or the address on the estate. Vince made his decision and put the car into gear.

CHAPTER 94

"Where to now?"

Caleb turned to look at Leon, who was tapping his index fingers on the steering wheel of Syd's car.

"Do you know where Naomi lives?" Caleb asked him, knowing that he probably didn't.

"Um, no," Leon replied. "Sorry."

Caleb sighed in frustration. There was no reason at all for Naomi to let her clients know where she lived. On the contrary, them not knowing was a very good idea. Caleb closed his hand around the small gold earring he had found on the floor of the parking lot, close to the remains of a CCTV camera. The moment he picked the gold stud up, he knew it was Naomi's. He remembered her wearing them earlier that day.

He closed his eyes, forcing himself to concentrate. When they had been driving earlier, what landmarks had he seen? He tried to visualize their journey from the moment they had left her apartment to arriving on the estate. A vague image of a building floated into his mind's eye. Three stories. Cream walls. Black surrounds on the windows. An old building. Naomi had made a comment about the building as they had driven past.

In the driver's seat, Leon started to say something, but Caleb raised his hand to silence him. What had Naomi said? It was something about her sister. Her sister had been to the place. It was a bar, or more specifically in England, a pub. Was it last night her sister had been there?

Caleb furrowed his brow, knowing that the information he needed was right on the periphery of his memory. Then his eyes flashed open. He had it.

"The Last Pub," Caleb said, looking at Leon. "Do you know it?" Naomi had told Caleb that her sister, Jennifer, had been to the pub on a date. It might have been last night, but that wasn't what she had said. It was the name of the pub.

"No," Leon replied, reaching for his phone. Caleb waited as his fingers flew across the screen.

"Last Pub, Norwich," Leon muttered. He waited for a few seconds as his phone did its thing before showing Caleb the screen. "This the place?"

"Yes. Can we go there? I should be able to find Naomi's apartment from there."

As Leon drove, Caleb played back the earlier journey in his head again. The pub had been only a few moments into their journey, so Naomi's place was close by. He was desperate for Leon to drive faster, but knew he couldn't. All it would take was an eagle-eyed police officer to realize that the driver of the Ford Focus was a bit on the young side and it would be all over. A few moments later, Leon asked Caleb a question.

"What's going on, Caleb?" he said. "Is Naomi okay?"

"I don't know, but I think she's in danger."

"Who from?"

"It's a long story, Leon."

"King Street's a good fifteen minutes away."

Caleb thought for a moment before replying. Leon had every right to know what was going on. In a sense, although it wasn't on purpose, it had been his actions that had toppled the first domino, but at the same time, he was only a young man. Caleb sighed as he decided to tell Leon what had happened, or at least most of it.

"Do you remember the woman with the bag full of money? On the bus?" Leon paused for a few seconds before replying.

"Uh, yep."

"She was on the run from her abusive partner." The term abusive didn't even begin to cover Vince's activity or plans. "That's what the money was for. It was Suzy's and Leanne's escape fund."

"Is she okay? You're going to give her the money back, right?"

Caleb thought about the bag full of money that was still in Syd's apartment.

"No," he said. "She's dead." Caleb heard Leon swear under his breath and the car swerved momentarily. "So are a couple of other people who tried to help her."

"The kid?" Leon said, his face whitening.

"Missing. Vince, that's Suzy's partner, has got her."

"So she's the hypothetical smuggling victim?"

"Yes. Vince is a member of the security services, so is a pretty formidable man. MI5, or so Suzy said. It could all be a fallacy, but I have no reason to disbelieve her."

"Like James Bond?" Leon said, reminding Caleb that he was still only a boy.

"No," Caleb replied. "I'm pretty sure James Bond was one of the good guys. Vince isn't."

"He's the darkness?"

"Yes, Leon, he's the darkness," Caleb said with a sigh. "And he's got Naomi."

CHAPTER 95

Naomi gasped as the material that Vince had used to gag her finally fell away from her mouth. She took a deep, grateful, breath in through her mouth. It had taken her what seemed like ages, but she had managed to scrape it against the carpet on the floor of the trunk and work it away from her mouth. The gag now lay around her neck like a scarf.

After he had gagged her, Vince had taken a few moments before the car started up again. That had been, in Naomi's estimation, around twenty minutes ago. It was hard to judge time in the situation she was in though. It could have been much longer, it could have been much shorter. But Naomi thought they were still in or around Norwich. The car was speeding up and slowing down, pausing occasionally as if for a set of traffic lights, and she could hear the sound of other traffic. It was different to how it would have been if they were on a divided highway or a freeway, for example. Her mind drifting, Naomi thought back to a quiz she had attended a few months ago where one of the questions had been how many counties in England had no freeways. She couldn't remember what the correct answer had been, but Norfolk had been one of them.

So if they were still in Norwich, was that a good or a bad sign? Naomi had no idea. She knew nothing of this Vince character other than what Caleb had told her, and what Vince himself had said. She remembered his promise to her, and the memory started her heart racing again. Naomi forced herself to focus, not on what he had said, but on anything else. She needed to find a happy place.

As the car stopped and started again, she closed her eyes tightly and thought back to when she was just shy of her fifteenth birthday. She had gone to Cromer, a seaside town on the north Norfolk coast, with a group of school friends. Later in the day, after they had all eaten fish and chips on the seafront and were wandering along the beach underneath the pier, one of them, a young lad in her year called Michael, had pulled her to one side. When they were out of sight of the others, hidden behind a large, rusting support pillar, he had kissed her. Naomi couldn't remember much about the kiss other than the fact his lips were greasy and he tasted of cod, but it was her first proper kiss.

Naomi almost laughed at the memory and if she had been anywhere else, she would have done so. That memory didn't, she decided, qualify as a happy place. She was just in the process of trying to conjure up another one when she realized the car was slowing down. Her heart started thumping again when it stopped and the engine was turned off. One of the doors opened, and Naomi held her breath. Was this it? But the footsteps she could hear faded away and the car was still.

She remained motionless for some moments. Her arms and legs were aching, the pain in her joints from being in the same position for so long almost unbearable. Not only that, but she badly needed the bathroom. Where was Vince? Had he abandoned the car?

Naomi couldn't tell how much time had passed when she heard footsteps returning to the car. She could hear Vince talking, mumbling to himself. Then there was an odd scratching noise and he got back into the car. A moment after that, the engine started and they were off again.

If was different this time, though. Vince was driving much quicker, taking corners faster, and braking harder. Naomi tried as hard as she could to brace herself against the sides of the trunk. Maybe three or four minutes after that, the car again started to slow until it came to a complete halt. The next sound she heard was a metallic rattling and the car inched forward slowly before the she heard the rattling sound again. She could sense rather than tell that the car was now inside a building and that the sound she had just heard was a garage door closing. The car engine stopped and she heard the door opening, followed by the car bouncing slightly as Vince got out.

Naomi took a deep breath, partly to try to quell the overwhelming panic building in her chest and partly to prepare to scream as loudly as she could. Even if the car was in a garage, perhaps there would be neighbors who might hear her and call the police. Naomi knew she couldn't fight Vince. Not only was she still tied up, but her limbs were in agony from being in the same position for so long. All she could do was scream and hope for the best.

As the trunk opened, Naomi let out the loudest scream she possibly could.

CHAPTER 96

"That's the Last Pub Standing just there," Leon said, pointing at the slightly crooked building. Above the ancient roof the skies were darkening but that wasn't deterring the determined smokers outside the pub. He saw Caleb nodding and looking around. After a few moments, Caleb pointed toward the end of the street.

"Down that way, but drive slowly," Caleb replied. Leon did as instructed, following Caleb's directions. They took one or two wrong turns, but eventually Caleb's hand shot out a few moments later. "There!" he said, his voice almost excited. He was pointing at a small apartment block, one of the newer buildings on the road they were crawling down. "That's where she lives."

Leon pulled over outside the block and Caleb got out. He made his way to the front door, pressing the doorbells in turn just as he had done at the office block. But just as before, there was no reply. When he returned to the car, his frustration was almost palpable.

"Nothing," Caleb muttered. "What can I do?" Leon remained silent, sensing the question wasn't one that Caleb expected him to answer. They sat in silence for a few moments before Caleb appeared to make a decision. "Let's go back to the estate."

Leon pulled away from the curb, saying nothing. Caleb was deep in thought. When Leon glanced over at him, he had his eyes closed. Caleb's lips were moving as if he was talking to himself, but Leon could not hear any words. Was he praying? A light rain had started to fall outside, and it took Leon a moment to work out how to turn the wipers on.

A few minutes later, Caleb opened his eyes and looked at Leon.

"We have to find the girl," Caleb said. "Leanne. She's the key. We find her, and we can draw Vince in."

"Why has he taken Naomi?" Leon asked him. "That doesn't make sense."

"He's cleaning up," Caleb said. "He's going after everyone who knows about Suzy and Leanne." He paused, staring out of the window for a moment before continuing. "I should never have said anything to Naomi."

"Does anyone else know?"

"Well, the police know," Caleb replied with a look of frustration. "I don't think they believed me, though."

"If the Old Bill knows, why not go to them?" Leon said, thinking that it was the first time in his life he'd ever suggested approaching the police for help.

"What can they do? Naomi's only been missing for a short time, and she's a grown woman."

"But she's been kidnapped? Surely they'll do something. Naomi's got friends in the police. When they were interviewing me, she knew all of them at the nick."

"We've got no proof, Leon," Caleb replied. "No description of Vince. Nothing." Leon saw him pointing at a pedestrian on the sidewalk hurrying in the rain. "That could be him." He pointed at another man further down the road who was trying to hold on to a flimsy umbrella. "Or him. No, this is my mess. The police won't take her disappearance seriously for a couple of days." His face hardened. "Naomi won't have that long. It could already be too late."

"It's not your fault, Caleb," Leon said, almost on the verge of tears at the thought of something happening to Naomi. He liked her. She had been one of the few people who had actually tried to help him. "You weren't to know this nutter was going to go after her." When he looked over at Caleb, he had a faint smile on his face.

"I appreciate your sentiment, Leon, but with hindsight perhaps I should have."

"I don't see how. You shouldn't be beating yourself up over it, that's all I'm saying."

They drove in silence for a while, eventually turning into the estate. The only way to get to the towers was to drive right past his own house. Leon shuffled down in the seat and slowed down as they drove down his road, not wanting his mother to see his driving. With a sigh of relief as he turned into the parking lot at the base of the towers and parked in Syd's customary spot.

"We find Leanne, we can get to Vince that way." Leon saw Caleb nodding in agreement with himself. "Let's get Syd to set up a meeting with this Henry, and we can take it from there. Vince could be keeping Naomi as leverage to get to me." Caleb reached out his hand and placed it on Leon's arm. "Focus on that, okay?"

"So, what, you would trade yourself for Naomi?" Leon glanced at Caleb, whose face had darkened again.

"If that's what it takes, Leon, yes," Caleb said. "You must know the bible verse about walking through the valley of death?"

"Something about fearing no evil?"

"Very good, Leon," Caleb replied, his expression still one of stone. "Psalm twenty-three. Verse four."

"Okay," Leon said.

"If trading myself is what it takes, then so be it. I have no fear of evil." Caleb took a deep breath before continuing. "If anything, evil fears me."

CHAPTER 97

Caleb got out of the car and looked up at the sky. The rain had stopped, but the clouds were still dark and menacing, which mirrored his mood. As he made his way to the entrance door to Syd's tower, his thoughts turned to Naomi. Caleb had said nothing to Leon, but the probability was she was already dead. Vince wasn't wasting time cleaning up the witnesses. Suzy, Joan, and Father Martin. None of them had survived more than a few moments in Vince's company. Other than finding Leanne, and that was a stretch, Caleb had no options left. He couldn't find Vince, and Vince couldn't find him. But Caleb did have a familiar sensation building in his chest that he couldn't describe. He had felt it before. Evil was close, and it was getting closer.

He waited as Leon punched in the four-digit code to open the apartment door. There was a muted buzz as the lock opened, and Leon huffed as he pushed it open. Caleb followed him into the foyer and waited by the elevator as Leon pressed the bell for Syd's apartment. While they waited, Caleb rubbed the back of his neck.

"You okay, man?" Leon asked him. Caleb regarded the young man as he replied. He had thought there was more to Leon than it seemed, and he had been right. The way he had tried to reassure Caleb back in the car, and now the way he was asking after his welfare, showed a very different side to Leon than the one he presented to the outside world.

"I've got a headache brewing," Caleb said, but he knew the tight band of pressure that was wrapping itself around the back of his neck wasn't a headache. It was pure rage at the thought of Naomi's death. He closed his eyes briefly, offering up a quick prayer that it had been as swift and as painless as it could have been, but his prayer was interrupted by a vision of Suzy lying on her bed, her throat cut from ear to ear. Except it wasn't Suzy's face in his vision. It was Naomi's.

"Why's Syd taking so bloody long to answer the bell?" Leon said, jabbing again at the panel. A moment later, with still no reply from Syd, he turned to Caleb. "We'll have to take the stairs. He's probably off his head on something."

Caleb said nothing, but followed Leon to the stairwell. The air inside was just as pungent as he remembered from his earlier visit, and Caleb tried to put the thought that the smell was particulate matter to the back of his mind.

They climbed the stairs in silence, Caleb appreciating the exercise. It was helping to calm his thoughts and push the anger down to a manageable level. But when they reached Syd's floor and approached his front door, he could feel it ramping back up.

"I'm going to go to the roof, Leon," Caleb said. "I need some time out." Leon gave him a peculiar look, but nodded.

"I'll speak to Syd, get something set up with Henry, and we'll head to Yarmouth. You got money for the meeting?"

"No," Caleb said, shaking his head. "But I can take it

from Suzy's bag and pay it back somehow. Leanne will need that money." He paused before continuing. He had been about to say if we find her. "When we find her."

"I've got money," Leon replied without pausing. "I can pay so you don't have to borrow it from the girl. Let's just get this done."

Caleb nodded and turned for the final stairs leading to the roof, leaving Leon to speak to Syd. When he got to the open air, Caleb breathed in a deep breath. He needed to focus. The rage he was feeling was damaging and would limit his performance.

"A man of wrath stirs up strife, and one given to anger causes much transgression," he muttered under his breath and then, because he couldn't help himself, "Proverbs, chapter twenty-nine, verse twenty-two."

He made his way to the parapet of the roof and sat on a large metal duct, looking down at the city of Norwich. It was, like he was, sitting under a dark cloud. There was a dark gray smudge across the sky. The only thing piercing it was the tall pinnacle of the cathedral. There was, Caleb mused, something poetic about the fact something man had built to honor God was the only thing to reach into the darkness.

Caleb crossed his legs underneath him and closed his eyes, relishing the feeling of the cool breeze on his face. He placed his palms on his knees and started the methodical process of clearing his mind he had developed over the years. For a man of the cloth, Caleb was quite liberal about how he interpreted the seven deadly sins. On occasion, and this was such an occasion, he actively courted them. His actions with Naomi could be interpreted as lust, of that he was sure. But he was also sure he could account for that sin when the time came.

If the disciple Matthew was right in that every man who looked at a woman lustfully had already committed adultery with her in his heart, then the world was chock full of sinners, Caleb among them. But Caleb wasn't interested in lust at that point in time. He was interested in one of the other so called deadly sins. And in Caleb's case, it was almost always deadly. He thought again about the Proverbs verse. Caleb wanted to stir up strife. He wanted to cause transgression. For that to happen, he needed to channel one thing.

Wrath.

CHAPTER 98

As Caleb made his way up the stairs to the roof, Leon fished in his pocket for the keys to Syd's apartment. He cursed under his breath at the fact the man hadn't bothered to answer the doorbell, still out of breath from climbing ten flights of stairs. Even though Caleb was probably twice his age, the effort had hardly seemed to bother him.

Leon slid the key into the lock and turned it, opening the door a couple of inches.

"Syd?" he called out. "It's me, Leon." There was no reply.

When Leon entered the apartment, he paused. Something wasn't right. When he realized what it was, he laughed to himself. The fog of smoke that usually lingered in the place wasn't there, nor was the traditional smell of cannabis. Either Syd wasn't in, or whatever he had taken wasn't weed.

"Mate? Are you in here?" Leon called out, not expecting a response. Syd's front door opened straight into his lounge, which only left the kitchen and the bedroom unless he was in the can. Leon walked past the kitchen, glancing inside as he did so, and paused outside Syd's bedroom door. It wasn't closed, but ajar by an inch or so. Leon wasn't sure what to do. He didn't want to walk in on Syd if he was enjoying some personal time, either alone or with someone, but he couldn't hear anything so he leaned forward and pushed the door open.

"Fuck!" Leon gasped as the door opened. Syd was lying on the bed, his eyes wide open and a neat hole in the center of his forehead. Next to Syd's body was a pillow, torn to shreds, and a pile of feathers. Most of them were covered in blood and matter. "Fucking hell."

Leon started to turn, feeling a surge of vomit rising in his stomach. He was going to throw up. As he span around, he found himself looking down the barrel of a gun. He should have checked the bathroom.

"Not so fast, young man," the intruder said, making a gesture with the gun to usher Leon back into Syd's bedroom. "If you're going to vomit, do it in his bedroom. He won't mind."

Leon swallowed, trying to control his breathing. The man with the gun was around Caleb's age, and was wearing dark jeans, a hoodie with a small pink logo on the breast, and a pair of thin leather gloves. He was holding the gun, a matte black pistol that looked similar to Syd's Glock 17s, with the air of someone very used to using it.

"Who are you?" Leon asked, even though he knew the answer. He needed to think quickly or risk ending up with a hole in his own head.

"You can call me Vince," the man replied. Leon made a concerted effort to act as if he'd never heard the name before, remembering what Caleb had said about witnesses. "Who are you?"

"Leon," he replied, his mouth dry. "My name is Leon."

"Well, I'm pleased to meet you, Leon. I think I may have met your mother earlier." A shiver went down Leon's spine at the thought of this man talking to his mom. They may not always get on, Leon and her, but she was all he had. "She told me you might be up here. She also told me you've got a new friend. Is that right?"

Leon swallowed, or at least tried to. The inside of his mouth was like an emery board. He nodded before replying.

"So, I have a really simple question for you, young Leon." Vince was smiling, but it was a cold rictus grin. "Where is your new friend?" He glanced at Syd on the bed. "I would advise you not to lie to me. I can always tell when someone's lying."

Leon also glanced at Syd. There was no way Syd would have taken a bullet for Caleb, or anyone else for that matter. Leon imagined Syd desperately pleading with Vince, telling him he didn't know where Caleb was. But Syd would have been telling the truth. Caleb hadn't told him where they were going.

"I didn't kill your friend because he was lying," Vince said as if he had just read Leon's thoughts. "We were having a very civilized conversation until he came in here." Vince angled the pistol toward the floor. Leon saw one of Syd's Glocks, the one he kept under his pillow, lying on the floor. "That's no way to treat a visitor, is it?"

"Um, no?" Leon replied.

"You're a quick learner, Leon," Vince said, his grin broadening. "How old are you?"

"Fifteen."

"But very wise for one so young, perhaps?" Leon said nothing, unsure if it was a question or a statement. Vince's grin started to wane. "Wise enough to tell me where your new friend is. Tell me and I'll let you go. You have my word."

Leon knew he had two choices. He could lie and risk getting shot. Or he could tell the truth and risk Caleb dying.

But which was it to be?

CHAPTER 99

At the end of the scream, Naomi inhaled to prepare for another. As she did so, she opened her eyes just enough to peep through, expecting to see Vince about to strike her. But it wasn't Vince who she could see. It was three young men, all of whom looked as terrified as she was. In a bizarre parody of the three wise monkeys, one of them had his hand clasped over his own mouth. The other two were just staring at her.

"What the fuck?" the man in the middle said. "What the actual fuck?"

The man on the left reached into his pocket and pulled out a piece of metal. With a flick of his wrist and a metallic snap, the metal expanded into a knife.

"No, no, no," Naomi said when she saw the blade, wriggling to get away from it as he approached the trunk.

"It's okay, miss," the man with the knife said. "I'm not going to hurt you." He leaned forward and Naomi realized he was going to cut the zip ties around her wrists. He did so with exaggerated care, but the pain when her wrists were released made her cry out.

"I'm sorry, I'm sorry," the man said. Now that he was closer, Naomi saw that he wasn't a man at all, but could have been no more than fourteen. He wasn't even old enough to shave. He helped her into a half-sitting position.

The man who had sworn seemed to be the oldest of the three of them, but not by much. All of them were wearing hooded tops, jeans that seemed to defy gravity, and impossibly clean sneakers.

"Come on boys, let's get her out. Gently now."

Naomi cried out a couple of times as the three of them helped her out of the trunk. They were surprisingly gentle with her, holding her arms as she tried to stand. While she waited for her legs to stop shaking like a newborn foal, she looked at her surroundings. The car was in some sort of garage. There were tools attached to the walls, a large table full of car parts near one wall, and the garage door she had heard closing was a rusty orange color.

"Richie," the oldest of them said. "Get her a bottle of water and a chair. Quickly."

Naomi could feel tears of relief pricking at her eyes as the youth who had freed her hands scurried away.

"Where am I?" she asked the two men holding her arms. Her throat was scratchy from being locked up for so long. Screaming so loudly had hurt and it felt like she had actually torn something in the soft tissue.

"You're in my garage," the older man said. "I'm Bolt, and this here's Kenny."

"Are you a fast runner, then?" Naomi said, causing the man to smile.

"No," his friend replied before he could. "We call him Bolt because he shot himself in the ass with a nail gun."

"Shut up, Kenny, you muppet," Bolt replied, but he

remained smiling. "I've got to ask, how come you were in the trunk?"

"It's a long story," Naomi replied. Just as she spoke, Richie returned with a plastic folding chair. He put it next to her and the other two lowered her gently into it.

"Here," Richie said, thrusting a cold bottle of water into her hand. "It's a fresh one. Not filled from the tap." With Bolt nodding in agreement, Naomi opened the bottle and took a sip. The water was deliciously cold as it hit the back of her throat.

"Thank you," Naomi said. "For the water and for rescuing me. I think I owe you all a beer."

"Kenny can't handle beer," Bolt said, still grinning. "He'll swamp his bed if he has more than two pints."

"You're such a melt, Bolt," Kenny shot back. He was about to say something else when Naomi interrupted him.

"If you don't mind me asking," she said, "how come you've got my car?"

She saw the three of them exchange looks before Bolt replied.

"We, er, we borrowed it for a bit," he said.

"Yeah," Kenny added. "We were going to give it back." He glanced at his two friends, who were doing their best to look innocent.

"Are we in Norwich?" Naomi asked, not caring in the slightest that she was in the company of thieves. It was hardly the first time, and they had saved her life.

"Yeah," Bolt replied. "We're on the Lark's Cross."

"Do you know Leon? Leon Brockwell?"

"Syd's lad? Yeah, we know him." Bolt's eyebrows went up. "You a mate of his?"

"Kind of," Naomi replied as she stood, swaying slightly. She remembered Caleb saying he and Leon were going to the towers on the Lark's Cross estate. "Are we close to the towers?" She needed to get to Caleb and warn him that Vince was in the area. Once she knew he was safe, then it would be time to call the police. All of them.

"About a hundred yards that way," Bolt said, pointing at the garage door. "Syd's place is on the tenth floor of the closest tower. That's where Leon will be if you're looking for him. It's the one with the metal door."

"I need to go," Naomi said, causing Bolt's smile to falter.

"Okay," he replied uncertainly. "We'll, er, we'll look after your motor for you."

"Thanks," Naomi replied. "Can I ask you for two quick favors?"

"Sure," Bolt said, hiking his smile back up.

"Can I borrow a phone, please?" Naomi watched as Bolt nudged one of the others. Kenny, she thought his name was. He reluctantly reached into his pocket and handed her a cell phone.

"The code's one, two, three, four," Kenny said, earning a disparaging look from the other two young men.

"What's the other favor?" Bolt asked.

"I really, really, need the bathroom."

CHAPTER 100

Vince studied the young man in front of him, enjoying the mental anguish on his face. He saw him swallow a couple of times before licking his lips. But Vince knew his mouth would be as dry as sandpaper. Fear had a habit of doing that to people, as Vince well knew.

Do I lie, or do I tell the truth? Vince knew that was Leon's dilemma, but which way would he go? And did the young man truly appreciate how important the decision was? As Leon glanced at his dead friend, Vince could see that he probably did.

"Why are you looking for him?" Leon asked, no doubt playing for time. It's what Vince would have done, and he felt a grudging admiration for the young man emerging.

"That's between him and I, Leon," Vince replied. "Grown up stuff." He saw Leon open his mouth and then close it again. How much did he know? Vince hadn't yet worked out the relationship between Leon and Naomi, but as she was a public defender, he must be a client of hers. There was no other way their paths could have crossed.

"What are you doing talking to my mum, anyway?" Leon said a few seconds later. Another play for time. He could have that one, Vince thought.

"I borrowed a car that belongs to someone who's been spending time with Caleb."

"Who?"

Vince paused for a moment to consider his response before replying.

"Her name's Naomi."

"My solicitor?" Vince nodded at Leon's question. He had been right, but then again, he normally was. "Is she okay?"

"No, Leon, she's very much not okay. She's currently in the trunk of her car outside your house. And as soon as we're done here, we're going to have a bit of private time together." He let a smirk play across his face as he saw the expression on Leon's face. Was he a bit sweet on the lovely Naomi? Vince wouldn't blame him. "Grown up stuff, but I'm sure you get the gist of what I'm talking about." He was tempted to gyrate his hips, but that would be overkill. From the look on Leon's face, he knew exactly what Vince was talking about. But as he watched, a look of confusion spread across the young man's face. He opened his mouth to speak, but closed it again.

"That's not right, man," Leon said, a dark look appearing on his face. Vince sighed. He was getting bored with this conversation, and had no time for misplaced loyalty on Leon's part.

"Leon, I'm not sure you're appreciating the situation you're in. I've got a gun." Vince waved the pistol for effect. "And I've asked you a question which you've still not answered." Then he leveled the pistol pointing it at the center of Leon's forehead. "Where is he?" Vince watched as Leon closed his eyes.

"Caleb's on the roof," Leon said in a whisper as he opened his eyes few seconds later, a look of shame appearing on his face.

"What's he doing on the roof?"

"I don't know, praying or something."

"Why would he be praying?" Vince asked.

"Well, he is a preacher," Leon replied. Vince nodded in reply. He'd forgotten that Caleb was a man of the cloth. Not that it made a blind bit of difference to Vince. A bullet was a bullet, regardless of its victim's calling or even denomination.

"So he is." Vince studied Leon for a moment. He could tell that the young man was desperate to say more but was keeping his own counsel. It was by far the best thing he could do under the circumstances. "He is indeed a turbulent priest." If Leon recognized the reference to Thomas Becket, he didn't show it, which disappointed Vince.

"He's not a priest," Leon replied. "He's a preacher."

Vince inched the pistol in Leon's direction, tightening his grip on the trigger as he did so. "Shut the fuck up and turn around." Any minute now, Leon was going to start pleading for his life. Vince hated it when people did that. It was demeaning.

"No way, man," Leon said, the look of shame being replaced by one of anger. "You said you wouldn't shoot me if I told you the truth. He's on the roof. Go and look if you don't believe me."

"Leon, turn around or I swear by Caleb's God that I will put a bullet in your face."

"That's not fair," Leon shot back. "You said you wouldn't shoot me. You gave me your word."

Vince swore under his breath. Leon wasn't pleading for his life. He was arguing about the fact that Vince had said he wouldn't shoot him, as if his word was worth more than Leon's life.

"Just turn around." Vince said, trying to inject some reassurance into his voice, although why he was expending the effort, he had no idea.

Finally, Leon did as instructed, muttering something under his breath as he did so. Once he was sure Leon couldn't see his face, Vince allowed himself a smile as he tightened his finger on the trigger.

He might be a young man, but Leon had some balls.

CHAPTER 101

Naomi was breathing hard as she pounded along the pavement, the large grey tower block looming into view. Her mind was on only one thing. Warning Caleb. Vince was close by, but now that Naomi was out in the open, she wasn't as fearful of him as she had been. There were plenty of people about, several of whom were giving her strange looks as she ran. She knew that even if Vince saw her, he wouldn't do anything to her in public. That wasn't how men like him operated.

An elderly man walking a small dog stared at her as she swerved to avoid them, a look of incredulity on his face. She was hardly dressed for a run. But Naomi didn't care what she looked like, or what they thought. She had to reach Caleb before Vince did.

A voice in her head nagged her to slow down. Take a moment to call the authorities. The sooner she did, the sooner they would be here. But a louder voice told her to keep going. Get to Caleb first, then call the police. Those few seconds could be crucial. They could be the difference between Caleb living and dying.

Naomi slowed her pace as she approached the foot of the tower block. She placed one hand on her side where a painful stitch was reminding her it had been too long since she'd last been to the gym. She made her way to the panel outside the entrance. There were two vertical rows of buttons, each with a space for a name next to them. Only around half had actual names, and there appeared to be a lot of Disney characters who lived in the block.

"Tenth floor," Naomi muttered as she ran her finger up to the top of the rows. She saw a label for *S. Barrett* and stabbed at it a couple of times. The other apartments on the same floor, according to their labels, belonged to *R. Waters*, *N. Mason*, and *R. Wright*. She stabbed at them as well, noting that the labels for all the apartments were written in the same hand. "Come on, come on," Naomi said as she waited, the seconds ticking by inexorably. There was no reply from any of them.

Naomi made her way down the row of doorbells, pressing each of them but not knowing if the apartments were occupied or even if the bells were working. She was perhaps two-thirds of the way down the rows when there was a crackling noise from the speaker in the panel.

"What?" It was a male voice, made tinny by the intercom. Naomi couldn't tell which apartment it was that had answered their bell.

"Er, pizza delivery?" Naomi said.

"Nope, not me," the voice replied. It sounded slurred even though it was only lunchtime.

"Wait, wait." Naomi tried not to sound desperate. "I've got a large double pepperoni with extra cheese, garlic bread, and a large bottle of soda. All paid for. Are you sure it's not for you?"

There was a pause on the other end of the intercom before the unseen voice replied.

"Uh, yeah. That was me." There was a metallic buzz from the door in front of her. "Come on up."

Naomi shoved at the door to open it, surprised how heavy it was. She entered the small foyer, wrinkling her nose at the smell of stale urine, and made her way to the elevator. This time, there were only ten buttons. Naomi pressed the one to the tenth floor, hoping that the man expecting a free pizza wasn't on his way down to meet her. She looked up to see a small red light had come on underneath a CCTV camera, but there was no indication that there was anyone on the other side of it.

She glanced over at the stairs, wondering if she should just bite the bullet and go up to the tenth floor that way. Based on what the three men at the garage had said, Leon was up there as well. It wasn't just Caleb who was in danger. It was Leon as well.

Naomi pulled Kenny's cell phone from her pocket. She should call the police while she was waiting for someone to answer from the apartment above. If no one had replied by the time she finished the call, she would take the stairs and hope for the best. But to Naomi's frustration, she had no mobile phone signal, probably because of the thick walls of the apartment block. She looked over at the heavy entrance door and then around the foyer to see if there was something she could use to jam it open, but all she could see on the floor were flyers for takeout food. Nothing substantial enough to prop the metal door open.

With a groan, Naomi headed for the stairwell. Perhaps as she got higher, the signal would improve.

CHAPTER 102

Leon grunted as he put as much effort into teasing his wrists apart as he could. His shoulders felt as if they were on fire, but the zip ties around his arms wouldn't budge an inch. If he could somehow free his hands which were securely tied behind him then he could free his feet from the chair they were tied to. But as it was at that moment, he was tied up like the proverbial hog. At least he wasn't gagged, but from his current position in Syd's tiny kitchen, there was no one to hear him scream. The most frustrating thing was that Leon knew there were knives in Syd's drawer that would cut through the ties like butter, but Leon had no way of getting to them.

When Vince had told him to turn around a few moments earlier, Leon had been sure that he was going to die. At the time, to his surprise, he'd been more angry than scared. The latter emotion was the one he expected, but he couldn't get the fact Vince had told him he would let him go if he told the truth out of his head. He had told the truth, albeit reluctantly. Just before he'd given up Caleb's location, Leon had closed his eyes and come the closest to praying as he had done since one of his school friends had told him Santa didn't exist. But it hadn't been a prayer in Leon's mind. He'd been trying to work out what Caleb would do. The answer, which was to save himself, had come in a split second. Caleb wouldn't have wanted Leon to die for him, of that Leon was sure.

Leon had screwed his eyes tightly shut, wondering if you heard the bullet that killed you, when Vince rabbit punched him in the kidneys. The blow was harder than Leon had ever been punched in his life. It had felt like having explosive, jalapeño induced diarrhea, but instead of shooting out, it was shooting in. Leon had dropped to his knees, stunned and wanting to cry, but he'd not been able to summon up a single tear. It was all he could do to breathe while Vince secured his wrists in the small of his back before hauling him onto a kitchen chair and tying his ankles to the legs.

Just as Leon took a deep breath to prepare to try to free his wrists again, he heard Syd's elevator bell ring out. He stopped what he was doing, crunched his abdomen, and lowered his head. Then he arched his head up as powerfully as possible, putting all his effort into trying to edge the chair forward and toward the lounge. The chair moved perhaps six inches.

It took Leon perhaps another five or six lunges, but he managed to move the chair forward enough to see around the jamb and into the lounge. On the small screen next to the panel that sent the elevator down was a familiar face.

"Naomi!" Leon shouted as if she could hear him. But on the screen, Naomi was just peering up at the camera. "Naomi," he said again, realizing she couldn't hear him. "Thank goodness you're okay."

When Vince had told him earlier that Naomi was in the trunk of her car outside his house, it hadn't sounded right to

Leon. He and Caleb had driven past his house on the way to the towers, and Leon hadn't seen Naomi's car near his house. Being bright red and several years younger than almost every other car on the estate, it was quite distinctive. Leon had been about to say something to that effect to Vince but had kept his mouth shut. Now, he was pleased he had, but Naomi was potentially putting herself in danger by coming back here.

On the screen, Leon saw Naomi looking at her cell phone and frowning. Then she disappeared from view. From the way she had moved to the side, Leon thought she must be coming up the stairs.

He lunged forward again, moving another few inches toward Syd's desk. He wouldn't be able to open the door for Naomi if she was coming here, but there was a button on Syd's desk that opened the door remotely. And if Naomi got inside the apartment, she could free him.

That would mean he could go and help Caleb before it was too late.

CHAPTER 103

Caleb sat in silence, listening as a couple of seagulls called to each other. He watched the two enormous birds swooping and cawing as they circled around each other. They were too high to be looking for food on the ground, and as he watched, one of them snatched at the air with its large beak, plucking a winged insect of some sort from the sky. From their pink legs, Caleb knew they were herring gulls. Large, noisy, and opportunistic.

He envied the birds as they took it in turns to snatch at the sky. Not only for their ability to soar through the air, at times effortlessly, but for the simplicity of their lives. They were born, they were raised, they ate whatever they could find. Then they would reproduce, die, and the entire cycle would start again. Much like humans, but seagulls didn't have the trials and tribulations that people brought upon themselves.

Far below them, the estate sprawled. From his vantage point, Caleb could clearly tell where the estate ended and the more affluent housing began. He wondered if the seagulls were in this location because of the estate below. Whether it was rich pickings in terms of food. Perhaps the two gulls he was watching had chicks in a roof nest somewhere, waiting to be fed. He wouldn't have been surprised to see a nest here on the roof. If he were a gull, he would build one somewhere like this. Far away from any human visitors. Or perhaps not.

Beyond the gulls, Caleb could see the clouds that had briefly produced some rain earlier still building in the sky beyond the estate. But they weren't the only clouds that were building. There was another cloud, far more malevolent, that Caleb could feel in his heart. It was gathering speed, and Caleb knew a reckoning was past due. Unlike the many times he had felt this before, the reckoning was coming to him, not he to it. In seeking to be the hunter, he had become the hunted.

Caleb thought back to the first time he had experienced what he currently felt. The dark foreboding of evil. He thought he was perhaps eleven or twelve, back at home in Texas. He and his father had been on a hunting trip in the Big Thicket National Preserve, just north of Beaumont. It was one of the last memories he had of his father, and they had both been in a good mood as they were driving home. In the trunk was a large cooler full of white-tailed deer and wild boar. Everything they had hunted would be put to good use, whether for food or clothing. Caleb's first ever satchel had been made from a deer that he had shot. Caleb smiled as he remembered his father's response when he had asked him if he could shoot a squirrel, more to prove to his father that he could than any other reason.

"A rabbit, yes," his father had told him. "A squirrel, no." Then his eyes had wrinkled in the weather-beaten way they did when he smiled. "Unless you want to have squirrel stew for supper?"

As they had approached Huntsville, almost exactly the half-way point between the preserve and the patch of land they called home, Caleb's father had announced they were stopping for supper. They had gone into a roadside burger joint just off the highway. Caleb had first noticed the feeling as they waited for their burgers.

"Are you okay?" Caleb's father had asked him, realizing he wasn't feeling well. Caleb had shaken his head. He had a dull, heavy sensation in the center of his chest that he couldn't describe, accompanied by an alarming sensation of clarity in his head. Caleb had started crying, hating the sensation. Then the clock on the diner wall had ticked past six in the evening and with that, the feeling was gone in an instant. It had been years later that Caleb had been able to link that sensation with the proximity, and sudden departure, of evil personified. He had since learned to use it to his advantage, although as he sat on the roof and waited, Caleb knew he had no advantage to speak of.

A scraping noise sounded behind Caleb. It was the door to the roof being opened. Caleb had sprinkled some gravel near the door to ensure it couldn't be opened silently.

"Keep me safe, my God," Caleb muttered as he rose to his feet, "for in You I take refuge."

CHAPTER 104

Naomi reached the third floor, way more out of breath than she should have been after only three floors. She paused, partly to get her breath back and partly to check whether she had a phone signal. But her phone was still showing nothing. The stairwell was effectively an interior column inside the building, so she wasn't surprised. A few seconds later, she continued up the stairs, moving as fast as she could.

The higher Naomi climbed, the more labored her breathing became. Her legs became heavier and her pace slowed. She mentally chastised herself for not attending the gym more often as the stitch returned just below her left breast. Naomi paused for a few seconds to rub her side where it felt like someone was jabbing into her with a sharp object. She was almost there, and she forced herself to push through the pain and keep going. When she finally arrived at the tenth floor, she could feel a rivulet of perspiration running down between her shoulder blades.

She thought back to what Bolt had said back in the garage.

"It's the one with the metal door," she muttered as she made her way down the corridor. The last door she came to, and the closest one to the elevator, was metal. Naomi paused outside it, thinking. What if Vince was in the apartment? She would be right back where she started. She reached out a finger to the bell next to the door, noticing it was trembling. What should she do?

Naomi cursed herself for not calling the police when she had a chance earlier. It was a stupid decision. There could have been an army of police officers on their way. She knew that her call wouldn't have been dismissed as a prank call, but it was too late now. Unless she ran back down the stairs, went outside to call them, and then started over. But if Vince was in the apartment, then so would Caleb. It would be two against one. For what that was worth.

She swore under her breath as she jabbed at the bell, hearing a muted ding dong inside the apartment. Then she lowered both hands and clenched her fists. From inside the apartment, she heard a male voice shouting her name.

"Naomi," the voice said. "I'm coming." Was it Caleb? Naomi didn't think it was, but the door was muffling the voice. It sounded higher than Caleb's voice, but it could be stress, perhaps? She forced herself to unclench her hands, as her nails were digging into the palm of her hand. There was a series of thumps from the other side of the door and, a moment later, there was a buzz from the door.

Naomi shoved at the door as hard as she could. It opened with a hissing sound and she had to put all her weight behind it to open it. When she entered the apartment, she saw Leon grinning broadly at her from behind a large desk. As she rushed over toward him, she realized he was restrained to the chair he was sitting in. She threw her arms around him anyway and he made a sound as if he'd just been winded.

"Can you cut me loose?" he said when she unwrapped her arms from his shoulders. "There're some knives in the kitchen." She saw him nodding his head over his shoulder. Moving quickly, she made her way to the kitchen and threw open several draws until she found the cutlery.

A moment later, Leon was rubbing his wrists, a grateful expression on his face.

"Where's Caleb?" Naomi asked, her voice urgent.

"He's on the roof," Leon replied. He got to his feet, still rubbing his arms. "So's Vince. I'm going up there."

"No, you're not," Naomi said. "We need to get the police."

"I'm going up there, Naomi." Leon's voice was firm, but Naomi's was firmer.

"You are not, end of discussion." Naomi's relief at finding Leon was fast being outweighed by her concern for Caleb. Leaving Leon staring at her open-mouthed, she moved toward the windows of the apartment, her phone in front of her. She looked at her screen. Finally. A signal.

"Emergency. Which service?" a male voice said a few seconds later.

"Police, please," Naomi replied, trying to keep her voice even. There were a couple of clicks and another male voice spoke but, to Naomi's frustration, it was an automated message.

"You are through to the police," the voice said. "Press 55 to be put through to police call management." It took Naomi a couple of extra precious seconds to work out how to enter the digits on a mobile and she could see Leon glancing at the door. She fixed him with a hard stare in case he was thinking about going anywhere. She had messed this up once already by waiting so long to make this call. The last thing she needed was Leon in danger.

"Police, what's your emergency?" It was a female voice this time, and Naomi could have cried with relief that she was finally on the phone with someone who could help.

CHAPTER 105

Vince's first impression of Caleb when he saw him up close for the first time was one of disappointment. He was smaller than he had realized from the images and CCTV footage he had seen him on. Almost inconsequential.

"Caleb, I presume," Vince said as Caleb turned to face him, because manners cost nothing.

"Indeed. You must be Vince." His voice was deep, and his accent obvious. Vince wondered if he was accentuating it for effect. Vince took a few steps toward Caleb until they were perhaps twenty yards apart, separated by one of the wide metal ducts that crisscrossed the roof.

"You know," Vince said, "I thought you'd be bigger." To Vince's surprise, Caleb laughed.

"Gee," he replied a few seconds later. "I've never heard that before." His laughter faded and Vince could see how cold his eyes were. But looking at someone never hurt them. Vince's pistol was pressing against his abdomen, secure in its Kydex holster, but he was confident he could reach it long before the other man could reach him. He also had a knife strapped to his ankle, but Vince had another plan for that weapon.

"I've been looking for you for a while," Vince said. "You're a hard man to track down."

"Why have you been looking for me?"

"I like that in a man, you know," Vince replied with a smile. "Direct. To the point." He waited for a few seconds before Caleb raised his eyebrows at him. "I think you know why I've been looking for you. You have some information that I need suppressed."

"An interesting choice of words," Caleb said. "Suppressed. As in the way that you suppressed Suzy? And Joan? And Father Martin?" Vince looked at him carefully, noticing that he'd barely moved since standing up and turning to face him.

"I am a hunter, Caleb." Vince was already starting to get bored with the conversation. He was a man of action, after all. "It's in my blood."

"And Leanne? Where is she?"

"That is none of your business."

"You made it my business."

"How so?"

"When you killed her mother." Caleb's eyes had narrowed, but his eyes were still as cold as forged steel. "That is a debt which remains outstanding."

"So you're a debt collector now?" Vince asked him. "I thought you were a preacher?"

"A label is a label. Like the one you have given yourself. If you are hunter, then am I your prey?"

"I found you, didn't I?"

"Indeed you did."

The two men remained in silence for a few moments, regarding each other. Vince knew he could just end this by pulling out his pistol and putting a round between Caleb's eyes. That would be the sensible thing to do, and achieve the objective of silencing him. He could leave his body here for the animals, assuming no one came to investigate the sound of a gunshot. A sky burial of sorts. Vince doubted many people came up to this roof. Of course, he would be found at some point, but perhaps by then his body would have been picked to the bone by carrion crows. A fitting end for a preacher man.

"Aren't you curious?" Vince asked a moment later. "About how I found you?"

"Naomi told you?"

"Ah, the lovely Naomi," Vince replied. "I was wondering when you would ask after her. No, it wasn't Naomi who told me. Not directly."

"You took her and you took her car."

"Very good. Her sat nav told me all I needed to know."

"Where is she?"

"All these questions, Caleb," Vince replied. He faked a yawn, raising a gloved hand to his mouth for effect. "They really are quite tiresome. If you must know, she's waiting in the car." Vince watched as Caleb turned his head and gazed down at the estate below them. "Was she fun? In bed?" Vince narrowed his eyes as he looked at Caleb. It was time to turn up the heat on the man. See what he was made of. "I can't wait to find out."

Caleb turned back to look at Vince, but he still made no movement. Even his expression hadn't changed.

Vince slowly crouched down, one hand out toward Caleb. The other hand was reaching for the knife at his ankle. Moving slowly, he pulled it out of its holster and reversed it in his hand so he was holding it by the tip.

"Here, Caleb" Vince said as he pulled his hand back. "Catch."

CHAPTER 106

Leon saw Naomi breathe a large sigh of relief as she ended the call.

"They're on their way," she said, looking at him.

"We should do something." Leon rubbed his back where Vince had sucker punched him earlier. He probed the skin with his fingers, wondering if he had a cracked rib. It felt like he did, but Leon wasn't sure how far his ribs went down his back. "Not just sit here and wait."

"What can we do, Leon?" Naomi replied. "This Vince is some sort of trained assassin who's already got the better of the both of us." Her voice was breaking as she spoke, and Leon wasn't sure what to do. "If it wasn't for your idiot friends stealing my car, I would still be trussed up in the trunk waiting to be..." Her voice trailed away. "Waiting for Vince to come back," she said eventually, her voice quieter.

"What idiot friends?"

"One was called Bolt, like the runner."

"They nicked your car? Where was it?"

"Outside your house."

"The cheeky bastards," Leon replied. He pulled himself to his full height. "I'm going to have a word with them, so I am."

"Oh, Leon, calm down," Naomi said, brushing her hand across her cheek. "You're fifteen, for God's sake. Besides, they saved me from Vince. If they hadn't, you would still be tied to the chair."

Leon nodded, knowing Naomi was right. But there were still rules on the estate, and Bolt and the brothers had broken them. If someone was passing through the place, although few people did, and left their car unattended outside a shop or a bookies, then they were fair game. But a legitimate visitor to the estate was not to be targeted.

"We should do something," Leon said again. His voice was less confident, Naomi's words having made sense. Vince was not a man they could go up against on their own.

Leon watched as Naomi walked over to the Syd's desk. At some point, he should probably tell her about his friend's body in the bedroom, but at the same time he didn't want her freaking out.

"How does this work?" she asked him, pointing at the screen and panel that controlled the elevator.

"When someone presses the button, the screen comes on to show you who it is," Leon replied. "I could see you on it earlier." He pointed at the panel next to the screen where there were two buttons, both with arrows etched into the plastic. Leon's finger rested over the one pointing up. "That one opens the elevator door and then brings the car up to the tenth floor. The other one sends it down." He pressed the up button and the view on the screen changed to show the interior of the elevator. "The car's up here at the moment."

"Okay," Naomi said. "And you can't just press the button down in the lobby?"

"Not for this elevator, no. It can only be operated from here. There's another elevator, but it's rarely working."

"So you've got your own private elevator?" Naomi asked. She had a look of vague amusement on her face.

"I haven't, it's Syd's. He was the one who had these controls put in."

"Where is this Syd?"

Leon paused for a few seconds before replying.

"He'd dead," he said. Naomi's expression changed to one of horror.

"Vince?" she asked, her hand flying to her mouth.

"Who else?" Leon replied. "But don't go in the bedroom. Okay?"

"Right," Naomi said, nodding her head. Deep lines appeared on her forehead as she frowned. "Got it. Right, listen in. This is what we're going to do."

"I'm all ears," Leon replied, grateful that they were actually going to do something.

"You go down to the lobby to open the door for the police. I'll stay up here to work the elevator so they can get up here." Her eyes were bright and full of determination. "When they get up here, I'll send them to the roof."

"Why don't we do it the other way round?" Leon said. Naomi would be safer down there than she would be up here. Vince could return at any moment, although they were behind a metal door that he would have no way of accessing. Then he realized that was exactly why she was sending him instead of her. That, and perhaps she didn't trust him not to take matters into his own hands.

"Just do it, Leon," Naomi replied. From the expression on her face, it was clear the subject wasn't up for discussion.

A few moments later, Leon was in the elevator. He looked up at the camera in the corner and put his thumb in the air. A few seconds after that, the doors closed and the elevator started to descend.

Leon leant back against the wall, sighing as he did so. He knew the police wouldn't take long, not after what Naomi had told them on the phone.

It was almost over.

CHAPTER 107

As the knife left Vince's fingertips, Caleb knew he had three courses of action available to him.

He could do nothing. The way the knife was traveling, he had a fifty-fifty chance of it hitting him blade first. The blade was vertical, so he wasn't concerned about it actually penetrating his ribcage and it didn't seem to be traveling with enough force to get stuck in his ribs.

He could dodge out of the way of the knife, leaving it to sail past him and over the parapet. But that would leave him with one less weapon. Caleb knew that Vince would have a gun, either in a holster behind his back or an appendix holster. The knife might come in useful.

Or he could catch the knife, blade first, and return it to Vince with interest. To do that he would need to work out how quickly the knife was spinning so he could calculate the precise moment to catch it. That involved a lot of math, and math had never been his strongest subject. There was also the chance that Vince would merely sidestep the weapon. The time it would take Caleb to reach behind him to get enough momentum to throw the knife would give

Vince plenty of advance warning that it was coming back his way.

Caleb shifted his balance by a couple of inches, opting for a modified version of his first and second courses of action. A second or so later, the knife clattered into his sternum, handle first. There wasn't much force behind it at all and Caleb knew that Vince hadn't thrown the knife at him to try to hurt him. Even if it had hit Caleb blade first, it would have barely penetrated his skin. Caleb stooped down to pick up the knife, a cheap survival style knife with a serrated blade. It lacked the required balance for throwing, but was still a formidable weapon in the right hands, which Caleb's were. When he looked back at Vince, he saw that he had pulled his pistol out and was pointing it at him. Caleb started laughing.

"What's so funny?" Vince said. Caleb glanced at the knife before replying.

"I appear to have brought a knife to a gun fight." Caleb turned and placed the weapon on the parapet behind him. "Quite literally in this case." He regarded Vince, noticing that his grip on the pistol was relatively loose and his trigger finger was outside the guard. "Why don't we negotiate?"

"Negotiate?" It was Vince's turn to laugh. "I have a gun pointing at your head and you've just put the weapon I've given you down." Caleb raised his fists in an approximation of a boxer.

"We could settle this like gentlemen?" He lowered his hands. "Man to man. The old fashioned way. I have put my weapon down. Why don't you do the same?"

Caleb could see Vince was considering this. The other man was taller than Caleb. He was broader and heavier. And he was no doubt trained in unarmed combat. But there was a vast gulf between training and experience. Caleb was gambling on Vince not having much of the latter.

"And if you win?" Vince asked, a faint smile appearing on his face.

"You give me the location of Leanne and let Naomi go. After that, you walk away." Caleb offered up a small prayer to seek forgiveness for the lie.

"Really? You would let me go? Because if I win, you die."

"I accept that," Caleb replied, knowing that Vince was wavering. Men like him were full of pride. Caleb was tempted to offer Vince some spiritual guidance. From Proverbs, chapter eleven, verse two. *When pride comes, then comes disgrace.* But he thought better of it.

"They're not good odds in your favor, Caleb," Vince said. He let his hand drop to his side before taking a few steps back. Then he placed the pistol down on a duct next to the parapet, perhaps twenty yards from Caleb's knife. "Let's do this, preacher man."

Caleb watched as Vince approached him, crouching slightly with his hands loose at his sides. The stage was set. His eyes remained fixed on Caleb's. Caleb dropped into a similar stance and waited for Vince to make his first move.

He knew that only one of them would be walking away from this fight. The question was, who?

CHAPTER 108

Vince grinned as he saw Caleb dropping to his haunches, mirroring his own posture. The two men circled each other for a moment or two before Vince lobbed out a tentative swipe in Caleb's direction. The preacher stepped back to avoid it with ease, but he was sluggish in the way he did so. Vince tried another, faster jab with his left hand, followed by a feint with his right. As Caleb raised an arm to block the feint, Vince shifted most of his weight onto his rear foot and popped his left elbow into the air. Then he pivoted his rear foot, maximized his weight transfer forward and rotated his upper torso. The resulting rear hook landed just to the side of Caleb's right eye. Just before it landed, Caleb had jerked his head away, but there was still enough power in the resulting blow to open up an earlier cut.

Vince's grin broadened as he skipped back, chambering his hand back into his guard.

"First blood," Vince said, but there was no reply from Caleb. Technically, all he had done was open up an existing injury, but blood was blood. Vince jabbed and crossed into the air between them a couple of times, causing Caleb to step back in surprise. Vince continued smiling. This was going to be easy. When Caleb had suggested they settle things the old fashioned way, Vince had taken stock of the man. Caleb had just proven he was slow on his feet. He was also smaller than Vince was, both in height and in weight. Vince had trained for years in various types of combat, and mixed martial arts formed a core part of his physical regimen. But Vince had always preferred using his fists.

Vince raised his guard again as Caleb stepped forward. His right arm shot out, which Vince countered easily with his left. He left his right arm high, lowering his right shoulder and preparing to roll with Caleb's feint. But Caleb stepped in fast and delivered a short, stiff uppercut into the right upper quadrant of Vince's abdomen, just below his diaphragm. The blow wasn't particularly hard, but it was hard enough to knock the wind out of Vince, who was forced to deliver a couple of jabs of his own to push Caleb back. Just as he thought he'd gained enough space between them, Caleb's right leg shot out in a fierce stop kick that caught Vince square on his outer thigh. Vince took a couple of large steps back, the muscle in his right leg already burning.

"You know she's escaped, don't you?" Caleb said. A rivulet of blood was running down the side of his face. Vince looked at the red trickle. That would be his next target. If he could open the cut up more, the blood would be a distraction for his opponent.

"Who?" Vince asked, resisting the temptation to rub his thigh. Caleb's kick had been harder than he had first thought and he could feel the muscle starting to tighten up.

"Naomi," Caleb replied through gritted teeth. "Her car isn't outside Leon's house."

"Ah, this is the bit where you invite me to look so you can hit me." Vince took a couple of shuffling steps toward Caleb, considering his next move.

"No," Caleb replied, lowering his shoulders. "I'm going to hit you anyway. But I looked earlier. There isn't a bright red car to be seen anywhere on the estate."

Vince ignored Caleb's words. He knew he was trying to psych him out. The other man stepped forward, his right arm moving fast. Vince quickly switched his feet, driving up off the balls of his feet to extend his left leg into the air. At the same time, he thrust with his hips and shoulders. Just before his foot connected with Caleb's flank, he rotated his leg to maximize the impact. It was a classic Muay Thai switch kick, and one that Caleb would have been able to defend against if he was better. Vince noticed Caleb leaning to the side to deflect some of the power of the kick, but when it landed, it landed hard. Vince followed it up with a powerful right hook to Caleb's face. It landed right over the cut, and Caleb staggered back, breathing hard.

"This was your idea, preacher man," Vince said. He rolled his head from one side to the other, raising each shoulder as he did so. He was enjoying this. But from the look on his face, Caleb wasn't.

CHAPTER 109

The elevator seemed to take forever to reach the ground floor of the apartment. Knowing, or at least hoping, that Naomi was watching him on the screen, he glanced at the camera a couple of times. He'd told her not to go into the bedroom, and Leon really hoped she would heed that advice. Despite her age, Leon felt protective toward her, and he didn't like the thought of her being upset at the sight of a dead body.

Eventually, the elevator started to wheeze to a halt. When the doors opened, Leon pushed against them with relief. He didn't think he was claustrophobic, but at the same time he didn't enjoy the enclosed sensation of being in the car for so long.

He made his way across the foyer and pulled the exterior door open. Although it was only lunchtime, it was almost as dark as dusk outside. A fresh breeze was blowing and the air was musky, almost earthy. Leon looked up to see dark clouds overhead and birds wheeling through the air. As Leon leaned against the door to hold it open, he heard a low rumble of thunder in the distance. He looked up again to where two large birds were calling to each other as they moved through the sky. Even the seagulls were getting away from the coming storm.

It wasn't just the thunder that Leon could hear. In the distance, but gradually getting louder, he could hear the *whoop whoop* of sirens. Leon had never been a fan of the police, nor they of him, but this was different. There were people in danger. Caleb, certainly, and also Naomi. People he cared about.

A couple of fat drops of rain started to fall, sizzling on the dry pavement as they did so. Leon's grandfather, long since departed, had sworn he could smell rain coming. Leon remembered long, lazy summers on the farm he ran. He had always dreamed of running the farm one day, deep in the Norfolk countryside, but when Leon's grandfather had passed, they had discovered it was mortgaged to the hilt. The only inheritance that his mother had got was a massive headache. The sale of the farm to meet the debt had wiped her out, hence the council house they were living in now. He'd been too young at the time to understand what was going on, but his mother had explained it to him as best she could.

To his surprise, Leon felt a tightening sensation in his throat as tears pricked at his eyes. He'd not thought of his grandfather in years, so why now? All he wanted to do was to go home, give his mother a hug, and curl up on the sofa with a cup of tea. He didn't want to be here, waiting for the police to come and find Syd's dead body. Perhaps Caleb's too.

"For God's sake, Leon," he told himself as he brushed furiously at his eyes. "Get a grip."

In the distance, the sirens were getting louder. Leon thought he could detect three, perhaps even more. They would be here soon, and all this would be over. Leon's thoughts turned to Caleb. Was he alive? Was he dead? he remembered back to what Caleb had told him back in Syd's apartment. When Syd was still alive.

You've got a good heart in here, Caleb had said. Leon put his hand to his own chest, remembering the strange sensation he had felt when Caleb had touched him. Leon took a deep breath, listening to the approaching sirens.

For Caleb's sake, he hoped they got here quickly. Unless it was already too late.

CHAPTER 110

Caleb took a deep breath, ignoring the sharp pain in his side as he did so. He didn't think that Vince had struck him hard enough to break anything, but it sure felt like he had a cracked rib. As well as the pain in his rib cage, Caleb's head was pounding from the blows he had taken. As he shifted his weight from foot to foot, he considered the blows he had landed on Vince. One to the abdomen, one to the leg. The punch to Vince's abdomen should have been a lot harder. It was an opportunistic punch that Caleb had taken when he realized Vince still had his arm in his guard. But like Caleb's own rib cage, that area would be throbbing. The kick to his leg had been a tactical one. Having a dead leg made any further kicks much more difficult, not that it had stopped Vince's switch kick.

But Caleb now knew several things. He knew that Vince could kick, but preferred to use his hands. He had deliberately taken the switch kick to his side to encourage Vince to use his feet more, hopefully not realizing how much less power he could put into them from the dead leg. Vince probably didn't realize just how much he telegraphed his kicks as he prepared to take them. Caleb also knew that Vince left his abdomen exposed when he punched with his right hand. That left two major areas of weakness for him to exploit.

Caleb saw Vince's fight foot skip forward a couple of inches. Then his left leg swung out in a roundhouse kick. Caleb put the fingers of his right hand against his own temple and, keeping his elbow close to his body, dipped into it. As Vince's foot bounced harmlessly off Caleb's forearm, Caleb reached over with his left hand and wrapped his fingers around Vince's calf, spinning as he did so to push his opponent round. As he pulled Vince through the movement, using the other man's momentum, Caleb lashed out with his right foot and caught Vince on the ankle of his standing leg. Vince flew back, landing flat on his back with a rapid exhalation of air.

Resisting the temptation to step in and finish Vince with a throat strike, Caleb skipped backward and rolled his head the way Vince had done a few seconds earlier.

"What do you think, Vince?" he said as his opponent got to his feet. "When's this fight going to end?" Caleb was goading him, hoping for a rush of adrenalin from the man. It would make him sloppier than he was already. With a snarl, Vince leapt forward with a flurry of punches, some of which landed. But Caleb's arms were firmly in front of his head and none of them could do any damage. He pivoted away from the punches, lashing his hand out as he did so to slap Vince's cheek. There was nothing more humiliating in a brawl than being slapped by another man.

"This ends when you die, preacher," Vince said, his cheek coloring from the slap. He danced forward, attempting a roundhouse kick which Caleb just batted away. Then he tried a feint with his left arm followed by an uppercut which Caleb dipped below. Again, Vince had left his flank exposed, so Caleb drove a powerful punch into his diaphragm. Vince dropped to his knees as Caleb skipped away.

"You sure about that, Vince?" Caleb asked as a few fat raindrops started to fall. In the distance, Caleb could hear approaching sirens. If Naomi had managed to escape, then she would have called the police. But if they were on their way, that meant he didn't have much time. "Where's the girl?"

"Fuck you," Vince replied as he got to his feet, staggering slightly as he did so. Caleb looked at him with a touch of admiration. The man had to be hurting, but he wasn't giving up.

Vince tried a few more punches which Caleb stepped into, deflecting them with his forearms. Sure, he would be bruised for the next couple of weeks. Bare knuckle fights had a habit of doing that to you. But every punch that Vince failed to land weakened him.

The two men danced around each other for some moments, the sirens getting louder. They traded punches, but Caleb could tell Vince was tiring. It was time to finish this. Caleb needed to find out where Leanne was. Then he saw his opportunity.

Vince telegraphed with his feet, showing Caleb that he was shifting his weight to prepare for another switch kick, no doubt figuring that as the last one had landed, another could. When Vince's left leg shot out, Caleb reached down with his arm and grabbed it between his elbow and forearm. Then he stepped forward and raised his left leg into a knee strike that landed exactly where the two previous blows had. A point below and to the left of Vince's solar plexus, a few inches above where an appendectomy scar would be.

The result was instant and Caleb knew his liver kick had landed perfectly. Vince took a couple of large steps back before dropping to one knee. There was a look of abject agony on his face and he was gasping for breath. Then he turned and started crawling away from Caleb, retching as he did so.

"Where's the girl, Vince?" Caleb shouted after the retreating man. Vince didn't reply and Caleb turned around, looking at the sky just as a fork of lightning split the dark clouds overhead. A few seconds later, there was a loud crack of thunder that drowned the sound of the sirens. Vince had one more chance to give up Leanne's location. If he didn't, he would die. Caleb turned to face Vince, ready to give him one last opportunity before he met his maker.

When he did so, he saw Vince standing up, looking at him. Caleb realized his mistake instantly. Vince hadn't been crawling away to get away from Caleb. He had been crawling toward the gun.

Which was now pointing right at Caleb.

CHAPTER 111

Vince had never known such pain in his life as when Caleb's knee had impacted his abdomen. He was struggling to keep his arm out, the pistol feeling way heavier than it had done earlier.

"Move back!" he shouted as the rain started to fall in earnest. Caleb did as he was instructed and Vince followed him until they were both standing against the parapet, about twenty yards separating them.

"I thought we had a deal, Vince," Caleb said. Despite the situation, there was no trace of fear in his voice. It was something else. Sadness, perhaps?

"What did you expect, preacher man?" Vince shot back. "The Marquess of bloody Queensbury?" The sirens were much closer now. Vince risked a glance over the parapet and could see blue flashing lights on the edge of the estate. He returned his gaze to Caleb as the rain drops splattered around them. "In a few short seconds, Caleb, you'll know everything you've ever wondered about."

"And what's that?" It was definitely sadness in Caleb's voice.

"What it's like to die," Vince said. "Whether your God actually exists."

"He exists, Vince," Caleb replied. "Of that, I am sure."

"So where is he now, your God? I don't see him anywhere, rushing in to save you."

"That's not how He works." Caleb's voice was solemn, resigned almost.

Vince took a breath, sending a shooting pain through his diaphragm that took his breath away. The pistol in his hand wavered, but Caleb made no movement toward him.

"How are you going to get away with this, Vince?" Caleb asked. "The police are almost here. If you shoot me, you'll have shot an unarmed man."

Vince laughed at Caleb's naivety. "Sure, of course I will have." He changed the tone of his voice as if he was speaking in a courtroom. "Your Honor," he continued, "the suspect was armed with a knife. He was clearly agitated. I attempted to persuade him to drop the weapon. I gave him at three least clear and unambiguous warnings, but he came for me with the weapon and I was in fear of my life." Vince's laughter faded away. "You shouldn't have picked up the knife, Caleb. Your prints are now all over it."

He watched as Caleb closed his eyes and started moving his lips. "Don't be shy, preacher man. Let me hear your prayers." Caleb opened his eyes and regarded Vince with a somber look.

"Eternal rest, grant to him, O Lord, and let light perpetual shine upon him. May he rest in peace," Caleb said. "That's what I would say if it was anyone else's soul I was praying for. But I cannot pray for your soul. Do you read scripture?"

"Once a preacher man, always a preacher man," Vince

replied. "You'd better make this quick, Caleb. You're running out of time."

"For our struggle is not against flesh and blood, but against the powers of this dark world and against the spiritual forces of evil in the heavenly realms," Caleb said, his voice monotonous. "It's from Ephesians, chapter six, verse twelve."

"Very apt words for your last ones, Caleb."

Vince tightened his grip on the pistol and slipped his finger inside the trigger guard.

The gunshot, when it came, was deafening.

CHAPTER 112

Leon stood up straighter as the first police car rounded the corner. A few seconds later, as the first one screeched to a halt next to Syd's car, another marked vehicle appeared. The first car had barely stopped moving when the doors flew open and two uniformed police officers got out. One of them ran toward Leon, slipping on the wet ground, while the other ran round to the trunk of the car.

The police officer who ran up to Leon was in his mid-twenties, heavily built and dressed from head to toe in black tactical clothing. He had a variety of equipment attached to his belt, and was wearing a black baseball-type hat with the word POLICE at the front and a black and white checkered band around it.

"Location?" the police officer said, a look of fierce determination on his face. Leon glanced at the pistol attached to his hip as he replied.

"He's on the roof," Leon replied. "There's an elevator that'll take you to the tenth floor." He was talking too quickly, but the police officer didn't seem to mind. The second police officer, a woman perhaps in her late twenties wearing an identical uniform, jogged over with two serious looking weapons. She handed one weapon to her colleague before putting the sling of her own weapon around her neck.

"Rooftop, Melanie," the male officer said. She nodded in response. A few seconds later, two more armed officers arrived from the second vehicle. "We're going up in the elevator, boys."

Leon stepped back as the officers ran past him. He was about to call out to let them know that the elevator was being controlled from above, but he knew Naomi would be looking at the screen and would bring the car up as soon as she saw them enter. But when the police were in the elevator car, nothing happened. He saw one of the officers stabbing at the buttons, but the doors remained open. Leon's heart sank. Where was Naomi? Had Vince got to her somehow?

"Stairs!" the officer who had spoken to Leon shouted. As one unit, the four officers exited the elevator and barged through the door that led to the stairwell. Leon didn't envy them running up ten flights in body armor and carrying the amount of equipment they were. The sound of their stamping feet was cut off as the stairwell door closed.

The door to the stairwell closed as another crack of thunder split the air, making Leon jump. The storm must be directly overhead, although he'd not seen any lightning. He took a few steps inside the doorway to shelter from the rain, wondering what he was supposed to do now. In the parking lot, the police cars were just sitting there with their doors open and their lights flashing. Leon could see a few curious residents looking through their windows, but the rain kept them inside.

Leon was just trying to decide whether he should go home when another police car rounded the corner. This one wasn't marked, but had flashing blue lights recessed into the grill in the front of the car. Leon's eyebrows went up when he realized it was a brand new BMW X2 M35i xDrive. Forty grand for the most basic model, and this one looked far from basic. It screeched to a halt, its tires slipping on the wet concrete. The door flew open and a male police officer got out. He was wearing a suit, was unarmed, and as he ran through the rain to where Leon was standing, Leon realized he knew him. It was Dave, the detective who had interviewed him the other night.

"Where's Naomi?" Dave barked. "Is she okay?"

"She was on the tenth floor when I last saw her, and she was fine." The look of relief on the detective's face was almost palpable. He opened his mouth to reply to Leon when another sound rang out from far above them. It wasn't thunder, but it still reverberated around the towers. Leon saw Dave looking up into the air before swearing. He tried to run, but he couldn't get any traction in the rain. A second later, something smashed into the roof of the BMW, collapsing it completely and sending tiny fragments of glass from the vehicle windows across the parking lot. "Shitting hell," Leon said as he stared at what had just destroyed the brand new car.

It was a man's body.

CHAPTER 113

"Armed police! Drop the weapon!" Naomi kept her eyes tightly shut at the sound of the shouting. "Drop your weapon now or we will fire" She thought there were several voices shouting, but it wasn't until she heard a female voice issue the same demand that she opened her eyes. Then she realized they were shouting at her.

With a gasp, she threw the pistol in her hands to the roof floor. Then she ran to where Caleb was standing next to the parapet, throwing her arms around him when she reached him.

"Careful," she heard him whisper. It's a long way down."

When Leon had left to go to the bottom of the apartment block, Naomi had used the bathroom reluctantly. Whoever Syd had been, hygiene wasn't top of his priorities. There was no hand soap, no towel, and the toilet didn't look as if it had been cleaned for years. She had washed her hands using dish soap and dried them with a tea towel before leaving the kitchen. She had been standing outside the bedroom door. Leon's instruction not to go into the bedroom in her mind. But what if Syd wasn't actually dead, but badly injured? Would Leon have been able to tell the difference? He was only a child, after all. But when she had opened the bedroom door, it was plain to see that Syd was definitely dead. Then Naomi had seen the pistol on the floor.

Naomi had debated what to do for a few moments. She had retrieved the weapon and placed it on the coffee table, next to an overflowing ashtray. The police were on their way, but what if they were too late? She could be on the rooftop in a few seconds, but armed. The only flaw in her plan was the fact that, until just now, she had never handled a gun in her life, let alone fired one.

"Vince won't know that," Naomi had said to herself as she had picked up the pistol and made her way to the roof. When she had arrived, the door was already open. The first thing she had seen when she walked through was Vince, pointing a pistol at Caleb. Without thinking, Naomi had raised the pistol and pulled the trigger. She'd not expected to actually hit Vince, but he had disappeared over the parapet.

"Hell of a shot, Naomi," Caleb whispered in her ear. She clutched at his clothing and nuzzled into his neck. "Thank you."

"Is he dead?" she asked him, even though she knew the answer to that. She felt him nodding his head and she tightened her grip on him, not wanting to ever let him go.

"Move away from the edge, both of you," a female voice said. Naomi looked up to see a female police officer she recognized, her weapon now slung across her chest, beckoning to them. The rain was now teeming down and they were all soaked through. "Naomi, they said it was you but we weren't sure. We got here as quickly as we could."

"I shot him, Mel," Naomi replied, her voice trembling. "I killed him. I just killed a man."

"I know," Mel replied, reaching out a hand and placing it on Naomi's forearm. "I know you did. I saw what happened. You had no choice."

Twenty minutes or so later, Naomi and Caleb were sitting in the rear of an ambulance with foil blankets across their shoulders. The ambulance was parked facing away from a ruined car with a tarpaulin thrown over it. Knowing that was where Vince had landed, Naomi had averted her eyes as Dave led her to the ambulance. The parking lot was now a hive of activity and full of emergency vehicles, people in fluorescent jackets dashing about in the rain.

"What happens now, Caleb?" Naomi asked him, looking at him through teary eyes. She watched as he sipped a mug of tea that a local resident had brought out. Her own mug was cradled in her hands.

"We still need to find Leanne, Naomi," he replied. His voice was low and she could sense the concern in it. "It's not over until she's safe."

The ambulance door opened and Naomi saw Dave peering in. Behind him, the sky was beginning to lighten and rays of sunshine were beginning to poke through the cloud.

"Everything okay in here?" Dave asked. Naomi nodded in response. He climbed in, closing the door behind him and sat down on the paramedic's chair opposite Naomi and Caleb. "I've spoken to one of our liaison officers with the security services about this 'Vince'. He just needs to confirm it, but he thinks he is one of theirs."

"Okay," Naomi replied, glancing at Caleb. "What happens next?"

"The liaison officer said that once they've confirmed his identity, they'll turn his life upside down to find the girl." Dave took a deep breath. "If anyone can find her, they can."

"Leanne," Naomi whispered. "Her name's Leanne."

CHAPTER 114

Caleb sat in the back of the police car, Naomi next to him, as the first rays of dawn started to appear in the sky to the east. They were a few hundred yards away from a caravan on the north Norfolk coast, which was as close as Dave would allow them to be.

"You think she's in there?" Naomi asked him. Caleb stared at the squat white trailer in the distance. He could just see several tactical police units advancing on it, using other caravans in the park as cover.

"I hope so."

It was three days since Naomi had shot Vince. The security services had told them via Dave that his real name wasn't Vince, but wouldn't be drawn on what he was actually called. The one thing that Dave had told them was that they had turned their vast resources inwards and gone over every aspect of his life. One of the things they had found was the caravan, which Vince had bought years ago. It was close to the coast, and close to where Henry ran his operation. Perhaps Syd hadn't been that far from the mark, Caleb thought as he watched the police officers advancing.

Inside the caravan were two people, a man and a woman, with a girl Leanne's age, who was rarely seen by the other occupants of the holiday park. Dave had said that some agents had rented a caravan close by until they could confirm it was Leanne. How they had done this, Dave didn't know, but they were a hundred percent sure it was her. That was why they had handed the matter over to the Specialist Operations directorate of Norfolk Police to undertake the raid.

In the distance, dark figures were advancing on the caravan. Caleb watched as one of them raised an arm. A split second later, there were bright flashes in the windows of the caravan which momentarily blinded Caleb, followed a few seconds later by the sound of stun grenades rumbling over them. When his vision returned, he could see the door to the caravan was wide open and there were figures scurrying around inside.

"The poor child," Naomi said. "She must be terrified."

"Come on, let's go," Caleb said, opening the door to the police car. He snagged the hem of his robe on the catch for the seat belt as he did so.

"Shouldn't we wait for them to come and get us?" Naomi said, passing him his cloth bag.

"No," Caleb replied, taking the bag from her. There wasn't much in it, but there was one very important thing. "Like you said, she'll be terrified. At least my face is a friendly one."

"You think?" Naomi replied with a smile. "Have you seen yourself lately?" Then she put her hand on Caleb's arm as her smile faded. "Caleb, wait for a moment."

He paused, waiting for her to continue. She seemed to be trying to find the right words to say.

"You're wondering what happens after this?" he said.

She just nodded in response. "I think you know, Naomi," Caleb continued. "I don't belong here. Not now. He sent me here to deal with a problem. Now that's dealt with, He'll have other plans for me."

"But you didn't deal with it," Naomi replied, and he could tell she was trying not to cry. She did manage a wry smile. "I did." She sniffed loudly. "Can I tell you something if you promise not to tell anyone else?"

"Of course."

"When I pulled that trigger, I had my eyes screwed shut." Caleb laughed, and a few seconds later, Naomi joined in.

"He does indeed move in mysterious ways."

By the time Caleb and Naomi reached the caravan, it was surrounded by police officers. Two people, their hands cuffed behind them, were being led to a waiting van close by. Caleb didn't even look at them.

"The child's in the small bedroom on the left," a police officer at the door to the caravan said. "It's the only one we didn't put a stun grenade through, but she's pretty shaken up. One of our female police officers is in with her."

Caleb mounted the steps and stepped into the caravan. The air was fetid and stunk of cigarette smoke. He made his way to the door on the left, tapped lightly on it, and opened the door. Naomi, as if she sensed he wanted to do this alone, remained by the door. When he leaned around the door, there was a shriek of delight.

"Caleb!" Leanne screamed. He grinned broadly as she threw her duvet off and scrambled to her feet. He crouched down and put his arms out to hug her. She threw her arms around him, and he breathed in the scent of her shampoo. "You came back for me!"

"Hey, Leanne, I made you a pinky promise, didn't I?" Caleb said, looking at the child. She had been through so much, and still had so much else to go through. He hoped the money—Suzy's escape fund—that Naomi was keeping for her would help a small bit. "And I never break a pinky promise."

Leanne nodded enthusiastically as Caleb reached for his bag.

"Neither do I," Leanne said.

"I know," Caleb replied, pulling something out of the bag that forced another excited squeal from Leanne. He handed it to her, and she clutched the soft pink elephant to her chest. "And so does Boo Boo."

JOIN 'TEAM PREACHER'

To receive a complementary e-copy of the companion novella to The Preacher, you can join 'Team Preacher' now. The novella's called *First Rodeo*, and is a reader exclusive. It's not available in the stores, and never will be.

By joining the team, you'll be the first to hear about new releases, giveaways, competitions, and special bonuses.

Visit *nathanburrows.com/teampreacher* to join.

THE SOLDIER

Caleb returns in Book 3 of *The Preacher* series, *The Soldier*.

There's a saying that once you're a soldier, you're always a soldier.

But old habits die hard, and so do old soldiers.

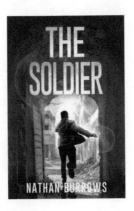

ALSO BY NATHAN BURROWS

The Preacher Series

The Preacher

The Soldier

The Keeper

British Military Thriller Series

Man Down

Incoming Fire

Enemy Within

Man Overboard

Gareth Dawson Series

Blind Justice

Finding Milly

Single Handed

Writing as N.D. Burrows

The Butcher

The Baker

The Candlestick Maker

Printed in the USA
CPSIA information can be obtained
at www.ICGtesting.com
LVHW092204220824
789056LV00032B/359

9 781917 016025